AMISH LOVE BLOOMS: 3 BOOKS-IN-1

AMISH ROSE: AMISH TULIP: AMISH DAISY

SAMANTHA PRICE

Amish Love Blooms Books 1 - 3

Amish Rose

Amish Tulip

Amish Daisy

AMISH ROSE

AMISH LOVE BLOOMS BOOK 1

SAMANTHA PRICE

CHAPTER 1

"HE SEEMS HAPPY," a deep voice boomed from behind Rose, jolting her from her daydreams.

Rose turned around to see her good friend, Mark. "Who does?"

"Your *bruder.*" Mark nodded his head while making a forward movement with the glass in his hand, both motions toward the wedding table where Trevor sat with his new wife.

It hadn't been easy for Trevor to decide on a wife. He'd had many women to choose from. Had it not been for the pressure on him from their parents, Rose was sure that Trevor would've happily stayed unmarried into his thirties. He'd made a good choice in Amy, Rose thought.

Even though Amy, her new sister-in-law, was a few years older than she, Amy had always been kind to Rose when she'd experienced trouble during her school years. It hadn't been easy for Rose being the eldest of four girls with two older brothers. Since her father was a deacon, there had always been pressure on her to be perfect. Rose had feared that she wouldn't live up to the standards that her older brothers had set.

"I guess he is," Rose commented, looking back to see Trevor laughing with Amy.

"It might be you soon."

Rose whipped her head around to look again at Mark. "What, marrying?"

"*Jah*, wedded bliss, some call it."

Rose glanced at the newly married pair, frowned, and then turned back to tell Mark exactly what she thought of that idea. "It'll be a long time before that happens." She shook her head to reinforce her feelings. Some girls might think Mark was a little bit handsome but he wasn't someone she would marry. He was slightly taller than she, but she'd always seen herself with a man who was much taller. Reaching five feet ten inches herself, there weren't that many men around who were taller.

"Don't you want to be happy, Rosie?" Mark was the only one who called her Rosie rather than Rose.

"I'm happy right now. Do you think a woman needs a man to make her happy?"

"*Jah*, I do."

Rose laughed, only because she knew Mark was teasing her. "Mark Schumacher, if I didn't know you any better I'd walk away right now."

"You'll marry me one day, Rosie Yoder. You just wait and see."

Rose shook her head at him. "Don't hold your breath waiting."

He laughed. Mark teasing Rose about marrying him had become an ongoing joke between them ever since Mark had

4

taken the stall right by the one she handled at the farmers market. Rose took his teasing in good humor. Whenever they weren't busy with customers, they'd talk and laugh to pass the time.

"Rose, there you are. *Mamm's* looking for you. She said you promised to help with the food." Tulip, Rose's younger sister by one year, looked shaken up and there was good reason. Their mother was helping organize the wedding feast for the three hundred guests. And to their mother, 'helping' meant taking over the task and delegating to the other ladies.

"Right now?" Rose asked.

"*Jah*, of course, right now. The food is being dished into the serving bowls as we speak and she's asked for you. Come on!" Tulip frowned and her dark eyes fixed upon Rose as though pleading.

"Okay. There's no need for dramatics."

Tulip took hold of Rose's arm and led her away.

"Hello, Tulip," Mark said as Tulip dragged Rose away.

"Hello, Mark," Tulip called over her shoulder.

When Mark was out of earshot, Rose said, "That was rude, Tulip. Mark and I were talking."

"You see him every day. What could you possibly have left to talk about?"

"I dunno—stuff."

"If I were you, I wouldn't tell *Mamm* you were off gossiping somewhere. She's mighty cranky that you weren't there to help from the start. *Mamm* said as her oldest *dochder* you should've stayed right by her side to learn from her."

Rose nodded as she hurried toward the annex outside Amy's parents' kitchen where the food was being prepared. The

5

kitchen in the house was far too small to suffice for the preparation of food for the large number of people who turned out for the Amish wedding.

"Here she is now," the bride's mother said to Tulip and Rose's mother.

"About time, too!" Nancy Yoder glared at her eldest daughter.

"Sorry, *Mamm*. I helped with the food earlier. I didn't know you needed me to do it for the whole time."

"If a job's worth doing it's—"

"I know. It's worth doing well. I know." Rose nodded, hoping to stop a lecture before it began.

"You stay until the job's complete!" Nancy shook her head at her and Rose knew if there hadn't been so many women fussing about, her mother would've delivered a lengthy stern lecture. "You're here now; that's the important thing."

"Please take the plates out to the tables, Rose," Amy's mother asked.

"Okay."

"You'll have to help her, Tulip," Nancy added.

Together, Rose and Tulip scooped up armfuls of white dinner plates and headed toward the tables spread across the yard. The wedding had taken place in the bride's home, as was the tradition in their community. Weddings were publicized and spread by word of mouth and there was never any way to tell exactly how many guests would attend. Typically, it was in the hundreds.

When Rose put the plates down on the table, she glanced over to see her two younger sisters, twins, giggling and running around with other girls in the distance. The twins were sixteen, but they still associated with people much younger than themselves. Rose knew that if her mother had been aware of how the twins were behaving, they too would've got a stern reprimand. They would've been told that they weren't behaving like young ladies, and since their father was a deacon and part of the oversight, their family had to set an example to others.

The twins, Daisy and Lily, had dark coloring and were pretty. They weren't as tall as Rose, but neither was Tulip. Rose wasn't jealous of her sisters, but had often wished she had their dark coloring rather than her red hair and the pale skin that always accompanied her shade of hair.

When she heard one of the twins let out an ear-splitting squeal, her mind drifted back to the lecture she thought the twins might get. It was a lecture that Rose had heard many a time before. She often wished her father hadn't been selected as part of the church oversight—their lives might be more enjoyable without the constant pressure. Rose always felt as though she were being watched—judged.

She glanced over at her second-eldest brother. Life had been a whole lot easier for her brothers; she was certain of that. Rose considered that life, in general, was easier for men—that was her secret thought. Amish women were restricted in what they could and couldn't do, more so than the men. Rose kept her rebellious thoughts to herself, apart from her many serious conversations with Mary, her best friend who'd gone on a *rumspringa.*

A *rumspringa* wasn't an option for Rose. Not because she wasn't allowed; it was just that she didn't want to live in the *Englisch* world. Her next best friend was Mark, and although there were many things that she never discussed with him because—being a man—he wouldn't understand, Mark was always good for someone to laugh with.

Rose turned around and went back for more plates. Each of the girls could only carry about twelve at a time, and there were a great many more plates that needed to be placed on each of the tables.

"We need some people to help us, *Mamm*," Rose said to her mother as she heaped some more plates into her arms.

Nancy ordered a few more women to help them with the plates. Nancy had taken over the organization of the food preparation from Amy's mother. That was Nancy's way— taking over and being in charge was what she did best.

Within minutes, all the cutlery and plates were on the tables, and now the only thing remaining was for the food to be brought out.

The bishop clapped his hands, causing the hum of the crowd's conversation to cease. He said a few words and everyone bowed their heads. When the bishop finished his prayer, he gave Nancy a nod, letting her know she could send the ladies out with the food.

When Rose had placed the last of the food onto one of the tables, she glanced at her mother to see her leaning against the house with her arms folded. A hint of a private smile turned the corners of her mother's lips upward.

Today, her mother was pleased to be getting her second son married off. A year before, the oldest, Peter, had gotten married. Peter and his wife were now expecting their first child. Somehow Nancy had persuaded her quilting bee, who met regularly every Tuesday afternoon, to start knitting baby clothing. It seemed no one was game to say no to Nancy.

"Are you eating, Rosie?"

"*Jah*, I've worked up an appetite."

"Sit with me?" Mark asked as he handed Rose a plate.

Rose nodded and followed Mark to a table at the far edge of the yard. There were around fifty tables that could each comfortably seat fifteen people, and each table had its own bowls of food in the center. Often there were so many guests that there were three sittings for the one meal. At some weddings, there were long food tables and people served themselves buffet-style before they sat down at the tables. The wedding had started just before midday, so it was a perfect time to eat a large meal.

She and Mark each heaped food onto their plates.

"It's a nice wedding," Mark said before he took a large mouthful.

"Aren't they all the same?" Rose asked.

Mark smiled and finished chewing. "You never agree with anything I say."

"I do when you're right."

"Aren't I always?"

Rose giggled. "*Nee*, but you're welcome to your delusions."

He shook his head and took another mouthful. Mark then talked to some of their tablemates who were visiting from another community.

Rose liked the way Mark could talk to anyone. She was too nervous to speak to someone new unless they spoke to her first.

The twins sat down at the table with them.

"It'll be you two next," Daisy said to Mark and Rose.

Mark laughed, raised his eyebrows, and looked at Rose as though waiting for her to say something.

"Don't be silly. That's what people always say at weddings. They look around for who'll be next." Rose looked at the other people at the table who were now staring at her. "She's only joking," she told them. It was an awkward moment and Rose looked down at her plate and pushed the food around with her fork.

Mark laughed. "I'm always asking her, but she always says no. One day she'll weaken."

The twins roared with laughter while digging each other in the ribs.

"You should marry him," Daisy, the older twin, said to Rose when she'd finished laughing.

"Hush, Daisy!" Rose just wanted the nonsense conversation to end.

"Stop hushing me all the time."

"Yeah, Rose, let her speak," Lily added.

Rose stood up and stepped over the bench seat. "Excuse me. I have to help *Mamm* with something." As she walked away, she could hear her twin sisters' faint giggles.

Mark would've been her perfect man if he were just a little different—a little taller and a little more mature-minded. She didn't need her sisters encouraging him. It would only lead to his disappointment.

Rose found her mother in the food annex. "Need some help?"

"Yeah! I'll need help washing the dishes as they come in."

"I'll do it."

"*Denke*, Rose. I was going to ask, but weddings are a good opportunity for you to meet people. Don't you want to mingle and see what new people you can meet? Amy has quite a few relations here you wouldn't have met."

Rose knew her mother meant it was a good place to meet potential husbands. Her mother was correct. Weddings were one of the best ways of meeting potential spouses. "I've already met quite a few people." Rose leaned in and whispered, "There are no men my age."

Her mother nodded. "Well, you might as well help me, then."

For the remainder of the celebrations, Rose stayed in the annex washing dishes. When the dishes were all nearly done, Rose took her hands out of the hot sudsy water. They were all wrinkled and her nails were pale and unsightly.

"Rose has got dishpan hands," she heard Daisy say to Lily.

"They'll come right soon, Rose. Do you want me to take over for a while?" Lily, the kinder of the twins, asked.

"Would you?"

"*Jah*. Move over." Lily rolled up her sleeves.

"I'll dry them," Daisy said.

Nancy walked up behind the three of them. "*Denke*, girls. You can go now, Rose. You've been enough help. You might be able to go home with your *vadder*. The girls and I will have someone take us home later."

"Okay. Are you sure?"

"*Jah*, now go."

By now, most of the guests had left. Rose looked around for Tulip and then caught sight of her father and Tulip heading for the buggy. She ran to catch them.

"Wait up."

They both turned and stopped until she caught up.

"*Mamm* and the twins are staying on. *Mamm* said I'd done enough work."

"I know; that's your *mudder*. She always stays late, until the end, at weddings. Let's go home," their father said.

"How did you get out of doing any work, Tulip?"

"I kept out of the way. You volunteered, I heard."

Hezekiah Yoder smiled as he listened quietly to his daughters. He never had much to say, but when he did, everyone listened.

"*Jah*, I did." Rose held out her hands.

"They look dreadful."

"They're very clean now, at least."

"We can put some olive oil on them when we get home."

Rose looked around to see if Mark had already left. She couldn't see his buggy and his chestnut horse anywhere.

Home was at least a thirty-minute buggy ride away. Rose let Tulip sit in the front while she settled in the back and looked out. She smiled as a rabbit scampered across their buggy's path and disappeared into the tall grass by the roadside. She closed her eyes and enjoyed the even rhythm of the horse's hooves as they clip-clopped their way up the dirt-packed road.

After a short rest, she moved closer to the opening so she could watch the cows grazing in the sun-drenched fields. Further up the road, two farmers mending fences straightened up and waved as they passed by. Their happy faces made her feel good and she waved back.

She looked across the patchwork of varying shades of green pastures and distant rolling hills, and wondered how her best friend could leave the serenity and beauty of this place to live in the city of New York.

CHAPTER 2

"Rose, can you collect the eggs for me? I just want to sleep in," Tulip asked the next morning from her bedroom as Rose passed by the doorway.

Rose stopped and stuck her head into Tulip's bedroom. "Okay, I'll do it this time, and then you'll owe me one."

"Deal!" Tulip replied.

Rose had learned early to negotiate with her sisters—to trade a favor for a favor. Otherwise, she'd be the only one doing anything. If she collected the eggs this morning, then Tulip would do something for her another time.

"Where are you going?" Her mother stared at Rose as she grabbed the wicker basket by the back door. "That's Tulip's job."

"I said I'd do it for her today."

"Okay. I suppose that's alright, but when you come back, I have something to tell you before the other girls come downstairs."

"What is it?"

"It can wait until you get the eggs."

"Have I done something wrong?"

Her mother laughed, her green eyes crinkling at the corners. Even though her mother was in her mid forties, she was still quite an attractive woman. Rose hoped she might look as good when she reached that age.

"Of course, you haven't done anything wrong, Rose. I couldn't have asked for a better *dochder.*"

Rose was relieved, but hated not knowing things. She couldn't wait to hear what her mother was going to tell her. "Can you tell me now, *Mamm?* I can't wait."

Her mother sighed. "Okay, sit down."

Once Rose was seated at the long wooden kitchen table, her mother sat opposite.

"Now that both of your brothers are married, I can turn my attention to helping you, and Tulip, and then the twins to find husbands."

"Is that it?"

"*Jah,* it wasn't a big secret I had to tell you."

Rose huffed. "I thought it was. Anyway, I don't need help, thanks all the same. I'd rather not look for a man. *He* can find *me.*"

Her mother shook her head. "That's not how it happens. You must listen to me, Rose. If you wait, you'll end up with no one!"

Rose frowned at the urgency and panic in her mother's voice.

Her mother grabbed her by the shoulders and looked into her eyes. "Men are in limited supply in the community. Girls Tulip's age are getting married, and girls the twins' age are dating. I don't want you to miss out."

Rose thought about that for a moment. It would certainly feel weird for her younger sisters to get married before she did —weirder still for either of the twins to date a man. They seemed far too young and definitely acted younger than their years. "I don't even know anybody that I want to marry."

"That's because you haven't been focused on looking for someone." Her mother slapped a hand hard on the table, which made Rose jump.

"You scared me."

"But that ends today!"

"What does?"

"You not looking for someone. You're old enough to be married and there's nothing wrong with giving me some *grosskinner.* Your *bruder's boppli* will be born soon and it would be *gut* if my *grosskinner* were all close in age."

"That doesn't sound like a good reason to get married to me."

Her mother laughed. "Everyone should be married. That's what *Gott* has planned. He planned for every *mann* to have a *fraa* and every woman to have a *mann.* That's the way *Gott* made us."

"I don't know."

"What don't you know, my dear girl?"

"I don't know about this whole thing. I've never even gone on a buggy ride with a boy … err, I mean, a man."

"Jah, I know. That's the problem, Rose. Can't you see that?"

Her mother cast her gaze downward and Rose felt bad for being such a disappointment.

"You see, Rose, if we don't plan in life we get nowhere."

Her mother wasn't making sense. "You want me to *plan* to

fall in love with someone?"

Nancy pressed her lips together and fine lines appeared around her mouth. "You're trying to make light of this, Rose."

"I'm not, *Mamm*, really, I'm not! I just don't see how you can plan to fall in love with someone."

Her mother leaned forward. "Love grows when you're married. You choose a husband with this." She tapped a finger on her head. "Not with your heart. Love grows from respect."

That was news to Rose—that her mother felt that way. A thought occurred to Rose. "Is that how you chose *Dat?*"

"*Jah.* Your *vadder* was a *gut* man of *Gott* and a hard-worker. He wasn't a deacon back then, though. That came when you were a *boppli*. He's never disappointed me and he's been a steady provider. Together, we've been happy."

Rose nibbled on a fingernail. She had never heard such a thing. She always thought that love was something whimsical and magical—something to be experienced once in a lifetime, when two like souls met and knew at once that they were meant for one another. "Are you saying you were never in love with *Dat* before you married him?" It was bold of Rose to ask that question at the risk of angering her mother, but she had to know. "I mean, when you first met him? I know you're in love with him now."

"*Nee*, I wasn't in love with him when I first met him. I had to get to know him. Now run and get those eggs so I can make the breakfast."

"Okay." Rose had a lot to think about. She stood up and grabbed the egg basket.

"I'm giving you a year, Rose."

Rose was nearly out the door. She stopped and turned

slightly to look at her mother. "A year for what?"

"To get married."

Rose's jaw dropped open. "What if I haven't found some-body in a year?"

"You will. Start talking to some men and that'll be a begin-ning. If you never talk to a man, how will you know which one suits you?"

Rose nodded. There was no point telling her mother that she did talk to men. If she told her mother that, she'd want to know which ones. It was easier just to keep quiet. With the basket looped over her arm, Rose hurried across the wet grass, fresh from the morning dew, as the crisp morning air bit into her cheeks.

Rose unlatched the wooden door of the chicken coop, closed it behind her, and leaned down. She and her sisters had raised most of the chickens by hand, and the others were just as tame. Each of the hens had their own distinct personality. She picked each one up and gave them a cuddle as she spoke to them softly. When she remembered her mother was waiting on the eggs, she stood up.

"How many eggs do you have for us this morning?" she asked as she looked in the straw bedding. She found eight eggs when there were normally twelve to fifteen every morning. Rose had a better look around and found two more.

"Better than nothing," she said aloud. *"Denke,* my little friends."

Leaving the basket of eggs by the door, she freshened their water and topped up their grain. She looked at the straw and wondered if she should change that too, but left that to Tulip.

"Well, that took you long enough," her mother said when

Rose got back to the house.

Rose placed the wicker basket of eggs on the table.

"Don't put them there. The basket's dirty. Put it on the floor. You should know these things by now. Why can't you remember anything?"

"Sorry, *Mamm.*" Rose obeyed her mother and placed the basket on the floor. She then proceeded to put the eggs in the ceramic bowl where they were kept, on the counter by the sink.

Her twin sisters suddenly appeared and sat down at the table, while Tulip was nowhere to be seen.

"*Mamm* says you've got to get married." Daisy, the older of the twins, laughed.

"Do you think you'll find someone with your head on fire like that?" Lily added.

The twins giggled. They always poked fun at her red hair. Their hair was dark, as was everyone else's in their family. Two generations ago, she'd been told, there were some red-haired family members, but Rose was the only one of this generation to have that color.

"That's not very nice," their mother reprimanded the twins. "And you know you shouldn't be eavesdropping. I won't warn you again."

"Sorry, *Mamm,*" the twins said in unison.

"Your turn is coming," Rose said to her sisters.

"I want to be married soon, and I'll have three sets of twins and then no more," Lily said.

Daisy gave a laugh, and said, "Me too. I'll have one set of girls, one set of boys, and then more girls. Then I'm done, too. There'll be fewer childbirths and pregnancies if I have all my *kinner* in sets of twins."

"What about triplets?" Lily asked her sister, which made Daisy giggle.

"So, who are you going to marry?" Rose asked them.

"I'd rather not talk about it," Daisy replied.

"What about you, Lily?" Rose figured she'd do some teasing of her own.

"Forget about us. You're the oldest *dochder*, Rose. Who are you going to marry?" Daisy stared at her. "That's more important right now. You are the one who has to set the example because you're the eldest. Isn't that right, *Mamm?*"

"I expect Rose to marry first but it doesn't have to be that way."

"Well, who's it going to be?" Lily asked Rose.

"You'll just have to wait and see."

"She's got no idea," Daisy said to Lily.

When both twins laughed, it was too much for Rose. "Make them stop, *Mamm*."

"We're going to wash the windows today," their mother announced to the twins.

Both sisters groaned and Rose couldn't help but giggle. She had a nice little job working at the farmers market. She ran a flower stall for the Walkers, an Amish family, who owned a wholesale flower business.

A job was far better than staying home every day, cooking, or scrubbing the house from top to bottom. And to make matters worse for her sisters, their mother always insisted on things being just so. With Rose having no horse and buggy of her own, Mrs. Walker collected Rose every day and also brought her home. This suited Mrs. Walker because after she took Rose to the market, she'd continue to her elderly mother's house and stay with her to help until the work day was done. It was also convenient that the Walkers lived right next door.

After breakfast, Rose grabbed her black shawl off the peg by the back door and yelled goodbye to everyone.

"Come here, Rose."

"*Jah*, what is it, *Mamm?* Do you want me to bring something home with me?"

"*Nee.*" Her mother hurried over to her and said, quietly, "I want you to spend the day thinking about what men you might like to marry. When you get home, we'll discuss them one by one."

"I can't, *Mamm*. I'll need time to think. Can I take a few weeks to think about it?" Rose bit her lip. "What if the man I'm supposed to marry doesn't even live in this community?"

Her mother's eyes opened wide. It was clearly something that her mother had never considered. "That wouldn't do at all. I think he'll be from around here somewhere. There are many to choose from, but you mustn't delay. This time next year, many of the single men will be spoken for. If you wait, you'll end up without."

Her mother's words sent a chill down her spine. The thought of ending up with no one to marry was something Rose had never considered. Surely God would put couples together without it being a race. "I'll definitely give it some serious thought, *Mamm*."

"*Gut* girl. We'll talk more about it tonight."

Rose nodded, knowing her mother only wanted the best for her.

She walked down the driveway listening to the crunch of the small white pebbles underneath her black lace-up boots.

At the end of the drive, she leaned against the gatepost and waited for her ride. Mornings were Rose's favorite time of the day. She loved to watch the birds going about their work, gathering small twigs and other odds and ends to make their nests, and plucking the occasional worm from the soft earth. It was spring and everything seemed fresh and new.

Once she saw Mrs. Walker's gray horse trotting toward her, she took some steps closer to the road, so she could get in quickly before the buggy would slow any passing traffic. Traffic was something they rarely saw down their road apart from the occasional weekend tourist looking at the countryside, but Rose was still careful.

"How are you this morning, Rose?" Mrs. Walker asked as soon as she stopped on the side of the road.

"Fine, *denke.* What about yourself?"

"I'll feel better when it rains."

"Jah, it hasn't rained for some time and we surely need it."

Every morning one of the Walkers' sons got to the market early and loaded the stall with fresh flowers. All Rose had to do was arrange them nicely, and, of course, sell them.

"Your *bruder* and Amy were very happy to be getting married," Mrs. Walker commented.

"Jah, Dat said they were made for each other."

"It certainly looks that way."

Rose was tempted to talk more about the wedding, but she didn't want to let on that her mother had given her what was close to an ultimatum about getting married within one year. Mrs. Walker had two sons who were single and Rose didn't want Mrs. Walker to think that she was hinting about one of her sons.

"How old were you when you got married, Mrs. Walker?"

"It was the day after I turned eighteen. Our parents made us wait to get married. We grew up together, right next door—side-by-side. We always knew we were going to marry each other."

"That must've been very comforting—knowing where your destiny lay."

"*Jah.* I always knew we would be together, and he knew it too." Mrs. Walker glanced at her. "What about you? Do you have a boy you're interested in?"

"*Nee,* not really."

"That sounds a bit doubtful. Have you got your eyes on someone?"

Laughter escaped Rose's lips. "I wish I did; then things might be easier for me."

"There's no rush; you're still young."

Tell my mother that, she thought. "That's true."

Mrs. Walker prattled on about what flowers were going to be at the stall that morning. "And the daisies aren't looking as fresh as they should be, so you can mark them down or give people more for their money. You know what to do."

"I do." Rose had to agree. If there was one thing she knew how to do, it was to sell flowers. She knew when they weren't looking their best and then the aim was to mark them down in price enough so they'd sell that day. It was better to get a little money before they wilted too far. The Walkers didn't freeze their flowers like many of the other flower wholesalers did, so the shelf life was considerably less. Fortunately, there was a strong demand for local produce. Retail florists were favoring locally-grown flowers, which helped the Walker family.

CHAPTER 3

AT WORK THAT DAY, Rose's mother's words played through her mind.

Since he had no customers, Mark took a few steps toward Rose. "What's got you so upset, Rosie?"

She looked into Mark's concerned face. "Who said I'm upset? I'm not, not at all."

"Maybe upset's the wrong word, but something's on your mind. Tell me what it is?"

She stared at the pink roses in the bucket by her feet, and answered, "It's nothing."

"It must be something."

Looking back at Mark, she said, *"Nee,* it's not."

"Tell me." He put his hands on his hips and stared at her, narrowing his eyes.

"It's just that I feel under pressure. Now that my *mudder* has got my two brothers married off, she's turning her attention to me. She tells me I must *plan* to be married by next year."

"Plan?" He chuckled. "Or what?"

"She didn't exactly say what would happen if I wasn't married by then. I think she is worried that I'll never get married if it doesn't happen by then, or something." Rose shrugged her shoulders.

"Rosie, if you want to marry me, just say it. You don't have to make up a story about something your *mudder* said."

She stared into Mark's smiling face. If only life were as simple as Mark made it out to be. "Ha ha; very funny."

"I'm sorry to be unsympathetic. Who does your *mudder* think you should marry? Has she got some man lined up for you?"

"She wants me to give her some names tonight. I've got today to think about it."

Mark roared with laughter.

"Don't laugh."

"Maybe I should pay your *mudder* a visit, and tell her I'm the man for you. She should know that already."

"Don't you dare!"

"You could do worse."

"Is that the best reason you can come up with for me to marry you—the fact that I could do worse?"

"I suppose not. I'll make a list of my good points and present them to Mrs. Yoder next time I see her. Perhaps I should stop by for dinner one night?" He tapped on his chin with his finger and looked upward. "I hope she is considering me for the job."

"I'm serious about this; it could become quite a problem. You know what my *mudder* is like when she gets her mind set on something."

"I don't know personally, but you've told me, so I have to take your word for that."

"I've got customers heading this way." Rose served some of her regular customers while Mark stayed behind his stall.

Mark ran a cheese stall at the end of the food line, and Rose's stall shared the corner of his where the flowers aisle started. Mark's family had a goat farm and made goat cheeses and other related products. The most popular products were the goats' milk and cheese. Mark had spent many an hour telling Rose how much better goats' milk was than cows' milk, mainly because it was easier to digest.

As THE DAY drew to a close, Mark walked over to Rose. "I've come up with a plan for you."

"A plan to do what?"

"If your *mudder* gets too high-pressured, we can always pretend that we're dating. You and me."

Rose considered what he said before she answered. "It might work for a while. Then she'll put pressure on us at the end of the year to marry."

He raised his eyebrows. "The offer's there."

"How do you see it would work? My *mudder's* not easily fooled. She's a very smart woman."

"It would take the focus off you if she thinks you've already got someone lined up to possibly marry. She could turn her energy onto one of your sisters."

Rose giggled. "It seems like a good plan. *Denke,* I'll definitely give it some thought."

Mark smiled, and then turned back to securing his stall for

the night. He'd never made a secret of liking her. Rose knew she'd only have to say the word and they'd be dating. But Mark was just a friend and Rose couldn't see herself marrying him. He was just a shade taller and he was an ordinary looking man. Rose had always known how she'd feel about her husband when she first laid eyes on him. There would be tingles running up and down her spine, and her heart would pitter-patter when he came close. He'd be tall, with dark eyes and dark hair, with olive tanned skin and dazzling white teeth.

Yes, she'd recognize him when she saw him, and that's something she'd always known in her heart. Rose hadn't met the man she'd share her life with. Perhaps her mother was right and she couldn't waste time. Her future husband was out there somewhere and she had to find him soon before he married another. What if his mother was also putting pressure on him to marry? He might marry someone else before they found each other.

CHAPTER 4

NANCY YODER LOOKED out the window to see Rose walking toward the house. Rose was a sweet girl, and nothing but a dreamer. If she didn't set the girl on the right path, what would become of her?

Rose was a tall and willowy girl, attractive with her brilliant red hair, but that would do her no good if she didn't get her head in the right space—and fast. Nancy had been blessed to find her husband when she was a young teenager, but if Rose didn't think about finding a man now, it might be too late. She could see in Rose's eyes from earlier that day she'd felt the pressure of her words. Rose was a girl who needed guidance, and besides, it was for her own good that she marry soon.

"Tulip, take your sisters upstairs. I want to have a word with Rose alone before your *vadder* gets home."

"*Mamm*, we're not three-years-old," Daisy said.

"Yeah! We don't need anyone to take us upstairs." Lily jumped to her feet.

"We'll go by ourselves, *Mamm,*" Tulip added in a tone of disgust.

Tulip never liked to be grouped with the twins, preferring to be treated as older along with Rose. Her three younger daughters made themselves scarce, while Nancy waited by the door for Rose.

When Rose pushed the door open, her mother was right in front of her.

"*Mamm!* Where is everyone?"

"The girls are upstairs. Sit down with me for a moment so we can talk alone."

Rose studied her mother's face to carefully judge her mood while she let the shawl slide from her shoulders. "Have I done something wrong?"

"*Nee.* I want to talk more about what I was saying this morning."

Rose hung her shawl on the peg behind the door, and walked into the living room. She sat on the couch and her mother sat down next to her.

Nancy inhaled deeply. "Rose, I know you think I'm meddling in your life, but I don't want you to have regrets about anything when you're older."

"I'm only twenty."

Nancy felt bad that she hadn't had this conversation with Rose two years ago. There had been many men who had gotten married in those years, and five of them she could name off the top of her head, any one of whom might've been perfect for her daughter.

"If you don't act now to find a husband—"

"I'll miss out," Rose finished her sentence for her while

nodding her head.

"*Jah,* you will. Now, you said you'd give it some thought today, so did you think of anyone you might like?" Nancy watched as Rose's eyes glazed over. "Perhaps I should get your *vadder* to talk to you?"

"*Nee, Mamm. Dat* wouldn't be comfortable talking about things like this."

"Well?"

"I … I have thought about it and …"

Nancy leaned forward, placing her fingertips behind her ear to pull her ear forward. It was something she used to do when her children were smaller to show them that she was listening intently. Old habits were hard to break. "And?"

"And I do like someone, but we've been keeping it quiet."

Keeping relationships quiet was often the Amish way among the young. Many people didn't know couples were together until their weddings were published, and a date for the wedding announced.

Nancy was relieved. "You have? You like someone and he likes you in return?"

Rose nodded. "That's right."

"Who is it?"

"If I tell you, it won't be keeping it quiet."

Nancy nodded. Rose had the right to privacy because she was an adult now and Nancy had to respect her rights. Still, Nancy hated it when there was something she didn't know. Who was this mystery man? Was he a suitable match? The thing that kept Nancy awake at night was that Rose was a girl who could easily be led astray. The girl just didn't think things through. Or was the whole thing a ruse made up by Rose to deflect attention and put off finding a man? "Perhaps we could have him over for dinner one night?"

Rose bit her lip. "Maybe."

"Rose, are you just saying this to stop me talking to you about marriage? Does this man exist other than in your daydreams?"

"*Mamm*, how could you possibly say that to me?"

"You're not denying it. This morning you made no mention of this man and that would've been the opportunity to do so. Why's that? Why didn't you talk about your man this morning?"

Rose crossed her arms over her chest and slumped back into the couch. "He does exist."

"Then who is he?"

"I don't want to make a big deal out of it. Can't we just leave it at that? I'll take notice of your warnings about finding myself missing out if I wait too long."

"Do I know him?"

"Of course you do. He's from our community. I'm not sneaking off to see an *Englischer.* You should at least be happy about that."

From Rose's response, it was more clear Rose knew Nancy wouldn't be happy about her choice in a man.

She thought about all the men she'd seen Rose with over the past weeks and the only man she could think of was Mark Schumacher. The two of them were always talking together to the exclusion of others. She closed her eyes, picturing them as a couple, and in the future, married. Then she opened them and locked eyes with Rose. "Mark Schumacher?"

"Why do you say it like that?"

"I'm just asking you a question. Is that who the mystery man is?"

"*Jah*, it's Mark, and there's nothing wrong with him."

"*Nee*, there isn't. I like Mark."

Rose sat on her hands. "You do?"

"*Jah.* He's a fine young man. And you clearly get along with one another."

"Please don't make a big fuss of it. I don't want you to scare him away."

Nancy laughed, trying to hide her amazement. Mark was an unusual choice. In her mind's eye, she'd always imagined Rose with someone older; someone who would act as a stabilizing influence on her. Mark was barely a year older than she. And, what's more, Mark struck Nancy as someone who seemed a little casual in his approach to life.

Then, another thought troubled Nancy. What if Mark was merely her first boyfriend and she'd grow tired of him? He would distract her, waste her time, and when their relationship was done, she'd be older and many of the men would've already married. She looked back at her daughter. "Are you sure about Mark?"

"Don't worry; we won't be getting married tomorrow." Rose laughed.

That wasn't what Nancy was concerned about, but she didn't want to worry Rose with her own troubling doubts since Rose was prone to nerves and anxiety. Rose had been better these past years, but any added stress on her oldest daughter wouldn't be good.

Nancy knew she'd have to let it go as best she could, and trust God. Rose was seeing someone and even if Nancy thought him not a good fit for her, she reminded herself that it was Rose's choice.

"Have I upset you or something, *Mamm?*"

She stared into her daughter's bright green eyes, which perfectly complemented the red tones of her crowning glory. Without saying a word, she leaned forward and kissed her daughter on her forehead. "You couldn't possibly upset me."

CHAPTER 5

ROSE WAS TAKEN ABACK. Her *mudder* was not one for physical affection with her grown children. She watched her mother stand and hurry into the kitchen.

Over her shoulder, *Mamm* called out, "Can you let your sisters know we've finished our talk?"

Sisters? Where are they? Still sitting, Rose leaned over to look up the stairs. Moving shadows proved that they had been listening in. Rose quietly bounded to her feet and caught sight of them. "I see you!"

The twins giggled and ran down the stairs while pushing and shoving each other.

"We heard *Mamm* say we could come down now." Lily stuck her nose in the air as she sailed past Rose.

Daisy was right behind Lily and poked out her tongue at Rose when she walked by.

Rose ignored her and looked back up the stairs, wondering where Tulip was. "You up there, Tulip?"

Tulip appeared. "Yeah."

Rose knew that Tulip was so gentle and polite that she didn't want to let on that she'd been listening along with the twins. "You heard?"

"I did." Her face twisted with guilt.

"It's okay."

Tulip walked down toward her. With Rose's best friend having left the community to go on *rumspringa,* Tulip had become her closest female friend.

"Is it true about Mark?"

Rose gulped. If Tulip didn't believe her, that meant her mother would also have doubts. "Not really."

"Then why did you say that to *Mamm?*"

"Are you two helping or what?" rang the raucous voice of one of the twins from the kitchen.

"We're coming in a minute," Rose yelled back.

"Well? I know it's not true," Tulip said.

Rose sighed. "I had to do something. *Mamm* told me I need to get married soon, but there's no one around for me to marry. She was putting me under pressure."

"Why don't we visit some relatives in other towns—just you and me? That way, we can meet more people and you might find someone."

"I'm not in a hurry. And I can't leave the stall. Mr. and Mrs. Walker need me."

"Someone else would be able to do it for a while. Think about it. It'll look like you're doing something to find a man and we can have a good time together."

"I can't. If I do that, *Mamm* will know that I lied to her and I'll never hear the end of it."

"She'll find out soon enough, won't she?"

"Nee. I hope not."

"You roped Mark into the lie with you?"

Rose cringed at the word 'lie.' "You make it sound as though it's something terrible." It was best to keep it to herself that Mark was the one who'd come up with the idea.

Tulip shook her head and her prayer *kapp* strings were thrown side-to-side. "This won't end well."

"Maybe and maybe not, but can't we keep this between the two of us?" Rose whispered.

Tulip nodded and the pair joined the others in the kitchen to help prepare the evening meal.

LATER THAT EVENING, Nancy was in her bedroom with her husband.

"Did you have a talk with Rose?" Hezekiah asked.

"About her getting married?"

"Jah."

"I did, and she says that she and Mark Schumacher have been seeing quite a bit of each other."

He drew his head back in surprise. "Besides seeing each other every day at the farmers market?"

"Jah, it seems so. She's fond of him."

Scratching his neck, he asked, "Do you think she's taking things more seriously now since your talk?"

"Maybe. I don't like to put pressure on the girl, but she's twenty now. I would've hoped she would have found someone before now, but it seems she wasn't seriously looking," Nancy said. "She must not have been taking her relationship with Mark seriously."

"We don't always know what's going on in our *kinner's* lives."

"*Jah,* especially when they get older. I just hope my talk didn't put too much pressure on her. You know what she's like."

"You did the right thing, Nancy. There's pressure in life and we can't escape that. She'll have to learn to deal with it."

"I suppose so, but I always feel overprotective, more protective of Rose than our other *kinner.* She's the sensitive one, while Tulip is the smart one. The twins—"

"The twins will mature in time." Hezekiah smiled as he often did when the twins were mentioned.

"What do you think of Mark?"

"He's a nice boy."

"Exactly! A boy. He's not a man, really, is he?" Nancy asked. "He's just a freckle-faced boy. I can't see him being a man and taking care of our Rose."

"He's still young—give him a chance."

Nancy's gaze swept upward to the ceiling. "I always saw Rose with someone older."

Hezekiah chuckled. "And he will be older in a few years. Stop worrying so much. Things have a way of following their natural course. She just needs to relax and the current of life will set her on the right course."

Nancy looked into her husband's eyes and was comforted. Maybe she was being overly concerned. She wanted Rose to be interested in a man, and now she'd found out she had something going on with Mark. He was an interesting choice and she'd have to keep a close eye on the two of them.

CHAPTER 6

ROSE COULDN'T WAIT to get to work to tell Mark that she'd taken him up on his offer of him being her pretend love-interest. As soon as Mrs. Walker dropped her off at the entrance of the farmers market, she hurried to their side-by-side stalls.

Mark had his back turned so she grabbed him by his arm and pulled him behind the stalls so no one would hear what she said.

"Whooaa! What are you doing, Rosie?"

"I need to tell you something important," Rose whispered.

"What is it?" He leaned forward and opened his eyes wide.

"It's my *mudder*—you know what we were talking about yesterday afternoon?"

"Jah?"

"I had to pretend that you were my boyfriend."

Mark appeared to be enjoying every moment of Rose's dilemma. A hint of smugness touched his lips as he leaned back on one foot and crossed his arms in front of his chest. Then he straightened up. "Hang on a minute. You're not joking with me?"

"*Nee.* I'm telling you what happened and what I had to say to *Mamm.*"

He sighed and rubbed his chin. "Tell me what happened. Tell me everything—who said what?"

"I was frightened she might send me away somewhere or try to find someone for me." Rose imagined what kind of man her mother would find for her. Probably someone old and stuffy who never laughed, who had a big farm somewhere, and would come home smelly and sweaty at the end of the day. "Anyway, it's all right, isn't it? It was you who suggested the whole thing."

"It was a joke, Rose. I wasn't serious."

Rose opened her mouth in surprise. "*Nee,* it was not a joke! You can't say this to me now, Mark. I more or less already told my *mudder* that you're my boyfriend."

"I wasn't serious. How do you think we'd ever pull that off?"

"I haven't thought it through, obviously. My *mudder* put me on the spot and then I just kept hearing your voice repeat what you said yesterday." She shook her head. "I can't believe you're letting me down when the whole thing was entirely your idea."

He rubbed his chin, not looking as smug as he had a moment before. "Are you blaming me for this whole thing, Rosie?"

"*Jah,* I am. I'm totally blaming you for everything. All of it. It was all your idea and now you're leaving me hanging. I'll look so foolish when I tell *Mamm* I made it all up." Rose huffed and folded her arms across her chest.

Mark shrugged his shoulders. "I'll go along with it, if it'll get you out of a jam." One side of his mouth tilted into a crooked smile.

"*Denke,* Mark, you're a lifesaver." She leaned forward and gave him a quick kiss on his cheek.

When she pulled her head away, he put his fingers where she'd kissed him.

"Now, about my benefits for pretending to be your boyfriend." His eyes sparkled with mischief.

"You'll simply do this as a friend—as a favor to help me. There'll be no payments made or benefits of any kind. Agreed? And we're only acting; this is not real. Okay?"

He rubbed his forehead and breathed out heavily. "Agreed. The things I get myself into. How well do we have to act this thing out?"

"Just well enough to fool my parents for as long as my *mudder* has this bug in her head about me marrying. It will probably pass in a couple of weeks. I'm sure it's just because of Trevor's wedding."

"Just a couple of weeks, eh?"

"I'm sure that's all it'll take. Anyway, this is all your fault, so don't pull that face."

"How could it be my fault? I'm not the one who wants to trick her *mudder.*"

"You should've just kept your mouth closed because if you hadn't said—"

"Okay, okay—lesson learned. I agree with you. Next time I'll shut my—"

"Hi, Rose."

Rose turned to see one of the Walker boys, who was delivering more flowers to the stall.

"Hello, Sam." Rose left Mark so she could instruct Sam where she wanted the flowers placed.

When Sam had delivered the last bucket off the trolley, he hung around talking for longer than usual. Rose thought it a little odd and wondered whether her mother was matchmaking already and had spoken to Sam about her. And if that was so, it meant *Mamm* didn't believe the story about Mark. Rose knew Sam had a second job to get to. He worked with his parents in the morning, and then worked for a building company throughout the day.

When Sam left, Mark walked over. "Were you trying to make your pretend boyfriend jealous just now?"

"Did it work?"

He laughed. "Not really."

"Well, you'll need more practice as a boyfriend. Am I your first girlfriend?"

"First pretend one." He laughed and went back to straightening his stall, ready for the day's customers.

Rose's mind danced around Mark and the memories of him for as far back as she could recall. She'd never heard about Mark having a girlfriend and she was convinced he'd never had one.

It was the middle of the day when Rose saw a dreadful sight. Her mother was walking toward her with the twins dawdling along behind.

Rose stopped and stared, waiting for them to get close. This wasn't good. She was only there to see the interaction between herself and Mark. What other reason would she have for being there? *"Mamm,* what are you doing here? I could've brought something home for you."

"Nee, I'm just looking around to see what I can see." She turned her head, looking at nothing in particular, in a false manner, until she caught Mark's eye. Then she waved to him. "Mark, it's so nice to see you again."

"Jah, we haven't seen each other since—it must have been as long ago as last week!"

Her mother giggled. "You're always full of jokes, Mark."

"Not always," Mark answered.

"Why don't you come over for dinner tomorrow night, Mark? We'd love to have you there."

He pointed to himself as his eyes bugged. "Me?"

"Jah, you. I can't remember that we've ever had you to the *haus* apart from when we have the Sunday meetings there."

Rose's heart skipped a beat. As Mark stammered a response, he glanced at Rose who was trying to hide behind her mother. Meanwhile, Rose's two youngest sisters were talking to each other, unaware of what was going on around them.

"I … I … I'd love to. *Denke,* Mrs. Yoder."

"I'll look forward to it. Mr. Yoder and I can get to know you better." Nancy turned to her eldest daughter. "I'll see you tonight, Rose."

When Nancy and the twins were in the distance, Rose said to Mark, who was also staring after them, "This is a disaster."

"Not really. It's only dinner."

"Don't you see? She didn't believe me and now she wants to question you."

"She didn't believe that you and I are in love?"

"I didn't say we were in love. I kind of just made out that we have been on a couple of dates."

"Did we enjoy them?"

"Mark, you agreed to do this for me. Don't give me a hard time about it."

"Don't worry about things. Everything will go smoothly. You're over-thinking things, besides, I'm a good actor. If you and I are dating, they want to see what kind of person I am. That's only normal. My parents would do the same—I think—if I were a female and you were my pretend boyfriend. Going on that scenario, you'd have to be a man, which would be kinda weird." He scratched his head. "Weirder still, me being female …"

Despite Mark's assurances and nonsense babbling, Rose knew what she'd said previously was true. "This is dreadful."

"What did you think would happen, Rosie? This is part of it —part of us pretending to be a couple." He shook his head, looking serious, with lines appearing on his normally smooth forehead.

Rose knew Mark was worried and trying his best to hide it. There was no other way but to go through with it. It was better they believed Mark was her boyfriend rather than have them pushing her onto someone else.

"I guess it might go okay tomorrow night."

He smiled. "Now you're talking. Don't worry so much."

"I just hope they don't ask you any hard questions."

"If they do, I'll answer them."

Even if Mark was nervous, his confident words gave Rose a slight amount of comfort.

The next two hours passed by quickly, with many customers keeping the two of them busy.

Then, just as Rose pulled a sandwich out of her lunchbox, she saw him striding her way. He was a large young Amish man in a billowing white shirt, and nicely tailored black pants held up by black suspenders.

CHAPTER 7

ROSE RUBBED her eyes and looked at the Amish man heading toward her.

He was as she'd always imagined he would be. He carried himself with a confidence unlike the regular Amish men from her community. Her sandwich dropped from her hands and she dusted off the crumbs, all the while watching to see which way he went.

On he walked, directly toward her. To her absolute delight, he was clean-shaven, signifying he was a single man. This had to be her future husband; she could feel it in every part of her body. Did he know it too? He smiled at her when he stopped in front of Mark's stall. To Rose, it was as though she'd waited all her life for this moment.

He turned his attention to Mark and Rose heard him whisper, "Do you know who that girl is?" He then nodded his head subtly in her direction.

Who was the man? Mark knew him, that was clear.

Clearing his throat, Mark moved away from behind his stall and closer to Rose. "Rose, come over and meet my cousin."

Rose took a few steps toward him. It was when she was closer that the warm sunlight lit up his eyes and she saw the flecks of amber in the brown eyes that gazed back at her.

"Nice to meet you ..." She glanced over at Mark, hoping Mark would say his cousin's name.

The handsome stranger took her hand in his. His hand was large and warm, and easily covered hers.

"I'm Jacob."

"Hello, Jacob."

"Hello, Rose," he said, still staring into her eyes.

"Where are you from?" Rose asked, amazed she could find her voice.

"I'm from Oakes County. I'm visiting for a few weeks, learning how to build buggies from Mark's and my *Onkel* Harry."

That was the best news Rose had heard for a long time. He released her hand and she dropped it by her side, still looking at him. She wanted to know more about the handsome stranger, but she couldn't think what else to ask.

"Is this your stall?" Jacob nodded his head toward the flowers.

"It's not mine, but I watch it. I look after it for the Walkers."

"Rose's flower stall," he said, grinning.

He wasn't the first person to comment on her name in connection to the flower stall.

She looked down at her feet and shuffled them. "I know. It's a funny thing."

Mark interrupted them. "Rose's mother named all her

daughters after flowers. There's Rose, as you know, then there are Tulip, and the twins, Lily and Daisy."

"That's delightful."

"Rose's aunty, that would be her *mudder's schweschder,* has two *kinner* and also called them after flowers. That made Rose's *mudder* angry and now Mrs. Yoder doesn't speak to her younger *schweschder* anymore—that would be Rose's aunt."

Rose frowned at Mark, wondering why he was jabbering on about things she'd told him in the strictest confidence. "Mark!"

Mark cleared his throat and appeared not to care in the slightest that he'd revealed something so sensitive. "Are you here to deliver a message to me or something, Jacob?"

Jacob frowned. *"Nee,* I just wanted to have a look around while I'm here." His face brightened when he turned back to Rose. "It would be good if I could find someone who knew the area to show me around."

From the way he smiled, Rose knew he was dropping a large hint. She wasted no time in responding. "I could show you around sometime if you'd like." This was an opportunity too good to allow to slip away.

"I'd like that very much."

"Gut! I'll drive us," Mark said. "You don't have your buggy here, Jacob, and Rose doesn't have a buggy of her own."

Rose's mouth dropped open and she stared at Mark. Why was he trying to ruin things for her? He was acting like they were dating for real.

"I'm sure I could borrow a buggy while I'm here," Jacob said as he looked down on his cousin. He was a good six inches taller than Mark.

Mark frowned. "Rose and I are …"

"*Ah*, I'm sorry." Jacob raised both hands in the air and took a step back. "I didn't realize. I had no idea."

"*Nee*, it's not like that," Rose shot back.

Mark swiveled his head and stared at Rose. He looked hurt; she could see it in his eyes, but at that moment, Rose couldn't let Jacob think that she was taken.

"I can show you around. Mark and I are only friends," Rose assured him. "And nothing more," she added for good measure.

"Enough said, Rose!" Mark raised his voice. "I'll work out a time with you tonight, Jacob. Tomorrow night, I'm having dinner at Rose's *haus*. Maybe you could arrange something for Saturday afternoon?"

"Sounds good." Jacob turned to Rose. "I'll see you again soon, Rose."

Rose smiled, but was too upset to speak. Mark had picked the worst time to be so bossy. She'd never seen him like that and neither had she known him to raise his voice in that manner.

As soon as Jacob was gone, Rose knew she needed to find out what had been going through Mark's mind. "Why did you do that? We aren't really dating! You acted like a jealous boyfriend and embarrassed me in front of your cousin."

"It was you who talked me into this, Rose. I have to go to your parents' *haus* tomorrow, have dinner with you all, and pretend we're in some kind of a relationship. How am I going to do that if we tell some people we aren't and some we are?" He shook his head. "I don't like being in a position like this. I respect your parents and I don't like lying to them. Now we'll both be found out, for sure and for certain."

Rose didn't know what to say. He had a point. Her father

had always told her that no good came from dishonesty. Now she was learning her lesson in the worst way possible. If she hadn't made up the lie about Mark and herself dating, she would have been able to be alone with Jacob without Mark getting in the way. She glanced over at Mark who was still fuming. "I'm sorry. I didn't think the whole thing through."

"We've got to stick to the story, Rosie. What do you want the story to be? You can go home today and tell your parents we ended things if that's what you want. You tell me what you want to tell them and I'll go along with it."

If she did as he suggested, there was no guarantee that Mark's cousin was just as taken with her as she was with him, but she had to try. Otherwise, Jacob might slip right through her fingers. He was the only man she'd ever been attracted to.

"Okay. I'll tell them that we thought it best to end things."

He raised his eyebrows, indicating he'd expected a different response. He nodded, and then turned away without saying a word.

Typical man, sulking, she thought. It would've suited Mark to pretend they were boyfriend and girlfriend, so he could be closer to her more often. After she'd given him time to cool down, she said, "I'm sorry, Mark."

He looked over at her. "For what?"

"To drag you into my silly schemes."

He laughed. "It wasn't all your fault. It was my stupid idea. I'm telling you right now you should never listen to anything I say."

"And why did you tell him all that private stuff about the spat my *mudder* is having with Aunt Nerida?"

"It's a little more than a spat. Spats are over quickly.

This has been going on for years." Rose frowned at him, until he said, "I know; I'm sorry. It came out without me thinking."

"Obviously! It was clear you weren't thinking." Rose shook her head.

"To make things up to you, why don't you come to dinner one night at my parents' *haus* while Jacob's here?"

"He's staying with you?"

"*Jah,* right there in the *haus.*"

He knew she liked Jacob. She didn't want to hurt Mark's feelings, but she was never going to marry Mark and he had to come to terms with that. She didn't want to lead him on in any way. "I'd like that, *denke.*"

"Tell your parents about our demise tonight, adding that we're still friends and you're coming over to my *haus* for dinner tomorrow night instead of me going over there. If that's okay with your *mudder.*"

"It will be. *Denke.* I'll do that."

"You might as well bring Tulip with you and that will look more believable."

That last part wasn't a good idea. *What if Jacob fancies Tulip before he gets to know me? I can't risk it.* "I can ask her. She might not come along."

He shrugged. "Suit yourself. If you want to, you can come home with me tomorrow night from here. Unless you need to go home to pretty yourself up, or something—not that you need to."

Rose giggled. "I'll let Mrs. Walker know she won't need to take me home tomorrow night."

The rest of the day flew by and Rose couldn't wait to get

home so she could tell Tulip all about Jacob, the man her instincts told her she would marry one day.

ROSE USUALLY ARRIVED home when everyone was preparing dinner and this night was no different. She walked into the kitchen, hoping to have a private moment with her mother to tell her that things were over with Mark. Her mother looked up when she walked into the room.

"There you are. Can you set the table?"

"Sure."

The twins were chattering amongst themselves while Tulip was busy making dessert. Rose opened the cutlery drawer and pulled out knives and forks. "Can I talk with you for a quick moment in the lounge room, *Mamm?*"

Her mother swung around and looked at her. "Right now?"

"*Jah.*"

"Lily, you're setting the table now."

Lily scowled as Rose handed her the knives and forks.

When Rose and her mother sat down on the couch in the living room, her mother started the conversation. "Is everything all right, Rose?"

"Everything is fine, but Mark and I decided to end things. It's regrettable, but that's how things turned out in the end." She placed her hands in her lap and tried to look a little forlorn.

Her mother leaned back and her eyebrows drew together. "Over before they even began?"

"Well, they began and then they ended."

"The whole thing doesn't seem believable, Rose."

"Mark and I decided we are more suited to be friends than

anything else. And we decided to remain just that—friends. It would've been a big mistake if we'd continued our relationship."

"Well, that is disappointing. I really like Mark."

"That's not what you said yesterday."

Her mother's mouth contracted into a straight line. "What I said was that I've always liked Mark. I distinctly remember that."

"It's probably not what you said, but how you said it. I got the feeling you thought we weren't suited."

"It's what you think that counts, Rose."

"Is that what you truly believe, *Mamm?*"

"Of course, it is."

"*Gut* because today, I met someone I really like. He's someone who's staying with Mark." She twirled one of the strings of her prayer *kapp* between her fingers as visions of Jacob came into her mind.

"Who is it?"

"Mark's cousin; his name is Jacob. He's come here to learn to make buggies from Harry. I think he might only be here for a few weeks."

"That is very awkward for you, Rose."

"Why?"

"Because of Mark."

"Not really."

"They're cousins."

"Oh, I see what you mean. Mark and I are such good friends that Mark invited me over to dinner tomorrow night and, well, he said if that's all right with you. It wouldn't be right for him to come over for dinner because we aren't a couple anymore and that's why you invited Mark."

"What you're saying is instead of Mark coming here for dinner tomorrow night for your *vadder* and me to get to know him better, you're having dinner at his place because you like his cousin and you're no longer interested in Mark?"

Rose carefully considered what her mother said. *"Jah."*

Her mother tipped her head to one side. "It all sounds very suspicious. Are you sure you're telling me everything?"

"I'm not keeping anything from you, if that's what you mean." At that moment there was a loud crash in the kitchen.

"I hope that wasn't the roast," Rose's mother called out to her daughters in the kitchen.

"It was just Tulip being clumsy again," Lily called out, which caused an argument in the kitchen between the three girls.

"As long as you know what you're doing, Rose."

"I do. I really like Jacob."

"But that's the thing I don't understand. You told me there was no one, and then suddenly there was Mark, and now Mark is finished then on the very same day Jacob appears." Her mother wagged a finger at her. "I know I'm not getting the full story here."

When the argument got louder, her mother stood up and headed to the kitchen. "We haven't finished talking about this, Rose," she said over her shoulder.

"That's fine, but can I go to Mark's for dinner tomorrow night? It's all been arranged."

"Okay, but I'll have to ask your *vadder* first. I'm not going to bother him with it until after dinner."

Rose was relieved. Even though her mother didn't quite believe her, Rose was certain her father would allow her to go to dinner. That meant only twenty-four hours to wait before she could see Jacob again.

AFTER DINNER THAT NIGHT, Tulip lay across Rose's bed on her stomach with her chin cupped in her palms while listening to Rose tell her again how handsome Jacob was.

"He's so tall, and his eyes are like dark liquid amber. They are dark with amber flecks."

"Brown eyes?" Tulip asked.

"Brown, but with flecks of gold. He looked at me, and I knew he felt something too. He even asked Mark about me. I heard him."

"Where was Mark?"

Mark? Rose was reminded she still hadn't gotten the full permission to go to dinner tomorrow night. She needed both her parents' approval.

"I feel bad about telling *Mamm* that I was dating Mark. It was a stupid thing to do."

"There's no real harm done," Tulip said.

Rose pouted. "It makes me feel bad."

"*Jah.* I know what you mean. Does Mark know you like Jacob?"

"I think he does and that's why he invited me to dinner."

"You and Mark were over before you even began," Tulip said.

"Pretend over, and pretend began. Don't forget that," Rose pointed out.

"Mark must be upset about you liking his cousin."

"*Nee.* Well, a little bit at first, but he invited me to dinner tomorrow night to see him. He knows I'm just a friend and that's all we'll ever be."

"How old is Jacob?"

"I don't know anything about him except that he's here to learn how to make buggies with his *onkel.* The rest doesn't matter. I'll find out all I can tomorrow night if *Mamm* and *Dat* let me go. I'll go downstairs now and hope *Mamm's* told him about it."

Before Rose made a move, a gentle knock sounded on her bedroom door. "Rose, your *vadder* and I would like to speak with you now."

Rose looked at Tulip for emotional and moral support. The next few minutes would determine if she was going to that dinner or not. "Okay. I'm coming," she called back.

"I hope things go well," Tulip whispered.

Rose whispered back, *"Denke.* Stay here and I'll tell you about it when I come back. I'm either going to be very happy or upset.*"*

"I'll wait. If *Mamm's* sort of said you can go, you've got a good chance."

Rose left Tulip and went downstairs to face what her parents had decided.

From the looks on both their faces, she felt she was in trouble.

Her mother began, as soon as Rose sat in front of them on the opposite couch, "I told your *vadder* that you and Mark are over and you're not interested in him any longer."

"That's right."

"So you were seeing him, and now you're not?" her mother asked.

"*Jah*, that's right."

"And exactly how long were you and he—"

"Rose doesn't have to tell us all the small details," her father said.

"I was just asking because it seems odd. She never mentioned a thing about him until the other day, and as soon as I asked him to come to dinner, she's not dating him anymore."

"Anyway, he won't be coming over for dinner tomorrow night because that would be awkward," Rose said. "He said he hoped you both don't mind and—"

"He can still come." Her mother frowned. "You're still friends, and I invited him."

"*Mamm*, do you forget I mentioned that I'm going to Mark's house for dinner because his cousin is visiting?"

"A man or a woman?" her father asked.

Before Rose could answer, her mother said, "It's Jacob Schumacher?"

"*Jah*, I guess that's his last name. His first name is Jacob and he's staying at Mark's *haus*. Do you know him, *Dat?*"

"I do."

Her mother turned toward Rose's father. "Well, what do you think of him?"

"I only met him today at the bishop's *haus*. He seems a nice young man."

Her mother wasn't finished. "And what community does he come from?"

"He comes from Oakes County," Rose's father said.

"Why did Mark ask you to dinner, Rose?"

"Because I met Jacob at the markets today. Mark thought it would be a good idea if we had dinner at his place. I don't know; maybe Jacob wants to meet people while he's here."

"Nee," her mother spat out the word.

"Mamm, what's the matter?"

"What you're saying isn't adding up. Something's not right here."

"Nancy, I can't think of a reason Rose shouldn't have dinner at Mark's *haus.* We know the family well. What harm could it do?"

"I didn't say it would do harm. I just don't think we're hearing the full story. That's why I wanted to talk with you in front of your *vadder,* Rose, because you might be more inclined to tell him what's really going on in your life."

"You know how young people can be, Nancy."

Nancy crossed her arms over her chest and Rose's father whispered, "We don't need to hear the whole story, Nancy."

Rose remained stony-faced, as though she hadn't heard his whispered words. She was grateful to her father for allowing her some space.

"Did you want to say anything else to Rose?" her father asked her mother.

Her mother shook her head. "Well, if you're happy with her explanation, we'll leave it at that."

"Well, *Dat?"* Rose asked.

"I think everything's been said. We trust you to make the right decision here, Rose, and not do anything behind our backs. The worst thing parents can face is their child getting into trouble or getting themselves into harm's way."

"Okay, but it's just dinner, *Dat,* and it's at the Schumachers'."

"Your *vadder* is talking about the other thing where you're not telling us the full story. You didn't have a boyfriend, the next day you do, and then the next day it's all over, and you've got your heart set on someone else. It doesn't add up."

Rose would've preferred if her mother hadn't said all those things in front of her father. Especially the thing about having her heart set on another man. "I'm not doing anything wrong, I'm safe, and I'm not putting myself in harm's way. Mark and I have ended things and we're still friends. We handled things like adults."

"That's very good to hear," her father said.

"Are you happy with what she's just said, Hezekiah?"

He turned to his wife. "I am, are you?"

"Not totally, but we'll leave it at that for now."

Rose leaped to her feet. "Can I go now?"

"Jah, you can go," her father said.

"And I can go to Mark's for dinner tomorrow, *jah?"*

"Okay," her mother said.

"Denke, Mamm, and *Dat."* She gave them both a quick kiss on the cheek and then wasted no time hurrying up the stairs. When she was back in her room, she threw herself onto her bed, missing Tulip by inches.

"What happened?" Tulip asked as she got up off the bed to shut the door.

When she sat back on the bed, Rose sighed. "Weren't you listening in?"

"I tried to, but I couldn't hear everything."

"Mamm doesn't believe that Mark and I were in a relation-ship and now she thinks something is odd about me liking

Jacob. She should be happy since she's trying to get me married off."

"Now both *Mamm* and *Dat* know you like Jacob?"

"I guess they do."

"That seems strange."

"I know, but I can't do anything about it now." Rose exhaled deeply.

"It's just that they might say something to someone. Parents have a habit of doing things like that and embarrassing their *kinner.*"

Rose giggled. "That's true, but I don't think it matters. I think that Jacob likes me just as much as I like him. I've got that feeling. We have a deep connection."

"I wish I had someone like that. Someone to love and admire."

"You will. I had no one and now I've got Jacob." Rose giggled. "I haven't really got him yet, but I've got him to think about."

"To daydream about," said Tulip.

"*Jah.*"

CHAPTER 8

ROSE WOKE EARLY the next morning. She had to make herself look the best she could because she wouldn't have time to change before going to Mark's house later that night for dinner.

She pulled on her dressing gown to shield herself from the chilly morning air, and when she took up her hairbrush, she placed it in her lap. Each night she carefully braided her hair, so it wouldn't tangle during the night while she slept. She untied her hair and it fell in waves well below her waist. Her hair had never been cut. After she'd brushed out her hair with one hundred long, smooth strokes, she re-braided it and pinned it flat against her head in order for it to fit under her white starched prayer *kapp*.

Rose turned her attention to her home-sewn dresses made with the treadle-machine. She had five dresses, each a different color. The pale yellow dress would give her skin a little more depth, she decided. She'd always felt good in yellow for some reason. She wondered which one Jacob would like. Maybe he'd prefer her in the green dress? Her eyes flickered over the grape-colored one, and then she decided to save that one to wear at the Sunday meeting. The dark green one was quickly discarded as that was a shade that many of the older ladies wore. She wanted to look young and vibrant, so she went back to her first choice of the yellow dress.

After she had pulled her dress on, she placed her apron over the top, expertly tying the strings behind her back. When she was fully dressed, she sat and looked out the window at the horizon. The sun was barely evident behind the distant hills, giving the sky around them a warm and happy glow.

The moon had set, its light all but faded, while one lone star twinkled brightly toward the west against the remaining backdrop of navy blue.

It was rare that Rose was awake so early and she reminded herself she should enjoy that hour more often. It was so beautiful to watch the night fade as it greeted the morning. It was a display of God's beauty.

Her wonder was interrupted when she heard a gentle tap on her door. She knew it couldn't have been her sisters awake so early because they never knocked. Instead, they'd just walk right in. It had to be her father.

She leaped off her bed and opened her door. "Morning, *Dat*," she said when she saw his smiling face.

"I thought I heard you awake."

"*Jah*, it's going to be a busy day because I'm going from work to Mark's *haus*."

"I know. I remember."

"It must be early if you haven't left for work yet."

"I'm just going down to eat. Your *mudder* has got my

breakfast ready. I just wanted to tell you to be careful. I know your *Mamm's* got it into her mind that you should marry someone and marry him fast. That's just how she is. She thinks of something and then she wants it done immediately." He chuckled quietly and had softness in his eyes the way he always did when he talked about his wife. "I'm not going against what she says. I'm just saying to be cautious."

Rose tilted her head to the side. They kept telling her to be cautious as though she were a child. "About what?"

"The decisions you make now, while you're young, can affect the rest of your life." There was a silent moment between them. "Do you know what I mean?"

"*Nee*, not really."

"Picture this, then: You get into a boat and you're on a journey. You pull up anchor and set your sail in a certain direction, and the current pulls you in that same direction faster and faster. Pretty soon you're a long way from where you started, and the problem is there's just no way to get back. Meaning you can't start over once you've set sail."

It sounded quite a frightening story the way he told it. "Doesn't the current go the other way?"

"In my story, the current is time, and it only goes in the one direction, and there's no way to go back and start over. Once you set the direction of the sails, that's it. Be careful which way you set them because you might fall asleep and when you wake, you'll find that you want to be over there and you're over here, with no way to get where you want to be."

She stared at her father's worried face and the deep lines in his forehead, knowing he didn't know a thing at all about boats.

She tried to interpret what he'd just said. "So be careful what direction I go in, and don't fall asleep?"

"You've got it." He put his hand gently on her shoulder and stared into her face. "Determine what direction you want to go and, if it turns out that that direction doesn't suit, adjust the sails quickly before you go too far in that other direction."

"The bad direction?"

He nodded. "But consider all directions carefully. The wrong direction might look like the right one when it isn't."

"Got it."

He stepped back and smiled. "Your *mudder* will be wondering where I am."

"Denke, Dat. I won't be late home tonight."

"Shall I come and collect you from the Schumachers'?"

"Nee, I'm sure Mark or his cousin will give me a ride home." Rose couldn't help the tiny smile that tugged at the corners of her lips. It would be wonderful and romantic if Jacob drove her home in the darkness under the starlit sky.

Her father walked away and Rose closed her door. She knew the translation of her father's boat talk; it was he telling her to be careful whom she married. If she chose the wrong man, she had to change her mind before she married him, otherwise, it would be too late. There was no divorce in their Amish community, and she'd seen a few unhappy marriages. In those cases, the couples had chosen to live separately. It seemed a miserable existence and she'd listen to her father's caution.

She gave a little chuckle thinking how funny her father was with his scenarios. Why couldn't he just speak his mind and talk about men and marriage? Rose went to the window and sat back down. The sun had just peeped over the horizon, giving a glow of light to the distant hills.

She closed her eyes and prayed that Jacob would realize that she was the woman for him. Hopefully, he felt the same attraction as she.

WHEN ROSE WALKED into the farmers market, she saw Mark talking to someone at the entrance. She walked right on past without saying a word.

"Hey," he called out to her.

She turned around to look at him.

He said goodbye to the person he'd been talking with and hurried to her. "Are we on, or are we off?"

"In our relationship? Or dinner tonight?"

"I meant our relationship." They continued walking to their stalls

"We're off," Rose said bluntly.

He rubbed his chin. "Oh, that's too bad."

She frowned at him. Yesterday he was upset with her about it, saying it would be too hard to pretend they were a couple.

He continued, "You can still make it for dinner tonight, can't you?"

"*Jah*, I can, if that's still alright. Jacob will be there, won't he?"

Mark nodded while they continued to walk inside the market. "Jacob will be there."

"Okay."

"You look nice today, Rosie. That color really suits you. It brings out the golden flecks in your eyes."

She laughed. "I don't have golden flecks in my eyes. My eyes are just green."

"You do. You have tiny flakes of gold surrounding your pupils. And the rest of your eyes are as green as precious emeralds."

She smiled because she recalled those same golden flecks in Jacob's brown eyes, which would mean their children would quite possibly have the golden flecks too.

"What did your folks say about dinner, and me not coming? Are they okay with that? I hope they weren't too sad that I'm not going to be there."

"I told them we were no longer together, and that you had your cousin visiting, so you invited me over. *Dat* said that he met Jacob at the bishop's *haus* yesterday."

"Oh, I didn't know that, but Jacob mentioned he was visiting a few people when he left here."

"I think *Mamm* thinks I'm a bit odd now."

"Her too?"

Rose giggled and slapped him on the shoulder. "Stop it."

"Why does she think you're odd? For ending things with me? If so, I totally understand that, and now I know for sure she's a wise woman."

"*Nee.* She thinks I'm odd because I told her we were a secret, and then suddenly I had to take it back and tell them we were no longer together. Not only that, I'm going to dinner at your *haus.*"

"That's not odd; that happens all the time."

"Not with me it doesn't," Rose said just as she reached her stall.

"Well, don't be too upset about us breaking up. We can still be friends." He sniggered.

"That's another thing my folks thought odd and strange—me going to your place for dinner after we're no longer together. Well, *Mamm* did more so than *Dat*. I explained to them that we're still friends and that your cousin would be there."

He shook his head. "You do get yourself into some awkward situations, Rosie."

"*Nee*, I don't! This was the first awkward thing that's happened, and don't forget it was your suggestion in the first place."

He chuckled. "And you're never going to let me live that down, are you?"

She shook her head. "Never!"

Rose kept busy by arranging the flowers. She loved working with them—she was happiest when flowers and their fragrance surrounded her. Despite her name being Rose, her favorite flowers were daisies. They were such happy flowers and filled her heart with joy, as she imagined their central section as smiling faces. Daisies also reminded her of when she was young when she'd sit in the fields on lazy summer days, making daisy chains with Tulip. The twins were babies back then. Her mother would spread out a large blanket, and Tulip and she would sit for hours after their mother had shown them how to make the flowers intersect one another to create the daisy chains.

For the remainder of the day, Rose purposefully tried not to think of Jacob and the wonderful life they'd have together. She didn't want to let her mind run away with her until she knew for sure that Jacob felt the same. Instead of daydreaming about Jacob, she concentrated on work. Every now and again, she got nervous pangs in her stomach about seeing him again. Her entire future hinged on this dinner. She'd surely find out if Jacob truly liked her.

CHAPTER 9

THE WORK DAY had been a struggle where Rose had to purposefully push her nerves aside and forget about the dinner she'd be going to that evening. Every time she thought about seeing Jacob again, she started to worry that he hadn't felt the same attraction, or if he had, he might change his mind over dinner.

At the end of the day, Mr. Walker himself collected the flowers and the takings, instead of one of his older sons. Rose waited for Mark to finish up serving the last of his customers.

"Are you ready now?" Rose asked when the customers walked away. She tried hard to keep the impatience from her voice.

"*Jah,* unless I get some more customers. That's why we're here, Rosie, to make money, remember?"

"I know, but it's after our normal closing time."

"Is it?" He glanced at the large clock that hung over the middle of the aisle. "So it is."

He was deliberately going slow just to annoy her, she was

certain. "I'll help you pack." All the cheese had to be locked down in the fridges overnight.

"No need. I do it by myself all the time."

"I insist," Rose said.

Minutes later, Rose walked with Mark to his buggy.

Before she got in, he said, "It's only about twenty minutes to my *haus.* I hope you can control yourself with me for that long —sitting so close to me in this luxurious buggy of mine."

Rose pulled a face at the ancient buggy that was barely road-worthy. "I could always sit in the back if you're that worried."

He laughed. "No need for that. I'm sure I can trust you." They headed out of the lot, where the horse and buggy had been for the day, and moved onto the road.

"I HOPE your parents weren't too upset when they learned we weren't together anymore."

Rose played along. "They were absolutely devastated. It will take them some time to recover. Maybe even years."

Mark chuckled. "I would imagine it would. They can see I am a reliable hard-working man and what more could they want in a husband for you?"

"Let's see now. One who is kind, caring, and unselfish?"

He glanced over at her, taking his eyes from the road for one second. "I'm all those things."

"I know you are," she said, hoping she hadn't gone too far with her teasing. The last thing she wanted to do was offend him.

"Well then, your search is over."

Even though Rose didn't want to hurt his feelings, neither

did she want him getting in the way when she was trying to talk to Jacob over dinner. "You will make someone happy one day, Mark."

"*Jah*, I believe I will."

Rose kept the conversation away from Jacob even though she was anxious to learn all she could about him.

"Here we are," Mark said when they finally pulled up beside his family home. "I'll take you in, and then I'll need to come back out and tend to the horse."

"You don't need to come in with me. I can go in by myself."

"Are you sure?"

"Of course I am." She got down from the buggy, looking all around to see if she could see Jacob, but he was nowhere in sight. He had to be inside the house. "*Denke,* Mark," she called over her shoulder as she walked to the house.

"No problem," she heard him call back.

She knocked on the door and Mark's mother opened it. Mark was the second youngest child of eleven children, all of whom had left home except for Mark and his younger brother, Matthew.

"Rose, how lovely to see you." With both hands, she reached out and clasped Rose's forearm. "Come inside. I'm always telling Mark to invite you for dinner. I don't know what took both of you so long."

"*Denke.* That's nice of you." Rose had struggled to find words. She hadn't expected such a friendly response. It was as though Mark's mother thought there was something between her and Mark. Could Mark have made out that there was? It *was* something he'd do.

"We've got a visitor, Mark's cousin from Oakes County."

"Jah, I've met Jacob. He stopped by the market stall yesterday."

Mark's mother ignored what she said, and continued to pull her into the living room where Jacob sat with Mr. Schumacher, Mark's father.

Both men stood when they entered the room. "Jacob, this is a good friend of Mark's, Rose."

Jacob nodded. *"Jah,* we've met before, just yesterday."

"Hello, Rose," Mr. Schumacher said.

"Hello, Mr. Schumacher," Rose answered, doing her best to look at the older man when all she wanted to do was fix her eyes onto Jacob.

They all stood there staring at Rose, and she licked her lips, wondering what she should do. She looked back at Mrs. Schumacher. "Would you like some help with anything in the kitchen?" Rose wanted to speak to Jacob alone, but didn't want to speak to him with Mr. Schumacher listening.

"Nee, you're our guest. Sit down and tell us what you've been doing lately. I never get a chance to speak to you at the meetings."

Mrs. Schumacher guided Rose to the couch, and Rose sat down next to Jacob.

When they were all seated, Rose looked around at the three sets of eyes on her. She felt like she was back in school where she had to stand and speak in front of the whole class. Her stomach clenched now, as it had then, and she felt she would be sick.

Rose took a deep breath to steady her nerves before she spoke. "I haven't been doing anything much. Just going to work."

"Rose works at the Walkers' flower stall at the farmers market," Mark's father explained to Jacob.

Jacob smiled. "I know, right next to Mark's stall. I saw Mark there yesterday and I met Rose at the same time."

Again, Rose felt nervous as the three of them stared at her. "That's all I've got to say." It was a lame response, but it was either that or silence.

"How many brothers and sisters do you have?" Jacob asked.

"I have two older brothers and three younger sisters."

"The younger two girls are twins," Mrs. Schumacher explained to Jacob.

Jacob smiled as he told Rose, "My two older brothers are twins and they married twin sisters."

"That is unusual, but I think I've heard of twins marrying twins before. I've never personally known anybody who did." Rose looked at Mark's parents, hoping they'd both leave the room so she could be alone with Jacob. Jacob was looking at her as though he were thinking the very same thing. At least, that's what Rose hoped was going on in his mind.

"How long are you here for, Jacob?" she asked, even though she knew the answer from the day before.

"I don't know exactly. I'm here for a few weeks, anyway, to learn about the buggy making from Harry. There's a permanent job on offer, but I'm not certain whether to take it or not. My uncle said to try it for a few weeks to see what I think so that's what I'm doing."

Rose was delighted to hear about the job offer. Harry was the local buggy maker and people came from far and wide to buy their buggies from him. Rose was sure Harry had around six men working for him.

"And have you done buggy making before?" she asked Jacob.

"Never, that's why I'm trying it." He laughed and Rose felt a little silly for asking a dumb question. It was just nerves. He continued, "It's something I've always thought about doing as a trade. I'm an upholsterer already, so I know how to do that side of things."

"Jah, which would come in handy, I'd imagine."

At that moment, Mark walked in and sat down with them.

His mother turned to look at him. "Mark, how was your day?"

"It was a fairly good day. We had above average takings."

"Gut!" his father said.

CHAPTER 10

"I DON'T KNOW how you do it, working at that stall all day," Jacob said to Mark.

"The market stall provides a good income for the whole family," Mr. Schumacher explained before Mark responded again.

"I quite enjoy it. I like meeting new people, and taking care of the same customers who come back week after week. I'm good friends with many of them now."

Mrs. Schumacher said, "Mark is a people person. He's always been outgoing and friendly, even when he was a little *bu.*"

Rose quietly agreed. Everyone liked Mark.

Jacob grimaced and looked at Mark. "Doesn't it get smelly working around goat cheese?" He waved his hand in front of his screwed-up nose.

Frowning at Jacob's rudeness, Mark said, *"Nee!* Anyway, we

sell nearly everything to do with goats. We have goats' milk soap, yoghurt, and milk; not just cheese."

"*Jah*, you'll need that soap to get the goats' smell off." Jacob laughed but no one joined him.

"It's no more smelly work than, say, buggy making," Mark replied, now looking either serious or annoyed at his cousin.

"That's not smelly at all." Jacob glared at Mark.

Sensing the mounting tension in the air, Rose said, "I have the smelliest job of all."

Everyone looked at Rose and laughed.

"I think the word you're looking for, Rose, is 'fragrant,'" Mr. Schumacher said.

"*Jah*, that sounds much better," Rose commented.

"Dinner smells delicious, Aunt Sally," Jacob said to Mrs. Schumacher.

"I hope you like it, it's—"

"Goat stew?" Jacob asked.

Mr. Schumacher laughed, while Mark scowled at him.

"I'm sorry, Mark, I was just trying to be funny," Jacob said. "Your *vadder* thought it was funny."

"Our goats are for milking, not eating," Mark said.

Jacob continued, "Surely you eat the older ones—"

"*Nee*, don't talk about that, please." Rose covered her ears.

"It's lamb stew, a recipe I got from your *onkel's* dear old *mudder*, your *Grossmammi* Schumacher, and Mark's." She looked at Rose. "She's gone to be with *Gott* now."

"I'm pretty sure I remember her," Rose said.

"It's Mark's favorite food," Mrs. Schumacher said, smiling at her son.

Rose kept talking, hoping Jacob wouldn't say anything else to upset Mark. "I can't wait to try it."

"Well you can, in about five minutes, as soon as Matthew gets home."

"Are you sure you don't need any help?" Rose asked.

"Maybe we could leave the men alone for a few minutes. Will you help me in the kitchen, Rose?"

Rose stood and followed Mark's mother into the kitchen while thinking that it might have been better if Mark had arranged some sort of outing with just a few young people, including her and Jacob. It was awkward having a family dinner at Mark's house with Mr. and Mrs. Schumacher listening to everything that was said.

HALFWAY THROUGH DINNER, Rose wished she had invited Tulip along after all. Rose wasn't much of a talker and it had been difficult to keep the conversation flowing as well as stopping the tension between Mark and Jacob. Matthew had sat there and barely said a word.

It was after dessert that Mark's younger brother excused himself and Mr. and Mrs. Schumacher left the other three young people alone in the kitchen to talk.

"Would you like coffee, Rosie?" Mark asked.

"*Jah*, I would. Do you want me to get it?"

"*Nee*, I can do it. What about you, Jacob?"

"*Jah*, I wouldn't mind one."

Mark went to the far end of the kitchen and put the pot on the stove to boil.

"Do you know what you're doing, Mark?" Rose asked with a giggle.

"Don't you worry about me, Rosie."

"He knows what he's doing in the kitchen. He'll make someone a good *fraa* one day." Jacob laughed hard at his own joke.

Rose smiled even though she didn't find it very funny, and Mark ignored him as he got the cups ready for the coffee.

Jacob turned his attention back to Rose. "So, is it Rose, or Rosie?"

"It's Rose, but Mark likes to call me Rosie for some reason."

"I'll call you Rose. I like the name Rose."

"Okay." It didn't matter what he called her. She liked the deep rich tones of his voice.

"Rose, we've got the meeting on Sunday morning. What are you doing after that?" Jacob asked.

"Nothing that I know of."

Jacob leaned closer and said quietly, "How about we do something together?"

The metal coffee container in Mark's hands slipped from his grasp and clanged heavily on the floor, scattering the ground coffee everywhere. The container bounced across the room and stopped just near the doorway.

Rose jumped up to help Mark clean up the mess while Jacob laughed.

"Thanks, Rosie," Mark said. "It looks like we won't be having coffee after all. How about some hot tea instead?"

"Tea will be fine. You go ahead and make the tea and I'll clean this up," Rose said. "Just tell me where the broom and the dustpan are."

"Through that door."

Jacob hadn't moved from his spot at the kitchen table. "I was looking forward to coffee."

"You still can have it. I'll scrape some off the floor for you," Mark said.

Jacob shook his head. "I'll take a pass on that one."

ROSE SAT on one side of the table sipping hot tea, while looking at both Jacob and Mark. It was like being between two roosters that wanted to fight each other. Jacob had attempted to ask her out, but she didn't know how to get the conversation back to where it had been before Mark's coffee-spilling incident.

Perhaps if she jogged Jacob's memory a little he'd ask her again, or would that appear too desperate? No, she would have to wait until Jacob mentioned something of his own accord.

"So, you have twins in your *familye?*" Jacob asked her.

"That's right. Daisy and Lily. They're younger than I am."

"I've got two older brothers who are twins."

Rose nodded politely, wondering why he didn't remember that they'd already talked about that before dinner. *"Jah,* I think I heard something along those lines."

Jacob turned to his cousin. "Mark, why don't you be a good son and see if your parents would like some hot tea?"

It was a large hint for Mark to leave them alone in the kitchen and Rose hoped he'd take it.

"Nee, they wouldn't. *Denke* for your concern. They never have hot tea after dinner. Sometimes they have coffee, but now they won't be having that."

Jacob turned back to look at Rose and from the way he

looked at her, she knew that if Mark had not been there he would've asked her out. All hope wasn't lost. Maybe at the meeting on Sunday he would ask her out again.

When the time came for her to go home, both Mark and Jacob insisted on driving her. It was Mark's buggy so he won the argument, but Jacob insisted on going along for the ride.

When they reached the house, Jacob looked out at it. "So this is where you live, Rose?"

"It is."

"It's quite big," Jacob said. "It looks so from the outside."

"Jah, none of us has ever had to share a bedroom even when the boys lived at home. There was a bedroom for each of us. Now *Mamm* has a sewing room and *Dat* uses one as an office since the boys are married and gone."

Through the windows, she could see warm light coming from both the kitchen and the dining room. Without walking inside, Rose knew that Tulip had been waiting up for her, wanting to hear what happened, and she couldn't wait to tell her everything.

"Denke for driving me home, Mark."

"Denke for coming to dinner."

"It was good to get to know you better, Rose. I'm sure I'll see a lot more of you soon," Jacob said. "And I would've driven you home if my cousin hadn't insisted on coming with us."

"I've driven Rose home. You've come with me," Mark pointed out to Jacob.

"Denke." Rose gave him a nod.

When Rose got down from the buggy, she headed into the house and the moment she opened the door, she turned and gave a little wave. It was too dark to see if the two men were looking at her as Mark's horse clip-clopped back down the driveway.

Rose closed the door behind her and leaned against it. She knew Mark liked her, but now there was Jacob, whom she hoped liked her. There had been tension between Jacob and Mark the whole night. Next time she'd have to get Jacob by himself somewhere away from Mark. If only Mark hadn't spilled that coffee right when he had. It had been such an awkward night. No wonder Matthew excused himself and went to bed early. He probably sensed the tension too.

"How was it?"

On hearing Tulip's voice, Rose looked up to see her sister rushing down the stairs toward her. Rose took off her shawl and hung it on the wooden peg by the door.

"Quickly tell me, or I'll simply burst."

Rose giggled and carefully looked around to ensure they were alone. "Let's sit by the fireplace where it's warm."

The two girls sat by the fire, which had nearly burned to nothing.

"I'm sure he likes me," Rose whispered.

"That's so great. How do you know?"

"I can tell. He tried to ask me out, but Mark got in the way."

"Oh, that's too bad. What does he look like?"

"I've already told you that."

"Tell me again. I have no boyfriend. I have to live through you and let your excitement be my excitement."

"He's not my boyfriend. Not yet anyway."

Both girls giggled and then Rose told Tulip about the awkward evening.

"Rose, he was just about to ask you out. Do you think Mark dropped that coffee tin deliberately?"

"He wouldn't have done that. At least, I don't think so. He was the one who invited me there in the first place."

"Jah, but it's no secret he likes you; he always has."

"I just wish that I could've been alone with Jacob and gotten to know him better."

"At least you found out a lot, and the reason he's here."

"The worst thing was that he mentioned going somewhere together after the meeting tomorrow."

"That's fantastic!"

Rose shook her head. "I don't know."

"Why is that bad?"

"Because he was interrupted when he was talking. I never got a chance to say yes and he never asked again."

"So you're not going anywhere with him tomorrow afternoon?"

"I don't know."

"It seems complicated. Tell me again what happened?"

"Haven't you been listening?"

"Jah, but I'm tired. Tell me again."

"That was when Mark had the accident with the coffee. I need you to do me a huge favor on Sunday."

Tulip leaned forward. "What is it?"

"I'll introduce you to Jacob and I want you to get friendly with him and then maybe mention that the four of us might go somewhere together."

"The four of us? Meaning you, me, him, and Mark?"

"Exactly! That way, I'll get to spend time with him and it won't look like I've asked him."

Tulip pouted. "*Nee,* it won't look like you've asked him because I would've asked him. That's not what I'd normally do."

"Well, will you do it? Do it for me?" Rose put her hands together and pouted, trying to make her sister feel sorry for her.

Tulip smiled. "Okay. I'll do it if you want me to, but only if you'll do the same for me one day, or something similar if I need you to."

Rose nodded. *"Jah.* We have a deal. *Gut!* When we're all together, just the four of us, you keep Mark talking and right out of the way so I can have time with Jacob."

Tulip giggled. "I hope that will work."

"There's no reason why it won't."

"Shall we have a cup of hot tea?"

Rose shook her head. *"Nee.* I had an early start this morning. I'll go to bed."

"And think about Jacob?"

"It's been hard not to think about him. I can't keep him out of my mind. I only hope that he feels the same."

"He does. I'm sure of it."

"I hope so."

Rose switched off the main overhead gaslight and carried a small lantern up the stairs to light their way. Then each girl went to her own room.

After she'd pushed her bedroom door open with her foot, Rose placed the lantern on her dresser and got ready for bed. She hoped that everything would turn out as she planned.

Once she was between the sheets, she imagined what it might be like to be married to Jacob and have children with him. Just like the twins often said, she too would like three sets of twins so there would only be three childbirths. The children would all have the golden flecks in their eyes, as Jacob and she shared that in common. Would Jacob be happy to stay on in this small community? Or would he go home in a few weeks? If he wanted to go back home, Rose would go with him if he asked her.

Once she was married with her own home, everyone would stop looking over her shoulder and trying to run her life. She'd be happy and independent. Rose drifted sweetly off to sleep while imagining she was married to Jacob, living in a clean, tidy house with their three adorable sets of twins. Life would be perfect.

CHAPTER 11

ROSE WAS UP EARLY on Sunday morning, making sure she looked her best for Jacob. Still, she was the last one down to the kitchen.

"Quick! You better hurry," Tulip said as she rinsed out a few dishes at the sink.

"I'm ready."

"You haven't eaten yet," her mother said.

"I'm not hungry."

"You'll need something in your stomach," her mother protested. She was always trying to force as much food into her children as she could.

Rose reached forward and grabbed an apple from the bowl in the center of the table. "I'll have one of these," she said before she bit into it.

"At least that's something, I suppose," her mother said.

"I'll eat after the meeting. There's always so much food."

"Don't look too hungry when you eat. I don't want people to

think we aren't feeding you enough or that you wait for after the meetings to have a decent feed."

"No one's going to think that. Everyone knows we get fed."

"You're thin because you don't eat enough, and there's nothing natural about that. I don't think men like women who are too skinny. You should keep that in mind. Men like women to have meat on their bones. And if you had more padding you wouldn't look so tall. Men like women to be shorter than them."

"Jah, Mamm." Rose wondered how her mother knew so much about what men liked, since *Mamm* had married young, and *Dat* had been her only boyfriend.

Her mother looked out the window. "Quick, your *vadder* has the buggy hitched. Come on, all of you. Now!"

Rose wore her grape-colored dress in the hopes that Jacob would like it. She got compliments when she wore it from girls her age.

THEY ARRIVED AT THE FULLERS' *haus* where the fortnightly Sunday meeting was being held. The twins hurried off to meet their friends while Tulip and Rose walked more slowly behind them.

"Don't forget what I said to do," Rose said.

"I remember. You'll introduce me to Jacob, then I'll get to talking to him and suggest the four of us go somewhere, right?"

"That's right."

"Got it. Do you think this will work?"

"I'm hoping so."

"You look pretty today, Rose. What have you done to yourself?"

"It's the fresh bloom of love."

Tulip giggled. "Well, if you could bottle that, we could sell it at the markets."

The two girls giggled again. Rose caught sight of Jacob heading into the house, and caught Tulip's arm. "That's him."

Tulip stood on her tiptoes. "I can't see anyone."

"That's because he's just now gone into the *haus*."

"Let's sit down at the back, and then you can point him out to me."

"Good idea, but you'll know him when you see him. He'll probably be the only stranger in the meeting."

"I like sitting at the back anyway, then I can watch everyone."

As soon as Rose walked into the house, Jacob was right there, smiling at her. She smiled back as she walked past him with Tulip beside her.

"Was that him?" Tulip whispered.

"*Jah.* What do you think?"

"He looks very nice. Isn't he too old for you?"

"*Nee,* of course not."

They slid into the back row.

"I've always seen you, in my mind, with someone more like Mark," Tulip said.

Rose's jaw fell open. "Don't be ridiculous! Mark is just a friend. I wouldn't marry a friend!"

"It'd be better than marrying an enemy."

Rose whispered back, "I'm not going to do either. The person I'm going to marry is sitting right there in the second row from the front."

"That's where Mark's sitting."

"That's also where Jacob's sitting and he's the one I'm going to marry. Don't be annoying."

"I'm just sayin' the truth of what I feel."

"It's what I feel that's important because it's my life."

"Okay."

Rose whispered, "Don't start getting to be like *Mamm.*"

Tulip dug her sister in the ribs. "I'm not like *Mamm.*"

"Well don't speak like her."

Tulip nodded. "I'll help you in any way that I can."

Rose looked at her sister and gave her a big smile. *"Denke."*

The girls' father stood and opened the meeting in prayer, and then Joseph Oleff sang a song in High German. When Joseph was finished, the bishop stood and began his sermon.

Rose always liked to hear what the bishop had to say. He usually told stories about real life situations, and then drew similarities from the stories in the Bible.

Rose's mother was one of the women who got up during the last ten minutes of the service to set out the food. There was always a big meal served after the meeting, and the other ladies yielded to *Mamm* as the organizer. Since Sunday was a day of rest, no one worked except to do the jobs that were necessities, such as feeding animals and the like, and the food for Sunday's meals was prepared the day before.

CHAPTER 12

ROSE WAS clever enough to arrange things so that the twins were helping their mother with the food after the meeting. And that left Rose and Tulip free to socialize, and talk with Jacob.

After the meeting had come to an end, people had walked out of the house into the yard where the food and refreshment tables were.

Rose whispered to Tulip, "Let's go up to the drinks table and get a soda. And then, we'll just wait there and hope Jacob comes over."

The two girls got a soda each and stayed back from the table while they talked to one another. It wasn't long before Jacob approached them and Rose introduced Jacob to Tulip.

"How long are you staying here for, Jacob?" asked Tulip.

"I'll be here for quite a few weeks. I'm staying with Mark's *familye.*"

"Do you know many people here in the community?" Tulip asked.

"Nee, I don't."

Rose stared at Tulip. This was the perfect time for her to say what they'd planned.

"The four of us should do something some time. The three of us and Mark."

"What a good idea," Rose commented as though she was hearing it for the first time.

"Okay, what do you think we should do?" Jacob asked with a smile.

Tulip answered, "I'm not sure. We could go on a picnic or something."

"Why don't we do it this afternoon?" Jacob asked, now turning to Rose. "Are you free later today, Rose?"

"Jah, I am. I guess we could do that." While she was talking, she saw Mark walking to them.

Tulip saw him too. "Mark, we're planning on doing something this afternoon. Can you join us?"

Rose couldn't help smiling as she listened and watched her brilliant plan unfold.

"Unless you had some other plans, Mark?" Jacob asked.

"Why don't we have a picnic?" Mark asked the girls, ignoring Jacob.

"A picnic sounds like a good idea," Tulip said. "That's what we were just talking about. I think it was my idea first."

Mark laughed and was just about to say something when Jacob interrupted him.

"How about we collect you girls at, say, around two o'clock this afternoon?" Jacob asked.

Tulip and Rose nodded.

"That suits us," Rose said.

"You don't want to stay on for the singing?" Mark asked.

"You can stay," Jacob said. "If I can borrow your buggy, I'll go on a picnic with the girls by myself."

"*Nee,* you won't. I'll go too. We'll collect you girls at two."

"We'll be ready," Tulip said. "So shall we bring the food?"

"We can bring the drink and the dessert if you girls can make some sandwiches," Mark suggested.

"We can do that," Rose said.

"Good. We'll see you at two."

Rose knew she'd have to do some careful negotiations with her parents. Of a Sunday, Rose normally took her parents home and then went back for the young people's singing where she would drive the twins and Tulip back home.

Rose found her father and considered he'd be the easiest to talk with first. *"Dat,* Tulip and I would like to go on a picnic with Mark and Jacob this afternoon at two. Do you mind if you collect the twins from the singing just this once?"

He rubbed his graying beard. "Have you asked your *mudder?"*

"*Nee,* I'm asking you first. Please don't say that I can if it's all right with her."

One dark eyebrow rose just slightly. "How did you know I was going to say that?"

Rose grunted. "Really?"

His mouth turned upward at the corners. "That's what I was going to say. I don't think she'll mind." He nodded his head. "There she is. Ask her."

She glanced where he'd pointed his head and saw her, and then said to her father, "So, if it's okay with her, I can go? You don't have a problem with it?"

"Nee. If it's okay with *Mamm,* it's okay with me. Just don't be late home."

"I don't know what time we'll be back. What if we want to go to dinner somewhere afterward?"

"Don't be later than eight thirty."

"Okay. I won't. I mean, we won't. Tulip's coming too."

"Very good."

Rose hurried over to her mother. To her surprise, her mother didn't seem to mind in the least. Either that, or she wanted to appear trusting of her daughter to those who'd overheard Rose's request.

Everything was falling neatly into place. Rose hurried to tell Tulip the good news.

BY THE TIME ROSE, Tulip, and their parents got home, the girls only had an hour before Mark and Jacob were due to collect them. Rose sat on her bed while Tulip tried to calm her.

"Why have you gotten so nervous all of a sudden?"

"Because I really like him."

"He likes you too or he wouldn't have agreed to go on the picnic."

Rose rubbed her forehead. "Do you think so?"

"Jah, I know it. Now, are you going to stay in that dress?"

Rose looked down. "Do you think I should change it? I don't want to look like I'm trying too hard. There is no reason to change the dress. It's not dirty or anything."

"You're making me nervous the way you keep chewing your fingernails. Stop it!"

Rose placed her hands in her lap.

"A cup of hot tea will soothe your nerves," Tulip said.

"Okay, but wait until *Mamm* and *Dat* leave to go visiting. It shouldn't be too long now. And we have to make those sandwiches, which I nearly forgot about."

Tulip giggled. "Me too. Anyway, that won't take long. I'll go down and put the teakettle on and find out how long it'll be before *Mamm* and *Dat* leave. Then, I'll see what we have to put on those sandwiches." Tulip stood and headed for the door.

"Don't make it obvious, or they'll think we're up to something," Rose whispered.

"Nee. They already know we're going on a picnic." Tulip left the room before Rose could say anything further.

Rose was pleased she wasn't nervous when she was with Jacob. It was only when she thought about him that she felt anxious. Her mother had told her whenever she felt like her head would explode, to take long deep breaths. She breathed in for ten counts and then out for ten counts. When she was on the third lot of repetitions, Tulip appeared before her and gave her a fright.

"They're leaving now." Tulip headed over to the window and looked down. *"Dat's* at the buggy and here comes *Mamm* right now. Now she's getting in."

Rose got off the bed and joined her sister at the window. "Do you think a hot tea will work? My stomach feels like a bundle of butterflies trying to escape."

"Jah, I'm sure it will. Come on." Tulip walked down the steps and Rose followed closely behind her.

As they sat drinking tea, Rose made a plan. "You keep Mark occupied and Jacob and I will go for a walk."

"How's that going to happen? Will you do that in the middle or the beginning or at the end of the picnic?"

"It'll have to be at the right time and I don't know when that'll be until it happens."

"Should we have a signal word, or something?" Tulip asked.

Rose pursed her lips. *"Nee.* We won't need anything like that. You won't need to instigate anything. When Jacob and I go for a walk, all you have to do is keep Mark talking and keep him away from us. The worst thing would be if he wants to go for a walk as well and he gets in the way. Do you know what I mean?"

"Ah, I see. I can do that." Tulip nodded.

"Good." Rose was so determined that nothing go wrong that while Tulip made the sandwiches, she carefully tutored her on what to do and say in every scenario that could possibly take place that afternoon.

When the girls heard a buggy, Tulip looked out the kitchen window. "It's them."

Rose jumped to her feet. "How do I look?"

Tulip looked her up and down. *"Wunderbaar."*

"Really? Or are you just saying that because you're my *schweschder* and you have to be nice?"

"You really do look good. Are you ready? We should go out and meet them rather than them come to the door. If they came to the door we'd have to ask them in and that wouldn't be allowed." Tulip bundled the wrapped sandwiches into a picnic basket and buckled it shut.

"I'm ready." Rose licked her lips. She was so nervous that her mouth was dry already.

"Do you want to carry the basket?"

"*Nee,* you do it," Rose said.

"Okay."

The men were out of the buggy already when Rose closed the front door behind her. Jacob was smiling so much that Rose found it hard to keep her eyes from him.

"Sit in the back with me, Rose," he called out. "Tulip can go in the front seat with Mark."

Rose was only too happy to sit close to him on the backseat. As they traveled to the park, Mark made certain that he was not left out of Rose and Jacob's conversation. That didn't bother Rose so much, as long as she could have some private time with Jacob later.

"This looks like a nice place to picnic," Mark said as he stopped the buggy at one end of the park.

"Looks good to me," said Tulip.

"Did you bring something to sit on, Mark? I totally forgot about that," Rose said.

"There should be a blanket in the back there just behind the seat."

Jacob reached behind them and found a blanket. "Got it," he said.

Rose hadn't needed to plan so intensely because after they'd finished eating, Tulip got Mark talking and then Jacob sprang to his feet and suggested Rose go for a walk with him. Jacob had done it in such a way that Mark couldn't have done a thing about it if he'd wanted to. It also helped that Tulip was distracting him by talking quickly and barely drawing a breath.

As they started on their walk alone, Jacob said, "Those were lovely sandwiches, Rose. Did you make them?"

"Tulip made them."

"The bread was so tasty. Did you bake the bread?"

Rose giggled. "I can't take credit for that either. I don't do much of the cooking now that I work full time at the farmers market. It's my *mudder* and sisters who do that now. I help cook the evening meal when I get home and do a few chores in the morning before I leave for work, and that's it."

"Seems like it's been good for you to have a lot of sisters."

"I guess so, otherwise, I'd have to do more chores." Rose had to get the conversation off her and onto him. "Are you hoping your *onkel* might give you a full time job? I mean, is that the only thing that brought you here?" Rose asked.

He smiled at her and then looked down at his feet as he walked. "I'm thinking the time has come for me to find a girl. My parents are always telling me that's something I need to do before too long."

Rose laughed. "They sound like my parents. Well, my *Mamm*, at least."

"It's good to know I'm not the only one who's being influenced by their parents."

"That's probably true. I guess our folks are older and have more experience in things." Rose suddenly felt bold, and wanted to let him know how she felt. "So, is that what you're doing here—looking for a wife?"

He glanced down, and then looked in the distance as he answered, "To be honest, that's one of the main reasons I'm here. There are many lovely women back home, but there's not been one that I feel a connection with."

"That's sad."

"It's not sad, it's merely so. Anyway, I got to thinking I should do something about it." He flashed her a smile.

Rose liked a man of action. She was getting to like him more as they spoke. "I hope you'll find your trip is going to be worthwhile."

He slightly raised one eyebrow. "Maybe I already have."

Rose giggled at the way he smiled at her.

"Tell me, Rose, what is your relationship with my cousin?"

"You mean with Mark?"

"Jah, with Mark."

"He's just a friend."

"Does he know that?"

Rose swallowed hard. "Of course, he knows that. We've been good friends for such a long time."

"I think he likes you as more than someone to pass the time with."

"Nee, he's always just joking around and we get along well. That's just how he is."

"That's good to know."

"Well, to be totally truthful, we had this dumb idea that he and I would pretend to be in a relationship so my mother would stop nagging at me."

He stopped walking and looked at her. "That sounds kind of dishonest."

"Oh, we never meant it to be like that. I can see how it sounds that way."

"I'd reckon it was Mark's idea."

Rose couldn't let Mark take the blame. "It was mine. It was a dumb idea and we never carried it through completely."

"I'm glad. Things like that have a way of backfiring on people. Dishonesty never pays."

"I agree with that. It was just a moment of silliness, nothing else."

They walked the next few steps in silence and then Jacob stopped in his tracks and Rose stopped along with him. "Rose, would you care to go on a buggy ride with me tomorrow?"

Rose hadn't expected this so soon. "I'd love to, but I can't because I work tomorrow."

"Perhaps I could collect you from work when you finish?"

Jah, that might be a good idea. I'll let Mrs. Walker know that I have a ride home. It's the Walkers' stall and Mrs. Walker brings me to work and takes me home. She'll be glad she doesn't have to do it."

"Shall I collect you from there at five?"

Rose nodded. "Five sounds good to me." She could see from Jacob's face that he was pleased she'd accepted his offer. Her plan with Tulip had worked brilliantly.

"Come on, we'd better get back to the others," he said. They turned around and as they headed back, Jacob started talking again. "I've got the idea that Mark likes you, as I said, but I think he's dating another girl. I find that confusing and a little odd. I never really understood Mark. He seems the odd one out in his family."

"Nee, that's not possible. He would've told me if he had a girlfriend. We talk about everything."

"Everything?"

"Jah." Rose nodded.

"Are you going to talk about me to my cousin?"

"Ach nee. I would never do that! I would never talk about personal things."

"Well, maybe Mark isn't telling you about things that are personal to him either."

Rose screwed up her face at the thought of Mark keeping something from her. It didn't seem likely. "I haven't heard that he is seeing anybody ..." Her voice trailed off. The thought of Mark dating someone and not telling her about it didn't sit well. And if Mark was dating someone, where was this mystery woman today?

Rose had grown used to the constant attention Mark had always given her and it was a little unsettling to think of that being taken away. Her mother always told Rose that she was the kind of person who wanted to have her cake and eat it too—and now she wanted to date Jacob, but she still wanted her special relationship with Mark. She had to admit that Mark's focused attention on her was kind of flattering. Suddenly she realized that she wouldn't be able to have that kind of relationship with Mark if she were dating his cousin, but it wasn't fair on Mark the way she occupied his attention.

"What are you thinking about right now, Rose?" Jacob asked.

She gave a little giggle. "You've got me thinking now. I'm thinking who Mark could have dated without me knowing. I normally get to find out about everything in the community. And I never thought Mark would have kept anything like that from me."

Jacob shrugged his shoulders. "Maybe I'm wrong. It's just the impression I got from a few things that Mark said. It's not unusual. A lot of couples keep relationships quiet until they're ready to go public. Everyone thought one of my cousins was single and then we found out he'd been dating a girl for two years. They announced their wedding and weeks later they were married." He snapped his fingers in the air. "As quick as that."

"I know it happens like that sometimes. My *bruder* just got married and they kept their relationship a secret for nearly a year before they told my parents they were getting married."

"Do you see? He could be secretly dating Tulip and you wouldn't know."

"What? Mark?" The thought of Mark and Tulip together was incomprehensible.

"Look at them over there now."

Rose looked to where Jacob was pointing. Mark and Tulip were sitting close together on the picnic rug, talking and laughing. She felt a pang in the pit of her stomach.

"Definitely not! Tulip is my *schweschder* and I know for a fact she's not dating Mark or anyone else."

Jacob laughed. "It's just an example. I didn't mean to worry you."

"I'm not worried. I'm not worried at all. It's just that Tulip tells me everything and so does Mark."

"People must trust you."

"I guess people who know me do."

When they'd walked two steps on, Jacob grabbed hold of Rose's arm and suddenly pulled her behind a tree. Now they were out of the sight of Mark and Tulip.

CHAPTER 13

Rose giggled. "What are you doing, Jacob?"

"Before we go back and sit down to talk about nothing, I want to be honest with you."

"About what?"

"About how I feel about you. I never dreamed that I'd meet a woman like you. I prayed to meet someone and since the first time I saw you, I knew you were the one—the one I've been waiting for."

Jacob's words were exactly what Rose wanted to hear. This was everything Rose had ever imagined and dreamed of. It had to have been love at first sight for him, too. He had exactly the same feelings for her that she had for him. The image of him walking toward her that first day jumped into her mind.

"That's the same as I feel, too," Rose said.

"If I hadn't come here, I'd have never met you. I need to spend as much time with you as possible. Would your parents think it odd if I saw you again tomorrow night like we planned, or like we talked about?"

Rose giggled. *"Nee*. They want me to get married, but I don't want to do anything that would upset them, so I'll have to ask their permission."

"I meant for you to ask them. I would never go behind your parents' back with anything—not like Mark would."

Rose jolted her head back. "You're wrong about Mark. It wasn't like that. Anyway, it was my fault."

"Enough about him. I hope your folks like me."

"Dat likes you already, he said so, but they wouldn't like it if things moved too quickly. I've heard them talk about couples who get married fast. They talk about it as though they don't like it." Rose knew she had blushed when she mentioned marriage. "I mean, I didn't mean to say that we were getting married or anything like that."

"I think I know what you mean. Your parents are conservative and want things to take their proper time."

"That's it exactly. They want things to take their own time. You're very good with words, Jacob."

"That's only because I'm a little older than you."

Rose nodded.

"I've only got a few weeks, Rose, and then I have to head back. That's why I want to spend every moment together with you. Can you sneak out of the house tomorrow night after our buggy ride so we can spend some more time with each other?"

She tried to work him out. He said he didn't want to mislead her parents, but then again, sneaking out of the house was fine? *"Nee*. I wouldn't feel right about that. They would find out, and then I'd be in real trouble. Then they'd punish me by making me stay in the house for a month."

"Wednesday night, then. Can I come and collect you on Wednesday night too as well as tomorrow night?"

"Maybe it would be better to go out Wednesday instead of both nights. And knowing my parents, they'll want you to come for dinner, so they can get to know you. How would you feel about that?"

"I can do that. I can come for dinner. Don't worry, I'll create a good impression."

Rose giggled. "I know you will. *Dat* already said he likes you from when he met you at the bishop's *haus.*"

"*Gut!* You mentioned that already."

"Oh, I didn't mean to say it again. It's just that I want you to feel comfortable that my parents like you."

"Your *mudder* does too?"

"She hasn't mentioned you specifically because she doesn't know you."

"Well since your *vadder* likes me, my job is half done already."

Rose glanced out from behind the tree and saw that Mark was now looking around for them. "We should join them now. It wouldn't look good if we stayed away any longer."

"You're right. I wish we were here by ourselves. Mark is really getting on my nerves even though he's my cousin."

"Just get along with him. You'll like him once you get to know him better. He's quite funny."

"I know him well enough. I've seen him at least once a year even though we live far apart. Once a year is more than enough." He put his hand on the small of Rose's back. "After you, my lady."

Rose walked forward and the two of them joined Tulip and Mark.

"I'm glad you've come back," Mark said as they sat down.

"Yeah, well, we got hungry again," Jacob said. "Are there any sandwiches left, or did you finish them all off, Mark?"

Mark glared at Jacob and then looked at Rose. "Picnics are about eating, not walking."

Jacob started to say something, but Rose gently touched him on his arm and he stopped. When Jacob grunted, he looked away from Mark and looked from Tulip to Rose. "The sandwiches were tasty. *Denke* to you two girls for preparing them," Jacob said.

"*Jah, denke,*" Mark said.

"There's more here." Tulip reached into the basket and pulled out more sandwiches. These ones were filled with pickles and roast meat. The first ones were a selection of chicken and ham. Each man took a sandwich and Rose handed everyone a paper napkin.

With more food and drink to occupy the two men, they each weren't focused on being irritated by the other.

While they ate, Rose knew she was smiling way too much, and hoped that Mark wouldn't ask what she was so happy about. Rose was thankful that Mark hadn't asked about the glow she knew must have been apparent on her face. He noticed though, she was certain of that.

When it was time to go home, Mark and Tulip carried the basket and blanket to the buggy ahead of Jacob and Rose, who dawdled behind.

Jacob moved himself closer to Rose. "I really want you to come out with me somewhere on Monday night as well as Wednesday night."

"I don't know."

"I've never met anyone like you, Rose. I can't stop thinking about you all the time. I can't wait until Wednesday to see you again. It's far too long a time away. Please see me tomorrow night?"

Rose giggled. That was exactly what she wanted to hear. He felt the same as she.

"The only thing is that if I go out with you on both nights, my parents will want you to come for dinner soon. What do you think about that?"

"I've already said I'd be happy to do that. I'd be delighted to do that any time your parents would like to invite me, or you'd like to invite me."

"Really?" She looked up into Jacob's soft brown eyes.

His lips drew upward at the corners. "Why are you so surprised?"

Now she knew he was serious about her. She couldn't tell him she was surprised because it would show how insecure she was. "I'm not sure."

"What is your answer then, about tomorrow night? Quick, tell me before we get to the buggy. I don't want Mark to know what we're talking about."

"It's not a secret, is it?"

"*Nee,* of course not, but he has a habit of ruining things for me. It's not a secret if you say yes." He stopped still and she stopped walking too. Then he looked down into her eyes. "What do you say, Rose?"

"Come on you two. It'll be dark by the time you get to the buggy," Mark called out as he waited by the buggy with Tulip.

"See what I mean? Come on, Rose. It'll make me really happy."

"Okay."

"Wunderbaar. I'll collect you at eight tomorrow night."

Before Rose could say another thing, Jacob was striding toward the buggy and Rose hurried to catch up to him.

WHEN ROSE and Tulip arrived home, their mother and father were back from their visiting, and the twins were still at the singing. Rose whispered to Tulip that she wanted to tell her parents about going out with Jacob the next night and on Wednesday night. She desperately hoped they wouldn't have a problem with that. Tulip offered to make herself scarce in her bedroom.

Her father was on the couch, reading the newspaper, and her mother sat next to him, knitting. When Rose sat down in front of them, they both looked up expectantly. "I just wanted to tell you that I'm going out with Jacob tomorrow night and Wednesday night, if that's okay."

Her mother got in quickly before her father could say anything, "That's fine. I'm pleased to see you're getting out more. That's all I wanted."

When Rose looked over at her father for a sign of approval, he smiled and nodded, which was his way of saying he had no problem with it. That had gone a lot easier than she thought it would. "Okay then. I might have an early night. Oh, unless you want me to pick up the girls from the singing, *Dat?"*

"Nee, I'll get them. I'll give them a couple more hours."

She rose to her feet. *"Gut nacht."*

"Gut nacht, Rose," her mother said.

"Night, Rose," her father said as she hurried up the stairs.

Rose burst into Tulip's room and told her the good news that she was allowed to see Jacob on both Monday and Wednesday nights.

WHEN EVERYONE WAS home for dinner the next night, Nancy was worried that Rose was too interested in Jacob and they didn't really know him as they'd know a man from their own community. She left the girls to finish cooking the evening meal in the kitchen while she sat beside her husband on the couch.

"Rose is going out with Jacob after dinner," she said to Hezekiah as he read the paper.

"I know." He put the paper down in his lap and looked up at her. "You were fine with that last night when she asked us."

"I know, but since then I've got to thinking about things, that's all. Do you think she'll invite him for dinner soon?"

"Ask her to, if that's what you want."

"Don't you?"

"Jah. I'd like to get to know him better if Rose likes him as much as she seems to."

Nancy rubbed her neck. *"Nee,* I'll wait for her to ask me if he can come to dinner."

"As you wish."

"Well, what do you really think should happen?"

"I think I want to read the paper." When she sighed, he added, "You worry too much about things, Nancy. You were worried that she was never going to get married and now she's interested in a man, you worry about that too."

"Only because we don't know him that well."

"We know the Schumachers."

"*Jah*, we know them, but not their extended family."

"If you're worried about it, ask her to invite him to dinner. Simple! And that will stop you worrying so much."

"It's not as though I'm worried. It's not unreasonable to be concerned."

Hezekiah gave a low chuckle. "No matter what you call it, it's still the same thing."

"You're probably right. Over dinner, I'll suggest she invite him one night this week, or perhaps next week. Given her history of short relationships, it could be over by next week, or even tomorrow."

Hezekiah laughed, seeming to find what she said particularly funny. "I thought you didn't believe Mark and she were having a relationship."

Tugging with agitation on her *kapp* strings, Nancy said, "I don't know. She's very secretive. I hope all the girls aren't going to be like this. My hair will go more gray, grayer than it is already."

Hezekiah shook his head.

"What was that for?" Nancy asked. The approval of her husband meant everything to her and she didn't like it when they disagreed about things.

"Nothing."

He had a definite gleam in his eye as though he were amused about something.

"Tell me what you think is so funny."

He took a long, deep breath, and then said, "I don't think she's secretive at all. She's not sneaking out to see anyone or lying to us. Now, if she did, I would say she was a secretive or a deceitful person, but she's not doing that. You need to calm down and stop expecting the worst of situations."

Nancy bit her lip. "Is that what I'm doing?"

"I think it's just because you're over-anxious and want the best for our girls. Trust in *Gott* and He will look after them and find them good husbands."

"You're right. *Jah,* I know you're right." There was a sudden clang in the kitchen, which sounded like a large saucepan had been dropped on the floor. Then an argument broke out between the girls. "I better get in there and supervise, or I'll have no kitchen left." She stood up and then leaned down and gave her husband a quick kiss on his cheek before she hurried off to the kitchen.

Nancy decided not to mention anything to Rose about inviting Jacob to dinner. Not tonight. She would wait to see if she also went out with him on Wednesday night like she'd planned. It wasn't as though she was thinking the worst, like Hezekiah said, but it was very likely Rose might cancel Wednesday night.

Rose was nervous about her buggy ride with Jacob. Earlier in the day at the markets, Mark had let her know that Jacob had asked to borrow his buggy to take her out. That was the only comment Mark had made about her going out with his cousin.

The twins teased her a little bit about Jacob over dinner, but after their father cleared his throat and glared at them, that was the end of that. Then their mother pointed out that Rose would get out of cleaning the kitchen and doing the washing up that night, and that made the twins grumble about the unfairness of being the youngest.

When Rose heard the buggy coming to the house, she was delighted. Not only would she get away from the twins' constant chatter and complaints, she'd get to be alone with Jacob.

"Bye, everyone," Rose called over her shoulder before she headed out the door. She got to the buggy before Jacob had a chance to jump down.

"Hi, Rose," he said in a deep, manly voice as she climbed in next to him.

"Hi."

He turned the buggy around and set off down the driveway. "I've got a lovely new buggy at home. It's embarrassing to collect you in a rickety buggy like this."

"It's fine. There's nothing wrong with it."

"Nothing wrong with it except it's fit for the scrap heap—the junk yard."

"It gets Mark to where he needs to go. That's all that concerns him. He's a practical man."

"Well, enough talk about Mark. You see him every day and I'm sure that's enough." He chuckled. "You must think I'm a dreadful person the way I speak about Mark sometimes."

"Nee, I don't. I know you don't mean it."

"I don't. I'm just fearful that you might like him if I'm totally honest with you. I guess that's immature. I'm working on being a better person because you deserve the best."

Rose was delighted that he was showing honesty as well as vulnerability. *"Denke.* That's a nice thing to say."

"It's true."

She hoped that meant he was going to stay longer. "How did you like your day at work?"

"Making buggies is nothing like I thought it would be."

"Do you like it better than upholstery?"

He leaned toward her and corrected her. "You mean uphol-stering?"

Rose giggled. "I don't know the right way to say it. I meant whatever it was that you used to do."

"I don't know that either of those things suit me, but I'm thinking of sticking with the buggy making for a little longer. I'm starting to like it here." He shot her a dazzling smile.

"I hope you'll stay a long time."

"Would you like to go back to the park where we were yesterday? I noticed that it had lights and a walking trail. It would be a perfect place."

"I'd like that."

"I don't want to keep you out too long tonight. I figured that your parents might not let you go out again on Wednesday night if they think I've kept you out too late tonight. Wednesday will be our real date night."

"I'm sure that will be fine with them, whatever time I get home."

"You might not know your parents as well as you think. I'm telling you now, they wouldn't be fine if you got home too late."

Rose wondered how many girls he'd been out with and how many parents had been cross with him for bringing them home late. She didn't ask because she didn't want to know.

When he stopped the buggy at the park, he stepped out and raced around to help Rose down before he secured his horse.

She loved the feel of her hand enclosed in his strong hand. He let go of her sooner than she wanted him to because he had to secure his horse to the post. To her delight, he took hold of her hand once more as they wandered onto the path.

"It's such a beautiful night," she said, staring up into the starry sky.

"It's a beautiful night because I'm with you," he said and then released her hand to put his arm around her shoulder. Then he pulled her close to him.

She was taken aback a little at the suddenness of his movements.

"Are you okay?" he asked, holding her firmly.

"*Jah,* I am."

"Me too."

They both laughed. They walked the next few minutes in silence.

"Why don't you put your arm around my waist?" Jacob suggested.

It didn't feel right, but Rose put her arm around him just the same. This was something she wasn't used to and it was the closest she'd been to a man. At the same time, it felt good.

"That's more like it," he said. "I'm so glad I met you, Rose."

"Me too."

"I have a serious question for you." He stopped abruptly and turned his body to face her, causing her hands to fall down by her sides.

"What is it?"

"How do you really feel about me?"

She gulped and didn't know how to answer. What if she told him how much she liked him and he didn't like her as much? The last thing she wanted was to embarrass herself or have him laugh at her. Pushing nerves aside and hoping God would reward her honesty, she said, "I like you."

"Like?"

"*Jah,* I do."

"*Gut* because I like you an awful lot." He started walking again. "I see good things in our future, Rose." He pulled her tighter toward him.

She put her arm lightly around him where it had been before. "Like what?"

He glanced down at her. "Marriage, of course. What do you think about that?"

"That sounds good."

"Don't get me wrong, I'm not asking you just yet, but if things keep going as well as they have been, I will ask you to marry me. How does that make you feel?"

"It makes me feel very happy."

"That's just how I want you to feel." He stopped again and then he slid both hands down to take hold of hers. Now he was looking down into her eyes. "You're so beautiful, Rose. One of the most beautiful girls I've ever seen. You're so pale and delicate, like a true rose."

Embarrassed and feeling heat rising in her cheeks, Rose went to walk away, but he wouldn't let her hands go.

"I mean it," he said.

He spoke with such intensity that Rose became a little nervous.

"I really want to kiss you right now," he said, letting go of one of her hands. With his fingertips, he pushed back her prayer *kapp* and took hold of some loose strands of her hair.

Rose had no idea what he was about to do next. She was surprised when he leaned forward and smelled her hair. He was so close that Rose could smell his musky masculine scent. She desperately wanted him to kiss her, but at the same time, wanted to reserve her first kiss for her future husband. Right now, she didn't know for certain if he was the one. Fearing that he would kiss her, she stepped back before he could do so.

"What's wrong? Have I offended you?" He took a step back.

"Not at all. We should probably head back now."

"Normally I would say no, but we've got Wednesday night to look forward to." Hand-in-hand, they walked back to the buggy under the moonlight.

It was the first romantic night Rose had ever had.

"Are you all right, Rose? Am I moving too fast with our relationship?"

"*Nee*, not at all. I'm looking forward to Wednesday night."

"Me too."

Their ride home was fairly quiet with neither of them speaking very much.

When they arrived at Rose's house, Jacob said, "Should I come in and say hello to your parents?"

"*Nee.* They're not expecting you to."

"Maybe I should walk you to the front door."

"I'm fine." Rose quickly got out of the buggy in case he tried to kiss her. When she was out completely, she turned back to face him. "I'll see you on Wednesday night."

"*Jah,* I'll be here at eight. *Gut nacht,* Rose. I won't be able to think about anything else until I see you again."

Rose giggled and said a quick goodbye before she turned and headed to the house. Her parents were awake and waiting for her. When she walked through the front door, they were sitting together on the couch and looked up as she closed the door behind her.

"You're early. Did things go alright?" her mother asked.

"Wonderfully well. I'm so looking forward to Wednesday night." Rose sailed past them and headed up the stairs, pleased that they didn't ask anything further.

THE NEXT DAY, and the following day, Mark was strangely quiet. Rose made no comment about it to him because she knew he was upset about her seeing Jacob. Rose wanted nothing to ruin her Wednesday night with Jacob because he'd said that Wednesday night would be special. Even though it was far too soon and she didn't really know him, Rose daydreamed about Jacob asking her to marry him. It would be wonderfully romantic if they both knew so soon after meeting that they were destined for each other.

AT LAST, Wednesday night arrived and as Rose waited on the couch to hear the clip-clopping of horse's hooves, her mother sat down beside her.

"Since after tonight you will have been out with Jacob twice, it would be nice to invite him to dinner. Your *vadder* and I would like to get to know him better."

It was no surprise to Rose that her mother said that. She'd been expecting she would be asked to invite him to dinner. "Sure. I'll ask him. Any particular night?"

"Before you go out with him again. It doesn't matter which night."

Rose leaped to her feet when she heard the buggy. *"Jah,* I'll ask, *Mamm.* That's him now." After she had grabbed her black shawl by the front door, she headed out of the house.

Her heart pounded when she jumped into the buggy beside him, and by the look on his face, he was just as pleased to see her.

"Hello, my sweet Rose."

"Hi."

"Let's go." He turned the buggy around and trotted the horse down the driveway.

"Where are we going tonight?"

"I don't know. Is there any particular place you'd like to go?"

As long as she was with him, she didn't care where they went. "Not really."

"I'll find a nice place where we can take a walk."

"That sounds good."

Jacob stopped the buggy on a deserted road. "This looks as good a place as any to take a walk in the moonlight. Just like we did on Monday."

"Okay."

He jumped down from the buggy and held out his hand to help Rose out. When she was on the ground, he kept hold of her hand. She liked the way he made her feel special. Pointing to the sky above, he said, "See the moon, Rose?"

Rose looked up at the moon that hung low in the sky—a crescent moon. "It's so beautiful."

He squeezed her hand as he stared at her. "Not half as beautiful as you."

When she glanced up at him, he stopped walking and looked into her eyes. Then he let go of her hand and placed his hand on the small of her back. He drew her close to him and lowered his head until she felt his warm breath tickle her face.

She stepped back. *"Nee."*

He took a pace forward. "What's wrong?"

"I want my first kiss to be when I'm married and not before then."

He stared at her in disbelief and then whispered, "Don't you see, Rose? I'm serious about you. If we both feel the same way, we will be married to each other."

"Really? You feel that way?"

"I do."

Once again, he put his hand behind her waist and this time he pressed her body against his. When he lowered his head, she turned her face and he was left to place his lips on her cheek. His lips were warm and soft. She wanted to kiss him on the lips, but had made the decision a long time ago to wait until her wedding day for her first real kiss.

He suddenly stepped back. "You're being quite ridiculous. Is there something wrong with you?"

"What do you mean?"

"If we're going to marry one day, why not kiss me now? Do you want to keep me waiting?"

Rose was upset at his outburst and didn't know what to say. Should she allow him to kiss her? She wanted to, so what was the harm? She stared at him open-mouthed, wondering what to say.

"I'm sorry, Rose. I shouldn't have gotten angry. It's just that my feelings for you are strong and you're beautiful. I find you irresistible."

His words made Rose feel good, and he had apologized to her, which made her feel better. She had been taught to forgive so she did just that.

"Say something," he said.

"I forgive you."

He put out his hand and she took it. Together they walked down the moonlit road.

"Where shall we live when we marry? How would you feel about coming back to live with me?" he asked.

"I'd like to live close to my parents, but it doesn't really matter." She gazed up at him and he smiled.

After ten or fifteen minutes, they turned back to the buggy.

"Are you cold?" he asked.

"A little."

He put his arm around her and held her close. When they got to the buggy, he stopped. "Rose, I just need to kiss you on your beautiful lips. We need to seal our future with a kiss." Before she could respond, he pushed her against the buggy and brought his lips down hard against hers.

He was kissing her before she could stop him. She knew that the right thing to do would be to push him away, but she didn't. As they kissed, he put his hands behind her back and pulled her hard into him until she found it hard to breathe. She finally pushed him away with both of her hands, and then gasped for air.

He laughed at her. "I think you liked that, didn't you?"

She wiped her moist mouth with the back of her hand. "I said I didn't want to kiss you and you made me."

"What's the difference if we kiss now or later?"

"It matters because you took away my choice." Rose wondered whether she was being silly about waiting for her wedding day to be kissed. Many girls didn't wait anymore.

He put his arm around her. "It's hard for a man to wait for a kiss from the woman he loves."

Her heart melted when she heard him say that he loved her.

"You do love me, don't you?" he asked.

"I do."

"Then that makes everything okay. Do you see that?"

Rose nodded, but would've felt better about things if she hadn't had her feelings overruled. "I suppose so."

"Anything we do is okay because we're in love, and soon, when it's time, we'll tell people."

"Okay." Rose nodded again, pleased to be almost engaged, and she knew that would make her mother thrilled.

"Let's walk some more." With his arm around her, they walked quite a distance in the darkness with the only light coming from the moon above them. "One day, I'll ask you to marry me. I'll ask you properly."

Rose would scarcely be able to wait. "My mother said to ask you to come to dinner."

He laughed. "See? Your parents like me. That should make you feel better about that kiss just now."

"I don't feel bad about it; it's just that I didn't expect it."

"You should have. All couples kiss and some do more. It's only the normal thing that everyone does."

If only someone had told Rose how things worked.

"How about tomorrow night for dinner at your folks'?" he asked Rose.

"*Jah,* that'll be fine. *Mamm* said any day would be okay."

"Come on. Let's head back," he said, swinging her around to face the buggy.

When they arrived back at Rose's house, he pulled her close to him before she got out. This time, it was easier to kiss him because she'd already done so before.

"Don't forget I love you, Rose."

"I love you too, Jacob." She got out of the buggy and headed into the house, wiping her mouth with her fingers. He was a little forceful, but perhaps that was what men were like when they were alone with a woman they were dating. At times like these, she could've done with an older sister who would've been able to give her advice.

CHAPTER 14

ROSE KNEW from the warm glow coming from the living room that everyone had gone to bed. There was a sole lamp burning, which had been left on so she would have enough light when she got home. Once she was inside, she closed the front door behind her, and turned off the lamp before she carefully made her way up the now darkened wooden stairs to tell Tulip all about her night.

She leaned over Tulip's bed. "Are you awake?"

Tulip sat up. *"Jah,* I've been waiting up for you."

Rose told Tulip everything that was said between her and Jacob, leaving out the fact that she kissed Jacob not once but twice.

"I'm glad you're happy, but I don't like it how he asked you to sneak out," Tulip said. "It seems a little dishonest or something."

"That's because he's so in love with me that he wants to see me all the time. Anyway, I'd forgotten he said that. He only mentioned it the once. You've got a good memory."

"I remember everything you tell me and I still think it's wrong that he asked you to do something he knew *Mamm* and *Dat* would be against."

"You'll understand when you're in love. Anyway, you shouldn't be so judgmental."

"Why's he moving so fast?" Tulip asked.

"We're in love and he's only got a few weeks before he has to go home. Unless I can persuade him to stay on for longer."

"Just be careful. You don't really know him."

"He's in the community, so he must be okay. He's coming for dinner tomorrow night."

"Okay. Then we'll see what *Mamm* thinks of him."

"Will you do something for me, Tulip?"

"What is it?"

"Will you work instead of me for a couple of hours tomorrow in the middle of the day? I want to surprise Jacob at the buggy workshop. It's not far from the markets."

"Okay. I'll go in with you in the morning."

"*Denke,* Tulip. I knew I could rely on you."

THE NEXT DAY, just before lunchtime, Rose left Tulip to mind the stall while she went to surprise Jacob. She kept it quiet from Mark that she was surprising his cousin with a visit.

The taxi took Rose to the front of the buggy workshop and she walked into the office, which was in a large trailer. At one end, there was a large desk and filing cabinets and behind that desk was Marta Bontrager.

"Hello, Marta," Rose said as she walked forward, glancing at two Amish women, who were sitting on chairs at the opposite end of the office.

"Hi, Rose. What can I do for you?"

"You have Jacob Schumacher working here and I was hoping I might have a word with him." Rose was secretly hoping that Jacob would be able to have lunch with her. Even if he couldn't, he'd love it that she'd thought to surprise him.

"Okay. Have a seat. I'll see if I can find him. He's popular today. I think he's due for a break soon."

Rose sat down while Marta left the trailer. With a sideways glance, Rose saw that one of the Amish women was young and the other was much older. They weren't from her community.

The young woman lurched forward. "Excuse me. I heard you were asking about Jacob?"

"Jah, do you know him?"

"Very well."

Rose studied the girl, wondering if she might be Jacob's sister.

"How long have you known him for?" the girl asked.

"Only since he's been here. Are you a relation of his?"

The old woman sitting next to the girl spoke. "Jessica is Jacob's girlfriend. He said he was going to marry her and then he just up and disappeared. Now we found out he's here. And that's why we've come."

"Please don't!" Jessica said to the older woman.

"Well, that's how it is," the woman replied with a scowl.

Rose's heart sank. It didn't seem real. It couldn't be true. "You're his girlfriend?"

"I thought that's what I was until he disappeared. Now, I don't know what I am. That's what I've come here to find out."

Rose sat there dumbfounded. Now it was all clear. Jacob had wanted to see if there was another woman out there better suited to him before he made his commitment to marry Jessica.

Rose stood up. "It was very nice to meet you both." She rushed out of the small office before they could see the tears that had formed in her eyes. She'd allowed this man to kiss her. Now she felt violated by him. He'd cruelly used her.

The first person she wanted to rush to was Tulip, but that would mean she'd also have to see Mark and she wasn't ready for that.

I'm such a fool!

She decided to leave Tulip there for the rest of the day and Mrs. Walker could drive her home. Tulip wouldn't mind a bit when she explained what had happened.

NANCY YODER WAS in the midst of sewing her daughters some new prayer *kapps* when Rose walked into the house, slamming the front door behind her.

"Rose! I didn't expect you home so soon. Did you leave Tulip at the markets?" She looked around and Rose was nowhere to be seen, but she heard her footsteps trudging up the wooden steps.

After giving Rose a little time alone, she made a cup of hot tea and took it up to her. Nancy gently knocked on the door, opened it, and saw her daughter in bed with tears flooding down her cheeks.

"What's wrong?" She knew in her heart Rose was crying over Jacob.

"Nothing!"

Nancy moved forward and placed the cup and saucer down on the nightstand. She sat on the end of the bed. "I can see there is something wrong."

"I'll not talk about it, *Mamm.*"

"Is it about Jacob?"

Rose sat higher in the bed, licked her lips, and then brought her knees up to hug them. "He's got a girlfriend."

Nancy couldn't stop the gasp that escaped her lips. *"Nee!"*

"Jah! And she's here! She followed him over here and she's with an older lady who might be her *mudder.* It was all such a shock."

"How did you find out?"

"I met them. I went to surprise Jacob where he worked and Jessica, that's his girlfriend, and the older lady were sitting there waiting for him, too."

"Nee! That's a horrible thing."

"She said they were to be married and he just walked out on her and came here. I think he was looking around to make sure he was making the right decision. Like a boat setting sail out on the water. He wanted to make sure he was sailing in the right direction."

"Your *vadder's* been talking to you about sailing again?"

"How did you know?"

"It sounds like something he would say. He often talks about sailing and boats when he's trying to explain things."

Rose grabbed her mother's arm. "What do I do now, *Mamm?*"

"Not everyone marries the first girl they go out with, Rose. Maybe he just didn't feel the girl was suited to him and there's nothing wrong with that."

"Maybe so, but I don't like that he was keeping the relationship going on while looking around for somebody else. He should've ended things with her first. From what she said, he just left her not knowing."

"He wanted to have his cake and eat it too."

"Exactly right." Rose nodded. "But I don't like being the cake."

CHAPTER 15

NANCY HATED to see her daughter in so much pain and torment. She sat on the edge of Rose's bed, looking into her green eyes in silence for a few moments before she spoke again. "Jacob needs to give you an explanation."

Rose held her head. "I don't know."

"Jah, you do. There are two sides to every story. Maybe this girl only told you half of what had gone on. Maybe Jacob *had* ended things with her and she hadn't accepted it. You've got to give him a chance to explain. That's what adults do."

Rose shook her head. "I suppose you're right, but I can't see that the girl was making any of this up."

"Your *grossdaddi* always used to say that there are two sides to every story and the truth lies somewhere in the middle. Jacob sees things from his point of view and she sees things from her point of view and they're not the same."

Rose sighed and rubbed her eyes. *"Dat* says a person should stick to their word. If you say you're going to do something then you should do it. Jacob said he was going to marry her and then walked out on her just like that."

"Maybe she misunderstood what he said about their relationship. If you really like Jacob, you should listen to what he says about it when you ask him."

Rose stared at her mother. "Maybe the girl misunderstood and maybe she's one of those girls who thought she was in a relationship and she really wasn't."

"Jah. Maybe. Do you think so? It could be that Jacob wasn't at fault." Nancy smiled, trying to be encouraging until the truth was discovered. "It's quite possible. Talk to him and see what he says. He's still coming to dinner tonight, isn't he, and then you're going on a buggy ride?"

"Jah, if that's still on, and he's not spending tonight with his girlfriend."

"Don't be like that. If he comes here tonight, talk to him after dinner about what this young lady said, and see what he's got to say."

"Okay, I will."

"And don't be too hard on yourself, or on him. We all make mistakes."

"But shouldn't I be harsh on him? I don't want to make any mistakes choosing my husband."

"Nobody is perfect, Rose. Remember that."

"I know that. I'm not expecting my husband to be perfect, but I do need a man who sticks to his word. That's important to me. I need someone I can feel safe with."

"Drink your tea and then you'll feel better."

Rose looked down at the tea beside her. *"Denke, Mamm.*

Maybe you're right and Jessica did misunderstand him. I'll wait to hear what he says."

"That would be a *gut* idea."

Nancy walked downstairs and out of the house, determined to get to the bottom of things. She went into the barn and made a couple of calls, intending to find the truth. She knew a couple of families who lived in Oakes County. Her first call was to Jean Davis, a woman she was sure knew everyone in Jacob's community.

Once Nancy opened her address book, she dialed Jean's number. The call was answered almost immediately.

"Hello, Jean. It's Nancy Yoder."

"Nancy! Is anything wrong?"

"Nee. I've called to ask you a couple of quick questions if you don't mind."

"I don't mind at all. What is it?"

Nancy said, "There's a young man who's arrived here who comes from your community. He's staying with his relations who are friends of ours. Rumor has it that he's got a girlfriend back there and I was wondering—"

"Jacob Schumacher?"

"Jah, how did you know?"

"I'm afraid it's true, Nancy. The poor girl's devastated. I know her *mudder* well and she told me just yesterday. They were keeping their relationship quiet and Jessica thought things were going well and they'd even spoken of marriage and he disappeared without saying a word."

'Spoken of marriage' is quite different from being engaged. "I'm sorry to hear that," Nancy said.

Jean continued, "And, Jessica had to find out where he'd gone from Jacob's parents. It had to be embarrassing for her."

"There's no doubt it would've been."

"Why are you asking, Nancy?"

Nancy swallowed hard. She didn't want to lie and neither did she want to gossip. If poor Jessica found out that her daughter and Jacob had been dating, that could quite possibly escalate a storm. That's not what she wanted to do.

"Some people had some questions, that's all. Then, Jessica's here with another lady, and I just wondered. I hope you don't mind me asking you those questions."

"*Nee*, not at all. The lady she's with would most likely be her aunt, Becca."

"*Denke.*" Nancy talked a little bit more about other things before she hung up. She'd told her daughter to give Jacob the benefit of the doubt, but now she knew that he'd walked out on that poor girl without an explanation. That wasn't the kind of man she wanted her daughter to marry. She wanted Rose to marry someone true to his word, just like Rose's father.

As Nancy walked toward the house, she made up her mind that she'd allow Rose to figure things out for herself. She hoped that Rose would tell Jacob that she didn't want to see him anymore. Rose had to grow up sometime and this adult decision would help turn her into a woman.

CHAPTER 16

ROSE MADE sure she was right there at the front gate to meet Tulip when Mrs. Walker dropped her at home. When Tulip got out of the buggy, Rose rushed forward to explain to Mrs. Walker that she had been unwell and had gone home. Then she walked with Tulip to the house and told her everything that had happened during the day.

"So what's your opinion?" Rose asked.

"I feel sorry for Jessica, but if he'd changed his mind about her, what was he to do? You can't marry someone just because you feel sorry for them. He made a mistake, and now he likes you. That's how it seems to me."

"*Jah*, but didn't he—I mean, shouldn't he have told her how he felt before he just up and left? She was left to wonder what was going on and now she must be so embarrassed."

"Sometimes we do things without thinking. You shouldn't be so harsh on him, but at the same time you have to be careful."

"Do you think I'm being harsh?" What would Tulip think if

she told her how he'd forced her to kiss him? Rose couldn't bring herself to tell her sister that!

"You're a perfectionist, Rose, but sometimes life and people aren't how you want them to be."

"I'm not expecting Jacob to be perfect, but there are a few principles that I want the man I'm going to marry to have."

"And who's to say that he doesn't have all of those? You've only known him for a little over a week. You should wait at least a few months before you start assessing him."

"Do you think so? I thought you'd decide you didn't like him, and would tell me not to see him anymore."

"I don't think it's about that. I think you've built up an image of what you want in a man—this whole perfect man, and you've made that man too idealistic. Real people have flaws and if you want a real husband rather than one who only lives in your mind, you'll have to accept a few imperfections."

"*Jah,* the man I will marry will be everything I want him to be, or I just won't get married. If he wasn't perfect, why would I marry him?"

Tulip giggled. "Don't say that around *Mamm* or she'll have a heart attack."

Rose laughed a little. "I'm glad I can talk with you. You might be right; he could have a reasonable explanation for everything."

"Exactly. This girl could've thought the relationship was serious, more so than it was. They might have only been on one date together and she expected him to marry her."

"You could be right. But the woman with her agreed with everything she said."

"It's possible that the woman has only heard Jessica's side of things."

Rose nodded. Her sister and her mother were saying the same kind of things.

"Let's go and help *Mamm* with the dinner," Tulip said. "But you didn't ask me how work was today."

"How was it?" Rose asked.

"It was good. It got really busy around lunchtime and then toward the end of the day it was quiet."

"That's how it usually is."

"I think Mark's in love with you," Tulip said with a grin.

"Do you think so? I knew he liked me a bit. Love is a strong word."

"He talked of little else in between customers."

Rose knew it was true. His teasing and jokes about them getting married one day had an element of truth in them, from his side. That's what he wanted—for them to marry.

"So?" Tulip stared at her.

"You know I don't like him in that way. I'm in love with Jacob."

"I know, but Mark is so nice."

"*You* marry him, then." Rose giggled.

"You wouldn't mind?" Tulip asked. "I mean, truly wouldn't mind?"

Rose glanced at her sister's face as they walked up the driveway to their house. "Go ahead. You'd make a nice couple." Rose suddenly had a hollow feeling in the pit of her stomach. It would be weird if her sister married her good friend. She'd grown used to him and his company. Things wouldn't be the same in their friendship if Mark were dating Tulip.

"Jacob is coming for dinner tonight, isn't he?"

"Jah, he's coming here and then we're going on a buggy ride after dinner. I'm going to make dessert and show him what a good cook I am."

"That would be a good idea. When do you think you might get married?"

"He's here for a few weeks, and then I guess we'll write to each other. After that, he might ask me to come and visit him."

Tulip giggled. "You've got it all worked out."

"I have. I hope he'll want to come back here to live, though. I don't want to live in a strange place where I don't know anyone."

"You'll make friends and besides, it's not that far away."

"Maybe he'll propose to me in a letter. That would be romantic, and then I'll have it to keep forever, and one day I could show our *kinner.* That is, if he gives me a good explanation tonight about Jessica."

ROSE PACED UP AND DOWN, waiting for Jacob to arrive for dinner. Then, when she heard the clip-clopping of horse's hooves and saw that it was him heading toward the house, she opened the front door and went outside to meet him.

He gave her a wave and then brought the horse closer to the house. When he got out of the buggy, she saw he looked upset. Maybe he'd had a talk with Jessica and sorted things out. She hoped that Jessica wasn't too upset and that he'd let her down gently.

"Hello, Rose."

"Hello. Is everything alright? You don't look too happy."

He looked down at the ground and then took a couple of steps before he looked back up at her. "There have been some developments."

"*Jah,* I know. I was there at your work today and I ran into Jessica."

"So you know?"

Rose nodded. "I do."

He gave a relieved sigh. "That's good. I thought you'd be upset with me."

He was here, so he must've sorted things out with Jessica, she thought. "There are always two sides to every story. I'm not upset with you at all. I only hope that Jessica isn't upset."

His eyebrows drew together. "Why would she be upset?"

"When you told her that you weren't going to marry her."

He looked away and then shuffled his foot, rolling a couple of pebbles back and forth under his shoe. He looked up at her. "Jessica and I had a long talk today, and to make a long story short, we're getting married."

Rose felt all life drain from her. It couldn't be true. "What are you talking about? She said you just left her and came here. She said you were going to marry her and then you changed your mind, or something."

"I had to clear my head. I had to think what I really felt about her before I made the next step. I'm only here to tell you in person. I'm not here to stay for the meal."

Rose's fingertips flew to the sides of her head. "You wanted to see who else was out there? Was that it?"

"I'm sorry, Rose. I never meant to hurt you."

"We kissed! You kissed me!"

"It was only a kiss—nothing more."

"I told you I didn't want to." She was hurt, desperately hurt. He preferred someone else. Nothing he'd ever said was true. She scowled, not the slightest bit concerned about how unattractive her face looked in that moment.

He took a step toward her. "Rose, it's not like that. I honestly prefer you, but—"

"But what?"

"It's complicated."

"It's not complicated in the least. You chose her over me, so there's nothing difficult about that. I don't know what you're thinking by even coming here. I even made a special dessert for you. I'll throw it in the trash!"

"I won't come in. I didn't expect that I would be staying for dinner after I said what I came to say. I only came to tell you in person. Let your parents know I'm sorry, but … tell them I'm unwell. I'm sorry, Rose. I didn't … I didn't mean it to end like this. I didn't mean to hurt you. That was the last thing I wanted."

"What about all those things you said to me? Were you lying about everything?"

He looked down at the ground once more. "I can't answer that."

Rose stamped her foot. "You can't answer that because you were lying. Go! Leave my place now and never come back!" Rose turned to leave, but he caught her by her elbow and abruptly swung her around to face him.

"Rose, there are some things you don't know."

"Well, tell me."

"I can't."

"You forced me to kiss you and you said it would be okay because we'd be married. I wanted my first kiss to be on my wedding day, or at least with my husband, and you stole that from me."

He shook his head. "Grow up, Rose. You're not so special that a man would wait for you to kiss him. Maybe that's how things were two hundred years ago, but today a man needs more. More than a kiss, even."

Rose's jaw dropped open and she turned on her heel and stomped away without saying another word. Now she knew the truth. Jacob was just horrid, and she'd made an awful, terrible mistake.

CHAPTER 17

Minutes before…

FROM THE KITCHEN WINDOW, Nancy watched her daughter hurry to meet Jacob outside. The scene brought her mind back to when she and her husband were getting to know one another. She'd told herself she'd never spy on her daughters, but she found herself doing just that.

"I'll set the table, *Mamm,*" Tulip said.

"Denke." Nancy didn't want Tulip to see she was watching the young couple so she busied herself preparing for her daughter's boyfriend's dinner at the house.

When Tulip's back was turned, she glanced out the window again to see what looked like some kind of a disagreement. Nancy guessed there was more to the story of Jessica, the young woman who was visiting their community. Could he have chosen Jessica over her daughter? It certainly looked that way from Rose's body movements and it looked like she was even yelling at him.

Now Rose headed to the house and Jacob was wasting no time getting back into his buggy. Nancy hurried to meet Rose at the front door. "What's happened? Where's Jacob?"

"He's not coming to dinner tonight, or any other night. We're through—it's over!" Rose burst into tears before she ran up the stairs.

Nancy stood there frozen, not knowing what to do. She hadn't had any dramas like this with her sons. The sound of Rose's bedroom door slamming echoed through the house.

Tulip ran out of the kitchen. "What's going on?"

Nancy swung around to face her. "Rose and Jacob had some kind of argument."

"I'll go to her."

"Nee, don't. I'll give her a few minutes and then I'll talk with her."

"What's happening? Isn't Jacob coming to dinner now?" Daisy asked as she also ran from the kitchen to her mother.

"Did they have an argument?" Lily yelled out from the kitchen.

"Hush!" their mother said, not wanting Rose to hear them discussing her. It'd only upset her more. She looked at Daisy. "He's not coming to dinner now. Go and tell your *schweschder* to be quiet."

"Which one? Rose or Lily?"

"Lily, of course. Now's not the time for game playing. You know who I meant."

Daisy's mouth turned down at the corners as she flounced back into the kitchen.

"He's not coming now," Daisy yelled to her twin on the way.

"*Gut!* There'll be more food for us," Lily called back.

Nancy shook her head. "Hush, all of you."

"*Mamm,* it's best if I go up and talk with her," Tulip said over the top of the twins' sniggers.

Nancy was a little disturbed that the twins seemed to be enjoying the drama. She looked at Tulip, her second oldest daughter, and put her hands on her shoulders and looked her directly into her face to hold her attention. "This is something that is a *mudder dochder* thing. I'll have a talk with your *vadder* when he gets home, which should be soon, and then I'll go to her. Until then, help me with the dinner, *jah?*"

Rather than answer, Tulip pulled her mouth to one side.

"Trust me, Tulip, I know what I'm doing," *Mamm* said, taking hold of Tulip's arm and guiding her back to the kitchen.

"I could talk to her," Lily suggested.

"*Nee!*" Tulip and their mother said at the same time.

"That's a little harsh," Daisy said.

"It's okay, I'm used to being left out of things," Lily replied, stifling a giggle.

"Stop it, both of you!" Nancy wagged a finger at her twin daughters. "This is a serious thing. Rose is upset, and you're being very unkind."

"He was too handsome anyway," Daisy said in a small voice.

Nancy frowned. "What has that got to do with anything?"

"The more handsome a man is, the less kind he is," Daisy said, which made Lily giggle. "It's true. I know these things," Daisy insisted.

"You'll marry an ugly man and have ugly *kinner* then," Lily replied.

Daisy stuck her nose in the air. "As long as he loves me, I don't care."

Nancy sighed in despair. Her two sons had been so easy to deal with and she hadn't appreciated it at the time. They'd found wives without any problems. Something gave Nancy the feeling that all of her girls would be challenging in the romance sector of life.

A horrible thought occurred to Nancy and she clutched at her throat. What if her four daughters all remained single? She would be an old lady with four middle-aged daughters still living in her house squabbling and bickering. When would she have a chance to be alone and enjoy her last years with Hezekiah? "All of you concentrate on cooking."

"It's all done," Lily said with her arms raised.

"The table's still not set. You know how your *vadder* likes his dinner as soon as he gets home."

To Nancy's relief, the three girls found something else to talk about other than Rose's disaster.

As soon as Nancy walked into Rose's room, she looked up from her seated position on her bed. "I'm never going to marry anyone—ever. I'll never be able to trust anybody. I trusted Jacob and look what happened. He lied to me. He told me how much he liked me, and he knew it was all lies. He didn't mean a word of it."

"What happened?"

"He's going to marry Jessica. That's what happened. After

telling me he loved me. I don't know how Jessica can trust him after he walked out on her."

Nancy gasped and put her hand on her heart. "That's a surprise."

"Why would she take him back? It doesn't make sense."

"She probably has forgiveness in her heart."

Rose's green eyes flashed. "I have none! I will never forgive him and I will never marry anyone because I'll never be able to trust anyone ever again as long as I live."

"Rose, you can't mean that. You're just upset."

"Why would I love and put myself at risk for being hurt again?"

"You only knew him for a couple of weeks or less. It can't have been real love. You can't tell me you could have fallen in love with him in that short amount of time."

"I didn't know there was a time limit on love, *Mamm.*"

"I don't know that there is, but you wouldn't have had time to find out what kind of person he was."

"Well I certainly know what kind of person he is now! He's a person who can't be trusted, and if I'm so dumb and easily fooled who can I ever trust again?"

Her mother pushed some strands of hair away from Rose's face.

"Anyway, *Mamm, denke* for coming to talk with me, but I'd rather be alone if that's okay."

"Of course it is. I understand. I'll bring some dinner up to you."

"*Nee,* don't." Rose shook her head and then ripped off her prayer *kapp* and held it with both hands. "The last thing I feel like is food."

"You've got to keep your strength up, Rose."

"You can bring the food up if you want, but I won't eat it. It'll only be wasted." Rose lay down across her bed, wiggled herself lower, and pulled the covers over her head.

THE NEXT MORNING, Rose had to go back to work. She couldn't miss two days in a row. And she'd quite possibly feel better back in her normal routine. Some time with Mark would make her feel happy again. She wondered what Mark would say about his cousin and Jessica. Rose only hoped Jacob would go home sooner than he'd planned. It would be hurtful and embarrassing to see him out and about with his girlfriend. What a fool she'd made of herself by liking him.

As soon as Mrs. Walker let her out at the farmers market, she saw Mark in the distance and hurried toward him. When she got closer, he saw her and waited for her.

"I'm so sorry I was mean to you, Mark," she blurted out.

"You were?"

"Jah."

"*Nee*, it's me who should apologize to you. I had no right to tell you what to do."

"You've heard about Jacob?"

"Have you?" Mark asked.

"He told me he's marrying Jessica. After he told me ..."

Mark frowned and his eyes narrowed.

Rose's shoulders drooped. "Never mind. It's just a weird thing that's happened."

"It is, and I'm sorry things didn't work out for you and Jacob. I know you liked him."

Rose sighed. "At least I know now that I'll never marry."

"Never marry anyone?"

"Never."

"You can't mean that, Rosie."

"I do."

"Unless it's to marry me, right?" Mark asked jokingly.

Rose was pleased they were back to the old Mark and Rose. She had to giggle at his words and the silly expression now on his face. "I'm sorry to disappoint you, Mark. I won't even marry you."

"You'll change your mind one day. I'll grow on you; you just wait and see. I'll grow on you like ivy grows on a tree—slowly but surely, never giving up."

"We'll see." Rose giggled again.

During the day, Rose learned that Jacob and Jessica were leaving that day, along with Jessica's aunt, to head back home.

Rose was relieved that she wouldn't have to see them. She felt foolish to have believed everything Jacob had said to her. Not only had he robbed her potential husband of her first kiss, he'd robbed her of her desire to marry.

CHAPTER 18

When Rose arrived home from work that night, her gloomy mood returned. Somehow everything reminded her of Jacob.

Rose knew she was in a depression and she couldn't pull herself out of it. She had been dumped; she had been cheated by the man she thought she would marry, and no one except Tulip understood.

The twins weren't sympathetic because they didn't understand how she could develop real feelings for someone in such a short space of time. They poked fun at her and told their mother that Rose was just trying to get attention. Her mother was worried about her, and her father always stayed out of what he called, 'girl problems.'

After dinner that night, while they were washing up, Rose's mother told her she wanted to have a chat with her. The twins and Tulip were sent to sit with their father in the living room.

"I'm troubled about you, Rose."

"Why? I'm fine. There's nothing to worry about." Rose dried

the plate too many times back and front until she noticed her mother staring at her. She quickly put the plate with the other dry ones.

"You're not yourself."

"I am, I'm the new me. This is how I am now."

"Don't be like that. Just because you've had one bad experience with a man doesn't mean you're never going to find someone who suits you."

"I'm not going to marry, and I don't have to. Even the Bible says that people don't need to marry if they don't want to. I think it was Paul who said it was preferable not to marry but if people had to do so, then it was okay. So, I'm going to be like Paul and stay single. It's a Godly choice."

"Leave the dishes. Let's sit at the table. I'll have the twins do it."

Rose sat down and her mother sat opposite.

Then her mother's fingertips drummed on the kitchen table. "You're not making your decision out of a Godly choice. You're making it out of hurt. Besides, Paul was a man. Maybe things were different for men and women back then. Those were different times and in a different culture."

"Ask *Dat* about it. He'd know. I'm sure it's okay for a woman just as it would be for a man not to marry. No one can force me; it's my choice."

"I just want you to be happy, and in an ideal situation you would be happily married."

"That's not what I want anymore, *Mamm*. I thought I did, but it only leads to disappointment. I want to be happy and being in love is okay when it's *gut*, but I don't think I've ever been so low. I feel as though there's no point to life, almost."

"Honey, that was just one man. They're not all like that."

Rose swallowed hard. "He was the *only* man for me and then it all turned bad."

"Is he the only man you want?"

Rose nodded. "He is."

"Do you think you should find out if he and Jessica are still engaged? They had a rocky relationship, so maybe they're off again. I could make some calls and—"

"*Nee,* I don't like him anymore! I wouldn't marry him now. He could change his mind about me just as easily as he changed his mind about her. The perfect man for me would never have walked away and left me."

Her mother was silent for a while before she spoke again. "Your *vadder* and I have talked about it and we've arranged for you to speak with Bishop John and his *fraa.*"

Rose leaped to her feet, knocking the chair over as she did so. "Talk to the bishop about my personal things?"

"We're worried about you. And we both think it's best that you speak with him and tell him how you feel."

Rose picked up her chair and sat back down. Maybe talking it over with someone would help her sort out her feelings. "I guess it wouldn't hurt if that's what you want me to do. But I'm not sure what you think it's going to accomplish. I can't be the only girl in the community who has chosen never to marry."

"It's not only that. You just don't seem to be yourself."

"And what do you think the bishop can do about that? I'm upset, that's all."

"He has a lot of experience about everything—all life's situations. He'll give you some good advice, I'm sure."

"I can't imagine what about."

"See that there—that attitude? That 'don't care' attitude? I think you're feeling sorry for yourself. You've never spoken out like that to me before. You've always been so polite."

Rose didn't make a comment. No one cared about her, so why should she care about herself? "And when have you arranged for me to go and see them—the bishop and Olga?"

"On Thursday, after you finish work. *Dat* will collect you from work and take you there. You can tell Mrs. Walker tomorrow that she won't need to collect you on Thursday night."

Rose shrugged, too tired to be bothered with arguing. "Okay, *Mamm.* Whatever you want."

THE NEXT MORNING, Rose couldn't wait to tell Mark that her parents were sending her to talk to the bishop and his wife. Mark had overprotective parents as well, and he'd have a good chuckle about it with her.

When Rose got to her stall, Mark was nowhere to be seen and he always arrived before she did. Instead of Mark, she saw his younger brother, Matthew.

"Matthew, what are you doing here?"

"I thought Mark would've told you. I'm taking over the store from him."

"What? Why?"

"He got an offer to learn the trade from *Onkel* Harry. He's going to be making buggies."

Rose frowned. Just when she really needed Mark, he'd left her. "Isn't that what Jacob was doing?"

"*Jah,* but Jacob has gone and … so it goes."

"Jacob and Jessica have gone now?"

"They left yesterday. Didn't you know?"

"I did. I was just making sure. Jacob told me they were leaving. I was just checking that they'd actually left."

"No one had heard about Jessica until she showed up here." Matthew laughed. "Jacob will be under the thumb soon if he doesn't watch himself."

"What?" Rose frowned. "What do you mean?"

"She snaps her fingers and then he goes running back home. He was supposed to be here for a few months." Matthew shook his head as though disgusted. "I don't know what happened there."

Rose kept silent and set about readying the stall for the day's trade. She tried to make the display as attractive as possible.

She glanced over at Matthew and knew it wouldn't be as much fun working there without Mark; she knew that right away.

Rose had been right—the day dragged by without her friend.

She wondered if Mark was angry with her. "Matthew, why does Mark want to work with your *onkel?*"

"I dunno. He doesn't have a lot of choices. He doesn't like to work in the dairy. That's why he chose to work here, and now he's gonna make buggies."

"I know he doesn't like to work in the dairy, but he never said a thing about wanting to make buggies."

Matthew shrugged his shoulders. "Like I said, I dunno. Maybe that's not his ideal thing, but we've all gotta work."

"I suppose that's right—it is a job. And what were you doing before you came here?"

"Working the dairy."

It was Rose's worst fear that Mark and she would grow apart. Now she would only see him at the young peoples' 'singings,' the fortnightly Sunday meetings, and the various social events. "When did he decide to work with Harry?"

"You sure ask a lot of questions about my *bruder.*"

Matthew smiled at Rose and she knew he thought that she liked Mark. She did, but not in the way that Matthew might have thought.

He finally answered, "When he heard Jacob was leaving was when he said he'd work with Harry. Harry had been asking him for some time."

"Do you think you'll like this job?" Rose only asked because she had to talk about something other than Mark.

"Anything that will get me away from the dairy is good. The dairy is hard work. Not that I mind the work; it's just nice to have a change."

Mark and Matthew were fortunate to be the youngest of the Schumacher boys. The older ones had all worked in the dairy at some point. Rose considered that Mr. Schumacher must be pleased to have had so many boys to help with everything.

Toward the end of the day, Rose remembered that there was a volleyball game on that night. Normally she wouldn't attend, but tonight she'd go and hope that Mark would be there. Seeing his friendly face would make her feel better.

CHAPTER 19

THE VOLLEYBALL GAME was already under way when Rose arrived with Tulip and the twins in tow. Before Rose brought the family buggy to a complete stop, the twins leaped out and ran off to join their friends.

"They'd be in trouble now if *Mamm* or *Dat* were here," Tulip said, watching her younger sisters disappear into the crowd.

"Don't worry about them. Can you see Mark anywhere? I can't wait to talk with him."

Tulip craned her neck as she looked at the group of people. "*Jah*, I can see him now. He just got up to play." Tulip turned to look at Rose. "What do you want to talk with him about?"

"I want to know why he didn't tell me he was changing jobs."

"I don't know, but maybe you can ask him tonight."

Rose stepped out of the buggy. "I intend to." She looped the reins over the fence and secured the horse. Then together she and Tulip headed to join the onlookers.

Throughout the night, Rose avoided looking directly at

Mark. She could see him turning around, trying to catch her eye, but she deliberately didn't look back.

As soon as the games were over, Mark walked over to her just like she had wanted. "I hoped you'd come tonight, Rosie."

"I'm here."

He chuckled quietly. "I can see that. I'm glad."

"Well, did you win?"

"Volleyball?"

"Yeah."

"We won two games."

"Is that good?"

He laughed. *"Nee.* We played ten games and the team I was playing on only won two."

Rose couldn't wait to talk about his new job. "You didn't tell me you were leaving the market stall."

"I didn't have time. It was a sudden last-minute thing when Jacob left."

"Do you like making buggies?"

"I guess so. It's too soon to tell for certain. I've always wanted to have some kind of trade for myself. If I'm going to raise a *familye* one day, I'll need to have money to feed all those little mouths." Mark chuckled.

"It wasn't much fun today without you there."

"Yeah, I can imagine that. My *bruder's* a little dull." Mark stared at her when she didn't laugh. "Can I get you some soda?"

Rose nodded and together they walked to the refreshments table. For the first time ever, Rose wondered whether she liked Mark as more than a friend. Or was it just that she'd missed him as one would miss the companionship of any good friend?

He picked up a jug, poured her a glass, and then handed it to her.

"Denke."

When he poured one for himself and took a sip, Rose wondered if he felt just as awkward as she did.

"I missed you today," he said.

"Me too. I missed talking with you, too."

"We had a lot of fun. Well, not really fun, but having you there helped pass the time when things got quiet."

Had? Was their time together over just like that? She nodded and then looked down at the ground, wondering what to say.

"I'm sorry about the Jacob thing," he said.

"I'm over it now. There's no need to say anything. Things always turn out for the best."

"That's exactly right; they do." He nodded.

She smiled at the way he said his last words with such enthusiasm.

"I hear your parents are forcing you to go to the bishop tomorrow night."

"What? How in the world did you hear that?" Rose asked.

"My aunt just happened to be at Bishop John's *haus* and overheard a conversation between him and his *fraa* about you going there."

Rose slapped a hand to her forehead while she tried not to spill the drink in her other hand. *"Ach,* that's so embarrassing. Did they say what it was about?"

"Nee. Don't you know?"

"My *mudder* thinks I'm in some kind of a depression. Only because I said that I won't get married."

"Well there's nothing wrong with that."

Rose smiled at him. Finally someone understood her. "Do you think so?"

"I think it's a good decision."

"I'm glad you think so. I hope you're not the only one in the whole community who thinks that. And why do other people think it's any of their business?"

"Mmm, I don't think they do."

Rose was half waiting for him to say that she shouldn't marry anyone but him. That's what he always said, but today, he said no more. Right then, she wanted to go away somewhere where she knew no one. If she had a complete break, that might clear her head. Maybe she could go to Pinecraft and be near the water.

"What are you thinking, Rosie?"

"I'm thinking of going somewhere warm, near the water."

"On a vacation?"

"*Jah,* I think I need one, away by myself somewhere."

"Why don't you ask the bishop if he can arrange for you to stay with someone somewhere? He knows lots of people."

"You know, I just might."

They were interrupted by a group of people who wanted Mark's opinion on something. Rose wasn't included in the conversation so she gradually backed away.

Several minutes later, she was talking to the twins, telling them they had to leave soon, when Mark asked to speak with her again.

The twins giggled as their older sister walked away with Mark.

"What is it?" Rose asked when they were far enough away not to be overheard.

"I just wanted to make sure you're okay."

"I'm fine. I'm just nervous about going to the bishop's *haus* tomorrow. I mean, what do I say?"

"Just smile a lot and nod. Agree to pray about everything and ask the bishop some questions about the bible. He loves to answer questions."

"Does he?"

"Jah, he'll forget about the reason you're there and start talking about the Scriptures."

"Really?"

Mark nodded. "Have a couple of questions ready."

Rose giggled. "I'll do that. *Denke."*

CHAPTER 20

WHEN ROSE WAS COMFORTABLY SEATED in the bishop's living room, Olga sat down beside Bishop John, and then he began, "Rose, you're here because your parents are concerned. There was a situation with Jacob Schumacher."

Rose looked at the bishop and then Olga, wondering how much they'd heard. "Oh, that's all been resolved."

"They said you took it hard when he left with Jessica," the bishop said.

"Do you know Jessica?" Rose asked, trying to deflect the comment.

Olga interrupted, "We met Jessica and her aunt when they came here about Jacob and the dreadful, sinful situation they were in."

Rose wondered what Olga was talking about and then noticed that the bishop shot a look of disapproval toward his wife, as though she'd revealed information that was confidential. Sin? Had Jacob done something wrong?

Olga glanced at her husband who was still staring at her, and said, "I'll get us some hot tea."

"I'll help you," the bishop said. "I'll be back in a moment, Rose." Before he left the room, he turned back to Rose, and explained, "The pot is too heavy for Olga to lift once it's full."

"Okay."

Once Bishop John and Olga were in the kitchen, Rose decided she wanted coffee instead. She jumped up and walked to the kitchen door and found it closed. Then she didn't want to go in, in case they were talking about something private. She listened while she decided whether she should walk in or not.

She heard the bishop say, "Olga, you've got to keep things quiet about Jessica and Jacob. If anyone finds out that Jessica is expecting a *boppli* out of wedlock, things will be uncomfortable for them. Once they're married, no one needs be any the wiser."

Rose clapped her hand over her mouth in shock. That's why things had been so sudden. That's why the old lady with Jessica was so cross, and that explained why Jacob had gone back to Jessica.

Rose shook her head, feeling a little faint. She'd had a close call. If Jacob hadn't been taken away from her so quickly, she could've fallen victim to him just like Jessica had. He'd forced her to kiss him, and then he'd even hinted that more than kissing would be okay. It was odd, but Rose was relieved and grateful for the experience, as awful as it was. Jacob wasn't the man for her—not at all. But if she'd been wrong about Jacob, how could she trust her feelings again? He had made it all sound so right.

She heard the bishop's hushed voice once more. "Just be careful what you say," he said to Olga.

Rose scurried back to the couch and had just reached it when the kitchen door opened.

"Sorry to leave you alone like that, Rose."

"That's okay."

"Now, where were we?" the bishop asked.

Remembering what Mark told her, Rose asked, "I forget quite honestly, but I have a question about Moses."

He smiled and with a slight raise of his bushy black eyebrows, asked, "What is it?"

"How did he divide the Red Sea? I've always wondered. Did it really happen literally?"

"Ah, I'm glad you asked. It was a miracle. You see …"

Rose settled back in the couch and listened to the bishop talk about Moses and the crossing of the Red Sea on dry land.

While she watched the bishop's mouth open and close above his long bushy beard, she thought about Mark. He wasn't tall, and he wasn't over-confident, but he was someone she could trust. Without a doubt, she knew she could trust him with everything she held dear. She didn't love Mark with her heart the way she'd loved Jacob, but then and there she decided she would open her mind and her heart to the possibility of love with Mark. If, of course, he still felt the same way about her after she'd paid him no mind for years.

Olga brought the tea out on a large tray and set it down on a table in front of Rose. "Here you go, dear."

"Denke." Rose leaned forward and picked up a teacup.

"Did I answer the question sufficiently, Rose? Do you understand all I said about Moses?"

"Jah. It was really interesting. I've wondered about all that for some time."

An hour later, Rose left the bishop's house and got into the buggy with her father.

"Did his talk help you?" he asked.

"It really did. You and *Mamm* were right to have me talk with him and Olga. I found out some things." Rose smiled. She found out some things because she'd overheard the truth about Jacob.

"*Gut!* Then, let's go home and tell your *mudder* you're feeling better."

Rose nodded.

WITH MARK'S change of vocation, Rose had to wait until the next Sunday meeting before she saw him again. When she sat with Tulip at the back of the room, she watched Mark enter the house and sit down with his younger brother.

There was a different feeling when she saw him, she was certain about it. She probably just missed seeing him every day.

Tulip leaned over closer to her, and whispered, "Just because things ended badly with Jacob, don't rebound onto Mark. I've noticed people do things like that and it's not good. Be sure about who you want first."

Rose stared at Tulip. Tulip must've seen her looking at Mark, and somehow guessed that Rose was thinking of him as a possible boyfriend. Was she rebounding, though? She'd never considered Mark as a serious marriage partner before this, so why now? "I'm not sure how I feel."

"That's why you should wait. Don't rush into things. You

gave your heart too early to Jacob and look how that ended. There's plenty of time. It's not a race."

Rose nodded. Tulip had a good point. She should keep her distance from Mark and then wait to see what happened. She leaned over to her sister. *"Mamm's* the one who doesn't want me to wait. She's putting pressure on me to marry, saying she'll give me a year."

"I think she feels different now, since things happened the way they did with Jacob."

Rose was relieved and only hoped that was true. "Are you sure?"

"Jah, she was talking about it yesterday."

"Not in front of the twins, I hope."

"Nee, just with me," Tulip said.

"What did she say exactly?"

"Just that she blames herself for the whole Jacob thing."

Rose frowned. "It's not her fault."

"I tried to tell her that. It was Jacob's fault."

The deacon, Rose's father, stood before the congregation and said a prayer. Rose and Tulip could no longer whisper in the back row or he'd see them. It saddened Rose to learn that her mother blamed herself for what had happened.

AFTER THE MEETING, Rose sat alone by a tree, feeling sorry for herself. She hadn't even noticed anyone approach.

"Why so gloomy?"

She looked up to see Mark, and then she forced a laugh. "I don't know. I'm just thinking about some things."

He stood next to her. "Mind if I sit?"

"Would it matter?"

"It would."

She nodded. "You can sit down."

"Mighty nice of you." He sat beside her on the wooden log seat.

Rose smiled and gazed into the distance.

"Does this gloominess have anything to do with Jacob?"

She nodded. "I made a fool of myself."

"You didn't."

"I feel like I have and everyone probably knows about it by now. News travels fast."

"It's plain to see that you were … fond of him, I'll say that."

She shook her head and shuddered. "That was a big mistake."

"The mistake was his and he made it before he met you, Rosie."

She whipped her head around to look at him. "You know?"

"There's not much that escapes me. I might act dopey, but it's just an act. I'm actually a genius. Too many people would become jealous if they knew the truth about the power of my brain." He looked from side to side as though he was worried that someone might be listening.

Rose couldn't help but laugh at him. He always made her feel better. If only she could still see him every day.

"What I'm hoping is that I can take advantage of someone else's mistake," Mark said.

"That sounds ruthless."

"I'm a ruthless genius."

"And how would you go about taking advantage of some-one's mistake anyway?"

"That's my secret."

"You can't tell me something like that, Mark, and not follow through with an explanation."

He sighed. "It's pretty clear, Rosie. Jacob has to marry someone else other than you. How would I turn that to my advantage?" He stared at her with such intensity that she had to look away. He still liked her just as she'd hoped and he hadn't been put off by her liking Jacob.

Mark continued, "I've always felt a certain way toward you, and I've always hoped that you might feel the same way about me. I love you, Rosie."

She turned her head around once more to look into his eyes. "You do?"

He nodded.

"Why did you encourage me with Jacob? Why did you ask me to have dinner at your *haus* when he was there?"

He shrugged his shoulders. "I've just been hanging around, hoping you'd feel the same one day. There are only so many hints I can drop. All those jokes and what-not that I say to you —I mean them. I've always meant them. I've always hoped you'll marry me and perhaps one day see something in me that you've never seen before. That's my hope, anyway."

Rose looked down. Her heart was bruised and not ready to let anyone else in.

"You don't have to say anything, Rosie. I'll have to settle for your friendship if that's all you have to offer. I need you in my life and if it'll only ever be that you and I stay friends then I'll consider myself a man most blessed. Blessed because …" He put his hand on his heart. "You are … I can't find the words. You are just *wunderbaar!*"

She laughed. No one had ever talked that way about her before. With Jacob it had all been lies and it somehow felt as though he was always out of reach. Here was Mark who had all the goodness, principles, and kindness that she'd always wanted in a man, but did she love him? There were no butterflies in her tummy.

"I don't know what to say, Mark."

He shook his head slightly, smiling at her. "You don't need to say anything, but I need to ask you something."

She gulped. "What?"

"Rosie, will you marry me?"

She gulped again. "I don't know … it's too soon because …"

"Don't say anything more. I didn't think you would. I just wanted to let you know in all honesty how much I would love you to be my *fraa.*" He stood up. "I'll never be far away, Rosie, if you ever change your mind."

Rose sat there and watched him walk away. Part of her wanted to run after him, but there was another part that told her Mark wasn't her perfect man. He wasn't the one she'd always imagined. Tulip had been right to caution her. Just because Jacob had been a disaster, she shouldn't settle for someone who was nice and wouldn't break her heart. Someone else might come along who suited her better than Mark and be more like the dream man she'd always imagined.

CHAPTER 21

A WHOLE YEAR PASSED. Months ago, Rose had held her oldest brother's newborn baby in her arms, and she desperately wanted to have a baby of her own. Some weeks after that, she heard whispers that a child had been born to Jessica and Jacob. Of course, the child had been born less than nine months after their marriage, but that was swept under the rug and not mentioned. Still, the news of the birth reminded Rose of how she'd been fooled by Jacob and it sent her into a dark depression.

Nancy Yoder sat her oldest daughter down one Monday morning before Rose left for work.

"Rose, it's been more than a year now since I spoke to you about you getting married. You haven't been out with anyone since Jacob. Your *vadder* told me to let you be, but what's going on? There are ten weddings booked now in the time since Jacob left. One of those weddings should've been yours."

"I told you, *Mamm,* getting married is something I won't do until I find someone who suits me. I won't be forced into something just for the sake of it."

"There are a dozen men, any of which would suit you. What are you waiting, or looking, for? It's not setting a good example for your sisters. They seem just as uninterested in the whole idea of marriage as you are and I can only blame you for that."

Rose tugged at the strings of her prayer *kapp*. "I don't know."

"You don't know about what?" Her mother was using her angry voice.

"Anything, really … I guess."

"Well, perhaps that's where we should start. We shall work out what problem you have with marriage and clear it up. Perhaps another talk with the bishop would be in order?"

"Nee, not the bishop again, please, *Mamm."*

"Okay, but you can't escape talking with me. Tonight's the night, right after dinner."

Rose stood up. "Okay, tonight it is, but right now I need to go to work. Mrs. Walker needs me to start a little earlier today. She'll be here soon. They're redoing the roof over the market and we might need to move the stall to the other end for a few days. The managers are letting us know today."

"Okay, Rose, but we will speak tonight. And we'll put a plan into place. You're making too big a thing out of this. One man is as *gut* as another."

"Really?" Rose raised her eyebrows. "I wonder what *Dat* would think about that?"

Mrs. Yoder giggled and wagged her finger at her daughter. "I didn't mean it like that."

Rose smiled and then leaned over and kissed her mother on her cheek. "I'll see you later, *Mamm."*

"Don't forget we need to talk tonight."

"There's no danger of that. You've talked about nothing else these last few minutes."

Rose hurried down the driveway to meet Mrs. Walker. She'd long since gotten over Jacob and the hurt he'd caused her heart. Jacob hadn't been respectful toward her and now that more time had passed, she could see that clearly. She felt sorry for Jessica, the girl he'd married.

Mark and she hadn't been as close as they once were. It was kind of awkward between them ever since Mark had asked her to marry him. She'd thought about Mark and his proposal every single day. She couldn't find a reason not to accept his proposal except for a nagging doubt. After months of self-examination, Rose realized that her doubt was purely based on the fact that she'd always seen herself with someone different from Mark. She was a tall girl and Mark was barely a shade taller and she'd always imagined herself married to someone so much taller, as tall as Jacob. Besides that, Mark was easily available to her and there was something within her that wanted the excitement of the exotic stranger, someone new and exciting—as Jacob had been.

Is it that simple? She slowed down when she nearly reached the road. Looking down, she kicked the pebbles along the driveway. Rose missed talking and laughing with Mark every day. What if he no longer wanted her? Could he have grown tired of waiting? She knew he wasn't dating anyone—she hadn't heard he was, at least.

She leaned against the gatepost at the end of the drive, waiting for Mrs. Walker while she thought about men. Her relationship with Jacob had been exciting, but it had also caused her pain. Jacob wasn't honest and forthright, whereas Mark had told her exactly how he felt about her and that had taken great courage. Rose could appreciate that now that time had passed.

Maybe she loved Mark. Or was it love? Could it be love or simply that there was no one else around? Was that why she now felt as though she might love him?

She heaved a loud sigh. *This is all too confusing!*

When she heard the clip-clopping of hooves, she looked up to see Mrs. Walker's gray horse pulling the buggy.

WHEN THEY ARRIVED at the markets, Rose found out that the Walkers had to move their stall to the other side while the roof was being repaired. That also meant that Rose wouldn't be next to Mark's younger brother and the goat-cheese stall.

When the midday rush was over, she looked up and saw Mark walking toward her. Her heart pounded in her ears while at the same time she hoped she looked all right.

"Hi Mark. It's nice to see you."

"Hello, Rosie. I've come to check on Matthew."

"They've had to move us all around."

"I know. I hope it won't be for too long. Our regular customers mightn't be able to find us."

"You're not working today?" Rose asked.

He laughed. "I've got the day off. It's the advantage of *not* working in the *familye* business. Goats have to be milked every day."

"That sounds *gut,* that you can have a day off."

She stared at him. Had he grown a little taller and was he a little heavier? He looked more of a man now rather than a teenager. How great a difference a year had made. Sure, she'd seen him every couple of weeks at the meetings, but she'd never really 'looked' at him like she was now.

"How have you been, Rosie?"

She desperately wanted to tell him that she'd missed him. She swallowed hard against the lump that had formed in her throat. "I've been okay."

"You look lovely."

Rose giggled. *"Denke."*

"Well, I'd better have a look to see where our stall's been placed."

"I'm sure it's over that way." She pointed to the western corner of the building.

"I'll come back and talk after I see Matthew."

Rose nodded. "I'd like that."

She watched him walk away and to her surprise she was tingling, and she could only put that down to being nervous.

A loud boom shook the ground underneath her and Rose grabbed hold of the table in front of her. The roof that was being fixed had collapsed, and billows of dust filled the air. Her stall was outside under an annex and had escaped the disaster. Everything took place in slow motion, as though she were in a dream. There was an eerie silence and then all at once screams and cries rang through the air. Seconds later, Rose stood stunned as people ran to and fro.

CHAPTER 22

"MARK!" Rose screamed as she ran toward the rubble.

Suddenly Mark appeared amongst the dust and debris. He yelled for someone to call Emergency Services. Then he organized men in the crowd that had gathered, forming teams to start moving the rubble aside to get people out.

When Mark saw Rose, he yelled at her to stay back.

All Rose could do was stand there and watch the scene unfold as though it wasn't really happening. It was too awful to be true. Mark could've been killed, and where was Matthew? Rose knew Matthew was somewhere under the pile of wooden beams and roofing fragments with many of the other workers.

Soon Mark and the men he'd organized were pulling out the wounded. A sense of relief came at the sound of the sirens of the police, fire, and paramedic vehicles.

Rose closed her eyes tightly and prayed that Matthew was somewhere safe where he wasn't harmed. When Rose opened her eyes, she saw an upright beam tilt, and Mark was directly underneath it. She screamed and ran to him, but she was too late. He was lying there, still and motionless.

"Mark." She picked up his hand. The lower half of his body was trapped.

A pair of strong arms lifted her up and away. She turned to see a fireman.

"Stay clear, Ma'am."

"Help him!" Rose screamed pointing to Mark. Rose stayed on the side and watched as three firemen levered the wooden beam off him. Once it was off, the paramedics were called over to tend to him.

"Is he okay?" Rose leaned over and asked them.

"He's alive."

Rose looked around and couldn't see Matthew. She knew that would be Mark's first concern. "His brother's still in there somewhere."

"They're doing all they can to get everyone out. Stand back, Ma'am. We're ready to move him." The paramedics moved Mark onto a stretcher and Rose ran alongside until they put him in an ambulance.

"Are you his wife?" one of them asked as he closed the double doors at the rear of the vehicle.

"No, I'm just a friend." Thinking it didn't reflect their relationship, she added, "A really good friend."

After the paramedic had told Rose which hospital he'd be taken to, Rose ran back to look for Matthew. To her relief, she found Matthew sitting with people who were waiting for medical attention.

She silently thanked God that he was still alive. "Matthew, are you okay?"

"*Jah,* Rose, nothing major. How are you?"

"I'm okay, but they've just taken Mark to the hospital. A huge wooden beam fell on him and he's been knocked out."

Matthew's bottom lip trembled. "Mark was here?"

"*Jah.* He came to see where your stall had been placed. I've got to go to him to make sure he'll be fine. I mean, I'm sure he is. He's in good hands. Are you sure you're okay?"

Matthew gulped and nodded. "I'm just a bit dizzy. Go and be with him please, Rose. He'll want you to be with him."

Rose nodded and ran to grab her belongings from behind the flower stall. At least that had escaped the damage. Then she headed out to the main road to catch a taxi.

ROSE WAS RELIEVED when she arrived at the hospital. She was told that Mark had regained consciousness; he had a slight concussion, and a broken leg.

He was still in the emergency section and she was shown to his bedside where a nurse was adjusting his drip.

"What are you doing here?" His eyes were half open and his speech was slurred.

"I'm here to make certain you'll be okay." She grabbed his hand.

"I'm fine, but I can't marry you."

A nurse was adjusting his IV drip, and whispered to Rose, "It's the drugs talking."

Rose nodded and smoothed back Mark's hair, careful of the bandage on his head. "You can't?"

"*Nee,* I can't. I can't marry you in here."

"The doctor will be back to see him soon." The nurse shot Rose a big smile before she made her way through the curtains that separated Mark from the other patients in Emergency.

"But you still want to marry me?" Rose asked Mark.

He smiled back. "Nothing I'd like better," he whispered before his eyes gradually closed.

Rose leaned closer to check that he was still breathing. What part of his words were his and what part was the pain medication? Would he still want to marry her after so long? She looked down at their hands clasped together and tears fell down her face. As long as he got healthy again, that's all that mattered.

Suddenly the curtains were pulled aside. A man in a white coat stepped through and introduced himself as a doctor.

"Will he be okay?" Rose asked.

"Are you a relative?"

"No." She then realized she should've called Mark's parents.

The doctor glanced down at their clasped hands.

"We're engaged," she announced.

"Congratulations!" The doctor smiled and then told her about Mark's injuries and what he expected of his recovery. "He'll sleep now. He's had strong medication and you won't get any sense out of him. He'll be out of Emergency and in a ward tomorrow if you want to come back in the morning."

Rose nodded. "Is it okay if I sit with him for a while?"

"Of course, but he won't know you're here."

Rose stayed by his side another hour before she thought about her family and the Walker family. They would've heard about the disaster by now and would be wondering where she was. She leaned over and left a soft kiss on Mark's forehead. Before she left the hospital, her first call was to Mark and

Matthew's mother to tell her what had happened and where her sons were.

When the taxi stopped at Rose's house, her mother rushed out the front door.

"Rose, you're okay."

Rose finished paying the driver and quickly got out of the car because she knew how her mother was prone to panicking at the slightest thing. *"Jah, Mamm."* Rose repeated everything she'd told her on the phone. "I'm okay. I just had to leave the stall because there was so much devastation everywhere. Mark is in the hospital with a broken leg and concussion and Matthew has got something wrong with him but he's not too bad. The paramedics were looking after him when I left for the hospital to see how Mark was."

Her mother wrapped her arms around her. "I'm so grateful you're okay."

As they walked to the house, Tulip ran out and she was promptly instructed by their mother to call the Walkers to tell them Rose was fine.

"I had to leave the flowers," Rose said as Tulip hurried to the phone in the barn.

"I've had Mrs. Walker over here and she told me everything that happened. She was very worried about you because no one knew where you were."

Rose bit her lip and stopped still at the bottom of the porch steps. "I don't know why I didn't call her. I thought of it, but everything was happening so fast. I called Mrs. Schumacher and told her where Matthew and Mark were."

"That would've been a hard call to make. Come inside now. You look all pale, much paler than usual. You need something to eat and drink."

That was the last thing Rose felt like, but she didn't have enough energy to argue with her mother after all that had happened.

As soon as she stepped into the house, she was faced with the twins who rapidly asked her questions one after the other. Rose answered as many of them as she could. "As far as I know, no one died, but many were injured."

Their mother ordered, "Stop asking so many things. Daisy, make her a cup of tea."

"Okay," Daisy said.

"It's okay, *Mamm,* I don't mind answering questions."

"What would you like to eat?" Lily asked.

"Would you like to eat in the kitchen or the living room?" Daisy asked.

Rose was touched that her twin sisters were being so nice to her. They usually kept to themselves. "In the kitchen is fine, *denke.*"

"Mrs. Walker said that she's glad you're okay and they're heading into the markets to see what's left of their stall."

"Denke, for calling her, Tulip," Rose said. "Their stall's okay. It wasn't in the badly damaged area."

They sat in the kitchen, the four girls and their mother, while Rose told them all about the horrible event she had witnessed. "And you should have seen the way Mark took charge before the paramedics and emergency team got there. It was as though he was somebody else."

"I wonder if that will be in the papers tomorrow," Daisy said.

"Of course it would be," their mother said. "Things like that are always in the papers."

Lily said, "I wonder if they will have something about Mark in the paper if he was such a hero like Rose said."

"Are you doubting what Rose said, really?" Tulip asked.

"*Nee,* not so much. It's just that she likes Mark, so she thinks anything he does is spectacular. I was wondering what other people thought, that's all."

Their mother shook her head. "I'm sure Rose wasn't making anything up."

"I didn't say she was, *Mamm.*" Lily heaved a sigh. "Why does this always happen? Everyone in this family always takes everything I say the wrong way."

"I don't," said Daisy.

"I didn't mean you. Everyone except you turns everything around to make me look like I'm the bad one."

"I know what you mean," Daisy said, nodding.

"You two always stick up for each other," Tulip said. "Anyway, I don't know why everything has to turn into an argument. Mark did a good thing in helping people and what does it matter if no one else noticed that apart from Rose?"

Rose remained silent as she hugged her warm teacup with both hands.

"Rose is in love with Mark," Lily said.

"Everyone knows that," Daisy added with a high-pitched giggle.

"Come on, girls, Rose doesn't need this right now. Up to your rooms the both of you."

The twins looked at each other with pouting faces.

Daisy asked, "Can we go to the same room?"

Their mother sighed. *"Jah,* do what you want as long as it's upstairs and you leave Rose alone for the rest of the night."

"How long do we have to stay in our rooms?" Lily asked.

"Until morning."

"Come on, Lily, there's no use arguing. They don't think we're adults." Daisy stood up and grabbed Lily's arm.

Their mother narrowed her eyes. "When you behave like adults, I'll treat you like adults."

The twins left the room and Rose took another sip of tea.

Her mother put a hand on Rose's arm. "I'm so glad you're unharmed."

"Me too," Tulip added.

"It was so dreadful. I don't know how it happened. I'm just glad no one was killed. I hope no one was killed. Unless they found someone after I left." Rose put her teacup on the table and covered her face with both hands. "It was awful. And it was horrible to see Mark lying in the hospital."

"How is he?" Tulip asked.

"Broken leg and concussion. They said I can go see him tomorrow morning and he might be able to talk. He barely said two words to me and what he said didn't make much sense."

"Lie down on the couch and have a rest, Rose."

"Okay." The couch in the living room was where the girls went when they didn't feel well but weren't really ill. It was comforting to sit by the fire on the soft couch, looking out the large window at the trees and the distant fields.

THAT NIGHT, Rose lay in bed worrying. Had she missed her chance with Mark by foolishly choosing his cousin a year ago?

It was an embarrassing mistake, which thankfully not many people knew about. Her door opened slightly and she saw Tulip's silhouette at the door. "Come in."

"I didn't know whether you'd still be awake." Tulip came further into her room and sat down on her bed while Rose pushed herself up into a seated position.

"I have so many things going around in my head."

"I thought you would. You still like Mark, don't you?"

"I do, but it's a different thing that I feel. I don't want to be without Mark in my life and I want to see him every day. I didn't think he gave me butterflies, but when I saw him yesterday, I felt something in my tummy."

"Was that before or after he was saving everybody?"

Rose smiled. "That was before. Helping everyone like that showed what type of man he is."

"He's a brave man and a man of action."

Rose nodded. *"Jah,* he's a real man and that's what I want."

"Mmm. That's very attractive in a man."

"Tulip, what if he had died yesterday? I mean today. It's still today, isn't it?"

"Jah, it's still today. It's only about eleven o'clock."

"He could've died and then I would've regretted things. He was always asking me to marry him but what about now? Does he still want me after all this time?"

"That's something you'll have to find out from him."

Rose put a hand over her stomach. "I hope I haven't left things too late."

"I don't think you have. He's always liked you."

Rose nibbled on the end of her fingernail. "I'll have to call the Walkers tomorrow to see what's happening with the stall. I guess I won't be working again for a while. I don't know what will happen."

"I guess so. They'll probably shut the markets down for repair."

"I'll go to the hospital first thing and see him," Rose said.

"Good idea."

THE NEXT MORNING, knowing that he would be out of the emergency room, Rose found out from the reception desk that Mark was in room 209. She hurried to the second floor and when she walked into his room, she saw four occupied beds and then she saw two Amish women talking to the person in the far bed.

Taking a step closer, she recognized the backs of the young women. They were Lucy Stoltzfuz and Becky Miller. Rose had grown up with them and so too had Mark. The two young women turned around and greeted her. She gave a quick nod and then focused her attention on Mark, who looked pale, but was smiling.

"Rose, you came back."

"You remember I was here yesterday?"

"Of course I do."

Lucy said, "It's all over the papers what happened at the markets and they're calling Mark a local hero."

"Really? I wondered if it was going to be in the papers."

"Did you really save all those people?" Becky asked him.

"*Nee.* I didn't save anyone. That's what the paramedics did. I didn't do much at all."

"That's not what everyone's saying." Lucy's face beamed.

Mark gave a low chuckle. "I can't help what others say."

"Has the doctor been to see you this morning?" Rose asked.

"Not yet, but no doubt I'll see him sometime today."

"How did you hear about Mark being in the hospital?" Rose asked the two young women.

"My mother heard it from someone," Lucy said. "They said that the roof in the farmers market had collapsed, Mark and Matthew were injured, and Mark was in the hospital. We had to come and see how he was."

"You can see I'm perfectly fine. No need for anybody to worry."

Becky sat on his bed and grabbed hold of his hand. "Oh, Mark, I don't know what I would've done if something bad had happened to you."

"Me either," Lucy said.

Rose could tell that Mark was lapping up all the attention. She never realized that Lucy or Becky were that close to him and that was because she hadn't had much to do with him over the past year. Perhaps the article in the paper made them look at him in a different light. It was uncomfortable watching the two women throw themselves at him.

Rose waited for a break in the conversation, and then said, "I might come back a little later."

"You could come back at visiting hours, Rose," Becky said.

"*Jah,* we just sneaked in," Lucy said.

Becky added, "Because visiting hours aren't until later. Ten to twelve in the morning and then between one and three in the afternoon."

Rose nodded. "I'll be back soon, Mark." She smiled at Mark and said goodbye to the two women before she left the room.

Mark hadn't even urged her to stay and she took that as a bad sign. She was only going to wait half an hour or so in the hospital cafeteria until they left so she could talk to Mark alone, but he hadn't known that.

He seemed happy enough with the company of the two women. For all he knew, she could've been heading home and not coming back until the next day.

When Rose found the cafeteria, she slumped into one of the chairs at one of the several round tables. There she wondered what to do. Then she decided if Mark wanted one of those women over her, there was nothing she could do about it. She was the one who didn't know what she had until she'd lost it and she couldn't blame Mark for that. He'd waited for her for a long time without her giving him an ounce of encouragement. And how would he have felt several months ago when he found out she'd liked Jacob? She put her elbows on the table and held her head in both hands.

"Are you alright, dear?" An old lady had sat down beside her and she hadn't even noticed.

"Oh, yes, I'm okay."

"Do you have a loved one in the hospital?"

She stared into the old woman's face and noticed how her beady blue eyes studied her. "I do, but he's not seriously ill. He's got a concussion and a broken leg, so he'll live."

"That is good news."

Rose took her elbows off the table and straightened her back. "Yes, it is. You're right. It is good news."

"I thought you had lost somebody."

Rose smiled at the kindly woman. "I haven't. Not yet."

The old lady smiled back and then turned her attention to

her teacup, ripped open a packet of sugar, and poured it into her tea.

Rose went to the counter and ordered a coffee. Once she finished drinking her coffee, she planned to go back to Mark. Hopefully by then, his admirers would've left.

ROSE PUT her head around Mark's door and saw that Lucy and Becky had gone. She was instantly relieved and was just about to walk into the room when she heard a voice behind her.

"I'm sorry, but it's not visiting hours yet."

Rose swung around and in front of her was one of the blue uniformed hospital staff. "I'm sorry. I didn't know there were particular visiting hours until I got here. Can I just say a quick hello?"

The female worker frowned at her.

"Please? I won't be long and then I'll go."

The worker gave a curt nod and walked away.

Rose wasted no time in hurrying to see Mark. His face lit up when he noticed her walking toward him. "Rosie, you're back."

She liked him calling her Rosie; it was just like old times.

"There were too many people here before, so I thought I'd wait until they were gone."

"Denke for coming."

"Why wouldn't I visit you?"

"I didn't mean it like that. I'm glad that you did, that's all. Come closer and sit on the bed."

She glanced over her shoulder, and then said, "I just got into trouble for being here out of visiting hours, so I can't stay long."

"Just a moment longer."

She sat on the edge of his bed, pleased that he was so happy to see her. "You're looking good today. I was worried about you yesterday."

"I'm feeling a lot better. The nurse said I'd feel tingling or itching on my leg as the drugs wear off."

"How long do they think you'll be in here?"

"I guess that's up to the doctor whenever he gets here."

"I didn't know you were particularly close friends with Becky and Lucy."

"A lot has changed in the last year, Rosie."

Rose would've asked more questions but considering the state of his health they were questions best left for another day. "Can I bring you anything while you're in here?"

"Nee denke. There's nothing I need except to see your friendly face. You'll come back and see me again, won't you?"

Those words pleased her immensely. "I will. I'll be back to see you every day. Have your parents been here yet?"

"They were here last night and they said they were coming back this afternoon. Matthew just had cuts and bruises; nothing serious."

"That's good. I was wondering about that." She looked over her shoulder at the door, hoping that the person who told her about the visiting hours wasn't going to come back and check on her. It was then that she noticed the people in the other beds. Two of them were old men who were asleep, the other one was a young man watching the television with earphones in his ears. "I should go before they kick me out."

"You'll come back tomorrow?" he asked again.

"I will. I don't think that the Walkers can have their flower stall at the markets now. I'm not sure what's going to happen. Either way, I'll get here and see you tomorrow."

His eyes started closing. "I'll see you tomorrow, Rosie."

She got off the bed. "Bye, Mark."

"Bye, Rosie."

She turned and headed out the door. Before she got to the end of the corridor, Mark's doctor stepped out of the last door. They made eye contact and the doctor stopped and smiled at her. "Mark's fiancée?"

"Yes. You have a good memory."

He chuckled. "We don't get that many Amish people in here."

"I've just been to see him. He seems a lot better. When do you think he'll be able to go home?"

"Perhaps tomorrow or the day after."

"That soon?"

"Most likely the day after. It depends on his progress."

"I see. Thank you, doctor." Rose hurried away, glad that nobody heard him calling her Mark's fiancée. She probably shouldn't have told him that, but she couldn't go back in time and change things.

Rose took a taxi directly to Mrs. Walker's house to find out what was going on with the flower stall. The damage caused from the collapse of the roof would take weeks and maybe even months to repair.

The Walkers had made the decision to set up a roadside stall. The market stall was only a small part of their business and their only retail outlet of their large wholesale flower business. They wouldn't suffer too much financially from what had happened, but that wasn't the case for the Schumachers. The bulk of their goats' milk products were sold through the market stall and they would need to find another outlet to sell their goods.

ROSE WALKED HOME FROM THE WALKERS'. Even though they lived on the next-door property, they weren't close enough to be able to see the Walkers' home from their house. Only the rows of temperature-controlled greenhouses could be seen.

As soon as Rose opened her front door, her mother rushed toward her, followed closely by the twins, and then Tulip.

"How is he?" her mother asked.

"He's fine and he'll need to stay in for a couple more days. That's what the doctor said."

"That's good, and have you heard how Matthew is?"

"Just scrapes and some bruises. He's fine. Mark was in the papers and they called him a hero."

"Who was in the papers?" Daisy asked. "Mark was in the papers?"

"Jah, he was."

"I said he was going to be," Lily said.

Daisy stuck her chin out. *"Nee,* I said it."

"Quiet, girls," their mother said. "It doesn't matter who said it." She looked at Rose. "Did you get one of the newspapers?"

"I didn't think to get it."

"Why not?"

"Dat doesn't like the *Englisch* papers." Rose hoped her mother wouldn't send her back out to get a paper. She was too tired to go anywhere.

"It wouldn't hurt to just get one to see what they said about Mark."

"Rose, why don't you and I go out and get one now?"

Rose looked at Tulip. Even though she was weary, getting out of the house and being with Tulip sounded like a good idea. *Jah,* why don't we do that? Is that okay with you, *Mamm?*"

"*Jah,* go on."

"Let's go, Rose." Tulip stepped forward and grabbed Rose's arm and pulled her back toward the front door.

The two girls set about hitching the buggy.

"What happened at the hospital? It's like something's bothering you."

"You can tell?" Rose asked.

"It's written all over your face. I'm surprised *Mamm* couldn't tell."

Rose rubbed her forehead. "When I got there, to Mark's hospital room, Lucy and Becky were there."

"Do you think one of them likes him?"

Rose nodded. "Or both of them do because that's how they were acting. They were telling Mark how brave he was and what a hero he was, and all that. And then one of them grabbed his hand. I can't remember which one it was. At that point, I left. I went and had a cup of coffee and waited for them to leave. Then I went back again."

"Had they left when you went back?"

"*Jah,* but I couldn't stay long because it wasn't visiting hours."

"Do you think Mark likes one of them?"

"It's hard to say. He didn't look upset to have them there, put it that way."

"He couldn't, though, because that would've been rude. He would've liked to have visitors no matter who they were. Besides that, he probably sees them as just friends."

Rose nibbled on a fingernail. "Do you think that's it? Do you think they're just friends?"

"I don't know. I haven't noticed them talking to him at the meetings or anything. How would we find out?"

"I suppose we could ask around, but that would be a little nosey and I wouldn't like to do that."

While Tulip backed the horse into the harness, she said, "So, we just wait and see how things unfold?"

"I guess that's what we do." When the horse was hitched to the buggy, Rose patted him on his neck. "I said I'd go back and see him tomorrow."

"Do you want me to go too? That way, if he has visitors besides you, I can talk to them while you talk with Mark."

"*Denke.* That's a *gut* idea."

WHEN ROSE and Tulip got to the small supermarket that sold the daily newspapers, they saw that the news about the farmers market had made the front page. Tulip grabbed the paper and scanned the article while Rose looked for Mark's name over Tulip's shoulder.

"It says here a local Amish man, Mark Schumacher, pulled people from the rubble and took charge until the paramedics arrived."

"That's pretty much how it happened," Rose said.

Tulip took the paper to the counter to pay for it and then they headed back to the buggy. "Rose, if you want Mark, I think you have to move fast because women would want a man like Mark—a man who would put others before himself and risk his life to help others. There's something very attractive about a man who would do that."

Rose could barely speak and she hoped she hadn't left things too long. She'd only just realized how she felt, and now she would have to compete with other women for his attention. A year ago, no one gave him a second look or a second thought, including her.

"Well, what do you think?" Tulip asked as they both climbed into the buggy.

"You're right. I don't know what to do. I've got to sort my feelings out first."

"I think you know your feelings and you don't want to admit them to yourself."Tulip moved the horse forward.

"That doesn't make much sense."

"It does. It makes perfect sense. You've always been in love with Mark and you didn't know it. You expected love to be something else."

Tulip was right in a sense. Rose thought back to Jacob. He was tall and handsome and had a dazzling smile and he'd said all the right things, but it was deep inside a man that mattered. Jacob wasn't half the man Mark was. She knew that if she married Mark he would always put her first and look after her.

"Why have you gone quiet, Rose?"

"I'm thinking about Jacob and how he made my heart pound. The first time I saw him I was sure we would be married."

"It wasn't real, though. He's more handsome than Mark and probably more handsome than most men, but he's too in love with himself to ever be in love with a woman. That's what I reckon. You can easily do without Jacob, but can you do without Mark in your life?"

"I've really missed him over this past year. I always thought of him as a friend until he wasn't there."

"And that's when you started to think of him as something else?"

Rose covered her face with her hands. "I'm so confused."

"There's nothing confusing about it. Either you love him, or you don't. And if you don't, you must release him from your heart and your mind, so some other woman can have him and make him happy."

Rose was a little embarrassed to admit to her sister that she loved Mark because if she said it out loud she would feel bad about not realizing it earlier. "I wonder what *Dat* will say when he sees the thing about Mark in the paper?"

"He'll be pleased, of course."

When they got home, their mother told Rose that Mrs. Walker had stopped by to let Rose know that, along with other stallholders, they'd set up shop down the road from the markets. Rose was selfishly disappointed because it meant she wouldn't be free to visit Mark.

"I can work on the stall instead of you for a few days if you like, Rose."

"Would you?"

Tulip nodded. "I don't mind at all."

Rose looked back at her mother. "When are they going to start?"

"The day after tomorrow."

"Perfect. I'll walk over and talk to Mrs. Walker now and

tell her that Tulip will do a couple of days for me." Rose knew she wouldn't mind. Tulip often filled in for her at the flower stall.

∾

THE NEXT DAY, Tulip and Rose walked into Mark's hospital room at the start of visiting hours, and to Rose's delight, they were the only visitors.

Mark turned to look at them and smiled as they walked over. "I've got two visitors today. I can't pull any chairs closer for you. They tell me I can't walk just yet."

"It looks like it'll be some time before you can," Tulip said while Rose pulled the two chairs by the wall close to his bed.

"It's not a bad break. The doctor just wanted to keep me in here because of the concussion. I feel fine. What's going on with you two?"

They sat down and Rose was the one who answered, "Tomorrow the Walkers are setting up a stall for their flowers not far from the markets with a few stallholders. Are your parents doing the same?"

"I'm not certain. Our generator was destroyed and now we're borrowing one and setting up somewhere. My folks didn't say where."

"It's a shame about the generator being destroyed. One that size would cost a lot of money."

"It did."

While Rose listened to Mark talk, she was pleased that there was no sign of Becky or Lucy. "Have you been getting many visitors?"

"Quite a few. The bishop and his wife came yesterday after-noon along with a couple of my brothers."

"Tulip is looking after the stall for me, so I can come back and see you tomorrow."

"That's very nice of you, Tulip. *Denke.*"

"I know how worried Rose has been about you."

Mark smiled at Rose. "I'm fine, Rosie, you don't need to worry."

"I know, but it's hard to see you in the hospital like this, so helpless."

His lips turn down at the corners. "I'm not that helpless. They showed me how to walk on the crutches this morning. A broken leg won't hold me back too much. It could've been worse."

"Don't talk about it," Rose said. "It was very dangerous, you going back into the building like that."

"If I remember correctly, I was out of the building when something fell on me."

Tulip stood. "I'm going to get a soda. Can I bring you back anything, Mark? Tea or coffee?"

"I'd love a strong coffee."

"Coming up. And you, Rose?"

"Nothing for me, *denke.*" Tulip walked out of the room and Rose was pleased to be alone with Mark—alone apart from the three other patients in the room. None of them were listening. One had his earphones in again, one was reading a book, and the other was asleep.

"I'll be out of here tomorrow or the next day. Most likely tomorrow."

"That's good. They seem to be looking after you in here."

"Yeah, they are, but I'd much rather be at home. *Denke* for coming to see me again. I was hoping you would."

Heat rose to her cheeks. She'd never been embarrassed or shy in front of him before. Now things were different. Now that Tulip was out of the room and she was alone with him, she desperately wanted him to know that she liked him. He wasn't joking about marrying her like he used to when they'd worked side-by-side at the markets. "What about your job? Will you still be able to make the buggies with a broken leg?"

"I'll be able to do some parts of my job. I'll work around things somehow."

"That's good." When Rose heard loud voices in the corridor, she recognized them as belonging to the two girls who had visited him the other day. Her heart sank. "It sounds like you have some more visitors heading your way."

"*Jah,* their voices are unmistakable, aren't they?"

"I'll leave you alone with them and find Tulip."

"Will you come back?"

"*Jah,* we'll have to come back to give you your coffee."

"That's right. I'll see you soon, then." As she was about to leave, he lunged forward and grabbed her hand. Then he whispered, "Don't leave me alone with them for too long."

Rose giggled. "I won't. We'll be back soon."

That confirmed to Rose that he didn't like either of them. He still liked her, she was sure of it. He let go of her hand when the two girls walked through the door.

"Rose, you're here again!" Lucy walked through the door, followed closely by Becky.

"I am. I'm just leaving."

"Bye, Rose," Becky said as Rose walked past them.

It didn't sit well with Rose that they were visiting Mark again. She tried her best not to let it bother her. Just as she was walking into the café, Mark's doctor was walking out carrying a take-out drink container.

"Ah, Mark's fiancée again."

Rose gave a small giggle. "Yes, it's me again."

"You'll be happy to know he might be coming home to you tomorrow. I'll be here around six in the morning doing my rounds, and if all's good he can go home."

"Thank you, Doctor. I'm so happy he'll be home soon."

He smiled and gave her a nod and kept walking. Rose found Tulip at the counter paying for the coffee and the soda.

Tulip saw Rose as she walked away from the counter. "What are you doing here?"

"We might as well sit down for a few minutes because Mark has visitors."

Tulip raised his take out coffee. "The coffee will get cold."

"It'll stay hot for ages in that container."

The two girls sat down at one of the tables. "Who's visiting him?"

"Three guesses."

"I'd reckon I would only need two. Becky and Lucy."

"That's right. We heard them coming and he asked me not to leave him alone with them for too long."

Tulip raised her eyebrows. "That's good. That means he doesn't like them and he likes you." Tulip sucked on her straw while still keeping her eyes fixed on Rose.

"Do you think so?"

"It's pretty obvious if you ask me."

Rose sighed. "I wish I knew for certain."

"Ask him."

Rose gasped. "I couldn't."

Tulip shrugged. "There are many instances in the bible where women did bold things regarding men. It worked for them. Anyway, so much for our plan of me talking with them. It might work if we head back now."

"*Nee*, just stay here."

While Tulip continued encouraging Rose to be more forthright with Mark, Rose considered that maybe her sister could be right. In the past, Mark had revealed how he'd felt, so maybe the time had come for her to do the same. Especially now that she had competition. If she didn't do something now, it might be too late. She wasn't an expert on love. All she knew was that her days were much better and happier with Mark in them.

"We should go now and take him his coffee," Tulip said when she finished her soda.

"I hope they've gone by now." Rose stood and pushed her chair under the table.

"If they haven't, we will just give him his coffee and then leave. Or did you want to stay? It's up to you."

"I think we'll just give him the coffee and then go. It'll be too awkward to stay around there with them there."

"I agree."

When they got back to Mark's hospital room, the two girls had made themselves comfortable. They looked like they'd be there until the visiting hours were over. After Tulip had handed Mark the coffee, Mark shot Rose a pleading look that said, 'save me.' Rose had to stifle a giggle. At that moment, she knew for certain that he liked her and no one else.

CHAPTER 23

THE NEXT DAY, Rose entered the hospital alone and hurried to room 209. Today was the day that the doctor had said Mark might be released.

Rose poked her head around the doorway of Mark's room and saw him sitting up in bed, looking brighter.

"There you are," Mark said.

She walked to his bedside and then sat close to him on the bed. *"Jah,* here I am."

"You don't have to come here every day, Rosie."

"Of course, I do. Tulip's looking after the stall today and everything's just fine. Are you getting out today?"

"Before I answer that, do you have any idea where my fiancée is?"

Rose frowned at him. "What do you mean?"

"My doctor keeps talking to me about my fiancée. Tell your fiancée this, tell her that, this is something your fiancée needs to know. I'm just wondering where she is, that's all." He dipped his head when Rose giggled. "Have you seen her?"

"I told him we were engaged the first day you were here. I've run into him two more times and he thinks I'm your fiancée."

"Oh, it's you?"

Rose nodded. She figured she'd made him wait long enough. He'd always been honest and held nothing back. She took hold of his hand. "Mark, do you still want to marry me like you used to?"

"I've always wanted to marry you, Rosie, always. That's something that'll never change as long as the sun keeps coming up every morning and sets every evening."

Peace swept over Rose and she knew in her heart that this man would never fail her or let her down in any way. She didn't want to go on without him in her life. It had taken her some time, and certainly more time than her parents were happy about, to find the perfect man for her. "Will you marry me, Mark?"

He smiled and stared at her for some time before he spoke. "Are you serious right now, Rosie? Don't joke with me about something like this."

"I've never been more serious." She leaned forward and placed her lips softly on his, knowing she was kissing her husband—the one who had been made just for her. She pulled back.

"We're getting married, then, it seems."

Rose smiled at him and all was right with her world. "I'm glad."

"As soon as we possibly can?" he asked.

"*Jah*, very soon."

"That's all I've ever wanted, Rosie. That's all. I don't know why it took you so long to see that I was the man for you."

"It probably shouldn't have taken me so long, but it did."

"None of that matters now that we're together. This is the happiest day of my life."

When she saw him blinking back tears, she laughed and fought back tears of her own. "Don't you cry, or I'll cry and I won't be able to stop."

"Cry? I never cry. Well, maybe just a little every time someone accepts my marriage proposal."

Rose laughed. "Exactly how many marriage proposals have you given out?"

"Only ever the one. And I was right. I knew if I waited for you long enough you'd marry me." He squeezed her hand.

Rose held his hand tightly while she thought back to over a year ago. He'd always said there was never anybody else for him. It didn't matter now that he wasn't tall and handsome. He was Mark, and that was all she needed. Contentment and peace flooded her heart.

THREE MONTHS LATER...

MRS. NANCY YODER leaned against the wall of her house. This was the first wedding that had taken place at her home. She looked over at Mark and Rose as they talked to one another at their wedding table in the yard. Her oldest daughter was finally married, and if it hadn't been for her pushing Rose, it might never have happened.

Mark had been an excellent choice of a husband for her daughter. She wondered why she hadn't seen sooner how Mark was the one.

Nancy sighed. She was tired. She had just, with the help of five other women, served over three hundred people for the wedding breakfast.

It had been an exhausting eighteen months trying to get Rose married off. Firstly encouraging her, goading her, giving her ultimatums, and then leaving her alone. Now, her oldest daughter was finally married and she'd found someone who didn't mind that she was so tall and gangly.

Her sons, Peter and Trevor, were married, along with Rose, so that left only Tulip, and then the twins, Daisy and Lily. She was halfway there; three children were married and three were left. With Tulip about to turn twenty, there was no time to waste. She looked around amongst the food tables set up in the yard, searching for Tulip. She finally saw her at the far end of the yard talking with three young men who appeared very interested in what she had to say.

"Ah, that looks like a fine start. I'll wander over there and find out who they are." She was pretty certain one was from their community, and the other two were visiting. In her ideal world, her daughters wouldn't go far from home when they married. If she managed things just so, she would see to it that what she wanted came to pass.

When she heard a squeal and raucous laughter, she looked and saw the twins playing with children. Nancy shook her head. A trip to the bishop might be required for those two. Out of her four daughters, Tulip was her smart one, Rose was the soft and gentle one, and the twins—the twins seemed to be a lost cause. As Nancy walked over to Tulip, to find out more about the young men she was speaking with, Nancy shook her head about the twins—they were a puzzle for later.

End of Book 1 Amish Rose

AMISH TULIP

AMISH LOVE BLOOMS BOOK 2

SAMANTHA PRICE

CHAPTER 1

NANCY YODER HAD BEEN successful in getting her oldest daughter, Rose, married in a timely fashion. Organizing people and events was what Nancy did best, and with her encouragement, Rose had finally seen the sense in getting married young. With the wedding held at their house now coming to a close, Nancy leaned against the outside wall, feeling a deep sense of satisfaction. The guests were just finishing the main meal, and the desserts were ready to be distributed—a perfect time to have a break.

Now that they were married, Rose and Mark would be moving into a small house on Mark's uncle's land, which left only the twins and Tulip still in the family home. Once they were all off her hands, Nancy figured she would take life easier and enjoy some time alone with her husband, Hezekiah. Of course, there would be the added benefit of the grandchildren that would follow the marriages and she was looking forward to watching them arrive. Her oldest son and his wife had already had a daughter and she'd been a blessing to the whole family. It was high time for her second eldest son who'd been married for more than a year to give her a grandchild.

Nancy looked around for Tulip, her next project. Squinting hard, Nancy saw that her daughter was at the far end of the yard speaking with three young men. Wasting no time, she hurried over to find out exactly who these young men were. As she drew closer, she noticed that only one man looked familiar and she didn't recognize the other two.

Tulip glanced at her mother as she approached and didn't look happy to see her. Nancy knew Tulip didn't like her knowing too much about her friends. She'd developed a habit of being far too private and that didn't suit Nancy one little bit.

"*Mamm!* Do you want me to help with the food again?"

"It's a bit late for that, Tulip. Why don't you introduce me to your friends?"

"*Jah,* okay. Sorry. *Mamm,* this is Andrew, and this is Nathanial, and of course you know Phillip." She turned to the young men and almost as an apology said, "This is my *mudder,* Nancy Yoder."

"Hello, Mrs. Yoder," one of the young men said, while the other two nodded politely.

"And where are you all from?" Nancy swept her gaze across the three of them. As they talked, she found out that one young man was from Oakes County, another was from their community, and the third one of them belonged to people from Ohio. It was all too much for her to remember, the three names let alone where each of them was from. She told herself she'd find out more from Tulip later in the night and whether Tulip might be interested in one of them in particular. Her job of finding Tulip a husband might well be easier than she thought it would be, but only if Tulip didn't carry on in the ridiculous secretive manner she'd had of late.

"Are you going to say hello to Aunt Nerida, *Mamm?* It looks like she's leaving," Tulip said, staring at the row of buggies.

Nancy glanced over at her only sister, who she didn't get along with. Tulip was simply trying to get rid of her mother, Nancy knew that, but she kept staring at Nerida and her two daughters, surprised they'd bothered to come at all. They hadn't made any effort to come to either of her son's weddings. Not wanting to create a bad example to Tulip, she said, "*Jah,* I suppose I should thank her for coming and be cordial."

After she had nodded a goodbye to the young men, Nancy strode toward her sister. If Nerida really wanted to make amends with her, she would've stepped up and helped with the food. And if that wasn't the reason she'd come, then what was the reason? Perhaps Nerida and her girls were hungry and had come for the food? Nancy amused herself with that thought.

Nerida and she had been the only girls, with ten older brothers, and Nancy was a year older. The thing that had forever irritated Nancy was that her younger sister had a bad habit of copying everything she did. And Nerida knew that her copying had always bothered Nancy. The worst thing and the most unforgiveable thing Nerida had done was to steal Nancy's idea of calling her daughters names of flowers. That was *her* thing—her theme for the girls, and her sister should've known that she shouldn't have copied. Nerida had called her first child

Violet, and her second, Willow. When Nancy had confronted her about it, Nerida called her ridiculous and told her that 'Willow' wasn't even a flower. She'd acted like Nancy was making a fuss over nothing. The name Willow was close enough to Nancy's thinking, and from that moment, a rift developed between the sisters.

"Are you leaving already, Nerida?"

Nerida was already in the driver's seat of the buggy. She took hold of the reins before she looked at Nancy.

"Hello, Aunt Nancy," the two girls chorused from the buggy.

"Hello, Violet and Willow." She smiled at her pretty nieces who were both a little younger than Nancy's twins. "I haven't seen you all for some time."

"And whose fault is that?" Nerida quipped.

"Mamm!" Violet, the older of the girls looked shocked at the way her mother had spoken.

"Why don't you stay on a little so we can talk?" Nancy suggested to Nerida, After all, weddings were about families. Nerida's presence signaled a step to reconciliation, so Nancy was also taking a step.

Nerida tilted her chin high and said down the end of her nose, "I'm only here for Rose. She's a sweet girl, and the girls wanted to come to the wedding too."

"We love weddings," Willow said.

"We're just serving the dessert," Nancy said, hoping that would make at least the girls want to stay on. "Wouldn't you girls like to stay longer?"

"It's not their decision, Nancy."

"Couldn't we stay, *Mamm?"* Violet asked.

Willow added from the backseat of the buggy, "Just a little longer?"

"Nee. Goodbye, Nancy." Nerida slapped the reins against the horse's neck, and the horse walked forward.

Nancy stood and watched the buggy leave. They were the first guests to leave the wedding. *Well, Hezekiah can't say that I didn't try.*

CHAPTER 2

WHEN NANCY WAS STANDING BACK by the house, Rose and Nancy's eyes met and Rose gave her mother a little wave. Nancy smiled and waved back at her newly married daughter.

"Well, we've got three married off and three to go."

Nancy jumped at the sound of her husband's deep voice. She hadn't noticed him walking up behind her. "There you are. I was just thinking the very same thing. With the boys and Rose married now, there are only Tulip and the twins to go. Then we'll be alone again—at last. That will be the best outcome." Nancy giggled.

Hezekiah chuckled along with her. "Don't forget all the *grosskinner* we'll have."

"I'm not forgetting about that, or our little Shirley. She's been a blessing for the whole *familye*. She needs other children to play with; that's something I think about every day."

"There are plenty of children she can play with." Hezekiah

put a hand gently on his wife's shoulder. "That will all happen in time, Nancy, all in *Gott's* timing."

Nancy nodded and then her husband walked away. Hezekiah thought that things happened by themselves under God's general oversight, and she wasn't about to disagree with him, but sometimes God used people's actions to fulfill His will. That's all Nancy was doing; she was being God's helper to get her three remaining daughters married and off her hands.

Tulip was smart, so she needed a man equally smart, but where would she go to find one of those? Nancy looked around the crowd. It was getting harder just to find a single man, as many of them had married over the past year.

Seeing Tulip still talking with the same three young men, she decided to invite them all to Tulip's birthday. She left Hezekiah standing there and hurried back to Tulip's side. "It's your birthday soon and we always have a big party for you."

"That's not necessary, *Mamm.* I'm not interested in birthdays, not mine, anyway. I don't like a lot of fuss."

Nancy shook her head. "That's nonsense." She turned to the three young men. "I hope all of you will be able to come?"

"We would love to," one of them said. "At least, I'll be there. What day is it?"

"Wednesday upcoming."

"We'll be there," another of the men said, as the other two smiled.

Nancy was pleased that the three men appeared delighted to be invited. *"Gut!* Shall we say seven o'clock?"

All the boys nodded in agreement.

"If you'll excuse me, there are some other people I need to organize for serving the desserts." Nancy walked away, pleased with herself, and then hurried to find some more single men to invite to Tulip's birthday. Weddings were the best places for young men and women to gather, and they brought in many visitors from other communities far and wide. Tulip was stuck speaking to the same three men, so Nancy would have to do the legwork for her. She could not let this opportunity pass her by.

Nancy organized the serving of the desserts and then spent the next hour meeting as many young men as she could. She invited every one she could to her daughter's birthday.

TULIP WAS glad that her mother hadn't caught on to the fact that one of the boys she'd been speaking with was Jacob Schumacher's brother, Nathanial. Jacob had disappointed her sister, Rose, several months ago before she married, and then he left their community to go back to Oakes County to marry someone else. Jacob had gotten a young woman into a situation where they *had* to marry. Of course, none of that was Nathanial's fault, but her mother was stubborn and would fail to see it that way. Things turned out much better for Rose because the hurt from Jacob's deception opened her eyes to Mark, who had loved her since they were young. Rose and Mark were a far better match than Rose and Jacob would've ever been.

Now Tulip and Nathanial were alone, since the other two young men were talking with others nearby. Nathanial was a handsome man, much like his brother, Jacob. His hair was rich brown in color, and his eyes were a vivid blue-green that stood out against his tanned olive skin. He was so handsome that Tulip could barely take her eyes from him.

"I might stay on a few weeks more."

"That would be nice. Can you do that? What about your job?" Tulip asked.

"I'm in between jobs at the moment. I'm told there could be work around here."

Tulip smiled. She knew Nathanial liked her by the way he continually smiled and hung around making conversation. If she married him things could be awkward because Rose would be even more closely related—by two marriages—to Jacob, since Jacob was Mark's cousin.

"Your *schweschder* looks happy," he said, looking over at the wedding table at the end of the Yoder's yard.

Tulip glanced over at Rose. "She is. She's in love with Mark. He's always loved her."

"And what about you?"

She stared at him. "Me?"

"*Jah,* do you have a man in your life?"

"*Nee,* I don't right now." She giggled and looked down at her lace-up boots. The complete truth was that Tulip had never had a man in her life.

"Can I see you sometime? Alone, I mean."

She looked into his blue-green eyes and her heart gave a flutter. "I'd like that."

"I'm staying with my aunt and uncle, Mark and Matthew's parents." He nodded toward her house. "I already know where you live. Maybe I can see you before your birthday?"

Tulip nodded, wondering what her mother would say if she learned that she'd accidently invited Jacob's brother to her birthday. "Okay. What did you have in mind?"

"Can I see you—maybe Saturday afternoon? Can you get away and head into town?"

"I'll try."

"We could meet at Little Beans Café. It's a nice place. I went there yesterday with Matthew."

"I know where it is. What time?"

"Two?"

"I think I could do that." The only way she would be able to get away was to tell her mother she was meeting friends in town. She couldn't tell her she was meeting Jacob's brother. If she did, her mother wouldn't allow it, or worse, she'd send her younger twin sisters with her. That would completely ruin all her chances with him. The twins would tell stories to Nathanial and make Tulip look a fool. Either choice would be a complete disaster. She didn't like lying, so she hoped her mother wouldn't probe too far into where she was going on Saturday.

He smiled at her. "I'm looking forward to it."

"Me too." She glanced down at her boots and then looked back up at his handsome face. "I should see if *Mamm* needs my help."

He nodded. "I'll see you on Saturday."

"Okay." Tulip walked away as though she were floating. She pushed some loose strands of dark hair back under her *kapp* as she walked between rows of tables. The second seating of the meal had taken place and now the women were running the desserts out from the kitchen.

As soon as she walked into the house, a line of women with their arms full of either serving trays or bowls passed her. In the kitchen, her mother barked out orders at her. She too took several trips out with large serving bowls and trays of desserts to place on the tables.

When Tulip placed the last of the desserts down on one of the tables, she looked around at the hundreds of guests, most of whom were seated. She no longer felt hungry because of Nathanial. Not only had he made her feel light-headed, he'd taken her appetite away. She looked around for him and spotted him eating at a table next to his cousin, Matthew. He caught her eye and smiled at her. It was as though they had a secret that was their very own.

She turned around to see her father and the twins at the table in front of her, so she sat with them. Even though she wasn't hungry, she helped herself to a large piece of apple pie and spooned on a large helping of cream. If she sat there without eating, her twin sisters would say something about it and tease her. Tulip wasn't in the mood.

"It'll be you next, Tulip," Daisy, one of her sisters, said.

Tulip knew what she was teasing her about. It was time to do a little teasing of her own. *"Nee,* I think it will be both of you. *Mamm's* writing to all the communities and finding twin boys your age, or a little older, for you to marry."

"Is she?" Lily's face lit up like a lantern on a dark winter's night.

Their father chuckled. "Your *schweschder's* only having fun with you."

Daisy frowned at her. *"Jah,* having fun at my expense is what she's doing. How could you be so mean, Tulip? It sounds just like something *Mamm* would do."

"Jah, that would be *gut,* to marry twins, wouldn't it, Daisy?" Lily asked. "Then we could all live in one big *haus."*

"And each have twin *bopplis*," Daisy added with a giggle. "Three sets of twins each."

Lily added, "They can be the same ages so they can grow up together."

Tulip pulled a face. Did the world need more twins like her sisters? Tulip said, full of sarcasm, "Would you ever consider marrying someone who wasn't a twin?"

"*Nee*," both of them said at once.

"I don't think that'll happen. I haven't heard of twin boys your age," their father said as he helped himself to more dessert.

Lily said, "Don't be like that, *Dat.* You have to believe there are some out there somewhere."

Their father chuckled again. "You never know, but I would be surprised if that happened, so don't wait for these twins."

"I've found a man for you, Tulip."

Tulip leaned forward, not knowing whether Daisy was being serious or silly. "Where is he?"

"Over there."

She turned and looked where her sister was pointing to see Jonathon Byler, a quiet single man in his late twenties. He was very much overweight. Tulip wouldn't let on she knew they were teasing her and being mean about Jonathon. It would only draw attention to their meanness. "*Jah,* I like Jonathon, but not in that way."

"He's perfect for you." Lily giggled and poked Daisy in the ribs with her elbow.

Their father turned around to look at Jonathon, and then he glared at the twins. "It's been a long time since I had to scold the two of you, but if you can't behave, you'll spend the rest of the day in your rooms."

"Sorry, *Dat,*" Daisy said.

"Yeah, we didn't mean anything bad," Lily said, looking down at the table.

"I'm not sure what you meant, but you must watch your tongues. Small words can light great fires." He shook his head. "I'll be telling your *mudder* about this."

"Nee, Dat, please *nee,"* Lily pleaded.

"We'll go up to our rooms right now, but please don't tell *Mamm."* Daisy leaned over toward her father.

"She'll ask why you're in your rooms and I'll not lie," he said in a stern tone.

Lily nibbled a fingernail. "We won't do it again. We're sorry."

"See that you don't say anything like that again. And then we can forget the whole thing." His eyebrows pinched together as he shook his head. "I'll let it go this once if you watch your words."

"Denke, Dat." Lily glanced at Daisy with a look of relief. "We won't do it again. It was just a silly thing to say and we know that now."

"Just watch your tongues," he repeated.

Tulip did her best to hide her amusement at how scared the twins were of their mother. Most people she knew were more scared of their fathers than their mothers, but their mother could be very stern sometimes and thought nothing of dishing out harsh punishment. Most of the punishments were in the order of staying in the house for two weeks and only being allowed to go to the meetings. That also meant having no friends over to visit.

The twins were quiet for the remainder of the wedding, which was most unlike them. Tulip couldn't stop glancing over at Nathanial. It was a nice feeling to potentially have someone special in her life. Even if nothing came of their date, it was nice to have that feeling of harmony and light within. Now she had a little taste of what it would be like to have a special man in her life just as Rose now had Mark.

CHAPTER 3

THAT NIGHT, when Nancy was at home with her husband, she sat on a chair in their bedroom and brushed out her long hair with slow, smooth strokes while a single tear trickled down her cheek. It wouldn't be the same without Rose in the house; it already felt empty.

"What's wrong?" Hezekiah asked.

"Nothing."

"Now come on; I know it's something. Are you sad about Rose moving out of the *haus?*"

"I'm happy she's married."

"That's not what I asked you."

"I'm just a little sad that our *kinner* have all grown up, and now our first *dochder* is married. I want them all to be young again. I want to turn back time, and have all of them small again and gathered around my feet pulling on my apron strings, annoying me. Now I'd give anything to have them surrounding me like that again." She wiped away tears from her eyes.

Hezekiah got up and stood behind his wife. Placing his hands on her shoulders, he leaned over and kissed her on the cheek. "That's why we have to enjoy each and every moment. Each moment *Gott* gives us in this earthly home is precious."

"I wish I had enjoyed that time more when they were little. I kept looking forward to the time they'd be bigger, when I should've been enjoying them at the ages they were." She shook her head. "I had looked forward to the time when I could have an adult conversation with them and they would have their own opinions and ideas. Now that time has come, I miss their younger selves. You see, it is like they are each two different people—their younger selves and their older selves. I miss their younger selves. I know that doesn't make much sense and I'm babbling like a crazy woman."

"It makes perfect sense."

"People used to say to me, *Enjoy them while you can because they grow up so quickly.* I don't think I ever really did."

"There's no point in being upset about things that you cannot change, Nancy. Start now by enjoying each and every day for what joy it brings us."

"I suppose you're right." She inhaled deeply. "We can't turn back the clock."

"Now you can pass on your knowledge and your experience to our *kinner,* and to Shirley and soon to our other *grosskinner* when they arrive."

She laughed. "And they probably won't listen to me, just like I never listened to my parents."

Hezekiah chuckled. "You're probably right. We can only give them advice. It's up to them to follow it. Life's a journey, and we don't know in which direction the wind will blow our sails. All we can do is set our sails in the one we think is the right direction, with *Gott's* help, naturally."

Nancy breathed out heavily and then sighed. "I know I can't get the time back. I should enjoy the time I have with Tulip and the twins before they get married. And then when that happens it will feel very strange indeed. Do you realize that means the *haus* will be empty?"

"*Jah,* it'll be just like when we were newlyweds. We'll have the place to ourselves."

"I can look forward to that while also enjoying what's happening now."

"*Gut!* With the love you and I have for each other, our life together will be *wunderbaar.* I don't see that it could be any other way. We've been very blessed, you and I. We've always enjoyed each other's company and we'll go on doing that into our old age."

"I hope I go to *Gott* before you do," Nancy said while wondering why she was suddenly feeling so emotional. Normally, she wasn't a sensitive person prone to sudden pangs of nostalgia.

"There's no point talking about things like that. *Gott* takes us when he chooses."

"I know that, but what would I do without you?" She began to cry once again, and he encircled his arms about her.

"Whoever goes first, we won't be long without the other. We'll be together forever in *Gott's* Kingdom. This life is brief in comparison with eternity. And we'll spend eternity together. I think we can cope with maybe one or two years without the other, don't you?" He patted her on the shoulder and kissed her again.

"I know." She grabbed his hand and held it tight. "I know I'm being silly."

"*Nee,* you're not being silly. It's nice to hear how much you care for me. I haven't heard that in a while."

She turned to look him in the eyes. "You haven't?"

"I know how much you care for me, but it's nice to hear it every now and again."

"I'm sorry if I've been distracted. I've always done my best to be a good *fraa.*"

"You've been the best *fraa* to me, and the best *mudder* to my *kinner,* that a man could have. And I don't know how you do half of the things that you do. You're truly an amazing woman."

She got up, stood in front of him, and wrapped her arms around him as he enfolded her in a hug. "I've truly been blessed. Rose has a perfect man and now it must be Tulip's turn."

"All in *Gott's* timing, Nancy, all in *Gott's* timing."

"That's exactly right." Nancy said with a little smirk turning the corners of her lips upward. Nancy closed her eyes and thought back to earlier that day. Rose's wedding had been beautiful. The ceremony had taken place outdoors between two overhanging trees. It was a beautiful sight to see how Rose looked adoringly into her husband's eyes.

She had seen that Jonathon's cousin, Wilhem, was sitting next to him and she noticed many girls looking at him while ignoring Jonathon. She thought it funny that girls placed such a high priority on the way men looked before getting to know them. Jonathon was a lovely man but because he was quiet and a little overweight, girls didn't give him a chance.

His handsome cousin won't be single for long, Nancy thought. Her worst nightmare would be that Tulip or any of her daughters would get married and go to live far away. She was certain that Tulip hadn't even noticed the handsome stranger who spent most of the wedding by his cousin, Jonathon's, side.

CHAPTER 4

TULIP MANAGED to get out of the house on Saturday afternoon by telling her parents she was visiting friends. That wasn't a lie; Nathanial could be classed as a friend. She certainly didn't know him well enough to call him more than that. Because her mother was reprimanding the twins over something they'd forgotten to do, she just told Tulip she could go without asking any questions at all.

Tulip had taken the most reliable of their buggy horses and the smallest buggy. Once she found a spot near the café to park the buggy, she secured the horse and then smoothed down her dress with both hands. There was another horse and buggy on the same road and she wondered whether that might have been one that Nathanial had borrowed from the relatives he was staying with.

As soon as she turned the corner onto the main road, the café came into sight. She could see Nathanial's smiling face through the large window. He stood up and waved to her.

Walking on the rough floorboards, she breathed in her favorite aroma—the smell of freshly-ground coffee.

"You look lovely, Tulip," he said as soon as she sat opposite him.

"Denke."

He'd made her feel relaxed right away. She took in her surroundings. The café was large, with around twenty small tables inside and more tables outside under the awning on the broad sidewalk. On the mottled brown walls hung two large paintings that looked more like graffiti than art.

"I thought you wouldn't come."

Looking back at him, she gave a little giggle. "Why wouldn't I?"

"I thought your parents mightn't like me."

Tulip realized that he'd expected her to tell her parents where she was going. Somehow she'd gotten the opposite impression. She couldn't tell him that she hadn't told them because they might not approve of her seeing Jacob's brother—that might make him feel bad. "They don't know you."

"I met your *mudder* at the wedding. I haven't met your *vadder* yet, but I will since I'm staying longer. Now, what would you like to eat?"

"Just a coffee for me."

He pushed a menu over to her. "Nothing to eat?"

"Nee, denke. I've just eaten at home."

"I've just eaten too, but I can always eat more." He took the menu back and looked at it for a while before he said, "I'm going to have a steak sandwich. Can you help me eat it?"

"I could have a little."

"*Gut!*" He sprang to his feet to place their order at the register.

While he was gone, Tulip looked around, hoping that there was no one there who might happen to tell her parents she was sitting alone with a man. No, there was no one around that she knew. They were the only Amish couple in sight.

When he sat back down, she asked, "How is your *bruder?*"

"Jacob? He's okay. He's married now to Jessica. I'm not sure if you know that? And they've had a *boppli.*"

"That's nice. *Jah,* I did hear that." She had to change the embarrassing subject of Jacob and Jessica. "So, what kind of work are you looking for?"

"Anything. I learned the upholstery trade just like Jacob, but it's not something I want to do for the rest of my life. I like being out in the fresh air, and I like to build things."

"There should be plenty of that sort of work around."

"Which one?"

"Either, I suppose."

He chuckled. "I hope so. I'm starting my search on Monday. My *onkel* is asking around for me. He knows some builders. What is it that you like doing?"

"I don't have a job. I stay at home helping my *mudder.* There are only me and my two younger sisters at home now."

"Do you like doing that?"

She shuddered. "Not really. I'd rather be out of the *haus.* I want to get some kind of a job, I just haven't worked out what I'd like to do."

"So, you want to get a job soon?"

"I do, if I could figure out what direction to go in. I like cooking, but that's all I can think of doing. Most jobs go to people with experience and I've heard it's hard to get a job without having worked somewhere else."

"You could work somewhere for free to gain experience."

"I suppose I could. I didn't think of that."

The waiter brought over their coffees.

"Thank you," Nathanial said, pushing the black coffee Tulip's way and keeping the latte in front of himself.

"The steak sandwich won't be long," the waiter said before he left.

Tulip picked up a spoon and then poured some sugar into her coffee. She normally didn't have sugar but the man sitting in front of her was making her lightheaded. Surely sugar would help steady her nerves.

They were halfway through their coffees when the steak sandwich arrived. It was huge and there was an extra plate containing a heaped helping of salad.

"Are you going to get through all that?"

He laughed. "I said I'd need help. I didn't realize it was going to be quite this large."

He cut a slice off his sandwich, placed it on the saucer that his coffee cup had stood on, and pushed it over to her. "You can start on that."

"I'll try, but I might not even be able to get through that amount."

He picked up his sandwich with both hands and bit into it. Tulip picked up her portion and tried to eat in a ladylike manner, which was hard because butter was running onto her fingers and dripping onto the saucer.

Nathanial handed her a paper napkin and then used another one to wipe his hands.

"*Denke*. It's juicy."

He nodded because he still had a mouthful.

She ate a little, but that was enough. "I'm done. I can't possibly have any more."

He looked down at what was left of his sandwich. "Me too and we haven't even started on the salad."

"I'll just stick with my coffee."

"I hate wasting food," he commented.

"Maybe you can take it with you. They might put it into a container for you."

He shrugged. "Maybe. *Denke* for coming here today. I wanted to see you before your birthday."

She smiled at him, not knowing what to say. This was the first time she'd been alone with a man.

He picked up a napkin, leaned forward, and dabbed at her chin.

"What is it?" she asked.

"Just a little butter."

Now she felt embarrassed that she was smiling at him like a fool while she had melted butter on her chin. *"Denke."*

He scrunched up the napkin and put it on top of the salad.

"What does your *familye* think of you coming here for work?" she asked.

"They don't know yet. They think I'm visiting Matthew. I don't see they'll mind when they find out. I'm from a big *familye* and most of us have gone in different directions. Jacob's still close to home, but I've got one *bruder* who moved to Canada to start a community there."

"That is a long way away."

"We might never see him again."

233

"That's sad."

"That's what he wanted. He married a girl from the community and then they decided that's what they wanted to do. No one was going to stand in their way."

"I'm glad both my brothers have stayed close by after they married, and I don't think Rose will go anywhere."

"Your *familye* sounds like they want to be close together."

"We do."

"Not all families are like that."

Tulip nodded and wondered what his family was like. Had he come to the wedding looking for a wife? Many of the young people went to weddings hoping to meet that special someone.

"Would you go on a buggy ride with me if I can borrow a buggy?"

"I'd like that." If that happened, she'd have to tell her mother who he was because he'd have to collect her from the house.

"Gut! I'll see what I can do. I might be able to take Matthew to the markets one day and then borrow his buggy. He works at the markets, you see."

"I know. Rose works at the markets too."

"I borrowed Matthew's buggy today. Hopefully, he'll let me borrow it again soon."

Tulip nodded, but wanted to know when he was thinking of taking her on this buggy ride. Buggy rides were the traditional way the Amish dated. She would've felt better if he mentioned a day or a time to lock it in rather than it being fuzzy and open-ended. Why were these things so hard? She should've gotten some tips from Rose before having coffee with him.

She drained the last of her coffee, which had gone cold. In her heart, she wondered whether Nathanial might have had a girl at home much like his brother had when he'd fooled Rose. Tulip didn't want to let Jacob's downfall influence her feelings toward Nathanial, and they wouldn't have if Nathanial had just made a time for their buggy ride. Now, things didn't quite feel right to her. She had to examine things with her head and not be carried away by feelings of the heart. That's what *Mamm* always said.

"All done?" he asked.

She nodded, hoping he'd suggest a romantic walk in the woods since it was such a lovely day.

"Gut! I'll walk you to your buggy."

Was that it? Was that all? Tulip was more than a little disappointed that there wouldn't be more to their afternoon together than sharing a steak sandwich.

She stood up, and they both walked out of the café.

"My buggy is around the corner," she said, still holding onto the hope he'd suggest they do something else.

They walked side-by-side in silence. Tulip hoped hard he'd suggest a time for that buggy ride and didn't want the conversation to go in a different direction. He, too, remained quiet.

When they reached her buggy, he said, *"Denke* for meeting me here. I'll see you again soon."

When Tulip was in the driver's seat, she looked over at him as he stood straight and tall. "You're coming to my birthday, aren't you?" She hoped that would prompt him to make a time.

"Jah, of course I am. I wouldn't miss it." He smiled at her and then moved forward and slapped her horse on the rump.

The horse moved onward and Tulip kept her eyes on the road ahead. Did he like her or what? Men sure were confusing creatures. Perhaps he had to find out if he could borrow the buggy again first before he made a time. While driving along the streets, she thought back over their conversation; she recalled he'd said he liked the outdoors. If that was so, then why hadn't he taken a table on the pavement in the fresh air? Was he worried that someone might see them together? Had he come here to her community and left a girlfriend at home just as his older brother had done before him?

Tulip did not want to end up in a bad situation. She'd think long and hard before going out with Nathanial again. Asking people about him might be the best idea. That way she could find out everything about him. Surely Matthew would know a lot since he was his cousin, or even Mark. Since Mark was recently married, she'd have to find out what she could about Nathanial from Matthew.

CHAPTER 5

TULIP WOKE up and stretched her arms over her head before she got out of bed. She smiled when she realized that today was her twentieth birthday. But that was before she remembered her mother had invited as many single young men as she possibly could to her birthday dinner that night. Now she groaned aloud. She hoped her mother wouldn't do to her what she'd done with Rose—try to match her with a man. Tulip was certain that Mark hadn't been her mother's first choice for Rose, but they were very happy.

"Happy birthday, birthday girl." The twins ran in and jumped on the edge of her bed.

"Argh! Just as well I'm awake."

"You're always awake at this time," Daisy said.

"What if I'd wanted to sleep in for my birthday?"

Lily giggled. "You have to get the eggs so you're not allowed to sleep in."

"How about one of you gets the eggs for me today?"

"Nee!" Lily scowled.

"I'll do it," Daisy said.

Lily suddenly changed her mind. "I'll come with you, Daisy."

The twins were gone like a whirlwind, as fast as they'd come into the room.

Tulip closed her eyes to enjoy another ten minutes' sleep. Collecting the eggs was the first chore of the day and Tulip was only too happy when someone else did that for her.

She thought about the party and hoped her mother would make her a chocolate cake. No one could make a chocolate cake like her mother. The cakes her mother made were always so light and moist.

Unable to sleep, she pushed the blankets away from her and got out of bed. When she heard giggles, she walked over to the window and looked out. The twins were pushing and shoving each other as they walked toward the henhouse, tugging at the egg basket. It looked like they were arguing about who was to carry the basket. *I hope they don't do that when the basket is full of eggs.*

Tulip pulled on her bathrobe and popped her prayer *kapp* over her messy hair without even brushing it, and then headed downstairs. She'd have to tell her mother early that she wanted a chocolate cake because it had to be made with a special kind of cooking chocolate, and Tulip was certain they didn't have any more in the house—not with the twins around. The twins devoured any kind of chocolate as soon as it came through the door.

Tulip found her mother in the kitchen. "Morning, *Mamm.*"

Her mother looked over at her "Happy birthday, Tulip."

"Denke, Mamm."

Her mother glared at her. "Why aren't you dressed?"

"I'm going to have a shower, and then I'll get dressed. I just wanted to ask if you could make a chocolate cake for me?"

"Chocolate cake for your birthday tonight?"

"*Jah.*"

"You had days to ask me that. Why leave it until now? I don't even have any ingredients for the chocolate cake."

"I could go to the store and get some for you."

She looked her up and down. "Not like that, you can't."

Tulip giggled. "I'm going to shower and then dress."

"Just make sure you don't let your husband see you like that of a morning."

Tulip frowned. "I'm not married."

"One day you will be."

"I'm sure he won't mind seeing me like this. What's wrong with how I look?" She looked down at her dressing gown. "It's just a bathrobe."

"You must always present yourself well."

Tulip knew her mother was annoyed with her for having to make a chocolate cake on short notice, and that's why she was picking on her. Her mother would've already had every minute of the day planned, right up until the time the guests arrived.

"I'll be the first one at the store and then I'll help you make the cake when I get back. What do you think about that?"

"It's your birthday! You can get the things from the store, but the twins will help me cook."

"Are you sure they even know how to cook?" Tulip giggled. All of them could cook, of course.

"We can cook better than anybody," Daisy said as she sailed through the back door with the egg basket over her arm.

"Better than you," Lily added.

"That's good. Then you can both help *Mamm* cook all day while I go to the store."

"I want to go too." Daisy pouted.

"Me too," Lily added.

"You both have to stay here and help *Mamm* cook."

"That's right. I would appreciate your help," their mother said.

"That's what we do every day. We do nothing else but help you cook and clean every single day."

Lily nodded at what Daisy said. "Yeah."

"You're not helping *me*," their mother said. "You both live here too; you're helping yourselves."

"And since it's my birthday, I choose to go to the store by myself," Tulip said before she raced up the stairs.

"I'm writing you out a list of things to get," her mother called after her.

CHAPTER 6

TULIP WAS glad to be allowed to go to the store by herself since the family only went to the store every fortnight. It was a rare thing for her to be allowed out in the buggy by herself. That's why she was so pleased her mother had let her go into town when she'd met with Nathanial. The family used to have only one horse and buggy, but thanks to a neighbor who had moved far away, they now had three buggy horses and two buggies. She caught the black horse in the paddock and slipped a rope around his neck and led him to the barn. They mostly used the bay gelding, but today she wanted to take the younger black one.

Her father wouldn't like her taking Damon, or 'Demon,' as her sisters called the horse. *Dat* considered the bay to be safer.

It was a half-hour journey each way. She considered the peace and quiet of this time alone a nice birthday present. It was a perfect time of year. Winter would soon be upon them, but today, the sun was shining.

As the horse and buggy clip-clopped toward the store in the lazy morning sun, she felt drowsy, as though she could easily go to sleep.

Rose had warned Tulip that their mother would soon try to find a man for her, but Tulip didn't think that was likely. Rose had been a dreamer and that's why their mother thought she needed help in finding a husband. Although it was a little troubling that *Mamm* had gone to such great lengths to invite so many people to her birthday party. Was this her mother's way of getting all the eligible young men in the community in one place?

As she drove along the streets in town, she decided to treat herself at one of the local cafés. While she was drinking coffee, she could look in the paper at the jobs section.

Rose still had her job helping the Walkers sell their flowers at the markets. She'd held that job for many years and it'd given her a good income. Having a job to go to every day would be far better than staying at home with her mother and the twins.

Now that Tulip was the oldest daughter at home, she felt the need to be independent, and with some extra money she'd be able to spread her wings and feel more grown up.

She stopped her buggy close to the supermarket and secured her horse. Damon had traveled well and hadn't stepped one hoof wrong. She patted him on his neck as a thank-you before she headed to the coffee shop, which was next to the supermarket. As soon as she walked in the door, she headed to a stand where the daily newspapers were held. Picking one up, she checked that it was today's paper. Once she saw it was, she carried it along as she headed to a table in the back of the room. Flipping the pages over, she found the job section.

"What can I get for you?"

She looked up to see a smiling young waitress. "I'll have a cup of coffee, thank you."

"Sure. Anything to eat today?"

"Last time I was here I had a cheesecake. Do you have any of those today?"

"We've got lemon cheesecake or chocolate."

"I'll have the lemon one, please." When the waitress was just about to walk away, Tulip said, "Excuse me?"

The waitress spun around. "Yes?"

"Do you know if you've got any jobs open here?"

"Not that I know of, but you could drop in a resume. That's how I got my job here."

Tulip nodded. "Thank you." A resume? She guessed that was a list of where she'd previously worked and a list of her skills. She didn't even have one and she had no idea how to put one together. The only experience she had was helping her mother cook and serve at functions.

When the waitress had gone, Tulip opened the paper once more and scanned the jobs on offer. There was nothing there for her. All the jobs required experience or some kind of qualifications.

TULIP HAD JUST TAKEN a large bite of her lemon cheesecake when she looked up to see an Amish man walk through the door of the café. She looked hard to see if it was someone she knew, but she'd never seen him before. If he'd been one of the nearly three hundred guests at Rose's wedding, she certainly would've remembered. A man of his height and solid build would have made an impression.

He glanced in her direction and when their eyes met, he smiled at her and gave her a little nod. She gave the closest she could to a smile in return, as her mouth was still full of cheesecake. What bad timing!

When he turned back and grabbed a menu, she quickly swallowed and continued to study him. He'd removed his hat when he'd come inside, revealing unusual sandy-colored hair. Possibly it had started off light brown and the sun had streaked it with gold. It looked windswept and stopped above his shoulders. He was possibly one of the most handsome men she'd seen and he was definitely not from around the area.

After the waitress had said a few words to him, he took the menu with him and sat down at a table on the opposite side of the room. Now feeling awkward, she kept her head down, looking at the paper.

When the waitress approached him, Tulip listened to find out what he ordered, but she was too far away to hear anything. She looked in his direction. The waitress left, and the man turned his head in her direction. Tulip was quick to lower her gaze to the paper in front of her.

Tulip hurried to finish her coffee and the last mouthful of cheesecake. If she spent too much time away, her mother wouldn't have time to make her triple-layer chocolate cake.

She wiped her hands and mouth on the paper napkin and then hurried out of the coffee shop, careful not to look at the Amish man on the other side of the room. Tulip was only two steps out of the café when she heard someone calling.

"Miss! Miss!"

She turned around to see if the person was speaking to her. It was the waitress hurrying to catch up with her.

"Did I forget something?" Tulip asked.

"You forgot to pay."

Tulip covered her mouth with her hand. "I'm so sorry."

The girl offered a relieved smile.

"I'm not usually so forgetful." Her cheeks burning with embarrassment, Tulip walked back inside to pay. She daren't turn around to see if the man she'd been watching had noticed. "I normally go to places where I pay first," she explained to the woman as she handed over the money. When she'd paid, she hurried back outside.

Once she walked into the supermarket, she realized that she'd forgotten something else—the shopping list her mother had given her. She walked down each aisle trying to remember what was on that list. One thing Tulip recalled was the exact brand of cooking chocolate her mother liked to use. Now all they had to do was hide the chocolate from the twins until it was safely in the cake.

We have plenty of eggs and milk, also sugar, so what else could we possibly need? I know there's always lots of flour. She half filled her basket with things she thought her mother might need. As she tried again to remember what was on the list, she turned down the next aisle and nearly bumped into someone. She found herself face-to-face with the handsome Amish stranger who'd been in the coffee shop.

She stepped back. "I'm sorry."

He laughed and she walked around him.

"I saw you back there in the coffee shop."

She stared at him, not knowing what to say. All she could

utter was, *"Jah?"*

"You nearly got away with it."

Tulip looked into his deep brown eyes that now crinkled at the corners. She thought about how the scene had unfolded when she'd forgotten to pay and she laughed.

"Maybe next time you should try running?"

"I'll have to remember that." She shook her head. "I'm still so embarrassed. I've never done anything forgetful like that before." Glancing down at the basket, she added, "Except forgetting my *mudder's* shopping list this morning, so that's two forgetful things on the same day."

"If that's the worst thing that happens today, it will have been a good day."

She smiled at him—her father would've said something similar to that. He seemed to have an easy-going and relaxed nature. He was also clean-shaven, so she knew he wasn't married. "Are you new around here, or are you passing through?"

"I'm just visiting. What about you?"

"I've lived here all my life." Her eyes dropped to the basket in her hands. "I should go. I've got people waiting for me."

She walked past him and he said nothing more. Once she was at the counter, she pulled all the goods out so they could be rung through the cash register. Tulip was certain she could feel the man looking at her. Turning around, she saw he was watching her with a smile on his face. She turned back around, now even more embarrassed.

If she were a braver person, she would've stopped and talked with him longer, but what would she say? The community was quite small, so soon enough she'd find out who he was and where he was staying. When she'd paid, she took her two bags of groceries and hurried out of the store.

Now she had two men to dream about—Jacob's younger brother, Nathanial, and this handsome stranger. Then a thought occurred to Tulip: she didn't even know his name.

CHAPTER 7

ONCE THE BIRTHDAY celebrations got underway that evening, Tulip quickly forgot the stranger she'd seen twice earlier that day.

Her two older brothers were there with their wives, and her baby niece, Shirley. Then the newlyweds, Rose and Mark, arrived.

Tulip was the first to scoop Shirley into her arms. She wasn't even a year old and she was quite heavy. She could say a few words, but that was all. Tulip tried to teach her to say, "Aunty Tulip"—all Shirley did was giggle.

Rose came up with her hands outstretched to take Shirley from her.

Once Rose had her niece in her arms, Tulip asked, "How's married life?"

"Everyone's asking me that."

"Well?"

"It's good. In fact, things are perfect."

"Perfect? Well, that's a big word." Tulip was used to seeing Rose worrying about one thing after another. "You look satisfied and truly happy."

"I am. Now it's your turn to have *Mamm* trying to run your life."

Amy and Julie, their two sisters-in-law, joined their conversation.

"It never ends. First, everyone tells you that you should be married. When you get married, there's the pressure to have a child," said Amy.

Julie, Shirley's mother, continued, "Ah, but one's not good enough, because she'll need other children to play with. Meaning you have to produce another fast. And so it goes on. You have one child, then everyone's asking you when you'll have the second."

The girls giggled.

"I don't think we'll ever escape the pressure of other people's expectations. There always seems to be something else people think we should be doing," Tulip said.

Rose bounced Shirley on her hip. "My next project is to have one of these."

"Put your order in," Amy said, "but please don't have one before me because I got married first."

"I can't promise," Rose said with a grin.

Tulip was distracted by people coming through the front door.

"How many people are coming, Tulip?" Amy asked.

"I think *Mamm* invited the whole community and then some. Excuse me, I'll have to greet everyone."

The guests were served buffet-style in the kitchen. Everyone picked up a plate and, at her mother's direction, walked clockwise around the table serving themselves from the bowls in the center. Tulip's mother looked on, redirecting anyone who dared walk counterclockwise.

Taking center stage on the table was a large triple-layer chocolate cake. Tulip was upset that Nathanial hadn't come. Surely if he liked her enough to ask her on a buggy ride, he should've come to her birthday party. Especially after saying he would be there. Tulip hoped he was only late, held up by something, and he'd still arrive.

LATER THAT EVENING, Rose and Tulip were talking again.

"I want to get a job like you've got, Rose."

"What would you do?"

"I don't know exactly. I can cook and clean and I suppose I can sell things like you do. I've helped at the flower stall often enough."

"What about Audrey Fuller's cake shop? She's expanding it. She'll need more staff."

"Is she really?"

Rose nodded.

"That's a good idea. I'll get in before she starts advertising for people."

"Yeah, do it. I think you'd like working there." Rose looked around the room and then she fixed her eyes in one spot.

"What is it, Rose?" Tulip turned her head to see what Rose was staring at.

"Look at *Mamm* over there. It looks like she's interviewing for a new husband for you."

Tulip shook her head. "You're lucky you found Mark when you did."

"I didn't need to find him; he was there all the time."

Tulip sighed. "I've got nobody who's been there all the time like that. What am I going to do about *Mamm?*"

"If you get a job, she mightn't be so focused on you."

"I hope so, and then she can start on the twins," Tulip said.

"Yeah, they're nearly old enough to marry now."

The two sisters giggled.

CHAPTER 8

THE NEXT DAY, Tulip put Nathanial out of her mind and wasted no time in setting about looking for a job. She'd already done most of her morning chores when she walked into the kitchen to ask her mother for permission to be gone for a good part of the day.

"*Mamm,* can I take the buggy to go into town today?"

Her mother turned around from the stove where she was cooking breakfast.

"What for? You went into town yesterday."

"Rose told me that Audrey Fuller might be looking for someone to work in her cake store."

The twins giggled, and Daisy said, "Haven't you had enough cake? You ate your birthday cake nearly by yourself yesterday."

"Yep, and no one else could get any," Lily added.

"I only had two pieces and they were small ones." Tulip looked back at her mother as she sat down at the kitchen table.

"Rose said Audrey's expanding her store, and I want to get in first before she thinks about putting an ad in for someone."

"That sounds like a good idea, but I didn't even know you wanted a job." Her mother placed a plate of eggs in front of her.

"I do. I've been thinking about it for some time."

"Well, you better get into town and see her."

"Denke, Mamm."

"Now, eat your breakfast."

"If you can fit it in after all that cake you ate last night. It's a wonder you're not twice the size."

"Hush, Daisy," their mother said.

"You don't have to work, Tulip," Lily said.

Tulip had a mouthful of eggs, and when she swallowed, she answered, "I know that, Lily, but I want to."

"Could we go into town too, *Mamm?*" Daisy asked. "While she goes to the cake shop we can do something else by ourselves."

Tulip frowned, hoping her mother wouldn't let them. She didn't want them around distracting her or saying silly things when she was trying to get a job.

Thankfully, her mother read her anxious expression.

"Nee. It's best if you stay here. We've got a big clean-up day ahead of us."

The twins' mouths dropped open, and Daisy said, "That's not fair! Tulip should help; it was her party."

Tulip ate her breakfast in silence, feeling relieved that she was escaping the clean up.

Tulip walked into the cake shop to see that the space had already been extended. When she'd been there last, there was no room for anyone to sit down. Now there were tables inside, and more outside on the pavement. She stepped past the tables to speak to the young girl behind the counter.

"Is Mrs. Fuller in today?"

"Yeah, she's out in the back."

"Could I speak with her?"

"I'll get her."

The girl she'd been speaking to wasn't Amish, but she knew a couple of the girls who worked for Audrey were Amish.

When Audrey came into the front of the store, she looked pleased to see her. "Tulip! Happy birthday for yesterday. I heard you had a big birthday dinner at your place last night."

"*Denke.* I did." Tulip gave a little giggle.

"What can I do for you?"

"I was hoping you might be looking for an extra person to work here?"

Audrey narrowed her eyes as she scrutinized her. "I am looking for one more person. Have you had any experience?"

Tulip's shoulders drooped. "Not really. I've only worked for my *mudder* at weddings and things like that."

"That might count for experience. Your mother is a very good manager. I could give you a trial for three weeks and see how we work together. I start all my girls on trials. I'd have to show you how to work the register and how to make coffee barista-style."

"Really?"

"*Jah.*"

"I'd love to learn how to do everything. *Denke* so much."

255

"Are you looking for full time or part time work?" Audrey asked.

"Full time, but I can do whatever you'd like."

"I'm looking for someone full time. It wouldn't be until the first of next month. Would you be able to start then?"

"I certainly would. *Denke* again, Mrs. Fuller."

She chuckled. "The girls here all call me Audrey when we're in the shop."

"Okay."

CHAPTER 9

TULIP HAD BEEN WORKING at the cake shop for the past three months. She'd done well right from the start, and Audrey had quickly offered her a permanent position. She got along fine with the other staff. Stacey, the girl she'd met that first day, was the only *Englischer,* and the rest of the girls were Amish. Melinda, a girl in her mid-twenties, was the manager whenever Audrey was absent. Audrey started work early and generally left at eleven in the morning.

Tulip was wiping down the counter in the back room, and when she heard the girls giggling, she looked into the store and saw Jonathon Byler buying a cupcake. When Tulip went out front, she noticed that Jonathon was now outside by himself, drinking a cup of coffee with his cupcake on a plate on the table.

"Look at him, sitting out there by himself. That's why he's so fat! He eats cake every day. He looks ridiculous," one of the girls said while another one giggled.

"Back to work," Melinda said, trying to break things up.

"Why aren't you laughing, Tulip?" Stacey asked.

"I don't think it's funny to be like that with people."

"Tulip's in love with Jonathon," Stacey said.

"I'm not in love with him. I just know that he's nice, and it's mean to laugh at him." She glanced at him and hoped he didn't hear their laughs. "I'm going to wipe down the tables outside." After she had picked up a cloth, she headed outside.

"Hello, Jonathon," Tulip said as she wiped down the table next to his.

Jonathon glanced up at her. "Hello, Tulip. I didn't know you were working here. How are you today?"

"Fine! Is there anything else you'd like?"

"Nee, denke. My cousin's joining me today. You could join us if you'd like. Do you get a break or anything?"

"I'm actually due for a half hour break." She glanced at the girls inside who were smiling at the pair of them talking. "I'll get myself a cup of coffee and something to eat and I'll come back out."

"Okay, *gut."*

Tulip hurried inside and asked Melinda if she could take her break right now.

After Melinda agreed, one of the girls said, "You *are* in love with him; you're having coffee with him."

"So what?" Once she had paid for her coffee and a raisin bun, she made herself a coffee, placed a bun on a plate, and hurried outside with them to join Jonathon. She hated anyone to be made fun of.

"Which cousin are you waiting for?" Tulip asked.

"I don't know if you've met him. He comes here every now

and again when my *vadder* has work for him." He looked over her shoulder. "Here he is now."

Tulip glanced behind her. It was the same man she'd seen a few months ago, around the time of her birthday. She looked back to the front and he sat down with them.

Jonathon introduced the pair of them. The handsome man's name was Wilhem Byler.

"Actually, we've met before, but I didn't get your name last time."

Tulip giggled. "I remember."

His eyes dropped down to her food. "I hope you've paid for that?"

She laughed. "Your memory is too good. I paid for it and I work here." She told Jonathon about forgetting to pay and leaving the café and the waitress having to come running after her. Then the three of them laughed.

"Actually," Wilhem began, "I was at your *schewschder's* wedding a while back. That's when I first saw you."

"At Rose's wedding?"

He nodded.

"I didn't see you there."

One side of Wilhem's mouth twisted into a crooked smile. "I saw you."

Tulip was pleased about him saying that. He was almost flirting with her and his voice lowered when he spoke. "How often do you come here?" she asked.

"Every now and again when my *Onkel* Phillip has construction work for me."

"That's my *Dat,*" Jonathon said.

Tulip nodded at Jonathon. Of course she knew Jonathon's

father. She looked back at Wilhem. "Ah, so you do construction work—building work?"

"Jah. There are a few builders I work with back home, and now my *onkel* is going to be needing me from time to time. I'm happy to help out here."

Tulip smiled at the thought of him visiting their community more. Through the large glass window, Tulip looked to see that the girls weren't laughing anymore—not with the handsome man now sitting at the table with them.

Tulip was so nervous sitting next to him that she barely heard any more of the conversation. She hoped she was responding with the right words in the right places.

When Jonathon's cousin said goodbye and left, Tulip suddenly realized her break time had nearly run out. "I'll have to get back to work, Jonathon. *Denke* for inviting me."

"I'll see you soon. *Denke* for sitting with us."

Tulip stood and gathered the empty cups.

"Wait, Tulip!" Jonathon said.

"What is it?"

"Do you think you could put a good word in for me with Chelsea?"

Chelsea was one of the young Amish girls she worked with. "You like her?"

He nodded.

"Okay, I'll do it. But not right away, or it will seem phony. I'll wait for the right time."

"Denke, Tulip. I'll leave it in your hands."

Tulip walked back into the store with the plates and cups they'd used.

"You were a while," Chelsea said.

Glancing up at the clock, Tulip said, "I only had my half hour."

"Did you have fun with your new boyfriend?" Stacey asked.

Tulip spun around. "He's very nice."

"Who is? Jonathon, or that man who sat down with you? That was the real reason you sat out there with Jonathon, wasn't it?" Stacey asked. "He didn't stay very long."

"He's Jonathon's cousin." Tulip ignored the rest of the comment.

When Stacey said something else about Jonathon, Melinda cut across her, "Back to work now, and no more talk about the customers."

The girls stopped talking.

Later in the day, Stacey whispered to Tulip, "No need to get upset. Maybe you really are in love with Jonathon."

To Tulip, all the teasing and gossiping was just like being at home with the twins.

CHAPTER 10

Nathanial had never gotten back to her about the buggy ride he'd mentioned. Now that she'd met Jonathon's handsome cousin, Wilhem, she was dreaming about him instead.

The next time Tulip saw Nathanial again was at Lucy and Peter Bontrager's wedding. There were many visitors from out of town at the wedding, which was held at Lucy's parents' house, in their yard. As always, Tulip's mother was at the forefront of organizing the food, along with the bride's mother.

"Do you know who's here, Tulip?" her mother asked her.

"Who?"

"Jacob Schumacher's *bruder.* His name is Nathanial."

Tulip was pleased he was there. Maybe they would go on that buggy ride soon. She hadn't seen Wilhem again and didn't know if he'd ever be back. "Okay. I haven't seen him about."

"I think he was one of the boys you were talking with at Rose's wedding."

Tulip shrugged her shoulders. "Not sure. It was a long time ago."

"Stay away from him, if you happen to see him."

"Why, *Mamm?*"

Her mother's mouth fell open. "You know what happened when Jacob visited the community, don't you?"

"*Jah,* but his *bruder* can't be held responsible for Jacob's actions. Anyway, Jacob did the right thing and married that girl, so that's at least a *gut* thing." She had to make her mother think that he was okay, otherwise she'd never be able to go anywhere with him.

"Shh! Someone might hear." Her mother shook her head. "They are branches of the same tree. There are such things as bad seeds. I'm just warning you that if he's anything like Jacob, he'll be looking for prey. And by prey, I mean young girls who don't know any better."

"*Jah, Mamm.*"

"I mean it, Tulip. I have the benefit of many more years' experience than you do. You'd do well to listen to me."

"I do. I listen to you all the time."

"*Gut!* Now help Rosemary take those dishes out." Her mother pointed to the large collection of plates that had to be carried out and placed on each table.

Tulip did as she was asked. As she walked amongst the crowd, she looked around for Nathanial. Just as she placed half a dozen dinner plates on one of the tables, she caught a glimpse of him, and he caught her eye and smiled. She quickly looked away in case her mother was watching, and then she hurried back for more plates. Tulip believed there was no such thing as 'bad seeds.' Her mother was simply being over-protective.

When her mother allowed Tulip time to eat later that day, she hurried to one of the tables at the back of the yard, hoping there would be food left in the bowls in the center of that table. There was. She picked up an empty plate and spooned food onto it before she sat down.

"Did you cook the food?"

She looked up to see it was Nathanial who'd just walked up to her. He sat down next to her as she finished her mouthful. If only she knew why he'd never gotten back to her about going on the buggy ride. That really bothered her. Did that mean he wasn't interested in her after all?

"*Nee.* I just had the job of running the plates in and out. I'm on a break, and soon I'll have to take the plates back to the kitchen."

He put out his hand as though he was meeting her for the first time. "I'm Nathanial Schumacher."

She kept the charade going. "Hello, I'm Tulip Yoder."

His gaze dropped to her food and he tipped his head. "Go ahead. Don't let me stop you from eating."

"Have you moved here or are you visiting?" she asked to carry on with the act of having just met him.

"I'm doing some visiting around different places to see where I'd like to settle down."

Tulip finished what was in her mouth. "Where are you from?"

"Oakes County."

"Are you Jacob's *bruder?*"

"*Jah,* but don't hold that against me." He laughed.

"I met him. He visited here a while back to work for your *Onkel* Harry."

265

"Before your new *bruder*-in-law, Mark, stole his job."

Tulip narrowed her eyes at him. That's not how she remembered things at all.

"I'm joking. I'll have to brush up on my funny skills —humor."

She smiled. "It's not that. I was just trying to remember what happened. Jacob wasn't here long before he went back home and since then Mark's been working with your mutual *onkel* making buggies."

"That's correct."

When he smiled, Tulip saw kindness in his eyes. Her mother had to be wrong about him. Although she wasn't sure if she'd forgiven him about forgetting their buggy ride.

"And now you know all about me, Tulip, tell me something about yourself."

"There's not much to tell. I started working in a bakery a few months ago and that's what I do every day."

"Your *familye?*"

She pointed to her father who was talking with the bishop. "That's my *vadder,* and my mother is in the kitchen, unless she's spying on me right now to see who I'm speaking with. I've got three sisters around somewhere and two older brothers."

"Your *vadder's* a deacon?"

"*Jah.*"

"That must be hard."

"*Nee,* not really."

"I have a friend whose *vadder* is the bishop and she finds it awkward. She says that everyone thinks she should be perfect."

"It's a little like that sometimes."

"Where is the bakery?"

266

"Just off Church Street, in Baker's Lane."

"I might have to try some samples."

Tulip smiled as she ate another spoonful of food. Maybe he did have some unreliable traits, as his brother had.

"We never went on that buggy ride," he said.

"Buggy ride?" She wouldn't let on that she remembered anything about that.

"Jah, you promised you'd go on one with me."

"Did I?"

"Jah, you did." He laughed. "I'm not going to let you back out of it. How about we go on one this week?"

"What day were you thinking?"

"How about Wednesday night? I'll take you home after the softball game."

"Okay."

CHAPTER 11

LATER THAT DAY, Tulip regretted agreeing to the buggy ride with Nathanial when she saw Wilhem Byler again. Her hands were full of dishes and she was walking to the kitchen with Rose.

"Tulip."

She stopped to talk with him and Rose kept walking. "Hello, Wilhem. I didn't expect to see you here."

"Lucy's one of my cousins."

Tulip laughed. "Lucy is a cousin of yours, and Jonathon is too?"

"Yeah, Lucy is a cousin on my *mudder's* side and Jonathon is a cousin on my *vadder's* side."

"Everyone has so many cousins I can't keep track."

"I was hoping to see you here." He looked down at the plates. "Can I carry those for you?"

She shook her head. "I'll take these to the kitchen and come back out. Stay right there." Tulip scurried to the kitchen, dumped the dirty dishes with all the others beside the sink, wiped her hands on a dishtowel, and hurried outside to see Wilhem.

"Has your *onkel* got some work for you? Is that why you're back?" she asked.

"Jah, I'll be here for about six weeks." He looked around. "Shall we take a walk and get away from the crowd?"

She whipped her head around, looking for her mother, and when she couldn't see her anywhere, she said, "Okay."

Together they walked behind the food tables and out to a fence that separated two fields from the yard.

"Ah, silence," Tulip said.

"It's nice, isn't it?"

"It sure is."

"Tulip, I've been looking for you. I'm hoping I can see a bit more of you while I'm here."

"I'd like that."

"I've heard there's a softball game on one night soon. I normally wouldn't go, but if you're going I'd go there."

She had to think fast. Tulip couldn't let Wilhem see her with Nathanial. They both seemed nice, but she was now confused and didn't know which one she liked better. First there was no one and now she had two young men she liked. "I don't like softball." That was the truth.

"Okay. How about we go out somewhere else? Just the two of us?"

She nodded. "That sounds *gut.*"

"What if I collect you one day after you finish work?"

"Okay."

"We could go out for dinner somewhere nice."

"I'd like that."

It was when he smiled she knew she preferred Wilhem to Nathanial. And her mother would be pleased about her choice too, since *Mamm* still hadn't gotten over how Nathanial's brother had upset Rose.

"Monday, then?"

"Monday would be perfect." She glanced through the trees at the women collecting everything from the tables. "I'd better go back and help, or I'll face my *mudder's* wrath."

"I'll look forward to Monday," he called after her.

She hurried away, wondering how she could get herself out of this mess. She'd agreed to see Wilhem on Monday for dinner, and then on Wednesday she was going on a buggy ride with Nathanial. It wasn't right. She should've just chosen one or the other, but she hadn't expected Wilhem to suddenly turn up out of the blue like he had. To make matters worse, who would she tell her parents was driving her home from the softball game?

The best thing she could do, she decided, was tell Nathanial she couldn't make it on Wednesday.

After she took another load of dishes to the kitchen, she looked around for Nathanial. She couldn't see him, but found Matthew, the cousin he was staying with.

"Matthew, where's Nathanial?"

"Hi, Tulip. He's left already."

"Gone home? Back to Oakes County?"

"Back to our *haus,* not back to *his* home."

"I see."

"Do you want me to give him a message? I'm heading there now myself."

"Nee. It was nothing. *Denke,* Matthew."

. . .

THE REST OF THE DAY, Tulip was worried about the mess she'd created. She couldn't talk anything over with her younger sisters because they'd only spill the beans to their mother, who'd have an absolute fit if she learned she'd arranged to go out with Nathanial Schumacher.

Maybe Nathanial won't even go to the softball game. He forgot all about our buggy ride once before.

Tulip decided to do nothing and let things run their natural course.

THE NEXT DAY WAS SUNDAY. There was no meeting that day as they held their meetings fortnightly and had just met the previous Sunday.

As she was wondering what to do for the day, she remembered her words to Jonathon. She'd agreed to put a good word in for him with Chelsea. Work was sometimes hectic, and besides that, it wasn't a good place to talk about personal things. If the other girls heard them discussing Jonathon, they'd laugh about him and that wouldn't help Jonathon get closer to Chelsea.

Later that day, Tulip knocked on the door of Chelsea's home.

Chelsea's mother opened the door. "Hello, Tulip. Come in. Are you here to see Chelsea?"

"Jah, is she home?"

"Chelsea!" her mother hollered.

Chelsea came running down the stairs and stopped abruptly at the bottom. "Hello, Tulip."

"Hi, I was going for a long walk and saw your *haus* and thought I'd stop by and say hi."

"You walked all the way from your *haus?*"

"I'll get you girls some lemonade."

"Nee, we can get it, *Mamm,"* Chelsea said.

The two girls sat at the kitchen table. "So, tell me what's going on. What's the real reason you're here?" Chelsea's brown eyes bored through hers.

Tulip giggled. "I love to walk, to go on really long walks. And I saw your *haus."*

"Come on, Tulip. We've lived next to each other for a really long time and you've never come here and I've never gone to visit you. What is it?"

Tulip sipped on her lemonade. She couldn't betray a confidence.

"Is it about work? Is that it? Am I getting the sack—fired— cut loose?" She clutched at her throat.

"Nee, nothing like that. Anyway, no one would tell me anything like that. I was the last to start so I'd be the first to go."

"What is it, then?"

"Can't a girl talk to another girl?" Tulip asked.

"Jah, of course."

"You see, since Rose left and married Mark, I feel a little … a little lonely."

"You need a friend?"

"Kind of. I mean, there's the twins, but …"

"Yeah, well, I know what *they're* like. They're all giggles all the time. I don't know how you live under the same roof as them."

"Me either!"

"Between you and me, I find them annoying," Chelsea said. "Oh, I shouldn't have said that. That was mean."

"See? We're quite alike," Tulip commented.

Chelsea smiled. "I suppose we are. I guess a girl can never have too many friends."

"Exactly."

"Cheers to that," Chelsea said, offering her glass to connect with Tulip's.

Tulip 'clinked' glasses with her, and the girls giggled. Now, how would she raise the subject of Jonathon without Chelsea knowing that was the real reason she was there? There was no way she could. The subject of Jonathon would have to wait for another day.

What she'd said was right, anyway. She really could use a friend now, since Rose had married. There was a gap in her life that Chelsea might be able to fill. Chelsea wasn't one of the girls at work who had been making fun of Jonathon. She'd remained quiet. That was a hopeful sign for Jonathon.

"I'm glad you came here, Tulip. I've always wanted to be friends with you, but you've always been surrounded by your sisters."

"I'm glad too."

"Do you want to see my room?"

Tulip nodded and together the girls left their half-full lemonade glasses on the kitchen table and climbed the stairs of the farmhouse.

. . .

Tulip told Chelsea about Wilhem collecting her from work on Monday and then taking her out for dinner.

Her friend told her that she'd officially met him at the Bontrager wedding.

She didn't tell Chelsea that she'd also agreed to be taken home from the softball game by Nathanial. She was still trying to figure out what to do about that.

CHAPTER 12

It was the middle of the day when Jonathon made his daily trip to the cake store.

"It's Jonathon."

"Why don't you serve him, Chelsea?" Tulip suggested.

"Okay. Don't you want to? Isn't he a friend of yours?"

Tulip nodded. "He is, but he'd rather you serve him."

Chelsea frowned at her but when Tulip disappeared into the back room, Chelsea had no choice but to serve Jonathon when he walked in.

Tulip looked at the other two girls talking as they worked in the backroom. It was nearly into their busy time of day and soon the store would be flooded with people. For now, Tulip was pleased they hadn't noticed Jonathon so they wouldn't say mean things.

When Tulip peeped out and saw Jonathon was now sitting at one of the tables on the pavement, she joined Chelsea behind the counter.

"Does he want a cup of coffee? I'll make him one if he does," Tulip said.

"You like him, don't you, Tulip?"

"Yes, of course I do."

"But not as a boyfriend?"

"*Nee*, just as a friend," Tulip said.

Chelsea asked, "Why not as a boyfriend?"

Tulip looked up at the ceiling while trying to examine why she didn't like him as a boyfriend.

"Is it because he's quiet and doesn't talk to many people or is it because he's fat?"

Tulip knew Chelsea wasn't being mean.

"I don't think it's either of those. There just isn't that spark I feel when I like a boy."

"Not like the spark you have with Wilhem?"

"I suppose that's true."

"I'm glad you don't say rude things about him like the other girls," Chelsea whispered.

"Everyone's different. They should put themselves in Jonathon's shoes and see how they'd feel about the sniggers. I reckon he can feel it even if he can't hear them. He's a good and kind person."

"That's true," Chelsea said.

Tulip was pleased she'd been able to do what Jonathon had asked. She didn't know if Chelsea would ever feel the way Jonathon wanted her to feel, but at least she was doing her best without being overly obvious. At least, that's what she hoped.

. . .

"A<small>RE YOU NERVOUS ABOUT TONIGHT</small>?" Chelsea whispered to Tulip just before closing time.

"I am, but I'm trying not to be nervous."

"It's very romantic."

"Is it?"

"*Jah,* a handsome stranger comes to the community and you're the only girl he's interested in."

Tulip giggled. "I didn't think of it like that."

When closing time came, Tulip waited outside the store, nervous about the situation she'd gotten herself into. She still hadn't canceled Wednesday night with Nathanial. She decided she had to put the situation about Wednesday night totally out of her mind for now in order to enjoy her time with Wilhem.

Her heart pounded in her chest when she saw Wilhem in the buggy heading toward her.

"It's nice to see you again," he said when she climbed in and sat next to him.

Looking into his soft brown eyes, she said, "And you."

He smiled and then gave the horse an order to move forward.

"Where are we going?" Tulip asked.

"I've made reservations at a place just outside town. It's an old Amish farmhouse that has been converted into a restaurant."

"I think I know the one. I've never been there but I've heard it's good."

THE WAITER PLACED their napkins on their laps, which Tulip thought an odd thing to do, but perhaps that's what they did in posh restaurants. She was only used to diners and coffee shops. The waiter then handed them menus before he disappeared. Soon after, another waiter came to take their drink order.

"Should we get a bottle of wine?" Wilhem asked studying the list in his hands.

"I don't drink alcohol," Tulip said.

He closed the drinks menu, leaned over, and said, "Neither do I."

Tulip was pleased that they had another thing in common. "Iced tea sounds good to me."

Once they'd made their orders and were alone, Wilhem leaned forward slightly. "Tulip, why is a girl like you still single?"

"I can't marry just anyone. I've been waiting for the right person."

"That's a good answer."

"Everyone thinks a girl should be married before she is twenty, but not everyone has to follow the usual pattern of things. I wouldn't mind if I never got married."

"Don't you want *kinner?*"

"I suppose that would be nice someday, but it's not the end of the world if I don't have any." Now she knew she'd let her mouth run away with her when she saw that Wilhem looked puzzled. She did her best to rectify the situation. "I guess I want what every girl wants, but if it doesn't happen …" She stopped abruptly. Perhaps she was digging herself a deeper hole. Here was a potential husband sitting right in front of her, a man who was obviously interested in her, and she was telling him she didn't care whether she got married or not. She looked into his eyes, wondering how to get herself out of the mess.

He gave a laugh. "You're quite different, compared with other girls I've met."

"And you've met a lot of girls on your travels?" she asked, trying to change the subject.

"Not really. I only go from home to here. They're the only places that I've been. Most girls think about nothing else other than being married, and that's all they talk about, and hint at."

Tulip tried to assess how the early part of the date was going. It was possibly a good thing that she was different from the other girls. She wondered exactly how many girls he'd been out with. A man as handsome as Wilhem could've been on many dates.

When they were halfway into their main course, he began to talk about what he wanted in life, and then added, "I'm thinking of moving here."

"You are?"

"I've been talking about it with Jonathon. He wants to move out of his parents' house and we figured we would share a *haus.*"

Tulip's immediate thoughts were about Chelsea. She knew Chelsea might be more interested in Jonathon if he were living away from his parents' home; it would make him seem more of a man and more independent.

"So what do you think of that idea?" he asked.

"I think it's a great idea. Would you get enough work here?"

"I would. Besides my *onkel,* there are other people I've met that said they could give me work."

Tulip licked her lips. That was the best news she'd heard for a long time.

"And when do you think this will happen?"

"Within the next few months. Jonathon is already looking for a *haus* and as soon as he finds one, I can put my plan into motion."

"So you've moved on from thinking about it. You're actually going to do it?"

He nodded. *"Jah.* I guess I should've said that. I hope you're pleased."

"Won't your parents miss you?"

"I won't be that far away and I can always visit them."

At the end of their meal, Wilhem looked across at her. "Can I see you again soon, Tulip?"

"I'd like that. Can we talk about that on Sunday after the meeting?"

He drew his eyebrows together. "Okay."

She hoped he wouldn't ask why and was glad when he didn't.

CHAPTER 13

ON WEDNESDAY, Tulip had every intention of not going to the softball game. If she wasn't there, then Nathanial wouldn't be able to drive her home. As she was eating dinner on Wednesday night, her father asked her to drive the twins to the game. The twins were old enough to drive the buggy, but their father had never allowed them to do so after a particularly nasty incident where they galloped a horse too hard against their father's instructions.

Tulip had no choice but to agree to take the twins. And it was too far to drop them off and then collect them when it finished, so she would have to stay through the whole thing. She only hoped that Nathanial would forget about their former arrangement. A smile twitched at the corners of her lips when she realized that she wouldn't be able to go on a buggy ride with him if she had to take the twins home. It was the perfect way out.

. . .

As soon as Tulip stopped the buggy at the field where the baseball game was being held, the twins jumped out and ran off to meet their friends, giggling all the way.

Tulip secured the horse and then looked into the crowd to find Nathanial.

She took a deep breath and walked toward the group of people. She saw him sitting by himself and then made her way to him.

"There you are," he said, looking up at her. "Sit with me."

She sat down. "I'm afraid I won't be able to go on a buggy ride tonight after all."

"That's disappointing. I was looking forward to it. I even borrowed the nicest buggy and best horse I could."

"I'm sorry. I have to drive my sisters home. *Dat* doesn't trust them to drive the buggy."

"That's no problem. I could follow you home and then we could go from there."

Tulip hadn't thought of that. "The thing is that—"

"You haven't told your folks we were planning on going on a buggy ride?"

She looked down at the dirt underneath her black lace-up boots. *"Nee,* I haven't."

"I see. They wouldn't like me taking you home because I'm Jacob's *bruder?"*

She shook her head, not wanting him to think her parents would judge him by what his brother had done. Her mother did, but her father probably wouldn't if he knew about Nathanial and him asking her out.

"That's all right; you don't need to say anything further."

She frowned. "You've got it all wrong. It's nothing like that."

284

"It looks like I'll have to prove myself to them. I'll introduce myself to your *vadder* at the Sunday meeting."

"What will you say?" Tulip hadn't figured on that.

"I'll just say, *Hi, I'm Jacob's brother, Nathanial.*" He laughed. "Don't look so worried."

"It's always a worry. You don't know what my parents are like."

"From the look on your face, I've got a pretty good idea."

Tulip laughed. It seemed he was making an effort to impress her family so that meant that he was taking her seriously. But where did that leave Wilhem? She'd gotten herself into a right mess. She liked Nathanial but she preferred Wilhem and what's more, Wilhem was moving to the community and she had no idea what Nathanial's plans were.

"I was really looking forward to our buggy ride," he said.

She remembered back to months ago when he'd first mentioned going on a buggy ride, and hadn't followed through.

He continued, "Like I said, I'll get your *vadder* on my side and then everything will be a whole lot easier."

"I don't know about that. There's still my *mudder.*" Tulip wished she'd kept quiet. If he talked to her mother, he might get an earful. Then, both her mother and father would think there was something happening between her and Nathanial.

When the game was underway, she looked over at the opposite side to a group of seats. There she saw Jonathon talking with Chelsea. They were sitting side-by-side and looking like they were good friends. Tulip smiled and hoped that she'd been instrumental in them speaking with one another like that.

Chelsea hadn't mentioned she was going to the softball game, but then neither had Tulip mentioned her plans to stay home, until she'd been asked to drive for her sisters. It wouldn't be a good idea for Chelsea to see her with Nathanial, as Chelsea knew about her dinner date with Wilhem.

"Who are you looking at?" Nathanial's eyes had followed her gaze.

"Just my friend over there. Her name is Chelsea. I work with her at the bakery."

"Is that her talking to that large man?"

"*Jah.* His name is Jonathan and he's also a good friend of mine."

"Tulip, are you sure that there isn't something standing in between us?"

"What do you mean? Like what?"

"Like what happened when my *bruder* was here in this community? And what he did before I got here? I wouldn't like to be judged by my *bruder.* I'm nothing like him and never have been. You're not that type of girl, are you?"

"What type of girl do you mean?"

"A judgmental kind of girl who won't give a man a chance."

"*Nee,* of course not. It's nothing like that. You've got every-thing all wrong. It's not about you. It's just that *Dat* recently got a new horse and buggy so us girls could use it, but he still doesn't trust the twins completely after what happened."

He crossed one leg over the other. "Why, what happened? Why doesn't he trust the twins?"

"A neighbor moved away and gave us their buggies and horses. One of the twins galloped one of the poor horses too hard and he was in a lather of sweat when he got home. It'll be a long time before she can drive the buggy again. I've never seen my *vadder* lose his temper, but that day he was close to it. I can tell you that much."

Nathanial laughed.

"It wasn't funny. You should've been there to see it."

"I'm sorry. I shouldn't laugh. Isn't that what horses are meant to do? It won't hurt the horse to have a good run."

"It wasn't that so much. It was because the horse was too young, or something, to race so hard like that. Anyway, *Dat* had already told them to take it easy with the horse and only walk him."

"Is your *vadder* a control freak or something?"

"*Nee*, not at all. He knows a lot about horses and cares for them well, and he gave the girls instructions and they didn't follow them. He is the head of the household, so they should've listened to him."

"Do you listen to your *vadder* all the time?"

"*Jah*, I try to."

"That doesn't answer my question, Tulip. You mean to tell me you always do what your parents say like a good little girl?"

"Mostly."

Nathanial threw his head back and laughed. "That's what I thought. What fun would we have if we obeyed our stuffy parents all the time?"

Tulip wasn't quite sure what he was getting at, or the point he was trying to make.

"So only one twin rode the horse too hard?"

"*Jah*."

"Do you realize you've just blamed both of them for that? You didn't name the twin, just said 'they.'"

"Oh."

"That's why I'm concerned that you've already done the same thing with me and my *bruder*. We're individuals you know."

"I know." Tulip realized he was right. Whenever one twin did anything wrong, she saw it as both of them. As though they came as a package. Anyway, Tulip had a sneaking suspicion that the twins never did anything without the other goading them on.

"Come on, stop pulling that face. The wind will change direction and your face will stay that way," he said as he leaned forward toward her, grinning.

The way he said it made Tulip laugh. Now she was certain he was a little devious as well as unreliable, but he was also a lot of fun to be around. And fun was probably what she was missing out on in life.

"That's better. You look so much more beautiful when you laugh, Tulip."

She looked down, embarrassment now heating her cheeks.

He leaned closer. "Hasn't anyone told you how beautiful you are?"

"I'm not used to people talking about such things as beauty."

"Well that's just nonsense in my opinion. If people can admire green fields, a beautiful sunset, a field of yellow corn, what's wrong with admiring a beautiful woman? *Gott* designed them all. They're all His handiwork."

"It's just that if people mention other people's looks in a positive manner, that person might get prideful if they think that they look beautiful. Anyway, that's just how I was raised. We don't give too many compliments in our household to guard against pride."

"I see your point. I won't tell you how much I like the color of your skin, or the way your eyes dance when you laugh, or how well your dark hair complements your eyes."

Tulip felt good about herself. It felt nice to hear all those things. "You know, saying that out loud is as good as telling me."

"Gut, because I wanted to let you know. You should know how beautiful you are, Tulip."

"Don't say that."

He laughed again. "Okay, I don't want to make you feel uncomfortable in any way."

"Denke."

He shook his head. "Now if someone were to tell me I was the best looking man they'd ever seen, I'd be quite pleased with that."

Tulip giggled. "Are you fishing for compliments?"

"Jah."

"And you think that's okay?" she asked.

He grinned and gave her a sharp nod.

"You certainly are very different from the men around here, Nathanial."

"Well, *denke.* That was your first compliment. See how easy that was?"

"Do you think it was, or was it an un-compliment? Something that was uncomplimentary is what I mean to say. You can't know what I think about the men around here. I could think the men around here are *wunderbaar* and since I just said that you're not like the men around here, perhaps I've just said something very awful to you."

"You're so smart, Tulip. I wouldn't have thought of any of that. Did you do well in *skul?"*

She shook her head. "There you go again."

He grinned cheekily. "Sorry, I just can't help myself, but that was genuine. I wasn't deliberately saying anything nice."

"So, the other things you were saying to me weren't genuine?"

"Tulip, you're tying me up in knots, and not in a good way. I mean everything I've ever said to you. You're smart and beautiful and that is a rare combination in a woman, and I don't care what you say. Someone needs to tell you the truth."

She looked down at her hands on her lap, not knowing what to say.

He chuckled again. "Aw, I've gone and embarrassed you now."

Tulip looked up at him. "I'm not embarrassed. I'm just not used to hearing such things."

"If I was your boyfriend, I would tell you that all the time. I hope you give me that chance. Cancelling our buggy ride is not a good start to our relationship."

"I told you why I have to do that."

"Still, it's not a good sign for me. Men have feelings too. Some women are so worried about getting hurt that they hurt all the men around them."

She exhaled deeply. This wasn't as easy as she thought it was going to be. "I'm sorry."

His face lit up. "Will you make it up to me?"

Tulip didn't want to make a promise that she couldn't keep.

When she hesitated, he said, "You're not the only beautiful woman around here, Tulip."

Now Tulip felt like he was threatening her. If she didn't jump to his commands and do things when he wanted, he'd find someone else. It made her feel dreadful inside. She stood. "I'll talk to you later. I've got something I need to tell Chelsea that I forgot to tell her earlier."

"Wait! We haven't finished talking yet."

Tulip swung around to face him. "Our conversation has become uncomfortable. I'll talk to you later when you're in a better mood."

He called after her, "I don't know what you're talking about. It's you who's in the bad mood. You're the one walking away."

Acting like his words didn't bother her, Tulip kept walking. Even though he had said nice things, there was a definite sting to his words. Now Tulip was sure that he was saying things to her in order to gain control—the upper hand. Well, it wouldn't work with her.

WHEN TULIP BROUGHT the twins home that night, her mother pulled her into the kitchen. "Tulip, there is a man in this community called Wilhem Byler."

"I know, *Mamm.* I went to dinner with him on Monday night."

Her mother looked at her openmouthed and it took a few seconds before she could speak again. "Was that who you went with? I thought you said you went with girlfriends. You didn't tell me you went with a man. Were you deliberately keeping things from me? Was it a date?"

"Many couples keep their relationship a secret. I wasn't doing anything wrong. I don't have to tell you everything when I'm this age, do I? I'm old enough to be married and have my own family and my own home by now."

"Quite right. So it was a date, a proper date?"

After Tulip nodded, her mother took a few steps and glanced out at Tulip's father, who was still reading his newspaper on the couch in the living room.

"I didn't realize. That's *wunderbaar!*" her mother said, grinning from ear-to-ear.

"I'm glad you're happy about it, but why do you look so pleased? What do you know about him?" She had thought her mother would be annoyed with her for keeping things from her.

"One of my friends wrote me a letter about him. Wilhem's thinking of moving here and taking a *haus* with his cousin. He comes with the highest recommendations. Your *vadder* and I give our approval of him. Well, I mean, your *vadder* would if he knew about the whole thing."

Tulip put her fingertips to her mouth and giggled. "That's *gut!*"

"Is that all you have to say?"

"*Jah.*" Tulip shrugged her shoulders. "What should I say?"

"Sit down," *Mamm* ordered. When they were both seated, her mother continued, "What's going on?"

"With Wilhem?"

"*Jah.*"

"I really like him. He's so nice and gentle, and he seems sweet and kind."

"*Gut!* I'm happy about that."

"Can I go to bed now? It's been a long day and I had to stay there longer because the twins wanted to wait until everyone went home."

"*Jah,* of course."

Tulip hurried off to bed, wondering what developments might happen on Sunday, at the next community gathering. Nathanial had said he was going to introduce himself to her parents. What if he mentioned that she'd agreed to go on a date with him, or worse, told them they'd already been out together? And what if Wilhem found out? She had gotten herself into a complicated mess and she hoped and prayed that things would work out smoothly and no one would get hurt.

CHAPTER 14

WHEN TULIP GOT to work the next day, Chelsea was waiting for her. As they readied things for their customers, Chelsea asked, "Why were you speaking to Nathanial so much last night? I thought you liked Wilhem."

"*Jah,* I do."

"You were talking and laughing with him. He looked like he was flirting with you."

"It was weird. It was a strange conversation." Tulip shook her head. "I can't even begin to tell you about it. The more time I spend with Nathanial the more odd I think he is. Don't tell anybody. I don't want people to think I'm gossiping."

"I won't. It's a shame. He's so handsome."

"He might be okay. I could be wrong about him. He might just be trying too hard or something like that."

"It's possible," Chelsea agreed.

"It can't be easy to come here, following his *bruder* being here."

"That's right."

Tulip took the chairs off the tables where they'd been stacked from the previous night's floor washing. Then she refilled the table shakers of their salt, pepper, and sugar, while Chelsea started up the coffee machine ready for their early morning breakfast crowd.

Not wanting to have her mind on Nathanial, when she had her next opportunity to talk with Chelsea, she asked her about Jonathan.

"Jonathan is great. I really like him."

"I'm glad. He's such a nice person. I'm glad you can see past his size. Oh, I don't mean anything rude by that."

"It's okay, I know what you mean. I've never been concerned with people's looks. It's the heart of the person that counts," Chelsea said.

When their boss walked in the back door, the two girls were quiet. Their boss didn't like them talking too much.

"Time to open the doors," Tulip said when she saw a regular customer by the door, waiting to get his regular take-out coffee. It was a few minutes before their official start time, but their boss was happy when the girls were ready early to open the doors for their customers.

CHAPTER 15

WHEN HEZEKIAH YODER stopped his buggy in the row with the other buggies on the Sunday morning, the twins were the first ones out.

Tulip got out next, and looked around. She had to avoid both Wilhem and Nathanial until things cooled down. Nathanial had been acting weird at the softball game and she hadn't seen him or heard from him since.

Tulip's parents were convinced she liked Wilhem, but what would they say about Nathanial? She sure hoped Nathanial would keep quiet.

She stuck close to her mother as she walked into the house where the Sunday morning meeting was being held.

As always, they were early. There were only two families who'd taken their seats in the house. Tulip's mother always sat at the front, while Tulip preferred to sit closer to the back. When her mother slid into the front row, Tulip headed to the back of the room where she'd soon be joined by Rose. She hadn't seen Rose for days and she wanted to tell her about the mess she'd gotten herself into. She hoped her big sister might be able to offer her a solution.

Ten minutes later, Rose and Mark came into the house. Tulip waved to Rose, and while Mark sat down with the men on one side of the room, Rose joined Tulip on the women's side. As was traditional at their Sunday meetings, men and women didn't sit together.

"Rose, I've got myself into a bit of a—well, it's a huge mess." Tulip managed to tell Rose the whole thing before the meeting began.

"You're worried about nothing, Tulip."

"Really?"

"*Jah.*"

"I'm not sure who I like best, but I think that Wilhem's the best man for me."

"How are you judging that so early on?"

"Because Nathanial talked about a buggy ride and then I didn't see him for weeks. He was too casual about the whole thing. He seems to be the kind of man who doesn't follow through with things. Then at the baseball game he was acting weird and I thought he might be controlling. He was telling me I was beautiful and smart and giving me compliments. It just made me feel weird. I didn't like hearing it. I told him so and he wouldn't stop. Then I think he got a bit mean, unless I was judging what he said wrongly."

"I see your point. And you're worried that Wilhem might find out that you went out for coffee, or wherever you went, with Nathanial?"

Tulip nodded.

"You're worried about nothing. You're quite entitled to do that. You don't necessarily marry the first man you go on a buggy ride with—or on a date. Don't forget the same kind of thing happened with me. Mark was there the whole time watching me go out with Jacob. It couldn't have been easy for him, but he understood in the end."

"That's because you finally chose him."

"Well, my situation was a lot more complicated than your situation is."

"That's true." Breathing out heavily, Tulip felt the tension she'd been holding in her shoulders float away. Rose was right. Her situation had been dreadfully uncomfortable. "I've been so worried."

"Is there something else you're not telling me?" Rose peered into her face.

"*Nee,* not unless I've left something out that I don't remember. The only thing is that Wilhem asked me if I was going to the softball game and I said I didn't like softball. That was the game that Nathanial was supposed to be driving me home from. Do you see? Wilhem thought I wasn't going to it. What if he finds out that I was there? He lives with Jonathon, and he *was* there. What if Jonathon said something to him? He probably will and then when Wilhem will think I'm a dreadful liar." Her shoulders stooped. "Come to think of it, that's probably what I am."

Tulip nudged Rose when Wilhem walked into the house followed closely by Nathanial. "Look! There they are. Both of them."

"Nathanial looks an awful lot like Jacob. Wilhem looks nice.

If Wilhem asks why you were at the softball game, just say you had to drive the twins at the last minute."

"That would be lying. It's close to the truth, but not the truth."

"You could always tell the truth, then."

Tulip frowned. Lying wasn't a good idea and neither was telling the truth. "Telling the truth would be better, but what would that sound like? *Oh, Wilhem, before I knew you'd be back here, I accepted a buggy ride from another man I like, but since you've turned back up I got out of that and now I'm hoping he doesn't ask again or tell anyone we went out on a date because now I like you better.*"

"*Jah,* that does sound bad, and kind of wacky," Rose agreed.

"I can't even explain myself. You see? Now I don't know what to do."

Rose and Tulip stopped their whispering and turned their eyes to the front when their father stood to open the meeting in prayer.

CHAPTER 16

FOR THE WHOLE MEETING, Tulip did her best to concentrate on what was being said. She didn't succeed very well, though, because she was too worried about what would happen afterward. What if both men approached her at the same time? She glanced over at Wilhem and Nathanial. Wilhem was sitting in the second row and Nathanial was sitting in the row directly behind him. What if the two men got to talking and her name came up? Her stomach churned at the thought.

When the meeting was over, Rose and Tulip stayed back until they were the last ones out of the house. After the Sunday meeting there was always food served. The men moved most of the long benches out of the house and replaced them with tables. In the warmer weather, the meal tables were set up in the yard.

"I'm going to help *Mamm* in the kitchen and hopefully avoid everyone," Tulip said.

"*Nee*, you shouldn't do that; not if you like Wilhem. You should go out and speak with him."

"I can speak to him later. Hopefully, when Nathanial's gone home."

"Don't let what happened between Jacob and me stop you from getting closer to Nathanial. He is not to be held responsible for his brother's shortcomings."

"I don't think I'm doing that. I'm not taking that into consideration at all."

Tulip headed back into the house and into the kitchen to help her mother and the other ladies with the food. Unfortunately, her mother kept giving her things to be taken outside even when she insisted she was happy to stay in the kitchen. Tulip went so far as to offer to do all the washing up as the dishes came back to the kitchen. Her mother wouldn't hear of it. It was as though her mother knew she wanted to hide away, and didn't want to help her do so.

When her mother loaded her up with bread to place on the tables, she saw Wilhem and to her amazement he headed straight to her.

"There you are."

She smiled at him, hoping he wasn't going to mention the softball game. Since he was smiling, it seemed like she was in the clear.

"How's everything going?" she asked as she placed one lot of bread on a table.

"I have some good news."

"What is it?" she asked.

By the smile on his face she thought it was something important

"Jonathon and I have found a nice *haus* to live in."

"That's *wunderbaar!* Is it close by? Wait, don't tell me yet. Stay here for a minute while I put this bread out." She placed four lots of bread on four tables and headed back to Wilhem. "Tell me about it."

"It's the small place on the corner of this road just before the creek."

"I know the one; it's the white one with the red roof?"

"That's it."

"That's quite exciting."

"We're moving in there on Wednesday."

"That happened quickly."

"I tend to move fast when I know something is right."

He said it in a way that made her giggle.

"Could I drive you home after the singing tonight, Tulip?"

Tulip glanced around before she answered, hoping Nathanial was nowhere close. She saw Nathanial and her father talking. Both men were smiling and seemed to be getting along well.

"Tulip?"

She turned to face him. "I'm... I'm not staying for the singing tonight."

"Can I drive you home before that, then? Or how about I pick you up from work one day next week?"

Tulip smiled. That would be a better plan and less likely for the two men to run into each other. "I'd like that."

"Tuesday after you finish work?"

"Perfect."

He gave her a beaming smile. "I look forward to seeing you on Tuesday."

Tulip turned around to head back into the kitchen. She had avoided a disaster, but now she wouldn't be able to stay on for the singing like she'd planned. That was a disappointment, but it would be worth it to avoid a disaster.

WHEN TULIP EMERGED from the kitchen after all the washing up had been done, she was relieved to see most of the people had gone home, leaving only the younger people who were staying for the singing. Thankfully, Nathanial was nowhere to be seen. She'd been successful at avoiding him—or so she had thought. As she was wiping the tables down before the men loaded them back onto the church wagon, he walked over to her.

"Have you been hiding from me?"

She smiled at him. "Of course not."

"That's what it seems like to me. Anyway, I spoke to your *vadder*, but I haven't been able to find your *mudder*."

"She spends most of her time on Sundays in the kitchen organizing the food."

"I think your *vadder* likes me."

"I saw the two of you talking together. What did you say to him?"

"I just talked about a little of this, a little of that. He knows I'm Jacob's *bruder* and he didn't mind at all."

"I'm surprised you think that that would make a difference to anyone."

He shrugged his shoulders. "Well, you never know."

Seeing the men were loading the tables she'd wiped down, she moved on to the other tables while Nathanial followed her.

"Can I drive you home soon, Tulip?"

"Nee, I'm not staying for the singing."

"What about now?"

"I have to stay back and then go home with my *mudder."*

He nodded. "Are you playing hard-to-get?"

She turned around and stared at him, wondering if he was joking or whether he was serious. "I'm not playing anything."

He laughed and she laughed too. When she turned back to one of the tables, she felt someone was staring at her. She looked over her shoulder to see that it was Jonathon.

"I must help with the cleaning up of the kitchen," she said.

"I'm not giving up on you. I'll see you soon."

"Bye, Nathanial."

"I'll see you soon," he said again.

She hurried into the kitchen, worried about the way Jonathon had been staring at her. He had to know that there was something between her and Nathanial the way they were laughing together. Jonathon could easily say something about it to Wilhem.

Wilhem would think that she was the kind of girl who would date one man and date another man at the same time, and that was not who she was—not at all. It concerned her that she liked both men.

CHAPTER 17

"I've been spending time with Jonathon," Chelsea said at work the next day.

"And?" Tulip asked. "I already know you like one another. We have talked about it." Chelsea had spoken as though she'd never mentioned Jonathan before.

"He's surprisingly mature. He knows some people laugh about him and his weight and it doesn't bother him. He's got a health condition and he ballooned up when he took the medication to keep it under control."

"Really? I didn't know he was sick."

"I know; neither did I. He wasn't always the size he is and I never knew why he suddenly gained weight."

"I feel awful. I had no idea."

Chelsea leaned in and whispered, "I like him as more than friends."

"You do? That's fantastic. He's such a nice man."

"He is, and he's so gentle and warm-hearted."

Tulip felt all warm and fuzzy. She was glad she might've played a small part in the two of them finding love with each other.

"What's happening with Wilhem?"

She shook her head. "I'm not sure. I'm going out with him tomorrow night. He's picking me up from here."

"That's good, isn't it?"

"Normally it would be, but I can't help worrying because I went out with Nathanial Schumacher once and he thinks I like him, and, well, maybe I do, but not as much as Wilhem."

"I see. You like both of them for different reasons."

"I guess, but Wilhem seems to be the more reliable one. I didn't tell you I liked Nathanial before because I didn't want to tell anyone."

"Are you choosing Wilhem because he's reliable, or does your heart tell you that he's the one you want?"

She shook her head. "Why is everything so complicated?"

"It's not. It shouldn't be."

"My *mudder* says a woman should choose a man with her head and not her heart," Tulip said.

"You're the one who has to live with your choice, so just be sure you choose right."

Tulip giggled. *"Denke,* but that was no help at all."

"I'm not your *mudder,"* Chelsea said with a grin. "Shh. Here comes Audrey."

Both girls stopped talking when their boss came into the bakery.

LATER THAT NIGHT, Tulip was sitting with her family around the dinner table.

"We met a new man today," Daisy said. "He said you know him, Tulip."

"Who is he?"

"His name is Nathanial Schumacher," Daisy replied.

Tulip gulped. She hadn't given the slightest thought to one of her sisters snatching away a man she liked. But she hadn't given him any encouragement yesterday when he wanted to drive her home.

Their mother dropped her fork onto her plate when she heard the man's name. "Where did you meet him?"

"At the supermarket."

Mr. Yoder frowned at his wife. "You let them go alone?"

"I thought they should start to take on some small responsibilities since they're getting older."

"We didn't have one accident with the buggy," Lily added. "We drove slow and the horse is fine."

"We hitched it and unhitched it by ourselves and rubbed the horse down and everything just like you showed us."

Their father scratched his beard in an agitated manner. "I suppose that's progress."

"Anyway, Nathanial's very nice. I thought we might be able to have him over for dinner one night," Daisy said.

Lily added, "Along with his cousin, Matthew Schumacher, because he's staying at Matthew's place."

Tulip stared at their mother. She knew *Mamm* liked Matthew because her oldest daughter was married to Mark, Matthew's older brother.

"We'll see." Mrs. Yoder picked up her fork and started eating.

"Mamm, you always say that when you mean 'no' and don't want to say it," Daisy said.

"Since *Dat* is the deacon, I think it's only reasonable to welcome visitors and newcomers to the community by having them over for dinner," Lily said.

Their father leaned back in his chair and stared at Lily, who was sitting next to him. "And since when have you developed this sense of what a deacon should do?"

Lily shrugged. "I've been watching my lovely *vadder* and how nice and hospitable he's always been to everyone."

Mr. Yoder laughed, while his wife was glaring at Daisy, the twin who'd raised the subject of Nathanial Schumacher.

He glanced at his wife's stern face. "It's your *mudder* who runs the *haus.* She has the say on the matter."

"And, as I already said, we'll see." Her tone was firm.

"Well, that makes things kind of awkward," Daisy said.

"Why?" Mrs. Yoder asked.

"We already invited them to dinner. They're coming on Wednesday night."

Tulip looked on in silence as their mother reprimanded the twins.

"Is there something you don't like about them, *Mamm?"* Daisy asked. "We always have people over for the evening meal. And many people drop by without being invited."

"Yeah, *Mamm.* Why are you like this about Nathanial and Matthew?"

She shook her head. "It's nothing. I've got no problem with either of them. Of course I don't."

"So, it's all right for Wednesday night?" Daisy asked.

"It would be embarrassing if we had to cancel," Lily added.

"Nee, you can't cancel. It'll be okay." She glanced at her husband and he remained silent.

IN HER ROOM later that night, Tulip was worried. Had Nathanial somehow gotten the twins to invite him because he liked her, or was it one of the twins he was interested in? What would happen when Wilhem found out that Nathanial had been invited to her house, but he hadn't been invited?

Tulip changed into her nightgown and ripped off her prayer *kapp* and threw it on her nightstand. Without brushing out her hair, she slipped between the covers.

Tossing and turning, many solutions traveled through her mind. Perhaps she should invite Wilhem as well? But then he'd be sure to find out that she'd been out with Nathanial.

One thing was for certain, if she found out that Nathanial was using the twins to get to her, she'd be mighty annoyed. She knew by the way the twins had been talking that one of them liked him.

CHAPTER 18

TULIP WAITED outside the cake store after closing on Tuesday for Wilhem to take her on their date. It wasn't long before she saw a buggy heading toward her. It was Wilhem driving it.

"Hello," she said as she climbed into the buggy.

"Hello."

"Where are we off to?"

"It's a surprise."

He didn't have to do anything special. She just liked to spend time with him and that would've been enough. But it sounded too gooey to tell him that, so she stayed silent.

"It's not too much of a surprise. I've just picked up the keys for the *haus.* I thought I'd take you there first and show you through it. I would've cooked you dinner, but there's no furniture there yet."

"That's exciting. When do you move in?"

"Tomorrow."

"I'm sorry, I missed that—you can cook?"

"Yeah. Why's that so surprising? I can do lots of things. I can even sew, and what's more it was my *grossdaddi* who showed me how to sew. He told me that he was out in the fields one day and cut himself on some wire. There were no hospitals in those days, not close by anyway. He either had to sew the cut closed or bleed to death. So, he sewed the cut shut."

"Ooohh! That's an awful story. I'm glad you didn't tell me that while we were eating. Yuck!"

Wilhem laughed. "Awful maybe, but it's true."

"And that's why he thought you should learn to sew? In case you cut yourself open?"

"Not exactly. Things like that do come in handy, though. Mind you, I didn't say I was a good cook, I just said I could cook. I'm not good at sewing either."

Tulip laughed.

He stopped the buggy close to the house. "We've still got some daylight left."

HE SHOWED Tulip through the small house that he was going to share with his cousin, Jonathon. Wilhem was acting like he hadn't heard anything about the friendly way she'd been speaking with Nathanial on the Sunday just gone and Tulip couldn't have been more relieved.

The house had only two bedrooms, one bathroom, a kitchen, and one living area. It was small but cozy. The living room and the kitchen were floored with gray slate tiles.

"It's nice. I think you'll be happy here."

"I'm sure we will be. Now let's have dinner."

He'd booked a table at an Italian restaurant in town. They had to travel back along the roads they'd just traveled down.

"I'm glad you like it here in this county, Wilhem."

"I do. There seems to be so much more happening here than back home."

"I've only ever lived here."

"Trust me, it's a nice place to live. And I've got work lined up for the next three months."

"I'm happy for you."

He smiled at her and when their eyes met, she knew she'd made the right decision, choosing him over Nathanial.

Once they'd parked the buggy close to the restaurant, they walked up the road together. The chill of the night air bit into her cheeks, causing her to shiver.

"Are you cold?" he asked.

"Not too cold."

When they arrived at the restaurant, he moved forward and held the door open for her so she could walk through first. She thanked him as she walked through the doorway. Once they were inside, they were greeted by a waiter who showed them to their table in the corner of the dimly lit room. William moved quickly to pull the chair out for her. He was being completely chivalrous and doing all the right things.

Two pink roses sat in the center of the table and in front of them a white candle flickered.

When he sat down opposite, Tulip said, "This is so nice and lovely."

He gave her a big smile. "You haven't even tried the food yet."

"I know I'll like it. I like the feel of the place."

"Gut. I'm glad you like it."

Soft music played in the background, creating a romantic mood.

"Do you think will be able to see our food? It's kind of dark in here."

"Will we be able to read the menus?" Tulip asked.

Wilhem looked over at the approaching waiter holding two menus. "It looks like we'll soon find out."

Tulip ordered salad and lasagna, figuring it would be easier to eat than spaghetti, which she'd probably have trouble getting onto a fork. Wilhem ordered the seafood pasta. For drinks they both opted for soda.

"Tell me more about yourself," Tulip said.

"You probably already know more about me than most people do. Even my own parents."

Tulip giggled. "I don't think that would be true."

"Well, what would you like to know specifically?"

"What are your hopes for the future?"

"I'd like to get married and have a large *familye.* Isn't that what everyone wants?"

"I guess so."

"What about you?"

"I want to get married and have a family as well. I would like to have an interesting life. Maybe I'd like to travel and see places."

"What kind of places?"

"I don't know. I just want to do something a little bit different."

He slowly nodded. "You don't want to be the same as everybody else?"

Tulip giggled. "You're probably right."

The waiter brought their drinks and warm bread, and told them their food wouldn't be long. Tulip was so hungry she felt like eating all the bread, but then she knew she wouldn't have room for the main meal.

She wondered if it might be best to come right out and say something to Wilhem about the softball game and Nathanial, but as she'd discussed with Rose, it would sound too strange. She didn't want Wilhem to think she was a strange girl.

Wilhem picked up the bread and offered it to her. "Would you like some?"

"Just a little bit." She broke off a small piece.

"Butter?"

She shook her head and then watched as he took a large slice of bread and scraped a great deal of butter on it.

"I see you like a little bit of bread with your butter."

He laughed. "I've always loved butter. Everything is always better with butter."

Tulip giggled. "I can't believe you just said that."

"It's true."

There was a moment of silence while they both ate the bread

"I've noticed that Jonathan and Chelsea are getting along well."

"*Jah*, they are."

"Jonathan tells me that you helped him. You put in a good word for him."

"I don't know if that did any good."

"I think it did and so does Jonathan, so *denke*."

"You are most welcome, if I did anything to help. I've always

317

liked Jonathan. Chelsea tells me he's got something happening with his health?"

Wilhem nodded. "He likes to keep that quiet because he doesn't want to be seen or treated as the sick person."

"I can understand that. I haven't told anyone and I won't tell anyone."

"Good." He finished eating his bread and butter.

They were getting along so well, but every now and again she was reminded that it could all end quickly if Wilhem found out she'd lied to him about being at the softball game. Rose had told her not to worry, but it was hard not to.

Their main meals arrived, taking her mind off her concerns.

"Yours looks nice," he said.

"So does yours," she said, studying his seafood. It had been a while since she'd enjoyed seafood. That's what she should've ordered.

"Do you want to swap?"

She giggled. "How about we go halves?"

"Half each?"

"Jah."

"Good idea."

She cut her lasagna down the middle and moved one half of it onto his plate. Then he gave her half his seafood pasta.

"The best of both worlds," he said.

"That's a bit dramatic. It's just food."

"I love food."

"Ah, now I am learning more about you. I've learned that you love butter and you also love food."

"That's right."

"Italian food in particular?"

"All kinds of food and I hope you're a good cook."

"Of course I am. I love cooking."

"That fits well because I love eating."

It was a silly conversation, but just being with him, talking about nothing in particular, made Tulip happier than she'd been in a long time. Her stress of earlier in the evening faded away.

When they finished their meals, Wilhem asked, "Dessert?"

Tulip patted her stomach. "I couldn't possibly, but you have some if you want. They might be able to bring you some more butter with a spoon."

He laughed at her. "I'll give dessert a miss if you aren't going to have any with me."

"Are you trying to make me feel guilty?"

He leaned over, close to her. "Is it working?

"*Nee*, it's not. There's nothing you could say that would make me be able to fit anything else in."

He chuckled. "Okay, but I'm not ready to go home yet. I'll keep you for a little longer, if that's all right with you."

"It is."

They talked easily for another hour and Tulip was pleased at how well they were getting along.

When they both noticed other people in the restaurant leaving, Wilhem said, "I should be getting you home, or your parents will be worried."

"Okay. *Denke* for a lovely dinner."

"Does that mean you'll go out with me again?"

"I will."

"That makes me happy."

As they walked to the buggy, Tulip again became worried about Nathanial. She felt that she might be sitting on a volcano that was about to erupt and she didn't want to lose Wilhem. She liked him even more after tonight.

Tulip shrugged off her fears and enjoyed the romantic walk beside the attractive man as they walked up the street in the chilly night air.

"I had the best night I've ever had," he said, glancing down at her.

"I've really enjoyed it too." It would've been the best night she'd had if she hadn't been so worried about what the future might hold.

When he stopped the buggy in front of her home, Tulip waited, hoping he'd make definite plans to see her again.

"I don't want the night to end. I'd like it if we could turn time back and start from the beginning and do tonight all over again."

Tulip laughed. He was a little silly and so carefree. She loved his easy manner.

"Would you care to come on a buggy ride with me on Friday night?" he asked.

"*Jah*, I'd like that."

"Shall I collect you at eight?"

She stared at him in the semi-darkness. The only light was coming from inside the house. "That sounds *gut*."

"Perfect."

Tulip climbed down from the buggy and before she got to the front door of her house, Wilhem had turned the buggy to face the road. Now the buggy was still. She turned when she got to the door and waved to him. When she saw that he waved back, she opened the door and stepped through. No one would be able to ruin how she felt, not the twins, not anyone. She felt so happy inside that she felt she might burst. She'd found her perfect man just like Rose had found hers.

She hung her shawl on the peg by the door and had expected to be faced with the twins asking her how her night had gone. Rather than the twins running up to her, it was her mother.

"I'm so glad you're home." Tulip's mother took her by the hand and dragged her into the kitchen. "I've been so worried and you weren't here for me to talk with. I'm so glad you're home."

"What is it?"

"The twins."

"I guessed it was something about one of them. What have they done now?" It would be just like the twins to ruin her slim chance of happiness.

"Nothing lately. It's just that I'm worried about Nathanial coming here. They knew I wouldn't want him here and that's why they didn't ask me first. You heard, didn't you, about Jacob?"

"*Jah*, but that's Jacob and not Nathanial."

"They're part of the same seed."

Tulip pulled her mouth to one side. "I don't think that's fair, *Mamm*."

"I've seen it before. Children of the same *familye* generally do the same things because they've got the same morals."

"I don't think that's what happened. Jacob, and the girl he

ended up marrying, made a mistake, but they made it right. Shouldn't people's sins be forgotten? *Gott* forgets them. Besides, don't forget that Nathanial and Jacob are cousins of Mark and Matthew, and there's nothing wrong with them. You allowed Mark to marry Rose."

"Generally you'd be right, but we're talking about the twins. I don't want to see them get into any trouble. I worry about them. They're too flighty and headstrong for their own good and they're immature—far too immature for their age."

"They'll be all right. They just need some time to grow up."

"But they're already keeping company with people like Nathanial Schumacher."

"You should be glad they asked the boys here to dinner; they aren't sneaking off somewhere with them."

Mrs. Yoder's face suddenly brightened. "You're right. I didn't see it like that. I feel much better now. Maybe I've been wrong about Nathanial. Your *vadder* said he seemed nice."

"You should know more about him by the end of dinner on Wednesday."

"You're right. *Denke,* Tulip." Her mother stood up and kissed her on her forehead. "I feel so much better. *Gut nacht.*" Mrs. Yoder hurried out of the room.

Tulip sat there alone at the kitchen table, thinking about what she'd just heard. She was more certain than ever that Nathanial had forced the invitation for dinner.

Her mother had been so worried about the twins and Nathanial that she hadn't even asked how Tulip's time with Wilhem had gone.

When she had time to sit there and think things through,

she realized she'd just made a big mistake. She had the opportunity to change her mother's mind about having Nathanial there. He could've possibly been uninvited and that would've been a good thing. Why did she defend him when he could very well ruin everything for her?

CHAPTER 19

On Wednesday night, Tulip decided she should have a quiet word with Nathanial before he came inside the house. That way she could possibly diffuse a bad situation before it happened. She watched the driveway from the living room so she could be first outside to speak with him. The twins were in the kitchen helping their mother with dinner when a buggy pulled up. Tulip raced outside and met Nathanial as he jumped out of the buggy. She looked around for Matthew.

"Hello, Nathanial. Where's Matthew?"

"He was working late, or doing something for his *vadder.* He'll be along soon. He told me to go ahead and get here first."

"I see. I wanted to talk with you about something so it worked out well that Matthew didn't come with you."

He drew his eyebrows together. "Wilhem? Is that why you didn't want me to take you home on Sunday?"

Tulip froze. "What do you know about Wilhem?"

"I know enough."

Tulip hated confrontation and didn't know what to say. "I was put in an awkward situation."

"And what was that?" He folded his arms across his chest. She shook her head and opened her mouth to speak and he butted in, "You've been two-timing me?"

Tulip frowned. That's what she'd been afraid of all along. She wasn't a two-timer but now people would think that she was. "I'm not. It just happened like that. I wasn't seeing you both at the same time. It was nothing like that."

"You led me to believe that you would be seeing me in the future at some point." He walked up close to her and, he being taller, she only came up to his chin. "Are you telling me that you've chosen Wilhem over me?"

"I haven't, I … er …"

"Haven't you heard about him?"

Tulip looked into his face and wondered why she'd ever found him handsome. Right now, his personality overshadowed his looks and he was anything but attractive. "What do you mean?"

"That's why Wilhem had to move here."

"Why?"

"*Nee!* I'm not going to be a talebearer. You can find that out for yourself."

Nathanial took a large stride to walk into her house, but she stepped in front of him to block his way.

"What is there to find out? He said he likes it better here and he's found work," Tulip said.

He shook his head at her. "You people gave my *bruder* such a hard time when he was here."

"Who did?"

"Never mind." He took a giant sideways step and walked past her into her house.

Now she'd have to sit through an awkward dinner with a man who'd been so horrible to her. And what if he'd said something to Wilhem about her? Tulip wasn't certain whether he knew something dreadful about Wilhem or whether he was just trying his best to make him seem like a bad choice. Besides, how would Nathanial know anything about him since they didn't even belong to the same community?

Now Tulip felt sick to her stomach. She shouldn't have rushed out to meet him. She didn't want to join them for dinner, but she had no choice.

THROUGHOUT THE DINNER, every time Tulip glanced up from her plate, she could see Nathanial scowling at her. It was plain to see that she'd hurt his feelings. As for Matthew, he seemed unaware of the tension between Nathanial and herself.

She wondered if Matthew was interested in one of the twins. She noticed his eyes kept glancing in Daisy's direction while Daisy had her eyes fixed on Nathanial. It would be her mother's worst nightmare-come-true if Daisy liked Nathanial. To be on the safe side, Tulip kept out of the dinner conversation as best she could, only speaking when she was spoken to.

When everyone finished dinner, it was time for coffee in the living room. Wanting to be on her own, Tulip volunteered to make the coffee, even telling her mother to go out and join their guests.

Just when she was in the middle of pouring the coffee into

the cups, Nathanial came into the kitchen. She glanced at him and said nothing.

"Were you stringing me along in case things didn't work out with someone else?" he asked her.

"It was nothing like that." She shook her head. "Nothing like that at all. Let me explain."

"Why would I listen to a liar like you?"

Tulip gasped. No one had ever spoken so rudely to her, not even her twin sisters. "If you think I'm a liar, why are you here having dinner at my *haus*? It's not nice to call me a liar in my own home."

"Would it be better to call you a liar outside the *haus*? Do you want to talk about this outside right now?"

"Shh! Someone will hear you."

"I don't mind if they do; then you can explain to them what you've done."

"You didn't answer my question. Why are you here?" She had to find out if he liked one of the twins, or whether he was just using them to get to her.

"Lily and Daisy asked Matthew and me to dinner. It would've been rude to say no, wouldn't it?"

"You could've easily refused."

He laughed in a cruel manner.

"Everything all right in here?"

They both turned to see Mrs. Yoder standing by the door with her hands on her hips.

"I just came here to help Tulip carry the coffee out," he said.

Tulip said nothing and walked past him with coffee cups on a tray.

"Stop, Tulip. Let me do that." He walked forward and

grabbed the tray from her so forcefully she had no choice but to let go.

Once Nathanial was clear of the kitchen, her mother asked, "What's really going on here, Tulip?"

"Nothing, nothing at all."

"I don't believe that. There is something going on between the two of you. Tell me—what is it?"

"I'll tell you when everyone goes home."

Her mother tilted her head. "So, there is something?"

"It's nothing much, really," Tulip said as she moved past her mother.

The boys only stayed for one cup of coffee. It was Matthew who suggested they go. Maybe he had sensed that something wasn't quite right.

When they left, the twins raced up to their rooms. Their father went to bed, while Tulip and her mother headed into the kitchen to wash the dinner dishes.

Tulip turned on the hot water tap and shook the soap in the holder to create the soapy washing up water.

"Do I have to drag it out of you?" Her mother placed a pile of dishes on the edge of the sink.

Tulip turned off the tap. "I wasn't going to tell you. I went out with Nathanial once, a while ago, for a cup of coffee. It was no big deal."

Her mother's jaw dropped open in shock. "Why didn't you tell me?"

"It was nothing. Except I agreed to go on a buggy ride with him and then nothing happened. He went away for weeks and came back as though nothing had happened and then said he wanted me to go on a buggy ride again, but by that time, I'd met Wilhem."

"The one you went out to dinner with? *Jah,* I like *him.*"

"I know you don't like Nathanial so that's why I didn't say anything. Anyway, now Nathanial is upset that I like Wilhem, or something. He said I two-timed him. I don't know how he found out about Wilhem."

"Someone would've told him. News always gets out. People like to talk about others."

Tulip sighed. "I know. Someone would've seen us together, I suppose."

Her mother tapped her chin. "I'm confused. Does he like either of the twins, or you?"

"I don't know. I was worried he might be using the twins to get back at me. Maybe I'm worrying about nothing and I don't want you to think the worst about him. I could be wrong." Tulip pushed the dirty plates under the water.

"Do the twins know what happened between the two of you?"

"*Nee,* I've not said anything to them."

"I think we should keep this between ourselves, don't you?"

"Okay, *Mamm.* I feel better now that you know. I've told Rose, but she won't say anything to anyone."

"If you've told Rose, you should've told me. You should never keep anything from me."

Tulip turned and smiled at her mother, feeling better that she'd told her the whole story. "The only thing I'm worried about is if Nathanial says something to Wilhem about me. He could talk to him alone and he might say that we were dating."

"He wouldn't say that if it wasn't true. You can't worry about that."

"I do, though. And it's making me feel sick whenever I think about it."

"Well, there's an easy cure for that."

"Don't think about it?" Tulip asked, predicting what her mother was about to say.

"Exactly."

It was a hard thing to do. Where would she find another nice man like Wilhem if things went sour between them?

CHAPTER 20

TULIP SPENT the rest of the time leading up to Friday night worried about Wilhem, and was continually fearful that he might find out about her spending time with Nathanial. She figured the only thing she could do was come clean to him and tell him what had happened.

A little before eight, she heard the buggy coming toward the house.

The twins had been unusually quiet that evening, and had been like that ever since Nathanial and Matthew's visit to the house. They hadn't even teased Tulip about going on a buggy ride. There was something going on with them and Tulip knew she'd have to find out what it was, but first she had to tell Wilhem what had been troubling her.

When she climbed into the buggy, she got the fright of her life. Instead of seeing Wilhem, it was Nathanial. She blinked hard, thinking that the semi-darkness might be playing tricks on her eyes. It was definitely Nathanial.

"What are you doing here?" she hissed.

"I told Wilhem what you were like and he said he no longer wanted anything to do with you."

"Why would you do that?"

He laughed. "It was my duty to tell my *bruder* in the Lord what he was getting himself in for."

"You had no right to interfere. Anyway, I was going to tell him what happened."

"Little late now."

She glared at him. "Why are you here?"

"To deliver the message."

"What message?"

"Wilhem's message that he wants nothing more to do with you."

She made to get out of the buggy, but he grabbed her arm.

"Let go, Nathanial! You're hurting me!"

"Wilhem can't find forgiveness in his heart for you, but maybe I can."

"I haven't done anything wrong."

"You're delusional."

"You're so rude!"

He laughed, and he still had a firm grip on her arm. "Look at things this way. Come on a buggy ride with me, or explain to your *familye* why Wilhem no longer wants to see you."

"That would be easier than explaining why I went on a buggy ride with you and not Wilhem. I thought you liked one of the twins."

"I could have either of them. They both like me."

She jumped out of the buggy, ripping her arm out of his

grasp as she did so. He jumped out of the buggy, caught up with her, and swung her around to face him.

"What you're saying is you prefer Wilhem?"

"*Jah*, I do."

"Well, too bad that's not going to happen now, but I'm still here, willing to forgive and forget."

She pushed him away and ran to the house, slamming the door behind her. Everyone was in the living room sitting around the fire and their heads turned to stare at her.

"What's wrong, Tulip?" her father said, bounding to his feet.

She kept back the tears that were threatening to spill from her eyes. "Nothing. I feel a little ill so I thought I should stay inside tonight. It's too cold out."

When her father sat down, Tulip raced to the kitchen. When she looked out the window, she saw that the buggy had gone. She sat down at the table, glad that Nathanial had gone. Tears ran down her face. Wilhem didn't want anything to do with her. Amish men chose their wives carefully and now he thought Tulip was a different kind of woman from the one that she was.

She quickly wiped her face with the end of her apron when she heard people heading to the kitchen. It was the twins.

"What's wrong, Tulip?" Daisy asked as she pulled out a chair to sit next to her.

She shook her head. "Nothing."

"Why did you come back inside so fast? You were looking forward to seeing Wilhem." Lily stood behind Daisy.

"It's complicated."

"Did you have a fight, or an argument?" Lily asked.

"Something like that. Make me a cup of tea?"

"I'll do it," Lily said.

"What's going on with the two of you? We haven't talked for a while," Tulip said.

Tulip and the twins sat, drank tea, and talked. Neither of the twins mentioned Nathanial—to Tulip's relief.

IT WAS Sunday meeting when Tulip saw Wilhem again. He caught her eye and to her surprise, he smiled and gave her a wave. She waved back. He didn't seem upset at all. Then he walked over to her. Perhaps he was a man who would forgive her.

What if she had been the reason he moved all that way and moved in with Jonathon? She half thought she might be the reason he'd moved away from his family and now he could be mightily disappointed and she couldn't blame him. She wished she had never laid eyes on Nathanial, but it was too late for that now.

"Are you feeling better, Tulip?" he asked with concern in his eyes.

"What do you mean?"

"You were sick on Friday and had to miss our buggy ride." Seeing her blank face, he added, "Didn't you send Matthew and his cousin to the house to tell me that?"

Tulip put the pieces together. Wilhem still knew nothing about what had happened between her and Nathanial. Nathanial had successfully ruined her planned time alone with Wilhem by telling him she was sick. He must've learned about her Friday-night date from the twins—that's all she could figure. The twins weren't good at keeping quiet about things.

"Not exactly," she said. "I didn't send them to the *haus* and I wasn't sick."

He drew his eyebrows together. "What do you mean?"

"It's a long story."

"Perhaps you can tell me about it over a walk with me in the park this afternoon?"

Tulip smiled. "I'd like that."

"How about we skip the singing? I'm too old for it anyway."

"Okay." Tulip looked around. "I better help *Mamm* now or I won't be going anywhere."

"I'll be here when you're ready to leave."

Tulip hurried away and left him standing there.

She was pleased that she'd have a chance to tell him the truth rather than him hearing half-truths from someone else. The only drawback to their time together that afternoon would be that she would have to tell him that she hadn't told the complete truth about the softball game that Wednesday night a couple of weeks back. And also that she had made the plans to go on the buggy ride before she saw him again. She hoped he would take the news well. At least she would no longer be lying.

CHAPTER 21

WILHEM HAD CHOSEN a deserted spot in a field for their time alone together. He spread out a blanket next to a patch of wild-flowers.

"It's beautiful here."

He looked around. "It is. Now, what did you have to tell me? You've been quiet all the way here in the buggy."

She gulped and looked around, wondering how to begin. "A picnic with no food?"

He laughed. "It was a little short notice. Next time, I'll be prepared."

"I think we've both had enough to eat anyway."

"I know I have," he said. "I think it's the company that creates a picnic. And right now, I'm having a happy time being with you. Now, tell me what's troubling you."

She took a deep breath. "Long before I knew you, well, days before I met you, I had coffee with Nathanial. I then agreed to go on a buggy ride with him later, but I heard nothing and forgot about it. Then I met you. Later, Nathanial came back expecting me to go on that buggy ride and by then I'd agreed to go out with you." She held her head and laughed when she saw him smirking. "It's not funny. I think that's what happened. It's confusing."

"I know I'm confused."

She looked into his brown eyes. "I wanted you to know what happened in case … well, in case you heard the story a different way than how it happened because I didn't want to go out with him after I met you. Then things became awkward between Nathanial and me."

"I'm pleased that you told me."

"You don't think badly of me?"

"I can't think why I would. You're not tied to a man just because you agree to go on a buggy ride or you have a cup of coffee with him."

Tulip's body relaxed and she let go of the breath she'd been holding onto. "I thought you might think me a two-timer."

He laughed. "Not at all. That's a silly thing to think. I'm glad you prefer me. It makes me feel good to know that my feelings for you are returned."

Tulip hadn't foreseen things going so well. She hadn't wanted to reveal to him she had feelings for him, but it had turned out for the best because now he'd admitted he liked her. "That's such a relief."

He frowned. "Is there something you're not telling me?"

"*Nee,* I've told you everything. Except, I didn't tell you that I wasn't sick on Friday night. Nathanial made that up. He came to collect me and I got into the buggy thinking that it was your buggy. I couldn't see in the darkness until I was sitting beside him."

"That's deceitful of him." He shook his head and pressed his lips firmly together, and then he asked, "Why would he do that?"

"He wanted to ruin things between us. He told me outright that you didn't want to see me anymore and he said that he told you I was a two-timer."

"Ah, that's why you were a little nervous with me earlier today."

Tulip nodded. "I didn't know then that he had been lying about what he'd told me in the buggy."

He took his hat off to run his large hand through his sandy-colored hair. "It's quite shocking that he'd do that."

"I know. It was awful."

"So, he did that hoping you'd forget about me and go on the buggy ride with him?"

Tulip shrugged her shoulders. "I guess so. *Nee,* come to think of it, the way he was acting he wouldn't have expected me to go out with him. I think he was getting back at me for rejecting him."

"That sounds more like it." He put his hat back on. "At least now the truth is out in the open. Don't ever be afraid to tell me anything, Tulip."

"I won't. It sounded too silly to tell you everything at the start, but I didn't know it was going to blow up." She ran her hand over thc delicate yellow wildflowers.

"Things tend to do that sometimes."

"It just got so complicated and I would rather be with you."

"I understand. Don't be upset."

Tulip could barely look at him and blinked back tears, not wanting to cry in front of him. "I feel better now that I've told you."

"He made you feel bad for no reason. Forget it and forget about him."

Tulip nodded. "I will."

"Are you sure you're okay? Look at me."

Tulip took her gaze away from the flowers and looked into his face.

"Everything's fine."

"I hope you don't think less of me now or think that I'm immature."

"If anything I think more of you. What you've just told me shows me what a caring and sensitive person you are."

"Really?"

"Jah." He put himself to his feet and held out his hand. "Let's go for a walk while the sun is still smiling down on us."

Tulip gave a little giggle at his words and reached her hand up. He pulled her to her feet. "Where are we going?" she asked, pleased that he still had hold of her hand.

"Nowhere in particular."

"That sounds good to me."

He looked down at her and smiled. She knew from the way he looked at her with softness in his eyes that he really liked her. They walked through a clump of trees. "I think there should be a creek along here."

"There is. I'm sure."

Tulip heard the running water before she saw it. There was no path running by the water, only thick trees growing from the water's edge and continuing along the banks.

"It doesn't look like a nice stretch of water. I was hoping we could walk along the side," Wilhem said.

"How about we walk up further and see if it gets any better?"

"Okay."

Tulip didn't care where they walked or what they did. She was just pleased to be with him and he was still holding her hand. They walked on, following the water for another fifteen minutes.

"I think we should go somewhere for a cup of coffee. Somewhere where we can sit down on a chair."

Tulip laughed. "That sounds good."

"Are you getting hungry?"

"Mmm, I'm starting to get hungry."

"Me too. Let's go." He swung her around and they headed back to his buggy. "Do you know any good food places?" he asked once they were in the buggy and he had hold of the reins.

"There's a diner just up this road a little way."

"How's the food?"

"Quite good from memory. I haven't been there in some time. I went there with Rose just before she got married."

"That wasn't long ago. This way?" He nodded his head to the left.

"That's right, and then left again at the crossroads, and then you'll run into it on the right hand side of the road. You can't miss it."

"That's what people always say. It's easy when you know where something is. I'm not good with directions."

"Just as well I know where it is. Most men aren't good with directions."

He pulled a face at her. "I'm not most men."

"Well, like I said, a lot of them aren't good with directions and neither are you. What does that tell you?"

He frowned. "I'm not sure. Nothing?" He clicked his horse forward. "I'll have you know that I'm different from other men."

"How so?"

His brow scrunched and he took a while to answer. "I don't know," he finally said as his face relaxed into a smile. "I was trying to impress you, and then I didn't have anything intelligent to say to follow it with."

Tulip giggled at him. She liked the way he was so relaxed and wasn't afraid to be silly. "You remind me a little of Mark, my new *bruder*-in-law."

"Ah, that's a *gut* thing?" He glanced at her.

"It is."

"And in what way do I remind you of him?"

"Just your easy-going manner. You're so calm and relaxed—easy to be around."

"I'm happy to hear it."

"I really miss her Rose. It feels strange to be in the *haus* without her. We used to do everything together. She was like my best friend."

"My *vadder* used to say that the one thing we can be sure of in life is change."

"That sounds like something my *vadder* would say, but he'd mention sailing down a river and he'd talk about the changing currents to go along with it."

"They sound similar, our two *vadders*."

"*Jah*. They do, but yours is right about change. Things are always changing whether we want them to or not. When each of my *bruders* got married and left the *haus*, things weren't the same, but it didn't matter so much because I was so close with Rose and now she's gone. It's like a part of me has left. I know that sounds dramatic, but it's so quiet at home without her."

"You were closest with her out of all your sisters?"

"*Jah*. The twins are practically inseparable, so it was always the twins and then there was Rose and me."

He stopped the buggy at the diner. "I'm close with all my siblings equally. I don't know why. We're all spread out in ages so maybe that's why."

"Could be." Tulip got out of the buggy and watched as Wilhem secured his horse.

THEY SAT in a booth looking at the menu. "What will you have, Tulip? My treat."

"*Nee*, it's my treat this time."

"*Nee* it's not. I'll pay."

"I work. I can afford it."

He chuckled. "That's not the point. I refuse to let you pay and that's that." He closed the menu and then snatched hers out of her hand.

She looked across at him in shock and saw his smiling face. "Okay, you can pay. Just give me back the menu."

He handed it back to her. "Now, what looks good?" he asked when he opened his menu once more.

"The hamburgers?"

"Is that what you'd like? You can have anything."

"I like hamburgers."

He glanced at her over the top of his menu. "I'll have to remember that. Favorite food hamburgers."

"Wait a minute. I didn't say they were my favorite food. They are just one of the things I like to eat."

"Ah, well then, is there anything else you see that you might prefer?"

"*Nee,* not today. Today seems like a hamburger day."

"What other food do you like?" He placed the menu on the table. "I want to learn everything about you, Tulip."

"My favorite food is apple pie and ice cream, but only the pies that *Mamm* makes. I don't know what she does, but they taste better than anyone else's. What about you?" Tulip asked.

"What's my best and favorite?"

"*Jah.*"

"Roasted lamb, with the skin slightly crisp on the outside, along with baked vegetables and thick gravy."

Tulip giggled at the look on his face as he spoke about the food. "Stop. You're making me hungry. I love the crispy part too. The thing is that you mentioned more than one food. You just named quite a few. I only asked for one favorite food."

He leaned back. "Oh, sorry. I didn't know there were rules."

"There are. I said favorite food—as in one food."

"Strictly speaking, you can't call gravy a food, and it's just not the same to eat roasted lamb without the vegetables that go along with it. They're a group of foods. How's that?"

A waitress walked to the table to take their order.

"Would you like your hamburger with the lot, Tulip?" he asked.

Tulip closed her menu. "*Jah* please."

He looked up at the waitress. "That's two with the lot." Then he looked back at Tulip. "And what about to drink?"

"Just a soda, *denke.*"

After their order had been taken, they sat there looking at one another until they both laughed.

He reached out for her hand and held it in his. "I'm so pleased I came to the community and met you."

"Me too."

He glanced out the window. "It's getting dark. Did you tell your parents you might be late home? I don't fancy getting on the wrong side of them."

"I told them to expect me when they saw me."

"Good. That is good news. Now what else can you tell me about yourself?"

She looked at their clasped hands, not even the slightest bit concerned that someone might see them. Being affectionate with him seemed like a natural thing to do. "I can't reveal all about myself in one go. There'd be nothing to look forward to and nothing to learn later, would there?"

He chuckled. "I just want to know more … well, the truth is that I want to know everything about you."

"That wouldn't do. You have to be content with just a little bit for now."

"Really? It seems you have rules that I don't know about. You'll have to let me in on them."

Tulip laughed. "There are no rules, not really."

"Okay. That's good to know. I'm happy with what I know about you so far. I'll have to be content with that for the time being."

They had to release each other's hands when the waitress brought their drinks to the table.

After they had a couple of mouthfuls of soda, their hamburgers arrived.

"That was fast," he said.

"It was and they look delicious."

When they finished eating, Tulip wanted to stay talking with him, but it wouldn't do to get home too late.

"Are you ready to go?" he asked.

Tulip nodded.

"Are you sure you don't want anything else?"

"I couldn't possibly fit another thing in."

He chuckled. "Neither could I and I very rarely say that."

When they walked out of the restaurant, he moved closer to her and held her hand.

"*Denke* for coming out with me tonight. I hope we have many more nights like these."

"Me too."

He helped her into the buggy, acting like a proper gentleman.

TULIP WALKED into her house after Wilhem had taken her home. Lily looked at her anxiously when she walked through the door.

"Oh, it's you," Lily said.

"Who were you expecting?" Tulip asked.

"Daisy, that's who! Nathanial was bringing her home after the singing and there's no sign of either of them."

"Do you mean Nathanial and Matthew are bringing Daisy home?"

"*Nee,* why don't you clean out your ears, Tulip? I'm here and Daisy isn't. Why would two men drive her home? That would be weird. Nathanial is bringing Daisy home. They like each other and don't pretend you didn't notice that when he was here for dinner."

"He doesn't like her!" Tulip blurted out before she could stop herself.

"What do you mean?"

"Forget it."

"*Nee,* tell me why you said that," Lily insisted.

"It's nothing." Tulip hurried to the kitchen and found her mother sitting down drinking a cup of tea.

"*Mamm,* did you know that Nathanial Schumacher is bringing Daisy home?"

"*Jah,* from the singing. Lily told me."

"*Mamm,* I said, *Nathanial Schumacher!*"

Lily had followed her into the kitchen. "What's wrong with you? You're saying that like he's a bad person or something. You're not the only one in the *haus* who can have a boyfriend."

Tulip ignored her sister and stared at her mother, looking for a different reaction.

"You were right, Tulip. Someone can't be judged by what their siblings have done. It's just not fair. Everyone is their own person," their mother said. "You told me yourself no one should hold him responsible for his *bruder's* actions."

"Maybe I was wrong!" Tulip said.

"You're jealous!" Lily said with a raised voice. "She doesn't

349

want Daisy or me to have a boyfriend, *Mamm*. She thinks she's the only one who can have one. Tell her, *Mamm*."

"Hush, both of you."

"Both of us? I'm not raising my voice," Tulip said. "I'm just worried, that's all."

"Go up to your rooms. I'll be glad when you're all married and out of the *haus*. Go to your rooms now!"

Tulip left the room before Lily. She knew Lily was scowling at her, but didn't look her way. Why was she getting into trouble? She was only trying to warn her mother that Nathanial was trouble.

For the next few hours, Tulip paced up and down her bedroom worrying about Daisy. The girl was immature and Nathanial, well, he was deceitful at best. And what if he was like his brother in other ways? Tulip feared the worst, but didn't know what to do.

NANCY LEFT her husband reading the bible in the living room, waiting for Daisy to come home, while she went to bed. She felt bad for saying mean things to the girls just now, but sometimes they pushed her and tested her patience to the limit. One minute Tulip was defending Nathanial, and the next minute she was making out he wasn't to be trusted. Hezekiah thought Nathanial was a good man so she'd have to trust her husband's judgment.

Trusting her daughters with men was another thing she was gradually trying to do as well. Each girl would have to rely on her own judgment at one point or another. She couldn't make every one of their decisions for them. Going on a buggy ride with a man might help Daisy mature a little. If one twin gained a little maturity it would surely influence the other. When Daisy came home, she would tell her not to be out so late in future.

After she took off her prayer *kapp* and brushed out her long hair, she changed into her nightgown. She'd kept out of Tulip's business as best she could in regard to Wilhem and things seemed to be working out well between them. She was there for Tulip to ask advice of and that seemed to be enough. Rose had needed a lot more guidance, but Tulip was the sensible one in the family out of all the girls.

Nancy walked to the window and looked out into the darkness. The warm glow of the moon lightened the darkness a little, and streetlights in the distance twinkled against the darkened landscape. There was no sign of a buggy bringing her daughter back home. It was then she saw a dark shadowy figure moving toward the house. She watched the figure come closer and saw a white prayer *kapp* and apron. The only girl who would be coming to the house this late at night would be Daisy. Why was she on foot?

"Hezekiah!" Nancy raced down the stairs and was met by Hezekiah's worried face. "It's Daisy coming to the house by herself!"

Hezekiah's eyes opened wide as though he couldn't believe his ears, and then he ran outside.

CHAPTER 22

Tulip heard her mother's screams and ran down the stairs right behind Lily.

As soon as she reached the bottom of the stairs, she saw her father bring Daisy into the house with his arm around her. She'd been crying, looked disheveled, and was out of breath, like she'd been running.

Their mother ran to Daisy and asked, "Where's Nathanial?"

"He tried to attack me. I ran away from him." Daisy sobbed into her father's shoulder and he encircled his arms around her.

Tulip and her mother gasped in shock.

"What?" their mother shrieked.

Lily ran to Daisy and hugged her. "He tried to attack you?"

Daisy nodded and then she rubbed her eyes.

"What happened?" their father asked, clearly trying to keep a level head.

"Didn't you hear her, *Dat?* He needs to be punished. Go punch him," Lily said.

Hezekiah shook his head. "It's not our way."

Lily curled her hands into fists. "So then—what? You can't let him get away with this."

"Are you hurt anywhere, Daisy?" their mother asked.

"*Nee.* I'm not. I should never have gone with him. You should've stopped me, *Mamm.* You'd never have let Rose go with someone you didn't know well. Don't you care about me as much as you care about Rose?"

Tulip looked at her mother and could see the hurt on her face at Daisy's words.

Tulip stepped in closer to Daisy. "You can't blame *Mamm.* Nathanial did this. He's the one to blame."

Their mother burst into tears. "It's all my fault. Daisy is right. I should never have let her go."

"Let's not find people to blame. Daisy, why don't you go into the kitchen with your *mudder* and have a cup of hot tea?"

Daisy wiped her eyes and nodded. "Okay."

He then said, "I'll talk to the bishop about this in the morning."

"*Gut!*" Lily yelled. "Finally, something will be done about him. I hope he's run out of town. I hate him! If I were a man, I'd go there right now and make him sorry he did what he did."

"That's not helping the matter, Lily," their father said quietly. "Now go help your *mudder* make the tea."

While the twins and their mother walked to the kitchen, Tulip stood by the bottom of the stairs, looking at her father. It couldn't have been easy not to head out the door and find Nathanial and have words with him. She could see by her father's face that he was dreadfully shaken. His whole face had turned a ghostly gray, almost a blue color.

"Are you okay, *Dat?*"

He nodded and then sat down in his chair, staring into the distance. She admired his self-control. Tulip was feeling the same outrage as Lily. They were both upset that a man would lay a hand on their sister and she could only imagine how their mother felt. If their father had raced out the door to confront Nathanial, she would've been scared for both of them. The Amish way was far better, as no good ever came from violence. The bishop would handle the whole thing and come up with some kind of resolution. In her heart, Tulip suspected that Nathanial would go back to Oakes County quite soon after everybody found out about this episode.

"*Dat,* would you like me to get you a cup of hot tea?"

"*Jah, denke,* Rose."

"It's Tulip, *Dat.*"

"Ah, sorry. *Denke,* Tulip."

Tulip walked into the kitchen to see Daisy dabbing at her eyes with a handkerchief.

"He tried to attack me, Tulip. I can't tell you more."

Tulip gasped. "That's just not right. Did you tell *Dat* anything else before you came inside the *haus?*"

She shook her head. "*Mamm* said she'll tell him again so that he can tell the bishop tomorrow."

"*Gut!*" Tulip put her arm around Daisy. "Don't you worry about anything. I'm sure he'll be leaving here soon."

"*Denke,* Tulip. I hope so."

When the pot boiled, Tulip made tea for everyone and then took a cup out to her father.

"Here's your tea, *Dat.*" She looked closer to see that he had his eyes closed. It seemed odd that he had been so wide-awake and now he was sleeping after the huge drama that had just taken place. She touched him gently on his shoulder. "Dat." He didn't wake. Tulip touched him again and when he didn't respond she was suddenly certain he was dead. She dropped the tea and screamed. *"Mamm!"*

Everyone ran out from the kitchen.

"I think *Dat's* dead! He won't wake up."

Their mother rushed to feel for his pulse. "He's not dead! Quick, call 911!"

Tulip grabbed a lantern and the three girls headed to the barn.

NANCY STARED at her husband's lifeless-looking body. He was still breathing and had a pulse, but he wouldn't wake.

"I can't lose you, Hezekiah. We told each other we'd have more years alone when the girls get married. I need those years with you." Tears ran down her face. "Don't leave me alone. You can't." She sobbed. It had never occurred to her that she might lose her husband so soon before they reached old age.

The twins ran back inside. "They're coming. They're sending an ambulance. Tulip is still on the phone with them. They're asking her a lot of questions."

"What's wrong with him, *Mamm?"*

"I don't know, Daisy. I don't know."

CHAPTER 23

TWENTY MINUTES LATER, Tulip stood with the twins at the front door, watching the ambulance leave with their father. Their mother had been allowed to travel to the hospital with him. They were told he might have fainted due to heart failure or possible hypertension.

"You know whose fault this is?" Lily said.

"It's Nathanial's fault. He gave *Dat* a heart attack. I could see by *Dat's* face something was wrong. He was filled with so much rage and he didn't let it out. I'm not going to let Nathanial get away with it," Tulip said.

"*Dat* said we shouldn't look for people to blame," Daisy said.

"*Dat's* not here! Lily, hand me that lantern." While Lily gave her the lantern, Tulip said, "Now come with me, both of you, and help me hitch the buggy."

"Where are we going?"

"We're not going anywhere. You're both staying here. I'm going to tell Nathanial what he did to our *vadder.*"

"You can't go there. It's too late. You'll wake Mr. and Mrs. Schumacher," Daisy said.

"And Matthew," Lily added.

"Then they'll all hear what he's done." Tulip marched to the barn with a twin on each side. "As soon as I'm gone, call Rose, Trevor, and Peter—tell them about *Dat.*"

Tulip had ordered the twins to stay home, and given the mood she was in they obeyed.

BEFORE SHE KNEW IT, Tulip was right outside the Schumachers' front door.

Matthew stepped outside before she got out of the buggy. He walked forward and squinted at her in the dark. "Tulip, is that you?"

She jumped out of the buggy. *"Jah.* I'm here to see Nathanial."

"Okay, I'll get him."

Nathanial walked outside. *"Jah?* Why are you here so late, Tulip? If you've got anything to say to me, can't you do that at a reasonable hour?"

"You attacked my *schweschder.*"

Matthew stepped forward. "Is that true, Nathanial?"

"She's lying," Nathanial said out of the side of his mouth while he glared at Tulip.

"Not only did you assault Daisy, you caused my *vadder* to have a heart attack. He's in the hospital right now."

Matthew stepped forward. "Is he okay?"

"She's lying about everything. They're a *familye* of liars, Matthew."

"*Nee,* they aren't, Nathanial. I've known them all my life and I've never known any of them to lie—not even once." He turned to Tulip. "Is there anything I can do?"

"*Nee,* Matthew. He's in the hospital. I hope he'll be all right. It's your fault, Nathanial."

Matthew stared at Nathanial, who turned away and walked back inside the house.

"Are you okay, Tulip? It must have given you all a dreadful fright. And Daisy, is she okay?"

"Daisy was really shaken over what he did to her. She ran away from him, and then she had to walk home all alone in the dark."

Matthew rubbed his chin. "*Mamm* and *Dat* won't want him to stay with us when they find out what's happened."

"I'm glad you came outside, Matthew. I wanted to hit him so badly just then when he denied what he did. *Dat* was going to tell the bishop about what he did in the morning. He won't be able to do that now. I'll have to go to the bishop and tell him myself."

"I know how you must feel. I'm sorry this whole thing has happened. I hope your *vadder* will be all right."

"Me too. I'll go home and call the hospital and see if they can tell me how he is."

"Do you want me to drive you home?"

"*Nee, denke,* Matthew. I'll need to cool down." Tulip was still mad, but felt better for telling Nathanial exactly how she felt. He wasn't a nice person at all. She was glad Matthew had been there to defend her from Nathanial's lies.

Tulip drove home in the darkness of night. She was very often scared of driving alone at night, but not this night.

Sadness and anger mixed together held her fear at bay. The twins rushed out of the house as soon as she arrived home.

"What happened?" Daisy asked.

"Did you speak to Nathanial himself?" Lily asked.

Tulip jumped down from the buggy. "Before I tell you, did you ring Rose and the boys?"

"I did," Daisy said.

"Gut, denke."

"They were very worried. Trevor and Peter said they'd go to the hospital and Rose and Mark were going too."

"It makes me wish we could've gone too," Lily said.

"Nee, they might not have let you see him with them treating him and trying to find out what was wrong with him. It would've been a wasted trip. Best that we all stayed here."

"Did you see Nathanial and talk to him?" Daisy asked.

"Jah, Matthew came out of the house first and he brought Nathanial out and stayed in the background. He heard everything. Nathanial denied he did anything and walked inside as if he didn't even care. Matthew said his parents won't want him there after they hear what happened."

"So Matthew is going to tell his parents?" Daisy asked.

"Jah. Now help me unhitch the buggy." While the three of them worked to unhitch the buggy and rub down the horse, Tulip told them she would speak to the bishop herself tomorrow morning.

"Do you think you should wait until *Dat* is well enough to tell him?" Lily asked.

"We don't know how long he'll be in the hospital," Tulip said. "I'll call as soon as we're finished here and find out how he is."

"Will they tell you?" Daisy asked.

"I don't know but I'll try to find out."

"Don't worry about talking to the bishop tomorrow," Daisy said. "It's more important that *Dat's* okay."

"*Jah,* but I don't want to let Nathanial get away with it," Tulip said.

Lily wheeled the buggy into the barn while Daisy and Tulip rubbed down the horse.

When Lily came back, she said, "He won't get away with it, Tulip, but I think Daisy is right. We should forget about it until we know how *Dat* is and he's back home."

Daisy stopped what she was doing and covered her face with both hands. "It's all my fault. *Dat* might die and its all my fault for going on that stupid buggy ride with that horrible man." She sobbed uncontrollably and both her sisters rushed to her side and placed their arms around her.

"It's not your fault at all," Lily said. "Stop crying."

"Lily is right. It's not your fault and *Dat* would want us to be strong. I'll call the hospital now if you stop crying."

Daisy put her hands by her side while Lily wiped the tears away from Daisy's face.

Tulip called the hospital with a younger twin sister on either side. When she finally got through to someone, she was told he was currently being treated and was stable. Then she was asked to ring back in the morning. When she hung up the receiver, she told her sisters that he was okay and they wouldn't know any more until the morning.

"*Mamm* would say that the best thing we could do is get a good night's sleep," Lily said.

"That sounds like a good idea," Tulip said. "Let's get inside. It's getting cold out here."

WHEN TULIP CALLED the hospital early the next morning, she learned that her father had heart disease, but he was okay for now. He was awake and was due to be released that afternoon. She called her two brothers and then Rose and learned that they'd all come home from the hospital in the early hours of the morning. Tulip headed back to the house to let her sisters know the news.

"Is he going to die soon?" Daisy asked Tulip.

"I don't think so. They're giving him medication that he has to take daily, so I think he'll be okay for a few more years."

"I thought he was dead, or going to die," Lily said. "I didn't get a wink of sleep all night."

"Me too. I don't think any of us would've gotten any sleep, especially *Mamm.*" Tulip thought back to the frightful moment when she couldn't wake her father and thought he had gone home to be with *Gott.* Until that moment, she'd never given any serious thought to losing either of her parents.

"Are you going to work today, Tulip?" Lily asked.

"I don't know. I had planned to go to the bishop. What do you think?"

"*Nee.* We talked about that last night and decided it's best that you don't," Daisy said. "Just wait until *Dat* is better and see what happens."

"Nathanial will probably leave of his own accord now that other people know what he's done," Lily said.

"*Jah,* I will go to work then. It sounds like *Dat* is not in any danger. You two can stay here and wait for *Mamm* and *Dat* to come home. See what you can fix for dinner."

"I hope Nathanial doesn't get away with everything that happened. Do you think he will?" Lily asked.

"Hopefully, he'll go away now after Tulip let Matthew know what happened." Daisy managed a laugh.

"I've never been so angry." Tulip placed a plate of eggs down on the table for the girls to help themselves. "It must've been a terrible fright for you, Daisy."

"It was. I jumped out of the buggy and ran away. At first I wasn't sure where I was, but then when I came to the corner I knew what street I was on. I was scared, too, because he kept yelling my name and I had to hide when he drove past looking for me."

TULIP WENT to work as usual. She didn't want to let Audrey down by calling in for a day off. She hoped that her father would be home by the time her shift was over.

When she finished work, she walked around the back of the shop to where the buggies were, and saw Wilhem waiting for her.

He stepped toward her. "Are you okay?"

She was pleased to see his friendly face. "You heard?"

"Everyone knows about Nathanial and about your *vadder* being in the hospital."

Tulip was glad everyone knew about Nathanial, but hoped it wouldn't be twisted around to reflect badly on Daisy's reputation.

"How is your *vadder* doing now?"

"He has heart disease, and he fainted because not enough blood was getting to his brain. It gave us all a terrible fright. He should be okay now that he'll have medicine to take. The doctor told me that people live for many years with it. He's coming home this afternoon. He might even be home now."

"That's good news! And you might be happy to know that Nathanial is leaving town this afternoon."

Tulip heaved a sigh. "I'm so glad. That does make me happy."

"I heard you had a few words to say to him and woke up the Schumacher household."

"How did you hear about that?"

He laughed. "News travels."

"It certainly does."

"Is there anything I can do, Tulip, for you or your *familye?*"

She shook her head. *"Nee,* I don't think so, but *denke."*

"I just wanted to let you know that I'm thinking of you."

She smiled back at him. *"Denke.* That means a lot.*"*

"I won't hold you up. You'll be anxious to see your *vadder."* He stepped away from her horse.

She climbed into the buggy. *"Denke.* It means a lot that you came here."

CHAPTER 24

ON HER DRIVE HOME, Tulip wondered if Wilhem would be attracted to a girl who would wake up a household to yell at their visitor. One thing she knew for certain, her mother wouldn't be happy to find out about her outburst and since Wilhem had learned of it, her mother would be sure to find out.

Tulip was pleased to be able to give the twins the news that Nathanial had left. Now it wasn't so urgent that they speak to the bishop.

Not long after Tulip arrived home, Peter and Trevor and their wives, as well as Rose and Mark, drove up to the house to wait for their father to arrive home.

Tulip was the first of her sisters to hurry over and ask her sister-in-law if she could hold Shirley, her young niece. It was usually the twins who got there first to hold Shirley, but they were too upset about recent events to race their sister to their only niece.

When everyone was settled in the house, the twins were

busy making tea when a taxi pulled up to the house. Tulip's older brothers went outside to help their father inside.

"Don't give me any more frights," their father joked to everyone as he walked inside the house. "The old ticker won't be able to take it."

Peter glared at each of the twins. "What's this about giving *Dat* a fright?"

"Why do you assume it was one of us?" Lily asked.

"Hush," Rose said. *"Dat* doesn't need to hear squabbles."

"It's nothing to worry about," Tulip told Peter as she shifted Shirley from one hip to the other.

"Sit down, *Dat,"* Lily said.

"We'll look after you," Daisy said.

Peter helped *Dat* to the couch. Once he was seated, *Mamm* sat next to him.

"Tell us the news. What did the doctor say?" Trevor asked as everyone sat down in the living room.

"I'll let your *mudder* tell you." His voice was quiet, almost breathless.

They all looked expectantly at *Mamm.*

"He needs to take daily medication and if he does that he'll be okay. He'll live long enough to see all his *grosskinner* come into the world." She particularly looked at Amy and Trevor when she said that since they'd been married well over a year and they still had no children and weren't even expecting.

TULIP LEANED down and kissed her father on his cheek, and then she looked at her mother, who looked like she needed a good sleep. "How are you, *Mamm?"*

"I need a hot shower."

"Did you get any sleep at all?" Julie, one of her daughters-in-law, asked.

"Nee, I was sitting up all night worried about Hezekiah."

"I'm sorry to put you through that," he said.

"No need to be sorry."

Their father chuckled. "I'm all right."

"Jah, you are now. Now that they've given you heart medication," Daisy said.

"Just don't forget to take them," Lily added.

Dat opened his mouth to speak but *Mamm* got in first. "There's no chance of that with all of us here to remind him. He has to go back to the hospital every day for a while until they get the levels right," *Mamm* told them. "We don't want him passing out again."

"Are you going to faint or something again?" Daisy asked her father.

He pulled a face. "I hope not."

"He won't as long as he does everything the doctor said." *Mamm* stared at her husband.

His lips turned upward at the corners. "I will."

"You look really tired, *Dat,*" Rose said. "And very pale."

"That won't make him feel any better," Lily said to Rose.

"I feel a bit weak, that's all."

"Did you say you have to go to the hospital every day?" Tulip asked.

"Jah, then I'd reckon I'll have to be checked every few weeks for a bit, and then months."

"Don't talk so much. Just rest," *Mamm* said, putting a hand on her husband's shoulder.

"Tulip said that Nathanial has already left, *Dat*," Lily said as she moved to sit on the floor by her father's feet.

Tulip glanced at her father, worried about how he'd take the mention of Nathanial. The last thing he needed was to hear that name, and now Trevor and Peter would want to know what was happening in regard to Nathanial. They hadn't heard what had happened as yet.

"All things work together for good," he said.

"What's going on with Nathanial?" Peter asked.

Trevor added, "Who is Nathanial?"

"It's a story for another day, but not today," Tulip said.

When they heard a buggy, Daisy ran to the window, followed close behind by Lily who had leaped off the couch.

"It's Aunt Nerida and it looks like she's come by herself," Daisy said.

Tulip looked at her mother. *Mamm* and her younger sister had been having a feud for some time. The twins ran and opened the door while their mother stood still, looking exhausted.

A LITTLE PART of Nancy was pleased that her sister cared enough to visit even though she was still annoyed with her. Nerida must've heard about Hezekiah landing in the hospital. Nancy placed one foot in front of the other and reached the door just as Nerida stepped into the house.

"Nancy, I just heard the news. How is he?"

"He's better; he's home now."

Nerida looked over at Hezekiah on the couch. "You gave everyone a scare."

He chuckled and everyone greeted Nerida and then there was silence in the room as the two women stood face-to-face, staring at each other. "Are you okay, Nancy?"

"As good as I can be. A night in the chair at the hospital has taken its toll."

"You need to rest, Nancy," Hezekiah called from the couch.

"Don't you worry about me, Hezekiah. You just worry about yourself."

Everyone laughed.

"*Denke* for coming, Nerida," Nancy said. Being with her sister gave her a sense of comfort and reminded her of days gone by.

"Of course I'd come. I came as soon as I heard. You should've called me."

"Would you like to stay for dinner?" Tulip asked her aunt.

Before Nerida could answer, Nancy said to Tulip, "Have you arranged dinner?"

Tulip said, "*Jah*. Everyone can stay for dinner. The twins fixed something, and there's plenty for all of us."

Everyone accepted the dinner invitation except for Nerida.

"Maybe another time," Nerida said. "I've left the girls at home alone. They wanted to come, but I told them I wouldn't be long. Now that I know you're okay, Hezekiah, I better get back to the girls and to John." Nerida turned and walked away, stepping out the door.

"*Denke* for coming," Nancy called after her younger sister.

"Of course I would come," came the reply.

It had been a while since Nancy had all her children in the home and, although she was pleased to have them there, the circumstances could've been better.

"It was very nice of Aunt Nerida, coming to see how *Dat* was, wasn't it *Mamm?*"

"Mmm. Now if you'll all excuse me, I need a shower. You girls see what you can do about getting dinner served and the table set."

"Jah Mamm," the twins chorused.

Nancy walked up the stairs, relieved that Hezekiah was going to be okay. He was always the one who'd told her to enjoy the day they were living right now rather than think they'd enjoy some future day in a future time. Nancy knew she had a habit of looking forward to the future, and particularly to the time when Hezekiah and she could be alone once more. It was a lesson learned now that she'd nearly lost him. Now she'd enjoy each day she got to spend with him.

As THE BEADS of hot water pelted over Nancy's body, all of the tension left her. She hadn't realized how tightly she'd been holding her body until she'd told herself to relax. Tonight, she'd enjoy having the whole family gathered around the table and under the one roof.

She would talk to her entire family and insist that they all have dinner at the house once a month. After the scare with Hezekiah, she intended to make the most of each and every day with her family. One day, things might mend between her sister and herself. Nerida had made a step, which had given Nancy hope. Now it was up to her to make the next step. If only Nerida had apologized years ago then things wouldn't have gotten this far. Maybe she had to let the whole thing slide rather than wait for an apology that she was clearly never going to get.

Nancy decided to put the step she'd make toward Nerida out of her mind for the moment. What was important right now was enjoying her entire family and thanking God that they were all together.

CHAPTER 25

The doctor at the hospital was pleased with Hezekiah's progress over the next few days and now they were satisfied that he was on the correct level of medication.

When Nancy went downstairs on Saturday morning, Tulip and the twins were already at the kitchen table, talking.

Tulip looked up at *Mamm* when she entered the room. "Can we all go today and choose some material for new dresses? We haven't had any for some time. I have enough money to pay for all of the material for the three of us."

"That's not necessary, Tulip," *Mamm* said, pleased by the sudden generosity.

"I don't mind. I've nothing else to spend my money on."

"I'm okay with her spending her money on me," Lily said with a giggle.

"Me too," Daisy added. "I'll pay you back when I get a job, Tulip."

Lily scowled at her twin. "You'll never get a job. You're not even looking for one."

"I've been thinking about it."

"You never told me you even wanted one."

"Quiet, girls. You can go into town by yourselves. I'm not feeling too well today, but the three of you can go if that's what you want. At least I might have some quiet around here while you're gone."

"We won't go if you're sick," Tulip said.

"I'll stay with *Mamm* if you and Lily want to get the material," Daisy said. "Just get me dark colored fabric. Maybe purple or something nice."

"*Denke* Daisy, but we can wait until *Mamm's* better so that all four of us can go together."

"You might as well go today. I can see how excited you are. The sooner you get the material, the sooner we can get started on sewing the dresses."

"Are you sure, *Mamm*?" Tulip asked.

"*Jah,* you and Lily can choose it and Daisy and I will stay here."

"Yeah, I don't mind at all," Daisy said, putting her arm around her mother. "I'll look after *Mamm.*"

Hezekiah was still in bed. It would be a long time before he'd be able to go back to work helping his brother on his farm —if ever. The girls made Nancy sit down on the couch while they made her breakfast.

It was rare that the twins did things separately and Nancy was glad to have the chance to speak to Daisy alone. They hadn't talked since Daisy had gone through the awful experience with Nathanial, and Nancy hoped that the scare she'd had wasn't going to affect her finding a husband. It was important for Daisy to know that what had happened to her was a very rare thing to happen in their community and totally not something that should be accepted. As soon as Hezekiah gained strength he'd let the bishop know what had happened and then Nathanial's bishop would certainly be informed of the event.

When Lily and Tulip headed off in the buggy after breakfast, Daisy sat down next to her mother. "Can I get you anything, *Mamm?* Some more tea?"

"*Nee,* I'm fine. I'm glad you stayed here with me. We haven't had much of a chance to talk lately."

"Is there something on your mind that you want to say?" Daisy asked.

"I hoped we might have a conversation about what happened with Nathanial."

Daisy scowled. "I don't want to talk about that. Anyway, I already told you what happened that night."

"Well, not really. What you said was quite vague and then he left so no one heard his side."

"What do you mean by 'his side?'" Daisy sprang to her feet. "Don't you believe me?"

Nancy closed her eyes for a moment. She was too tired for this. "Sit down! Of course I believe you. I just want to talk about it. I am your *mudder,* so you should be able to talk with me about everything, *jah?*"

Daisy obeyed her mother and sat back down. "Except that. I don't want to talk about him and how horrible he is. It just brings back awful memories. He's gone now anyway and I'm glad. He's back where he belongs, back where he came from, and far away from me."

Nancy stared at her daughter and she was sure that Daisy was keeping something from her, but now was not the time to find out what it was. She'd find out soon enough because she always managed to find out the secrets that her children kept from her.

Nancy's mind drifted back to her estranged sister. Her coming there to see how Hezekiah was showed her that they'd always be there for one another when it counted. Even when they didn't like each other, their bond as sisters would never be broken. Being the younger two in the family, and the only girls, they'd been so close years ago. It didn't feel right with her not being around. The feud had lasted years, each waiting for the other to be the first to make amends. Nancy sighed deeply.

She had to do something to show Nerida that she wanted her back in her life. That most likely meant she would have to forego that apology and that was something that didn't sit well with her.

"Is everything okay, *Mamm?*"

"*Jah,* it is."

"You look like you're worried about something. If it's me you're worried about, you don't need to be. Everything is perfectly fine. Nathanial has gone so everything is okay."

Nancy was slightly amused at her daughter's words. It was typical of her to think that everything was about her.

"That's better. You're smiling now."

"Maybe I'll have that hot tea now *denke,* Daisy."

"Sure, coming up." She leaned over and gave her mother a kiss on the cheek.

∽

WHEN TULIP and Lily had finished selecting the fabric for the new dresses, Lily suggested, "Why don't we visit Rose now?"

"At the markets?"

"*Jah.* She'd be working today, wouldn't she?"

"I think so. That's a good idea. We're not that far away. We can leave this parcel in the buggy so we don't lose it somewhere."

The girls stopped at their buggy and then continued to the farmers market where Rose worked at the flower stall. It was lunchtime when they arrived there and they walked through until they saw Rose's stall.

"She's got customers," Lily said.

"We'll just wait nearby to speak with her in between customers."

While they waited, they caught sight of Matthew Schumacher who was working at the stall next to Rose.

Seeing he had no customers, he walked the six strides over to them to say hello. "Hi, Tulip, and Lily."

Lily frowned at him. "How do you know I'm Lily?"

Tulip hadn't picked up on that, but now that Lily had mentioned it, Tulip found it odd. No one had ever been able to pick the identical twins apart—no one outside of the family, that was.

Matthew chuckled. "I know you're Lily because Daisy just looks different."

Lily pouted. "How so?"

Tulip noticed, by Matthew shifting his weight uncomfortably from one foot to the other, that he was uncomfortable with the question.

"Just different."

"We look the same. Many people say exactly the same and no one but our family can tell us apart. How can you tell us apart?"

"Well, Daisy has got three tiny freckles on each cheek. They're like small pinpoints and to me, her eyebrows look a little darker."

Lily frowned and stared at Tulip. "That's quite unbelievable. She does have those freckles."

"I know." Matthew excused himself when people walked up to his stall.

"What do you think about that, Tulip?" Lily asked in amazement.

"Weird."

"He's in love with Daisy."

Tulip couldn't resist saying, "How do you know he's not in love with you?"

"Do you think so?" Lily stared back at Matthew. "I've never thought of him in that way, but he doesn't have a twin and Daisy and I always said we would marry twins."

"It looks like Matthew misses out on both of you, then." Seeing Rose was now free, Tulip held onto Lily's arm and they both walked forward to say hello.

"So sorry. I've been busy like this all day."

"We came into town to get some material to make dresses," Lily said.

"Did you get any?" Rose asked.

"Oh, Tulip, we should've brought it with us to show Rose."

"*Jah*, I didn't even think of that."

Rose looked around. "Where's Daisy?"

"Home with *Mamm.* She didn't feel too good so Daisy said she would stay home with her."

"I think she's just tired," Tulip added so Rose wouldn't worry. It was bad enough worrying about one parent.

"And you've got the day off, Tulip?"

"Jah, a rare day off. I'm enjoying it."

"Can you come and have lunch with us, Rose?" Lily asked.

"Nee, she can't leave the stall. She brings food, and so do I when I work here."

"Boring!"

Rose and Tulip laughed.

"Can we bring you back something to eat, or a cup of coffee?" Lily asked.

"I'm fine, *denke.*"

"Okay."

Tulip noticed Lily give Matthew a sidelong glance.

"I guess we should keep going, Lily."

"We're going to have lunch somewhere, aren't we?"

"Jah, okay. We'll have lunch then we'll go home and sew."

They said goodbye to Rose and waved to Matthew, who was still serving customers. Just outside the markets, they found a café where they had lunch. All the while Tulip was doing her best to stop thinking about Wilhem, wondering where he was and what he was doing.

THE NEXT TIME Tulip saw Wilhem was Monday morning at the cake shop. He'd walked in, and now he was standing in front of her.

"Are you here to see me?" she asked. She had hoped to see him over the weekend. He'd certainly been on her mind every moment of the last couple of days.

"I'm here for a cup of coffee and to see you."

"You could've mentioned me first, before the coffee, at least."

He smiled and walked closer to her. A glass display cabinet that formed the counter stood between them.

"What will you have?" she asked.

"Just a black coffee today."

"Okay." She walked over and stood in front of the steel coffee machine, shook out a measure of freshly-ground coffee beans, and pressed it into the round container.

"How is your *vadder* today?" he asked.

"He's doing well. They say he'll be all right. He gave everyone a real scare."

"I can imagine he did."

After she pressed the button for the boiling water, she looked over the top of the machine. "How are you settling into the new *haus?*"

"It's great and I'm glad you brought that up. That's why I'm here. I wanted to ask you—"

"For decorating advice?" Tulip gave a little giggle at her own joke.

He laughed. *"Nee,* although some advice probably wouldn't go astray. We've gone for the functional look rather than the ..." He laughed. "I can't think of any other look."

Tulip was pleased that he was the only customer in the shop and the rest of the staff were working in the back.

"Tulip, have dinner with me tonight at my place?"

"I'd like that."

"Good. Shall we say, around seven? I'll come and collect you."

"*Nee*, I'll drive myself."

"Are you sure you want to do that?"

"*Jah.* Otherwise, you've got too much driving to do, back and forward, back and forward."

"I don't mind."

"*Nee*, it's okay. I'll drive myself. Would you like me to bring anything?"

He smiled again. "Just yourself."

Tulip took the filled-to-the-brim take-out cup and fitted a lid onto it. When she handed it to him, his fingertips brushed across hers. She withdrew her hand as a tingle rippled through her body. Had he done that on purpose?

He smiled as though he had. "I'll see you tonight, Tulip."

She nodded and then watched him turn and walk out of the shop. When her eyes dropped to the counter, she saw that at some point he'd placed the money there to pay for the coffee. Tulip giggled to herself. She'd been so distracted by him, she hadn't thought to ask for the money. It reminded her of their very first encounter, when she'd forgotten to pay at the café. Tulip placed the coins in the till and went into the back room to help the girls make tickets for the new cake varieties that Audrey was introducing.

AFTER WORK, Tulip walked into her house. Her father was sitting on the couch.

"Hi, *Dat.*"

"Hello, Tulip. How was your day?"

"Good. The same as most days. I can't complain."

"That's good."

"Will it be all right with you if I go to Wilhem's house for dinner tonight? I won't be home late."

"Who will be there?" he asked.

"Where do you want to go?" Her mother came out of the kitchen wiping her hands on a hand towel.

"I was just asking *Dat* if it is all right if I go to Wilhem's *haus* for dinner tonight?"

"Who else will be there?" she asked.

"No one. It'll just be the two of us. At least, I think it will be the two of us. He didn't mention that Jonathan would be there. Is that all right?"

She watched her mother and father exchange looks before her mother said, "That's fine, but don't be late home. And we're trusting you."

"Of course."

"Your *vadder* doesn't need any more surprises."

"None of us do," Tulip said.

"I must have known you were going out somewhere because I've just baked two batches of whoopie pies. You can take some with you."

"That's not necessary *denke, Mamm.*"

"You can't show up there empty-handed. It's rude." She looked her daughter up and down. "You go and clean yourself up and I'll find a basket for the whoopie pies."

"*Denke.*" Tulip headed to the shower before her parents changed their minds. They both liked Wilhem, that was clear, or they wouldn't have let her go to his house for dinner.

. . .

Just as Tulip approached Wilhem's place, she noticed smoke coming out of the half opened windows. There wasn't enough smoke for the house to be on fire; it seemed to Tulip that someone might have lit a fire in the fireplace and the chimney was blocked or needed cleaning.

After she got out of the buggy, she tied her horse to the post and walked in the already open door. "Hello?" she called out.

Wilhem appeared, coming out from the kitchen with a white tea towel in his hand and looking flustered.

"What's going on?" she asked.

"I burned the dinner."

"What?"

"I burned the dinner."

"I heard you. I'm just surprised that you could do that."

He shook his head. "I planned a nice dinner and now it's ruined."

"I thought the smoke was coming from the fireplace. Is all this smoke coming from what's left of our dinner?"

"I'm afraid so, and now we have nothing to eat. Unless you'd like some stale bread? Or we could get take-out?"

Tulip giggled. "We do have whoopie pies thanks to my *mudder*."

"We do?" His face brightened.

"She insisted I bring them. I'll get them out of the buggy." After she pulled the basket of pies out of the buggy, she moved back the lid of the basket and showed him the pies.

"That'll do me. Would it be bad if we had dessert and nothing else?"

"I wouldn't mind. I've always wanted to do that. Surely it wouldn't hurt us to do that just the once."

"Okay. I'm game." He looked back at the house. "It's too smoky to go inside. We could eat on the porch."

"That'll be fine as long as the fire's out and everything."

"No cause for alarm—literally—and no need for the fire department."

"I'm happy to hear it. As long as everything is under control."

"You sit down." He took the basket from her and then disappeared inside while she sat on one of the two chairs on the porch. Moments later, he returned with two blankets and the whoopie pies on a plate.

He placed the pies down on the table between the two chairs and then spread a blanket over her knees.

"Great, *denke.* It's a bit chilly."

Once he was seated, he pulled his blanket over his lap and leaned closer to her. "I'll make this up to you. I owe you a proper cooked dinner. As soon as I learn how to cook properly, that's what you'll get."

She giggled and picked up a whoopie pie. "Instead of waiting for something that'll never happen, why don't you come for dinner one night at my *haus?*"

"With your *familye?*"

"*Jah,* why not?"

"Yeah, I'd like that."

She took a bite of pie and when she'd swallowed her mouthful, she said, "I'm glad my *mudder* forced me to bring these."

"'Mother knows best'—isn't that what they say?"

"I haven't heard that, but maybe they do." She munched on her whoopie pie and then wondered where Jonathon was. "Where's your housemate tonight?"

Wilhem's brown eyes widened. "He's out with a girl."

"Really?"

He nodded with a hint of a smirk touching his lips.

"Who?"

He chuckled and shook his head at her. "You can't ask me things like that."

"It doesn't matter. I know who it is."

"Do you?"

"*Jah*, I do. It's obvious. How are you going to get all that smoke out of the *haus?*"

"I've opened all the doors and windows and with this breeze, I'm hoping all the smoke will be blown out."

"Everything will probably smell like smoke for a while."

He took a bite of pie and they ate in silence for the next few moments. "There's something I want to say to you, Tulip."

She frowned at him. "Good or bad?"

"Good—I think. Well, it's possibly good." He looked out across the fields and then back to her. "I don't want there to be any misunderstanding between the two of us. I would like it very much if you and I only saw each other and no one else."

"You mean like boyfriend and girlfriend?"

"Exactly like that."

"I would like that, too."

"You would?" When she nodded, he made a motion like wiping sweat off his forehead, causing her to giggle at him. "Phew. I was hoping you would agree. I thought you might have felt the same way as I do, but I didn't want there to be any misunderstanding just in case."

"I'm glad you said that; it's easy to have misunderstandings." Tulip was so happy she felt she would burst. Although it was too cold to be sitting outside and the dinner had been burned, it truly was the company that made the difference—nothing else mattered. "I do have to tell you that a long time ago Nathanial kind of made out to me that you had to leave your old community, or something. I think he was hinting to me that you had a girlfriend."

"He would've been saying that because he wanted you for himself mostly, but there was an element of truth in what he said."

Tulip stared at him, waiting for him to continue.

"I was nearly married to a girl and then changed my mind a few weeks before we married." He looked sad as his gaze fell to the boards of the porch underneath their feet. "It was a terrible thing to do and I felt really bad about it, but I just couldn't go through with it."

Although it wasn't the worst news Tulip could've heard, she still wasn't happy about it. Was he a man who didn't know his own mind? Shouldn't he have been sure about the girl before he asked for her to marry him?

He looked up at her. "Say something."

"Oh, I'm just a bit surprised, that's all."

"Does it make you think any less of me?"

"Not really, but it does give me some questions." Tulip answered as honestly as she possibly could.

"Tell me what questions you have and I'll do my best to answer them for you."

At that moment, all Tulip wanted to do was go home. She thought she'd found the perfect man and everything would work out perfectly and now she just wanted to be back in the safety of her house with her family. She sprang to her feet. "Can we talk about this another time? So much has happened with *Dat* being sick and what happened the other night with Daisy."

He stood up as well. "It does bother you."

"I don't really know. I just need some time to think about things." She took a couple of steps back.

"Don't go, Tulip. We can talk about this. Adele wasn't the right woman for me and I knew that."

Adele? Maybe she was being silly, but the fact that he had nearly married a woman called Adele that she didn't even know made Wilhem feel like a total stranger. Wilhem had been her picture of a perfect man and now she didn't know who he was. In her mind's eye, she saw a young woman called Adele crying over him and here he was in a different community asking another girl to be his girlfriend after he'd just broken Adele's heart. It didn't feel right.

Tulip looked at his pleading eyes and opened her mouth to speak but no words came out. She turned and walked to her buggy.

"Where are you going?" He followed after her.

"Home."

"Why has this upset you so much?" he asked.

She couldn't articulate why this felt wrong to her; there were so many reasons why it did. "I don't know, Wilhem. I don't think we should see each other for a while."

His mouth fell open in shock. "Is that what you really want? Because that's not what you said a moment ago."

"I didn't know that you are capable of breaking a woman's heart a moment ago."

He stepped closer to her. "Break ups aren't easy on anyone. It was better to happen before we got married than for us to go ahead with the wedding and have a miserable marriage. Don't you think so?"

"If you didn't get along, why did you ask her to marry you?" Tulip shook her head. "Don't answer that."

"I've got nothing to hide. I want to tell you everything."

Tulip had had too much drama over the past weeks, enough to last her for some time. As well as that, the horrible incidents that she'd had with Nathanial were still fresh in her mind. "Can we talk about this later? I need to go." She climbed up into the buggy and took hold of the leather reins.

He stepped closer to her. "We kind of fell into things because our parents wanted us to marry. I went along with it all without thinking too much about it, and then when I spent more time with her I realized we were totally unsuitable. By that time, I didn't have the courage to end things. That's why I left it so long."

Now he'd caught her attention. "What do you mean by the courage to end things?" To her, ending something seemed cowardly.

"It was a hard thing to do. I knew Adele would be upset, and all her friends and family, after they'd been planning the wedding. I had it in my mind I would just go along with it, but in the end I just couldn't go through with it. Everyone was mad with me and I knew they would be. I knew everybody was staring at me and talking about me, so I just had to get away for a while and that's why I came here. My parents weren't happy with me either because I'd gone back on my word. To me, it would have been worse to go ahead when I wasn't in love."

Tulip looked down at her hands and saw that she had been

holding onto the reins so tightly that her knuckles had gone white.

"You see, Tulip, I was caught in a trap and there was no way out where everyone would be happy. If I'd gone ahead and married her, things would've been bad, and if I didn't, they would've been bad too. In the end, Adele deserved to be with a man who truly loved her and that man wasn't me." He shook his head.

She appreciated the way he was so calm and explained things to her so nicely. *"Denke* for telling me all that."

"So, do you feel better about the whole thing now that I've told you how it was?"

"I do."

A slight frown marred his perfect forehead. "Are you going to get down from that buggy?"

"I really should get home to my parents. Things haven't been easy for them lately."

"I understand, but are things between us okay?"

Tulip nodded. "They are. I'm just not good with surprises and I tend to think the worst."

"Denke for coming here tonight. You will go out with me again, won't you?"

"Of course I will."

"Gut. I might see you at work tomorrow when I call in for coffee. And I'm sorry again about dinner."

Tulip managed a little laugh. "You should try and get the smoke smell out of the house before Jonathan comes home."

Wilhem grinned. *"Jah,* I'll do that right now." He took hold of the horse's cheek strap and turned him toward the road. "Bye,

Tulip," he said as he stopped and let go of the horse. The horse walked past him.

"I'll see you later." Tulip needed to process everything. It was a huge shock to learn that he'd gone back on his word. She'd always seen herself with someone who was upstanding and true to his word. It seemed like Wilhem wasn't the man she hoped he was. More than anything, Tulip wanted to marry a good man like her father. What she needed was to tell Rose what happened and listen to her opinion about the matter. She hoped Rose wouldn't mind her stopping by unexpectedly at this hour of the evening.

When she stopped her horse and buggy outside Rose and Mark's *haus*, Mark came outside to meet her.

"Oh, it's you, Tulip. I couldn't see who it was in the dark. Is your *vadder* okay?"

"*Jah*, he's fine. I wanted to steal your new *fraa* away for a couple of moments if that's okay. I need some older *schweschder* advice."

"Sure. She's in the kitchen. We've just finished dinner. You head inside and I'll secure your horse and give him some water."

"*Denke*, Mark."

"Hello," Tulip called out as she stepped through the doorway into Rose's house.

Rose came to the doorway of the kitchen and then went to hug her. "What are you doing here? Is everything okay?"

"*Dat's* fine if that's what you mean."

"What's going on? Why are you here so late? Not that I'm complaining. It's nice to have you here at whatever time of the day, or night."

"Can we sit down? I need to ask your advice about something."

"Come into the kitchen."

When they were both seated, Tulip began, "Wilhem invited me to dinner at his *haus* that he shares with Jonathon. He made a mess of things because the dinner got burned because he can't cook, and anyway, we ended up sitting out on the porch and then he told me something that shocked me. And if I hadn't brought it up, I might never have known."

"How could you have brought it up if you didn't know about it?"

"Nathanial hinted at something not been right with Wilhem and the reason he was here." She leaned in and whispered, "He hinted it was something like the reason that Jacob had come here."

"What did you find out?" Rose asked, leaning forward slightly.

"I don't know if I'm overreacting, and I need your advice. It wasn't as bad as the Jacob situation. I shouldn't have brought that up." Tulip took a deep breath. "Wilhem was supposed to be marrying someone and he ended the relationship just weeks before the wedding. He said their parents expected them to get married and he was just going along with it. Then he decided that they didn't really get along enough to be married."

"What's wrong with that?" Rose asked. "Is the girl—"

"*Nee,* nothing like that. I just keep picturing the poor girl being so upset that he ended things. He said she deserved to be married to someone who loved her."

"I can't see what the problem is. It's not as though he got married."

"I know, but I just wanted someone fresh, with no past. It was a shock for me to find that out. I wouldn't mind someone to have had a girlfriend or even two or three, but to have actually arranged a whole wedding and everything—"

"If he told you so soon, it doesn't sound like he was deliberately keeping it from you."

Tulip sighed. "Before he told me, he said he wanted me to be his girlfriend."

"That's *wunderbaar.* That's what you want, isn't it?"

"That's what I wanted. It's just that with all the drama you went through with Jacob and then all the fuss with Nathanial, I just want someone with no bad things in their past."

"He didn't want to marry the girl and he was honest. You can't blame him for that."

"I know that, but it sounded like he wasn't honest about it for a long time and he should've ended things sooner if that was the case." Tulip rubbed her forehead, hoping she was explaining her feelings properly to Rose.

"People learn from their mistakes. He was young at the time and probably thought he was doing the right thing going along with what his parents wanted, until he thought about the rest of his life with the woman he didn't love."

"I know, but did he love her and then change his mind? That's what I'm really worried about. I don't want to be with someone changeable like that."

"You have to ask him that."

Tulip slowly nodded. *"Denke* for talking to me. I feel a little better about things now."

"How's everyone at home?"

"Good. It feels a bit strange there without you."

"Come over here any time. You can even stay for a few days if you want to."

Tulip giggled. "You're newlyweds. I wouldn't want to get in the way."

"Do you want some hot tea or something to eat, perhaps?"

Right on cue, Tulip's stomach growled, possibly objecting to the whoopie pies that she'd eaten instead of a proper dinner. Tulip laughed. "Did you hear that?"

"Was that your stomach?"

"Jah. I wouldn't mind something to eat, *denke."*

"I can make you a sandwich with the leftover meat from dinner."

"Sounds delicious."

"We only had meatloaf."

"I love meatloaf."

Rose giggled and pulled out the leftovers from the gas-powered fridge. "You can give me a hand by slicing the bread."

Tulip stood up and opened the bread bin and pulled out the nearly full loaf. As she sawed through the bread with the serrated knife, her thoughts turned back to what Wilhem had told her. "Tell me honestly, Rose, do you think I'm worrying too much about nothing?"

"It sounds like you might be." She put a hand out for the bread and when Tulip handed her the two slices, she asked, "Butter?"

"Nee denke. It's fine like that."

"There you are." Rose handed her the sandwich on a plate and they both sat back down.

"I'm really hungry and this looks so good." She bit into the sandwich.

"I think you just worry because we've both had troubling things happen to us. Me with Jacob and you with Nathanial, and then there was what happened to Daisy with Nathanial. Wilhem's nothing like them from what I know of him and from what you've told me about him."

Tulip finished chewing. "I believe what he said, but it just doesn't feel perfect anymore."

"But maybe it is perfect and you should appreciate that rather than worrying about how you thought things should be or would be. He obviously really likes you a lot, so don't let what happened in the past come between the two of you. Besides, it wasn't his fault that his parents wanted him to marry that girl—the wrong girl. None of it was really his doing from what you told me."

"He shouldn't have let himself get dragged into it." Tulip looked down at the second-hand wooden kitchen table, scratched and marked from years of wear. Rose and Mark didn't have much to start their married lives, but they were happy. All they needed was each other. Mark was an honest man and she wanted someone like that. He'd only ever loved Rose. There had never been another woman in his life.

"I told you before, these things come with maturity and he was probably trying to please his parents and that's got to be a good thing." Rose leaned in closer, and whispered, "I always thought I would marry a man a lot taller than me and who looked different from Mark. There was this picture in my mind, and that picture became Jacob when I saw him."

"That was a total disaster."

"It was, and my perfect man was there all along right in front of me and I didn't know it. Maybe if Jacob hadn't jolted

394

me out of my silliness, or whatever it was, my eyes would never have opened to see Mark." Rose tapped on the side of her head with her finger. "It's the ideas we've stored in our head about how our husbands should be that ruin things for us."

"I suppose that's true."

"It is and just like I always thought my husband would look a certain way, it sounds to me that you wanted someone who had never had an upheaval with a woman in his past. I just don't think that's realistic if you want someone older than yourself. Most boys start going out with girls at sixteen or seventeen. If you find someone special, you have to hold onto them, overlook the small things, and be grateful that they have the qualities that are important."

Tulip exhaled deeply. "I know you're right, but it's not knowing all the details of when he was about to get married that worries me. Just think, if he and I get married, he would've gone through all the pre-wedding stuff before. It's kind of ruined."

"You should be pleased that he didn't get married. If he had, you would never have met him."

"I know, I know. I thought about that."

"Do you think he's lying to you about something or not telling you the whole truth?"

"*Nee.*"

"Then what are you worried about? Just ask him anything you want to know."

Tulip finished off the last portion of her sandwich while thinking about all that her older sister had just said.

Rose continued, "You're probably just upset about what

happened to *Dat* with his heart problem. That's upset everybody."

"It gave me a real scare. I thought he was dead there for a moment. You're right. I don't think I've gotten over that shock." Tulip dusted the crumbs from her hands. *"Denke* again for the sandwich. I should go now. I'm glad we talked."

"Me too."

The sisters hugged before Tulip walked with her sister to the front door. "Bye, Mark," she said when she saw him reading the paper on the couch. *"Denke* for taking care of the horse and letting me have ten minutes with Rose."

He chuckled. "Any time. Bye, Tulip. It was good to see you again."

"Bye." Tulip stepped out into the cold night air.

During the short ride back to her house, she decided to put Wilhem out of her mind for a day or two. Then she might be able to see things a little clearer. She was certain Rose was right, and she had to wait until she got used to the idea that things weren't as she thought they were. What probably annoyed her most was that Nathanial had hinted that Wilhem was there to get away from a problem and it turned out that he was right.

When Tulip walked into the house, instead of her mother and father on the couch, there were Daisy and Lily. "Have *Mamm* and *Dat* gone to bed already?"

"Jah. How was your big date night?" Lily asked.

Tulip put on a bright smile, not wanting the twins to know that she was upset. "It was a lot of fun." She sat down on the couch with them.

"What did you do?" asked Daisy.

"Just this and that. He cooked dinner for me but then

burned it. What did you two do tonight?"

Daisy nodded her head at some sewing on a table nearby. "We finished off some of our sewing that we started the other day."

"*Jah,* and then we got tired of doing that."

"And we were just about to go to bed when we heard the buggy outside, so we thought we'd wait up to hear about your night."

"Can you give us a few details about what happened on your date?" Daisy asked.

"Did you kiss him?" Lily asked, which made Daisy giggle.

"I can't tell you about things like that. *Nee,* I didn't, if you must know. Anyway, what about the two of you? I saw you both talking to men at Rose's wedding. Do either of you like anyone?"

"Why would we tell you if we did?" Lily asked.

"Because I just told you an answer to the question you asked me. That's why."

"*Jah,* Lily, tell her who you're interested in," Daisy said.

"Me? Why don't you tell her who you're interested in?"

Tulip giggled. As annoying as the twins were, she was glad to be home among everything that was familiar. When she was at home, she didn't have to worry about stepping out of her comfort zone. Maybe she wasn't ready for a real boyfriend just yet, even though many of the people her age in the community were now married. Perhaps she was just a late bloomer.

"What's funny?" Daisy asked, staring into Tulip's face.

"Life's funny in many ways."

Lily rolled her eyes. "You won't get any sense out of her because she's in love."

"Then why didn't you kiss him?" Daisy asked.

"I don't know him well enough."

When Tulip saw Daisy and Lily exchange glances, she explained, "I'm not going to kiss anyone until I know them really well, until I'm in love."

"See, Lily, she's not in love yet."

"I think she is because she keeps smiling. Unless she's not telling us the truth. Are you lying to us, Tulip?"

"I'd have absolutely no reason to do that."

"Why are you grinning like you've got a secret then?" Lily asked.

Tulip replied, "I didn't know I was."

"This is boring. I'm going to bed." Daisy jumped to her feet.

"Wait up." Lily stood as well and then they took a lamp upstairs with them, leaving Tulip alone.

Tulip leaned back on the couch with her hands behind her head. It wasn't often she could sit down in the peace and quiet. The house was always so noisy. To keep her mind off the man she was trying not to think about, she leaned forward and picked up one of the twins' sewing and began where she had left off.

THE NEXT TIME Tulip saw Wilhem was two days later when she was leaving work. She was pleased to see him leaning against her buggy.

He straightened up when he saw her approach. "Hello. I hope it's all right, me being here."

"It is."

"Things were kind of left a bit awkward the other night when I burned the food."

A small giggle escaped Tulip's lips when she thought about the smoke-filled house. He leaned down beside him and picked up a basket. "You left this basket at my *haus.*"

"You didn't have to make a special trip. We've got plenty of baskets."

"I wanted to see you." He took a step closer. "I know you were upset the other night to learn about Adele, but there's no reason to be."

"I'm just upset for her, that's all. She must've been very disappointed."

"She might've been more disappointed if we had married and the feelings weren't there between us."

"Wilhem, the thing that I think scares me is that I don't want to be *that* girl. The girl who thinks she's getting married and then the man runs away from her. And if I'm truthful, deep down in my heart, I wonder what will happen if we get close to marriage and then you do the same thing to me." She was being as honest with him as she possibly could.

"That would never happen, Tulip. I feel something for you in my heart that I've never felt for another girl—ever. Things are different with you."

"I'm scared."

He nodded. "I understand that, but I don't know what to do about it. All I can do is tell you how I feel and tell you that if my parents were forcing me to marry you, I would've gladly gone ahead with it."

She couldn't stop herself from smiling. "You would've?"

"Not only that, I would've told them to bring the wedding

forward." He laughed. "I don't know why you're looking so surprised. I thought you knew how I felt about you."

"Not so much, but I'm glad I know now. It makes me feel better."

"Can we start where we left off? You agreed to be my girl-friend, remember?"

"I remember."

"Let's start from there and then when we get to know one another better I might let you marry me."

Tulip put her hand to her mouth and giggled. "If we married, I have to tell you now that I would never allow you to cook."

"Not fair. I like cooking. You can't prevent me from cooking over one incident."

"I can if that one incident nearly caused you to burn your *haus* down."

He laughed. "I guess that's fair enough. If you agree to marry me, I'll stay out of the kitchen."

"Good."

"So was that a yes?"

"A yes to what?"

"To marrying me?"

She stared into his eyes to see if he was serious. "Really?"

"I would marry you tomorrow if you said yes."

"We've not known each other for that long."

He took a step toward her. "We have a lifetime to discover things about one another. I tell you what, why don't you take as much time as you want to decide, knowing that you already have my heart. When you're ready, I'll be ready to marry you."

She wondered if he was making this grand gesture to make

her feel secure. If he was doing it for that reason, it had worked. All fear left her now that she knew how serious he was about her and their relationship. "Okay. I like that idea."

"Can I be so bold as to take up that invitation from the other night for dinner with your *familye* once your *vadder* recovers enough for visitors?"

"*Jah,* I'd like that. *Dat's* okay now."

"What about Wednesday night next week?"

"Perfect. I'll cook your favorite food."

"You remember?"

"*Jah,* of course I do."

TULIP TOOK an early shift on Wednesday so she could cook the dinner just the way Wilhem had said he liked it. The twins weren't teasing her as they helped, as she thought they would. They seemed intrigued by Wilhem and were asking all kinds of questions.

"So he's Jonathan's cousin?" Daisy asked.

"*Jah,* that's right."

"So *Dat* knows the *familye?*" Lily asked.

"I'm not sure, but he knows Jonathan's family."

"If you marry him, will you have to move away?" Lily asked.

That hadn't even occurred to Tulip. She'd only thought as far as marrying him and not what their life would be like afterward. He could very well expect her to move anywhere. The last thing she wanted was to move away from her family. He'd said he would work there for a few months, then what after that? What if he was the type of man who liked to move around, staying a few months here and a few months there? She couldn't live like that.

"Well?" Daisy asked since Tulip was taking time to answer Lily's question.

"To answer your question properly, Lily, that's something I don't know."

"Yeah, well, would you move away if he wanted you to?"

"Can we talk about something else? You're making me nervous."

"It's just that we don't want you to move away," Lily said.

"We'd miss you," Daisy added.

"I'd miss both of you too and I wouldn't want to move away, but if I was really in love with someone and married, we might have to move to find work or something."

When their mother came into the kitchen, the girls stopped talking.

"How's the dinner coming along?"

"Fine, *Mamm.* I thought you agreed to have a rest and let us do the cooking?"

"I was trying to have a rest and then I heard a lot of talk from the kitchen. It smells good."

"Denke," Tulip and Daisy said at the same time.

Their mother fixed her eyes on Daisy. "When our guest arrives, don't forget it was Tulip who did all this. All you did was help her."

"I know that. She did most of it."

"Good, and it needs to be perceived that way as well, with no confusion."

Tulip turned away from her mother before she burst out laughing. Her mother was so desperate to get her married off to a nice man that she thought Tulip was trying to woo him with her cooking. Her mother was so old-fashioned that way.

"I feel like I can never do anything right," Daisy said. "I'll be sure to tell him that *she* did it all and I did nothing to help. Would you be happy then, *Mamm?*"

"Don't be ridiculous. You're close to being sent to your room and having dinner up there as well."

"Sorry."

"Now, no more silliness. This is an important dinner for Tulip, so you can apologize to her as well."

Tulip felt sorry for Daisy, but not sorry enough to intervene and risk getting on the wrong side of their mother.

"Sorry, Tulip."

"That's okay."

Mamm said, "I'll sit back down with your *vadder* if I'm not needed in here."

Tulip said, "We're fine in here *denke, Mamm.*"

When their mother had left the room, Daisy shook her head. "What's wrong with her? She must've got out on the wrong side of bed this morning."

"She's nervous about dinner." Tulip opened the oven door and checked on the meat.

"Why should she be nervous about dinner? If anyone should be nervous it should be you."

"She wants to get me married off." The meat was perfectly done. She switched the oven off. "Now for the gravy."

"Can I do that? I love making gravy. And I'll pretend you did it."

"You don't have to pretend I made it. That's silly," Tulip said.

Daisy raised her fine, dark eyebrows. "Tell *Mamm* that."

"Oh, yeah." Tulip giggled. "Well, just don't say anything in front of Wilhem because you'll get into trouble."

The girls placed the roasted lamb and vegetables into a separate pot to keep them hot while Daisy made gravy from the pan juices.

Lily had just finished setting the table when they heard a buggy.

"This'll be him," Lily squawked.

"Don't look too excited," Daisy whispered. "Just play it cool."

Tulip hoped she hadn't made a big mistake by inviting him there. Then she remembered he'd invited himself. If things got really bad she'd remind him of that. He'd see the funny side. How bad could her family be to the man she was interested in? She would soon find out because she could hear her mother opening the front door.

"Go out and greet him," Lily quietly urged.

"I will. I'm just checking on a few things in here first."

"We'll look at everything in here. You go."

"Okay, I'm going." Tulip grabbed a hand towel, wiped her hands, and then headed out to see Wilhem.

By the time she got to the living room, he was sandwiched on the couch between her mother and her father, looking most uncomfortable. He looked up and smiled when he saw Tulip approaching him and gave her a nod. She gave him a little wave and sat down to listen to what her mother was talking to him about.

"Well, Mrs. Yoder, I'm not totally certain how long I'll be here. I could stay longer depending on the job."

"Dinner is only going to be a couple of minutes away," Tulip said.

"Oh, Tulip. Look at what Wilhem brought me."

Tulip looked to where her mother pointed. There was a huge vase of flowers. He was certainly trying to win her mother over and it looked like it was working. "Oh, they look lovely and so colorful."

"It was so thoughtful. Every flower represents the name of each one of you girls—roses, tulips, lilies, and daisies."

Wilhem chuckled. "I couldn't come here empty-handed, Mrs. Yoder, not when you made all those lovely whoopie pies for Tulip and me the other night."

"Did you like them?"

"They were the best I've tasted."

"Nancy is a fine cook," Tulip's father told Wilhem. "Now, when I married her, she wasn't so good, but she's come a long way."

Nancy cackled. "We had a few mishaps along the way, but that was before I had a proper stove, Hezekiah."

Hezekiah teased his wife, saying, "Well, they say a poor workman blames his tools."

Nancy made *tsk tsk* sounds. "Don't listen to him, Wilhem."

Wilhem looked like he didn't know what to say, then after a few awkward seconds said, "The dinner smells *wunderbaar*."

"Our Tulip cooks well," her mother said. "She's rearranged her work to cook this meal. She said that roasted lamb with vegetables and gravy is your favorite meal."

He looked over at Tulip and smiled. "I'm glad you remembered."

"And I think there will be enough crispy pieces for you." She told her mother and father, "He likes the meat well done on the outside."

"*Jah*, it's tasty like that," her father said to Wilhem.

"I should see how it's coming along." Tulip went into the kitchen and checked on everything. Then she whispered to each twin to act naturally around her guest and not say anything to embarrass her. They said they would. Tulip stepped back into the living room and told everyone the dinner was ready.

They all sat down at the table with Mr. Yoder at the head. Everyone bowed their heads to say their silent prayer of thanks for the food.

When Tulip opened her eyes, she noticed that the meat had already been sliced. That was something that their father used to do. Mrs. Yoder took Wilhem's plate and filled it with food. It was an odd thing for her mother to do, but it reinforced to Tulip that her mother approved of him.

Tulip barely had to do any talking because her mother and father chatted away to Wilhem quite happily. They asked him about people they knew from his community. That was fine but then they got onto what kind of work he was capable of doing and what he'd done in the past. At one point, Tulip nearly had to tell her parents that they sounded like they were interviewing him for a job. Then she realized they kind of were. They were interviewing him as a potential husband for her. Thankfully, the twins had just eaten dinner quietly while looking bored throughout. All Tulip wanted was to be alone with him.

When it came time for dessert, Tulip was pleased to leave the table. The twins helped by clearing the dishes and helping Tulip place the dessert of fruit salad, ice-cream, and cheesecake in the center of the table.

Once her father started to help himself to the food, Tulip noticed that Wilhem quickly did the same—a sign that he too thought it a little odd that Tulip's mother put food on his plate. Since Tulip couldn't get a word in edgeways between her parents firing questions at Wilhem, she had time to notice these things. To think that she'd been worried about the twins making him feel uncomfortable! Wilhem was handling it all well, although his cheeks were getting a little rosy.

Her parents hadn't questioned Mark like that before he married Rose, but then again, Rose and Mark had grown up together and Wilhem was someone they'd met only recently.

Wilhem didn't wait long after dinner to thank everyone and say goodnight. He'd stayed for a cup of coffee and more talk in the living room—just long enough to be polite.

Tulip walked out to his buggy with him.

"I'm so sorry about all of that," Tulip said.

"About what?"

"The interrogation. Don't pretend you didn't notice. I saw you getting all hot and flustered."

He chuckled.

"Oh, and those flowers—you won *Mamm's* heart with the flowers."

"Good. I'm glad she liked them. I got them from your *schweschder* at the markets. I told her I was coming here and wanted to bring flowers."

"So having the four different flowers was Rose's idea?"

"Nee. I had the idea of getting her flowers to represent the four of her *dochders."*

Tulip giggled. "I think you passed the test."

"You think so?"

407

"Jah, I think *Mamm* wants to adopt you. She never puts food on people's plates like that. I didn't know what she was doing at first. She sometimes puts meat on plates for guests, but that's only when she's doing the same with everyone else."

"I like your parents."

They walked down the porch steps.

"Me too. You got off easy tonight. Usually the twins are talkative and out of control. I had to warn them not to embarrass me."

"You shouldn't have done that. It might have been entertaining."

Tulip giggled once more. "You don't think my parents were entertaining enough?"

"They were all right. It's only normal for them to want to know more about me. Do they know that we're … close?"

"Jah. They figured that out. *Denke* for coming tonight. I feel a little closer to you now that you've been here and survived dinner."

"I've passed the test, have I?" He reached for her hand and took it in his.

"Ten out of ten."

"Really? I've done well. How are you feeling now about the incident in my past?" They'd just reached the buggy and he turned to face her.

"It's not as though you got married."

"Jah, but you knew that the other day, yet it still bothered you."

"It doesn't any longer."

"I think it might bother you a little. It's hard to get over something that quickly. I could see it upset you."

"There are two different ways of looking at the situation and I was looking at it in the worst and most negative way." She shook her head. "It was silly of me."

"Your feelings aren't silly. You can't help the way you feel."

She was starting to like him more and more. It was as though she finally had someone of her very own. Someone who'd always be her special person and always be on her side no matter what. "That's nice of you to say."

"I'm not saying it to be nice. I want you to be sure about me and I don't want to pressure you into anything. I know I gave your parents the impression that I didn't know how long I'd be here for, but I can be here for as long as I want. There's permanent work available for me here if I want it."

"You'd stay on?"

He nodded. *"Jah.* I don't know how much to say to you because I don't want you to feel obligated to me. There's nothing worse than feeling trapped. I've decided to stay here because I want to build a future with you. There, I've said it." He leaned against his buggy, still holding onto her hand as they faced each other.

"Really?" Tulip licked her lips.

"Jah, but if you change your mind, I'll accept that. Don't think you have to be with me because I want to be with you." He picked up her other hand to hold it as well.

His words told her how much he liked her. They also showed her how he had felt when he'd felt obliged to marry someone his parents thought suitable.

He glanced over her shoulder at her house. "Tonight was special."

"It was a little tense and we hardly had time to say anything to each other."

"Tonight was for them—your parents. If they feel comfortable with me, maybe you'll trust me more. I'll never disappoint you, Tulip, and I'll never let you down."

As they stood there under the moon and the stars, Tulip knew what he said was true.

Six months later...

NANCY HAD MADE a new family rule since her husband's health scare six months ago and that was that they would all gather at her house on the first Saturday of every month for a *familye* dinner.

As the family sat down for one of their dinners, Wilhem, who had been invited to join them, spoke up. "I have an announcement to make tonight."

Mr. Yoder chuckled. "This will be an interesting dinner. I can't imagine what news there could be."

"I can," Daisy said.

Lily piped up. "I could take a good guess, too."

"Well, the sooner you make that announcement, the sooner we can say our thanks for the food," Trevor, the second oldest son, said.

Nancy looked around at her two sons and four daughters. They were all grown up and she had two lovely daughters-in-law, one granddaughter, and one wonderful son-in-law. She looked at her second oldest daughter and the man she'd been spending most of her spare time with, Wilhem. The two of them kept staring lovingly into each other's eyes and Nancy knew they were going to say they were going to marry.

Mr. Yoder cleared his throat. "We have Wilhem who wants to say something. Is there anyone else who wants to say something?"

Nancy knew that her husband was hoping that one of their sons, or maybe Rose, would tell them they were having a baby. Looking at them now, Nancy knew that they had no such news. Her eyes drifted to young Shirley in the highchair. She'd have to be the only one for a while yet, it seemed.

Everyone looked at Wilhem. "Shall I say it now, or after dinner? Or maybe after we give thanks for the food?"

Tulip gave an embarrassed giggle.

Mr. Yoder said, "You can't make us wait any longer. Tell us what you've got to say."

Wilhem smiled and glanced at Tulip before he looked at the others at the table. "Tulip has finally agreed to marry me."

"I knew it!" Daisy squealed.

"For real?" Lily asked.

Wilhem laughed. *"Jah,* for real."

Mrs. Yoder stood up and ran to hug Tulip and then Wilhem. Mr. Yoder and Tulip's brothers shook Wilhem's hand, while Tulip's sisters all got up to hug her. When everyone had congratulated the couple, they all sat back down.

"Well, I didn't expect that tonight," Mrs. Yoder said. "We'll have to start organizing everything tomorrow, Tulip. We'll go into town and buy material to make the dresses."

"Can Daisy and I be your attendants?" Lily asked Tulip.

"Of course you can. I want you both to be my attendants, if

you'll behave."

"What do you mean, Tulip? We always behave."

Tulip laughed. "We'll talk about that later."

"We should give thanks before this food gets cold," Peter said.

"*Jah*, we should," Mr. Yoder said.

They all closed their eyes and each gave their silent prayer of thanks for the food.

As everyone finished, they began to help themselves to the food in the center of the table. Except for young Shirley, who'd been happily mushing cooked vegetables onto the plate while managing to get some of them into her mouth.

The twins talked excitedly between themselves about what color their dresses would be and how they wanted them, while Nancy's daughters-in-law and Rose gave Tulip wedding advice.

WHEN THE DINNER was done and Wilhem was ready to leave, Tulip walked outside with him to say goodbye.

"I think that went well," he whispered as he leaned against his buggy. "Your *mudder* didn't cry, and your *vadder* didn't have another heart attack."

Tulip giggled and put her head on his shoulder. "They like you."

"The twins are excited."

"It's hard to tell. They're like that about most things." Tulip shivered. "It's cold."

Wilhem put his arms around her and held her close. "I can't wait until we're married and we can start our life together."

"Me too. I've never been happier." Tulip was pleased that

they had taken the time to get to know each other and hadn't rushed into anything. Without a doubt, she knew that he was the man for her.

"I must go. I've got an early start tomorrow. Go inside; it's cold." He leaned down and kissed her cheek. "I love you, Tulip."

"I love you too," she whispered back.

Wilhem climbed into his buggy and turned the horse around, and Tulip watched as he headed back down the driveway. She looked forward to the time when they could live together as man and wife. When a chilling gust of wind swept over her, she hurried back into the house.

To Tulip's surprise, the twins had ordered their parents to relax in the lounge room while they cleaned the kitchen and did the washing up. Tulip stayed in the kitchen helping the twins.

NANCY WAS PLEASED that everyone in their family seemed to have their life in good order.

"I don't think I can take any more happiness," Nancy said, as she held Hezekiah's hand. "I'm glad that Tulip will marry Wilhem; I really like him."

He leaned closer and whispered, "You weren't so certain about Mark at the start."

"I was sure he was a good man, but I wasn't convinced that he was a match for Rose, but he was. Look how happy they are now."

Hezekiah nodded. "They've all made *gut* choices."

"I'm worried about the twins. I think we'll have problems with those two."

Hezekiah chuckled. "I think you worry too much."

CHAPTER 26

TULIP STOOD next to Wilhem as they were pronounced man and wife. This was the day she'd waited many months for. Wilhem took her hand and gave her a quick kiss on the cheek and together they walked out of Tulip's parents' house. It was the second wedding there, the first being Rose's.

When Tulip stepped outside, she felt good in the blue dress her mother had sewn for her. She'd wanted to make it herself, but had given in to her mother's wishes and instead she'd helped the twins sew their dark green dresses. The twins hadn't been too happy about wearing that shade, but Tulip considered that it suited their coloring the best.

"We're finally married," he whispered to her as they walked over to the main wedding-breakfast table.

As the twins' giggles rang out close behind her, she said, "I'm glad."

"I hope I make you happy, Tulip."

"You already have, and you will."

He smiled and when they reached the table, he pulled out her chair for her. She sat down, and reminded herself to remember every single moment of the day. When Wilhem sat beside her, she looked across to the house to see her father step through the doorway. Tulip silently thanked God that He had spared her father from the close call he'd had many months ago. Her father was there to see her get married, and for that she was grateful.

After a minor squabble about who was going to sit beside her, the twins took their places next to her. Either Daisy won, or Lily forfeited, Tulip wasn't certain; all she knew was that Daisy sat closest to her and then Lily sat next to Daisy. Compared to their usual behavior, they were conducting themselves as mature young ladies. Tulip was proud of them for making the effort. Two of Wilhem's older married brothers sat on the other side of him.

Jonathon had moved back in with his parents to save money and, after this wedding, Tulip was certain that he and Chelsea would announce their wedding soon. She guessed that was why Jonathon had made the move. The house that Jonathon and Wilhem had shared would become the first house Tulip and Wilhem lived in as man and wife.

It felt strange to Tulip that she was on the other side of the wedding table this time and not running around helping with the food. This was one wedding she wanted her mother to enjoy. She had asked her mother to sit close to her and leave everything up to the other ladies, just this once.

. . .

Nancy looked at her second-oldest daughter sitting next to her new husband, and leaned into Hezekiah. "Do you feel old? Most of our *kinner* are married and we only have two to go."

He laughed. "You make it sound like some kind of game when you say 'two to go.' Like you're hitting balls and you've only the remaining two."

"*Nee*, I didn't mean it like that. Now that we're only going to have the twins at home, I want them to stay for a few more years."

"They'll work things out for themselves. If you've found out something, Nancy, it should be that no matter what you do or say, you have little influence over them when they become adults. And that's the way it should be. We bring them up as well as we can, and then we must trust that their values are sound."

"*Jah*," Nancy said, turning slightly to stare at her three daughters sitting at the wedding table, and then looking around for the remainder of her grown up children. "It's hard for a *mudder* to let them go, but at the same time, I want them to marry early so they have the best choice. The twins are already drawing close to their next birthday and if they wait too long …"

"They'll miss out," Hezekiah finished the sentence for her.

"I know you think I'm silly, but …"

"*Gott* needs people's actions to fulfill His will."

Nancy's mouth fell open. "How did you know I was going to say that?"

He shook his head. "And you think that the Lord needs your help to fulfill His plans?"

"It sounds silly when you say it." Nancy chortled.

"You've got one wedding where you can sit down and enjoy yourself. You're always so busy running here and there doing things for people. Do you think the world would stop if *you* stopped?"

Nancy stared into her husband's wise eyes and realized that she had been carrying many burdens.

He took hold of her hand. "Why do you think Tulip asked you to sit down for the meal rather than be in the kitchen? She wants you to share the enjoyment of today. And I want you to slow down and stop thinking of so many different things. The world will keep going without you being like an ox pulling the plow alone."

"I'm just trying to be helpful."

He squeezed her hand. "The time has come for you to be helpful to yourself and you might just find that things will work out the same without you. Maybe it's time to give others opportunities to be more helpful."

"That doesn't sound nice."

"You know what I mean."

She gave a little giggle. "All I can do is try."

"That's all I ask."

Nancy looked around her. There were some young men visiting that she hadn't met before and they looked about the right age for the twins. Her eyes were drawn to a particular young man because he was looking in one direction only. She glanced over her shoulder at the twins to work out which one he was staring at.

"Nancy, what did I just say?" Hezekiah asked her.

She narrowed her eyes and studied him for a moment. It was as though he knew what she'd been thinking.

When she opened her mouth to say something in her own defense, he said, "I know what you think before you do, and I know what you'll say before you say it. Just now, you were looking around for husbands for the twins, weren't you?"

She sighed. She'd been caught out.

He rubbed his knuckles against the beard on his chin. "Did you listen to a word I said just now? Let things follow their natural course like …"

"Like a boat sailing down the river?" Nancy tried to hold in her laughter. Hezekiah was always likening things in life to traveling down a river or a stream in a boat—mostly a sailboat. "You see, I know you pretty well too."

Hezekiah shook his head at her. Nancy leaned forward and when she had a quick look around and saw no one was looking, she gave her husband a kiss on his cheek. He smiled and Nancy knew that he knew she was going to continue doing what she'd always done. And she knew that he wouldn't mind.

∾

The End of Book 2.

AMISH DAISY

AMISH LOVE BLOOMS BOOK 3

SAMANTHA PRICE

CHAPTER 1

"Daisy May Yoder!"

Daisy cringed when she heard her mother's shrill voice calling to her from the kitchen. It was never good when *Mamm* used her full name. "I'll be right there, *Mamm!*"

"That's what you said five minutes ago. I need you here *now!*"

Knowing her mother wasn't going to give up, she stomped down the stairs. It was Tuesday, and every Tuesday her mother sent her and her twin sister, Lily, around the community with food for anyone who was ill, elderly, or for some reason couldn't get food for themselves. Lily had already left the house earlier to take a chicken meal to old Mary Stoltzfus, and now the second buggy was hitched and waiting outside for Daisy to take some food to recently widowed Valerie Miller.

It wasn't that she didn't want to take the food to Valerie; it was just that—what could she possibly say to her? Dirk Miller's funeral was only a week ago. He'd drowned in a nearby river, and Daisy had heard talk that Dirk had taken his own life. In Daisy's opinion he'd never looked a happy man.

"There you are," her mother said when Daisy entered the kitchen. Nancy Yoder looked her daughter up and down. "You look tidy enough, but you've got to put a smile on that face of yours."

"I can't smile when I see Valerie. Her husband's just died and she's all alone. She's probably wishing she died too. What's she got to live for now? She's so old and she wouldn't have anything to look forward to. She's got no *kinner,* so obviously, she'll never have any *grosskin.*"

"Nonsense! She's younger than me and she would've adjusted a long time ago when she knew she wasn't able to have *kinner.* Old people have a right to live, too. Life isn't just for the young, even though you young people tend to think that way."

"Well, you don't seem as old as she is."

"I am, every bit."

"What am I supposed to say to her?" Daisy whined, hoping her mother would roll her eyes at her and say she'd go instead.

"Just say that I sent you over with food. You don't have to stay long. In fact, with your attitude it's probably better that you don't. She's already upset, and we don't want her to get worse."

"Okay." Daisy blew out a deep breath. It was clear her mother was intent on staying put and not going anywhere. "I won't stay long."

"It's in that basket over there. And if you're not going to stay and talk to her, come right back—don't dillydally along the way."

"What time will Lily be back?"

Her mother had recently started giving the twins things to do separately, and Daisy and Lily knew that she was doing it because one day they'd get married and have to live separately. Their mother had never told them that she was doing that, but they knew exactly how she thought. What their mother didn't know was that they were going to marry twins and live in one large house with all of their children, who would also be several sets of twins.

"Lily will be back when she gets here and not a minute before. Off you go. I can't stand around talking all day. I've got things to do."

"Okay, but what if Valerie cries or something?"

"She won't cry. Her husband's been dead a week already. If she does, just give her a hug."

Daisy frowned at her mother. "Oh, is that all the time you'd take to get over *Dat* dying, just a week?"

Her mother frowned back at her and her mouth turned down at the corners. "Don't say things like that."

"I wasn't saying anything mean. I don't know. I've never been in love, but I would've thought Valerie would maybe take years to get over it. I thought she'd be crying every day for ages."

"*Jah,* but she won't cry when she sees a pretty young woman at her door with food. Now go!"

Recognizing her mother's angry tone, Daisy grabbed the handle of the food basket and wasted no time in getting out of the house.

.   .   .

NANCY YODER GRABBED a handkerchief from up her sleeve and dabbed at her eyes. With her husband's recent heart problems, she was scared that one day she'd be alone just like her good friend Valerie Miller. It was her biggest fear. At least her husband, Hezekiah, was now well enough to go back to work on his brother's farm, but only if he did 'light' work.

The next thing she had to do was find husbands for the twins, like she'd done for Rose and Tulip, her older daughters. Nancy shook her head, almost feeling sorry for the men who'd end up with Daisy and Lily as wives. What kinds of men would find the twins appealing? They were pretty enough, but at the same time they were immature and silly and showed no signs of growing up.

When Nancy heard the horse trotting rather than walking away from the house, she ran to the front door, looked down the driveway, and yelled, "Not too fast, Daisy!"

When the horse didn't slow down, Nancy knew Daisy was pretending she couldn't hear her. *I'm going to look at that horse when she gets home and if she's driven that horse too hard, I'm going to ban her from driving the buggy for a month,* Nancy thought as she closed the front door. The girls had been told to walk the horse down the driveway and only trot the horse when they got onto the road.

Daisy and Lily were identical twins, and they had given her more than a few problems over the years. They were impulsive, headstrong, and extremely stubborn.

ON THE WAY to Valerie's house, Daisy considered throwing the contents of the basket in the tall grass along the roadside and not going at all, but her mother would find out—somehow, some way, she always did.

Going to see Valerie was a job for her mother or someone older, Daisy was certain of that.

CHAPTER 2

Daisy pulled up her horse outside the home of their newly widowed neighbor, Valerie Miller. Still not knowing exactly what she'd say, she jumped out of the buggy and pulled the basket along with her, settling the handle over her arm.

She rolled the small pebbles of the driveway under her feet as she trudged to the front door. Just when she thought that Valerie might not be home, she heard voices coming from inside the house. If Valerie had visitors, she wouldn't have to stay too long.

Daisy knocked on the door, and when it opened, she found she was looking at a man's chest. Slowly, she worked her way up to see a pair of unusual amber-colored eyes looking back at her.

"Is Valerie in?" Daisy finally asked.

"She is. Come inside. I'm Bruno Weber."

She stepped inside when he stepped back to allow her in. "Hello, I'm Daisy Yoder."

He held out his hand and she shook it. "Pleased to meet you."

"And you as well." His hand was warm and large and it unnerved her slightly the way the man kept his eyes locked onto hers.

"Valerie's in here." He led the way into the living room.

Valerie stood up when she saw Daisy. "It's nice to see you."

"Hello, Mrs. Miller. My *mudder* sent me over … I think it's chicken casserole." She held up the basket.

"That's lovely of her. Bruno, can you take that from Daisy and put it in the kitchen?"

Daisy knew that Valerie must have heard her greet Bruno at the door, otherwise, she wouldn't have been able to tell if she was Daisy or Lily. Only their close family members knew which twin was which.

Bruno nodded, took the basket from her, and left the room.

"Come and sit by me, Daisy. Tell me some happy news."

Daisy sat down beside her, feeling awkward. Her mother should've been the one to visit. "I'm sorry about what happened … you know…"

"Denke. You're a sweet girl to visit an old lady."

"You're not old!" Daisy said, completely contradicting her comments in the earlier conversation she'd had with her mother.

"That's what I keep telling her," Bruno said when he came back into the room.

"Daisy, this is my youngest *bruder.*"

"Oh, hello. I didn't realize."

"I tried to get back here for the funeral, but one thing after another kept me in Ohio."

"You're from Ohio?"

He nodded as he sat on the couch opposite. "I'm visiting Valerie for a few weeks. I'm trying to talk her into coming back with me to live permanently."

"And I'm trying to talk *him* into moving here."

Daisy nodded. It was awkward talking to people without her twin sister there beside her. They'd always been together. Lily and she had separate bedrooms, but apart from that, they were with each other all day every day until recently when their mother thought she was being smart by giving them separate errands.

"Daisy's *vadder* is the deacon."

"Is he?" Bruno asked.

Daisy nodded and wondered what she should say. Normally Lily would speak and then she'd say something, or the other way around. *Say something!* she silently screamed in her own head. "And do you like chicken, Mrs. Miller?"

"I do. Be sure to thank your *mudder* for me. Did you help her cook it?"

Daisy nodded. "*Jah,* Lily and I help our mother cook." She glanced at the good-looking man staring at her. Why couldn't she think of something interesting to talk about?

"Do you live close by, Daisy?" he asked.

"*Jah,* not too far away. What kind of work do you do, Bruno?" she asked, not really caring about the answer, but knowing that was one of the usual questions people ask when they meet someone for the first time.

"I'm a horse trader. I run auctions too."

"That sounds like fun."

He laughed. "It can be sometimes. Mainly it's a lot of hard work. And what do you do?"

"I haven't got a job or anything like that. I stay at home and do work there."

"Daisy's *mudder* is very busy. She's the main woman in the community, the one who does everything."

"Jah, she's very *gut* at arranging everything. She's always doing the organizing at all the weddings and charity events."

"And do you take after her?"

Daisy recoiled. *"Nee!* Not at all."

Bruno laughed again.

The man was so handsome and so lovely that Daisy knew that if God had been listening to her prayers, the man would have a twin for Lily. She would marry him, and Lily could marry his twin brother. She'd never felt an attraction to a man like this before. "Do you have a twin?" she asked, staring at him.

He drew his dark eyebrows together. *"Nee.* Do I look like someone you've seen before?"

Daisy could barely speak as she watched his full lips form every syllable.

"I think what Daisy means to say is that she's a twin—an identical one."

His face lit up. "There's another young woman just like you?"

"Nee, there's not."

Valerie said, "What do you call Lily, then?"

"Who?" Daisy asked, a little annoyed that Valerie was interrupting when she was getting along so well with Bruno.

"Lily, your twin *schweschder."*

"Lily? Is she here?" Daisy frowned. She hadn't heard a buggy pull up.

Valerie smiled at her. *"Nee,* I think you came alone, didn't you?"

"Ach, jah."

Daisy noticed Bruno put his hand over his mouth to stifle a laugh, but she didn't care. She was lost in a world where it wouldn't matter if nothing existed except Bruno. If only they could be alone, so she could find out all about him.

"Daisy, does your *mudder* need the basket back today?"

"Huh?" Daisy thought hard. Basket? What basket was Valerie talking about? "Oh, the basket. *Nee,* she doesn't need it back. I could come and collect it tomorrow."

"Jah, do that." Bruno was now staring at her just as much as she'd been staring at him. "What time might you come back here?" he asked.

"Ten in the morning."

Valerie interrupted again. "Daisy, would you like to come back for dinner tonight?"

This time, Valerie wasn't being so annoying. "If that's not too much trouble, I'd love to."

"It's no trouble at all. What's one more for dinner? We'd enjoy the company."

"I'll bring dessert," Daisy said.

"Bring Lily too," Valerie said.

She was back to being annoying. Daisy thought quickly. "Lily won't be able to make it. She's busy tonight, but I'll be here. I could even come back early to help you, Mrs. Miller."

Bruno nodded. *"Jah,* my *schweschder* would like that."

Daisy rose to her feet. "I should go." If she was coming back there tonight, she didn't want to outstay her welcome.

"I'll walk you out," Bruno said, bounding to his feet.

"I'll see you tonight, Daisy," Valerie said.

Daisy offered her a bright smile and then stepped outside with Bruno. "How is she coping?" she asked Bruno.

"She's doing okay. It was a shock for everyone that he died so unexpectedly."

"I wouldn't like Valerie to move away. She has a lot of friends here. There are a lot of women her age."

"*Jah,* but they're probably married with families to look after. Valerie's got no *kinner* and no relatives."

"She'll be taken care of and my *mudder* is close to her age and there are so many people who'd miss her if she left. Everyone likes her. She's so kind and lovely."

He nodded as they continued walking to her buggy. "That's nice of you to say so."

"It's true."

When they reached the buggy, he said, "I'll see you later this evening."

"*Jah*, I'll be back in plenty of time to help Valerie cook. Or to cook for her."

He chuckled. "I'll look forward to it."

Daisy climbed into the buggy and then looked back and gave him a big smile. He grabbed the lower section of the reins and turned the horse until he was faced back down the driveway.

CHAPTER 3

DAISY ARRIVED home and couldn't remember how she'd gotten there. She was too busy thinking about the man she had just met. He was different from the men in her community, and she was sure that he liked her, too, because he kept smiling at her. She jumped out of the buggy and unhitched the horse just the way her father had shown her.

"What took you so long?"

Daisy glanced up at her mother who was walking through the barn toward her.

"Was I a long time?"

"Considering you said you weren't staying, you were."

"That's because Valerie had a visitor and she asked me to stay. I couldn't be rude." Daisy continued talking as she gave Damon, the black horse, a rubdown. "Anyway, you didn't say you were in a hurry for me to come back."

"I was. But you're right. I didn't tell you because I didn't need you to come back, but because of what you said I expected you earlier." Nancy looked over the horse carefully. "At least you didn't drive the horse too hard this time." When Nancy had finished running her hands over the horse's legs, she straightened up. "Valerie asked you to stay? Who were her visitors?"

"There was only one; her *bruder* from Ohio."

"Hmm, from the look on your face, I'm guessing he was young and handsome?"

"He's not married." Daisy giggled. "He's a bit older than me. They asked me to come back and have dinner with them tonight."

"'They,' or Valerie's *bruder?*"

Daisy looked at her mother and knew *Mamm* could see right through her. She couldn't put anything over on her. "Valerie asked me, and I said I'd bring dessert." Daisy couldn't remember if she'd said that, but if she hadn't, she should've. Anyway, she couldn't turn up empty-handed.

"I'm glad you offered to bring dessert. She shouldn't be entertaining; that's a lot of hard work."

"That's what I thought, so I also said I'd go early to help her cook dinner."

"Good girl. Finish with Damon and I'll figure out what you can take for dessert."

"Denke, Mamm."

Daisy couldn't get the smile off her face. She knew that her mother was going to make the dessert for her to take and her mother was a very good cook.

Glancing at the horse in the other stall, she knew that Lily was already home and, judging by the look of the horse, she'd been home for some time. She finished rubbing Damon down and headed into the house to tell her twin sister her news about meeting her future husband. She hoped Lily would take the news well. Bruno didn't have a twin and they'd agreed to only marry twins, or at the very least, brothers close in age. Maybe Bruno had a brother; that might soften the blow for Lily. Lily could marry Bruno's brother. She'd have to find out tonight over dinner how many single brothers he had.

She scraped the dirt off her feet before she walked into the mudroom to wash her hands. Once she dried them, she opened the back door to look for Lily.

Lily was sitting at the kitchen table eating a sandwich and their mother was nowhere about.

Lily looked up at her. "Where have you been?"

"I was visiting Valerie Miller. The one whose husband just died."

"Yeah, I know Valerie. We went to Dirk's funeral a week ago."

"That's right. Anyway, her *bruder* from Ohio is there staying with her."

"So that's where you've been for all this time? I've done three times the work while you've been sitting down talking, probably eating cake and having a *gut* time." Lily took another bite of her sandwich.

Daisy sat down next to her. "You should've seen Valerie's *bruder.*"

Lily swallowed her mouthful. "Oh, is that why you took your time?"

"*Jah.* Valerie invited me back there for dinner. And I really want to go."

"What's he like? Tell me everything." Lily pushed her half-eaten sandwich away.

Daisy hoped that Lily would be happy for her. If their situations were reversed, she'd be worried that she hadn't met the man her sister was interested in. "He's … I don't know."

"You must know. You've just seen him."

"He has amber eyes and full lips. That's all I remember. I'm certain he likes me. He was pleased when Valerie asked me to come back and have dinner with them."

"Did they invite me as well? Surely they would've."

"Sorry, but I guess she didn't think of it. She's under stress with her husband just dying and everything."

"First *Mamm* gives us separate things to do and now you're getting invitations that don't include me. Now you've met a man and I haven't. Tell me he's a twin at least."

There it was. It was like they were moving apart. Daisy knew Lily wasn't happy by the way her eyes had formed into narrow slits. "He doesn't have a twin."

"What do you mean he's not a twin? How could you even like him? That's just wrong. We planned on marrying twins."

"Shh. *Mamm* will hear you. Let's go up and talk in my room before she comes back and gives us more chores."

The twins raced up the stairs and then sat cross-legged on Daisy's bed.

"But we don't even know if there are any twins our age," Daisy said. "That's the problem. Even *Dat* doesn't know of any and he nearly knows everyone in the whole country."

"He couldn't nearly know everyone in the country."

"Near enough," Daisy said.

Lily pouted, and then continued with her objections. "I'm sure there's tons of them somewhere in all the communities across the whole country. There'd have to be. *Dat* said he'd ask around for us."

"I'd rather not marry at all than move a hundred miles away from everyone we know just for the silly idea of marrying twins." When Lily didn't respond, Daisy felt bad and looked down at her hands.

Lily groaned. "Silly now, is it? When did it become silly? The moment you met Valerie's *bruder?*"

"I'm sorry. I can't help liking him."

Slowly, Lily nodded. "You can't help who you fall in love with, I guess."

"I've only just met him. I might find out tonight that he's totally unsuitable."

Lily said, "Or you might fall in love with him. Don't mind me, I'm just being selfish. I guess … I guess I'll get used to the idea. But if you marry him, who will I marry?"

Daisy smiled and straightened up. "He could have a friend, and tonight I'm going to find out if he has a *bruder* close to his age. Don't worry." She reached forward and patted her twin on her knee.

"What time do you have to be there?"

"I said I'd be there early to help, and I've got to make dessert too, or help *Mamm* with it if she makes it."

"You better get downstairs and see what ingredients *Mamm* has for dessert. Have *her* make it and tell him you made it." Lily giggled.

Daisy's face lit up. "I'm already way ahead of you on that one. I'm glad you don't mind about Bruno."

"Are you certain he likes you too?"

"Yeah, why wouldn't he?"

Both girls giggled.

"Now to break the news to *Mamm* and *Dat.* What if they don't allow you to go?" Lily asked.

"Why wouldn't they? *Mamm's* already said it's okay."

"Really? I suppose that's because we've behaved lately and haven't gotten into trouble over anything in months."

They certainly had done everything that had been asked of them. Even helping their mother with her duties of helping people. That had to make her mother feel kindly toward her.

"Where is *Mamm* anyway?" Lily asked.

"I don't know. I saw her when I came home," Daisy said.

"Let's go find her."

When they walked back into the kitchen, their mother was right there waiting for them. "Where have you been, Lily? I heard you come home and then you disappeared. I was calling out to you."

"Oh, I didn't hear. We were up in Daisy's room just then," Lily answered.

"Cleaning your rooms, did you say?" Nancy asked.

From the tone of her mother's voice, Daisy knew she wasn't in a good mood.

"Actually, I was looking for you when I came home, *Mamm.* Where were you?" Lily asked. "I came home before Daisy and couldn't see you anywhere."

"You didn't look too far. I was in the vegetable garden seeing if anything had survived the frost we got the other night. Now, how did you two go on your outing?" she asked Lily.

"Fine," Lily said. "Daisy went to Valerie's and she has her *bruder* there from Ohio, and—"

"She only had one *schweschder* here for the funeral." Her mother looked at Daisy.

Daisy could see her mother was already forming an opinion of Bruno. *"Jah,* he said he couldn't get there. Anyway, he's there now keeping Valerie company. Don't forget about the dessert, *Mamm."*

"I won't forget. Are you sure Bruno didn't invite you? I hope Valerie's well enough for visitors."

Her mother peered at her with her mouth drawn tight. That meant that there was only one right answer and she hoped she'd make the right one. "Honestly, it was Valerie herself who invited me. I was worried about all the work, so that's when I said I'd come back early to help."

"Good."

Daisy licked her lips. Going to Valerie's early meant that she'd have less time to do chores about the house. "I mean, she's just lost her husband and things must be hard for her."

"Well, why wouldn't she eat the chicken casserole you took her?" *Mamm* asked.

"Oh, I don't know. I didn't think of that."

Her mother breathed out heavily and looked up at the ceiling. "That would make sense to me. Unless she intends to freeze it and eat it another time." She glanced at Lily, and then set her eyes back onto Daisy. "Did she only invite you?"

"Jah."

"I'm pleased that you said you'd help her. That was kindhearted."

Daisy smiled, pleased to be getting praise from her mother for something. While the going was good, she added, "I also said I'd bring dessert."

"You don't have to keep reminding me. I've been thinking about that and you can take the cherry pie I made yesterday. I was going to have one of you take it to old Mary tomorrow, but I'll find something else for Mary."

Lily grunted. "We don't have to go visiting again tomorrow, do we? I thought we only did that one day a week."

"We do it whenever we can. It's time effective to do it one day a week, but sometimes it's not always going to work like that. I just found out that Mary's not well."

"That's bad news about Mary. You really don't mind if I go tonight?"

"I already said you could. It's strange that she didn't invite your *schweschder.*"

Lily piped up. "That's what I thought."

"We're two separate people. You're giving us things to do separately. Lily wasn't there, so Valerie just didn't think about her."

"I think it had more to do with Bruno," Lily said with a pout.

Daisy glared at her sister. She had casually mentioned to her mother that Valerie had her brother staying with her, but she didn't want her mother's overactive mind too focused on Bruno.

"Bruno?" Her mother glared at Daisy.

"*Jah,* Valerie's *bruder.*"

"From Ohio," Lily added.

Daisy frowned at Lily, causing Lily to pull a face back at her, all without their mother noticing.

"What's he like, this *bruder* of Valerie's?" Their mother sat down at the kitchen table and the girls sat down too.

"Full lips and amber eyes is what she told me." Lily cackled an evil laugh.

"She asked me, not you," Daisy said, annoyed with her sister for a third time in less than two minutes. She could only figure that Lily was jealous, but why ruin things for her? Lily had made her sound foolish as well.

"Interesting. And the age of this young full-lipped, amber-eyed man?"

"I didn't ask." Daisy was only thankful she didn't tell Lily too much else.

Their mother leaned forward as though she was only just getting started. "Single?"

"*Jah,* he had no *fraa* with him and he's got no *baard.*"

Lily giggled again.

Their mother ignored Lily, still focused on Daisy and finding out more about the young man and his marriage worthiness. "What job does he have?"

"He said something about horse auctions. I wasn't really listening."

"He's an auctioneer?"

From her mother's tone, she seemed impressed that he was an auctioneer. Daisy shook her head. "I don't know if that's what he said exactly, but he said something about horse auctions."

"He probably goes around with a scoop and cleans up all the horse manure at the auctions," Lily suggested. "That's working at horse auctions."

"That's not nice, Lily," Daisy said.

"Well, for all you know that's what he could do. There are dozens of jobs at horse auctions. Clean out your ears next time,

Daisy," Lily said. "Do that before you go there tonight so you can answer all *Mamm's* questions."

"Lily, I'm trying to find out a few things and you're not helping."

"Sorry, *Mamm.*"

"Just be quiet while I'm talking to Daisy for just one minute."

"I'll try. It won't be easy, but I'll try."

Nancy turned her attention back to Daisy. "Valerie wouldn't have invited you back if she didn't appreciate you going there. You must've been a comfort to her."

"She's a lovely person. I like Valerie, and I always have."

"I'll have your *vadder* drive you there."

"Nee, don't do that. I said I'd go there early to help."

"Your *vadder* will be home early today."

"Why?" Lily asked.

"He's finishing earlier now the weather's getting so cold."

Daisy would feel awful if she arrived there driven by her father as though she were a child. *"Nee, Mamm,* I can drive myself. It's not even that far."

"Well, we'll see what he says when he gets home. If he's too tired, he might let you go alone."

There was no use saying anything further. If she protested too much, her mother would only dig her heels in further. She wanted Bruno to see her as an adult. Only a child would have their father drive them places.

As Daisy had feared, her father insisted on driving her to Valerie's house. It was obvious that her mother had whispered to him that Valerie's brother was staying there, and that Daisy liked him.

"I'll come in for a minute and say hello," her father said when they pulled up outside Valerie's house.

"Of course you will," Daisy said under her breath. It was embarrassing that her father was dropping her off and then collecting her later. To make things worse, he was coming inside deliberately to meet Bruno.

Furious at her mother's meddling, she buried her feelings and fixed a smile on her face so Bruno wouldn't think she was a grumpy person. She couldn't let Bruno see that small things angered her so much. He could find that out after they were married.

Hezekiah Yoder knocked on the door of Valerie's house and Bruno opened the door.

"*Dat,* this is Bruno, Valerie's *bruder.*"

They shook hands.

"I'm Hezekiah Yoder."

"*Jah,* Daisy's *vadder.* I'm pleased to meet you. Will you be joining us for dinner too?"

"*Nee, denke.* I'm just bringing Daisy and I thought I'd come in and see how Valerie's doing."

"Come right in," Bruno said, opening the door wide and stepping back to let them through.

Her father walked in first, and Bruno gave Daisy a big smile.

"I'll take the dessert to the kitchen," Daisy said, walking past him.

"Hezekiah, it's nice to see you," Daisy heard Valerie say from the kitchen. She stayed there to see what else she would hear.

Just as she stepped closer to listen in, Bruno walked into the kitchen and she nearly bumped into him.

"I can take you home after dinner, Daisy. There's no need for your *vadder* to come back and collect you late at night. Valerie told me he hasn't been well."

"That's nice of you. Perhaps you can suggest that to him before he leaves? If I mention it, he'll reject the idea."

"I'll insist I take you home." He looked over at the basket and smiled. "And what did you make for dessert?"

She took Lily's advice and carefully chose her words so he'd think she'd made it. "We have cherry pie for dessert."

"That's one of my favorites and barely anyone makes them nowadays. What a delight." He smiled at her and her heart melted. "I suppose we should join them," he said.

"Do we have to?"

He laughed. *"Jah.* Come on."

They sat down with Hezekiah and Valerie. Ten minutes later, Hezekiah stood up and announced he'd collect Daisy at nine thirty.

Bruno bounded to his feet. "You shouldn't have to come out so late. I'll take Daisy back to your *haus.* It's no trouble. I need to give Valerie's horse some exercise since Valerie hasn't been out for some days."

"Is that so, Valerie?"

"Jah, I was just asking Bruno today if he'd take the horse out soon."

"As long as it's no trouble for you, Bruno," Hezekiah said.

"You'd be doing me a favor, Hezekiah, really you would," Valerie said.

Daisy held her breath. She could tell her father was

weighing things up in his mind, like what Daisy's mother would say when she found out he wasn't going back to collect her.

Hezekiah nodded. "I'll see you when you get home, Daisy." He looked at Bruno and Valerie. "Enjoy the cherry pie. It's a recipe that's been handed down and my wife bakes the cherry pies so well."

Daisy bounded to her feet and slipped her arm around her father's, walking him to the door. *"Jah*, and there's nothing I like more than trying out all those old *familye* recipes—like that cherry pie. *Gut nacht, Dat."*

Her father turned around at the door and stared at his daughter.

"Gut nacht, Hezekiah," Valerie called out.

"I won't bring her home late, Mr. Yoder."

Hezekiah nodded and with gentle pressure on his arm from Daisy, he was further out the door. Daisy closed the door behind him and walked back to Valerie. "Now, how can I help you with the dinner?"

"If it's all right with you, we're going to have that chicken casserole your *mudder* was kind enough to send over with you earlier today."

"I don't mind at all. That's a good idea."

Bruno said, "I was at the markets early today and picked up plenty of fresh bread too."

"Good. Can I help you with anything else, Valerie?"

"Nee. All I have to do is heat up the food. I'm sorry to get you over here so early."

Daisy smiled, thinking of all the chores at home she missed out on. Besides that, it gave her more time with Bruno. "I don't mind at all. Do you have chores or housework I can do for you before dinner?"

"That's a kind offer. There's nothing to do. I've been able to do things. Keeping busy has helped me keep my mind off other things."

Bruno said, "Valerie likes to keep busy. She hasn't been out because she's had visitors coming and going with people stopping by to pay their respects."

Daisy wondered when dinner would be ready. It was awkward just sitting there trying to think of conversation. She could've talked to Bruno if they'd been alone and she wasn't sure what to say to Valerie. Finally she said, "You must have something I can help with."

"I can't think of anything. Why don't you relax and talk with Bruno and I'll make us a cup of tea." Valerie stood up and Daisy sprang to her feet.

"I can do it."

"*Nee.* You sit and I'll get you tea. It's still too early for dinner and tea won't ruin our appetites."

Valerie left the room and now Daisy smiled at Bruno who was staring at her.

"Did you make the cherry pie?" he asked.

Daisy was taken aback. Could he read her mind? It was a strange thing to ask and she didn't want to lie to him just in case he might be her future husband. *"Nee,* my *mudder* made it. She's an excellent baker. I hope I'm as good as she is one day."

He laughed.

"What's funny?"

"Nothing at all. I'm just happy. Happy to have met someone

my age. I'm glad Valerie invited you to dinner. I'm looking forward to finding out more about you."

"There's not much to know."

"I think there's a lot more to you. You're intriguing."

A giggle escaped her lips. She loved the attention he was giving her. "What would you like to know?"

"You said you live close by?"

"*Jah,* you'll see tonight when you drive me home that it's not that far."

"What sort of things are you interested in?"

"Just the normal things. I like baking and sewing."

"Do you sew quilts?"

"We used to a few years back. When I was younger, we all worked on one together. That's my two older sisters, my twin, and *Mamm.*"

"Do you have brothers?"

"Two. The oldest in the family are boys. They're both married."

"And the rest are married?"

"*Nee,* I'm not married and neither is my twin *schweschder.*"

"Ah, the lucky last in the family."

"And the youngest." Daisy giggled. "If I said something about being lucky in front of my *vadder,* I'd get a lecture that there's no such thing as luck."

Bruno nodded. "I was trying to be funny. Thanks for telling me. I'll watch what I say around him."

That was the right answer as far as Daisy was concerned. He showed he had it in his mind that he'd be around her father, and that meant he was interested in her, she was certain of that. "And what do you like doing, Bruno?"

449

"I like my work and that keeps me busy."

"That's a good thing." If only she could remember what he said that he did for a living. Was it horse trading, or something to do with horse auctions? She was sure he said something about horse auctions because that's what she told Lily, or was it her mother she told? Since she'd met him just a few hours ago, she couldn't concentrate on anything. Did that mean she was in love?

Valerie came back into the room. "Here we go." She placed a tray of tea items on the table near the couch.

"I could've helped you with that, Valerie," Bruno said.

"Or I could've," Daisy said.

"It's fine. It wasn't that heavy." She sat back down on the couch. "Milk or sugar, Daisy?"

"Just black for me, *denke.*"

"And you, Bruno?"

"However it comes, as long as it's not too sweet."

Valerie poured the tea from a teapot and handed them a cup of tea each before she settled back down on the couch with a cup for herself. After she had taken a sip, she said, "My late husband gave me that teapot." She looked downward. "Oh, it sounds funny to call him my late husband."

Daisy felt awkward and looked at the large white teapot. "What a nice teapot. It's a lovely shape."

"*Denke.*"

Daisy couldn't believe she'd picked the teapot to talk about. Amish wedding gifts were always practical things. Daisy recalled that her father gave her mother a treadle sewing machine for a wedding gift and it still worked as perfectly as the day he bought it. Daisy and all her sisters had learned to

450

sew on it. She didn't mention it to Valerie because she didn't want to make her sad. A sewing machine seemed a lot better gift than a teapot.

Valerie continued, *"Jah.* He surprised me with it. We'd been shopping weeks before we married, looking for something. I forget what it was we were shopping for. I admired the teapot, but it was too expensive and I never thought another thing about it. It just showed how thoughtful and caring he was." Valerie took another sip and looked at Daisy. "I hope you don't mind me talking about him. It helps to talk."

"I don't mind at all. I didn't think you'd want to talk about him." Daisy hadn't been around death. Both sets of grandparents had died before she was born and apart from people she knew in the community who'd died, she'd never lost anyone close to her.

"It helps. It makes me feel like he's still around. I feel like he is. I expect to see him walking through the door at any moment. It doesn't seem real that he's gone."

Daisy put both hands around her teacup, wondering what words of comfort she should be uttering. Nothing came to her. She took a sip of tea, hoping someone would say something.

"I'm glad you came to dinner, Daisy. I need some fresh young company for a change."

"What does that make me then?" Bruno asked, pulling a face at his sister.

Daisy giggled.

"You don't count. You're *familye.* Daisy's always been bright and happy." She turned away from Bruno and looked at Daisy. "Every time I see you and Lily, you're both so happy. I've never seen either of you downcast or sad."

"What's your secret, Daisy?" Bruno asked as he leaned forward.

"Secret for what?"

"The secret of happiness. It's a thing which makes many people struggle."

Daisy shrugged her shoulders. "It's just the way I am. Also, Lily makes me laugh all the time. We have a lot of fun together. I guess I make her laugh too." The mention of Lily made her feel bad that she hadn't brought her tonight too. As well as that, she felt guilty for saying that Lily was busy tonight. She hoped God wouldn't punish her for her lies.

"They say a merry heart is like a medicine," Valerie said. "You'll live to a very long age."

"I hope so." Daisy took a sip of tea, wondering what her life would be like at ninety.

"I'm going to throw myself into volunteer work to keep me busy. That'll keep my mind off my own troubles."

"What sort of things will you do?" Daisy asked Valerie.

"Just generally helping people. Things like your mother does."

"She always needs help with things."

"I'll visit her and see what I can help out with. Your *vadder* seems to have fully recovered from the scare he had a while back. Landed in hospital, didn't he?"

"*Jah,* he has a problem with his heart, but he's okay now as long as he takes the tablets every day." She turned to Bruno and explained, "We thought he was dead. He'd passed out in the living room after he had a fright."

"It must've been some fright," Bruno said. "What was it?"

Quick, change the subject. Daisy didn't want to go down that track of dredging up the dark family secrets of inappropriate men that she and her sisters might have been involved with, albeit briefly. "It might have happened anyway right at that moment. I don't think it was the fright. It must've been a fright for you, Valerie, because your husband wasn't even ill."

Valerie nodded. "That's right. I wasn't prepared. If he'd been sick or in the hospital, at least I would've known he wasn't well. To die in an accident like that was awful. I don't even know how it happened."

"The rescue people were vague in their explanations. That is, the paramedics who responded," Bruno said. "That's what Valerie told me."

"I'm very sorry, Valerie. I don't know what else to say," Daisy said.

Valerie wiped a tear from her eye. *"Denke."*

Bruno reached out a hand and touched Valerie on her shoulder. "There's nothing anyone can say, but it's touching to me and my *schweschder* that you care." Then he said to Valerie, "You wouldn't be alone if you'd come back with me."

She shook her head. "I've made a life for myself here. I don't want to start over at my age."

He slowly nodded. "The offer's always there."

"I know." She patted his hand, which still on her shoulder.

Daisy saw what a caring man Bruno was.

A little later in the evening, Daisy helped Valerie prepare the meal while Bruno set the table. Since the meal only had to be heated, there wasn't much to do apart from set the table, slice the bread, and put some butter in a serving dish.

CHAPTER 4

"You what?" Nancy shrieked at her husband when he got home and told her he'd given permission for Bruno to bring Daisy back home.

"He said he'd bring her home," he repeated, stroking his gray beard.

Nancy took a moment to take a couple of deep, calming breaths. Her husband had heart problems, so screaming at him might not be a good idea, but couldn't he think for himself? Why did everything have to fall on her shoulders? That's how it felt. He wasn't strict enough with the girls and never had been. Girls like Lily and Daisy needed strict discipline.

She tried the calm and reasonable approach, hoping her husband would see the error of his ways. "Hezekiah, do you remember what happened the last time that Daisy was in a buggy with a man? And we kind of knew him, and this man we don't know at all."

Hezekiah frowned. "That was two years ago, Nancy. We

can't be with the girl every moment. You want Daisy to get married someday, don't you?"

"You know I do, and the sooner, the better."

"We have to let her go sometime. We can't control her—not at her age. There comes a point that we have to let go and trust. Think of it like someone putting a sailboat in the water. There can either be a storm to endure, or a gentle breeze can well up and gently guide the boat to where it's supposed to be. There isn't any way we can control the weather."

Nancy shook her head. He was never going to see things her way. Life wasn't always to be compared with sailboats and water. "Think of it this way, Hezekiah, would you put a sailboat in the water when there were black storm clouds in the sky?"

He rubbed the side of his face. *"Nee.* I wouldn't. I'd wait until the storm clouds left."

"Exactly!"

"I don't see the meaning of your story, Nancy."

"I never see the meaning of your stories!" Nancy breathed slowly to calm herself. "The twins aren't like Rose and Tulip. They're stubborn, easily led, ignorant, and impulsive. And I left out completely selfish and not to be trusted."

Hezekiah's jaw dropped open. "I think you're being harsh. They're both bright young women and they like to have excitement."

"That's your interpretation because you don't see them day in and day out. I'm the one at home with them all the time, and I know them better than you do."

"You're seeing the worst in them. They've got such good qualities—"

"I'm being realistic. I want them to be married, but they

must be closely monitored. We can't leave them alone because they don't think clearly. They're easily led astray. That's why I asked you to take her there and collect her; otherwise, I never would have let her go without Lily. Now go change out of those clothes and then wash up for dinner."

"I'm sorry, dear."

"You must listen to me next time, Hezekiah."

He nodded. "I wouldn't dare not!" he murmured as he turned to get changed out of his clothes.

"What did you say?"

He turned around and smiled at her. "I will, dear."

As soon as they had said their silent prayer of thanks for the meal in front of them, Daisy was anxious to find out if Bruno had a brother. She was sure that he had a lot of siblings because she remembered that Valerie was the oldest and he was the youngest. She hoped the conversation would work its way around to the topic so she wouldn't have to ask.

"How long are you staying, Bruno?" Daisy asked casually as she buttered her bread.

"As long as my *schweschder* needs me."

Daisy looked over at Valerie and smiled.

"I shall need you for a very long time," Valerie said jokingly.

"Not if you move back to Ohio with me."

"What's so good about Ohio?" Daisy asked.

"You should come and see for yourself sometime."

"Maybe I will."

"I grew up there and so did Valerie. Valerie only moved here when she married Dirk."

Daisy's eyes flickered to Valerie to see if she minded her brother talking about her late husband after she had shed a few tears earlier. She didn't seem to.

"It's been my home ever since. I don't see any good reason to go back. It would've changed so much anyway. I'm used to being here now. All my memories are here. You should move here, Bruno," Valerie said.

"*Jah*, it's a *gut* place to live," Daisy added.

Bruno laughed. "I'm outnumbered here. It's not fair."

"Perhaps Daisy can show you around and you'll get a good idea of the place and what it's got to offer."

"I'd be only too happy to do that," Daisy said, trying to sound normal while inside she wanted to leap for joy.

He looked up from his food. "You wouldn't mind showing me around, Daisy?"

She loved the way he said her name so delicately, like butterfly wings tickling her ears. Her name had never sounded so beautiful. "I wouldn't mind one little bit."

"When might you be able to do that, Daisy? Tomorrow?" Valerie asked.

Bruno frowned at his sister. "You trying to get rid of me, sis?"

"I just want you to have a good look around, and I'm not up to showing you the sights."

"I could come back tomorrow," Daisy offered.

"I'll find out where you live tonight, and then I'll collect you tomorrow and we can explore. That'll give Valerie's horse plenty of work, too."

Daisy nodded. "Okay."

"That's settled, then," Valerie said.

Daisy smiled at Bruno and he smiled back at her. She longed to ask if he had a brother for her sister. Perhaps she could ask him tomorrow if the subject didn't come up tonight. Throughout the dinner, she used her very best table manners to make the very best impression that she could.

CHAPTER 5

LATER THAT NIGHT, Daisy was pleased to be in the buggy so close to Bruno.

"*Denke* for driving me home, Bruno."

"I'm happy to do it. It saves your *vadder* from coming back out. And, as I said, Valerie wants her horse to be worked."

"That's good."

"Are you certain it'll be okay with your parents if I take up most of your time tomorrow?"

Daisy was certain that he thought her to be much younger than she was, thanks to her father bringing her to Valerie's house. "I'm twenty-one—nearly," Daisy blurted out.

"Hmm, let me do the math. That means you're twenty, or possibly nineteen?"

"*Jah.* Something like that."

He laughed.

"And I don't need their permission," she added.

"My sisters had to ask my parents permission for everything when they were living under our parents' roof."

"What about your brothers?" Daisy asked, hoping he'd mention someone whom Lily could marry.

"I don't have any."

"What? Not at all?"

"Nee. I've got ten siblings, all females. My parents were certainly hoping I was a boy. I guess I was a pleasant surprise." He chuckled again.

She stared ahead at the darkened road. Now she had to go home, and not only tell Lily that she'd fallen in love, but tell her twin sister that Bruno didn't even have a brother. "Did you have a close male friend that you grew up with and have remained friends with ever since?"

He glanced over at her. *"Jah,* how did you know?"

"Just a guess."

"His name is Joel and he just got married last month."

Daisy was devastated. Things weren't looking good for Lily. How could she go home and tell Lily about her happiness when Lily had none? They'd always shared everything, and had always done everything at the same time. It wasn't right. Perhaps Bruno wasn't the man for her after all. Both of them had prayed to marry twin brothers ever since their oldest sister, Rose, had gotten married years before.

"Things are different now between Joel and me. We used to do everything together, but now that he's married he's busy with other things."

That would happen with Lily and her if she got married and Lily didn't. "That's too bad. I didn't expect Valerie to have a *bruder* as young as you."

"She's the oldest and I'm the youngest, and there are many sisters in between, don't forget. I only have a few memories of her in the house before she got married and moved away."

"That's a bit sad."

"We've seen a fair bit of each other. She always came home for one thing or another. She has to sell the farm, and that's why I'm trying to get her to come back to Ohio with me."

"Why does she have to sell the farm?"

"When Dirk died he left debts. The *familye* designated me as the one to come out here and bring her back—try to make her see sense."

It all fitted in with the rumors Daisy had heard of Dirk doing away with himself. If there was truth in it, maybe he did it because he had huge debts and was about to lose the farm, but she never thought an Amish man would do such a thing. She kept her thoughts to herself. "Sorry to hear that. I had no idea she was about to lose the farm. Does she know? Oh, I suppose that's a silly question. Of course she'd know."

"She does."

"She doesn't seem upset about it."

"I'd say it's too much for her to face at this time."

"Maybe the community can help. We could have a fundraiser."

He glanced over at her in the semi-darkness. "Possibly."

"Shall I talk to my *vadder* about it? He could work something out with the bishop. Maybe someone could lease her land, or something."

He nodded. "That might help. *Denke,* Daisy. There are various things that she could do, but she's not in the state of mind to make decisions right now. She could sell off the land

and keep the *haus*; that's the only thing I've thought of that could get her out of immediate trouble."

"That sounds like a *gut* idea."

"I need to wait until I can ask her some things. Perhaps don't talk to your *vadder* just yet."

"Okay, I won't. Oh, it's this driveway just off to the left."

When he stopped outside the house, he said, "I'm looking forward to tomorrow, Daisy. Shall I collect you at ten in the morning?"

She nodded. "Ten would be perfect." She got out of the buggy and walked toward the house. By the time she'd reached the front door, he'd turned the buggy around. She gave a wave into the darkness, not knowing if he was looking, and walked inside.

Daisy was surprised to see her mother sitting up in the chair. She'd obviously been waiting for her. "Am I late, *Mamm?*"

"Nee. I'm just glad you got home in one piece."

She could tell her mother was angry and she didn't know why. "Bruno drove me. He's Valcrie's *bruder.* Didn't *Dat* tell you Bruno was driving me home?"

"Jah, I've heard all about Bruno from your *vadder.* He thinks he's a nice young man."

"He is."

"That's what everyone thought about Nathanial and look what happened there."

"That was a long time ago. And anyway, you can't keep thinking about that."

"Why wouldn't I? He caused your *vadder* to have a heart attack."

"Dat didn't have a heart attack. He had some kind of a turn."

"It was a heart attack and now he's on medication for heart disease. He doesn't need any more stress from you."

Daisy sat down next to her mother. "Do you think I caused *Dat* to have a heart attack? Is that why you've been so angry with me these past two years? Do you hate me?"

"Of course I don't hate you. *Nee,* not you; it was Nathanial."

"You hate Nathanial?"

"I don't hate anyone. You shouldn't even use that word. I suppose, to be fair, your *vadder* had underlying issues with his heart. It might have been just as well all that fuss happened so he could get on the medication."

Nathanial had taken her for a buggy ride nearly two years ago and had displayed bad behavior, causing Daisy to jump out of the buggy to escape from his advances. When she'd found her way home, her parents went wild upon seeing her walking home by herself when Nathanial should've brought her home. Her mother hadn't trusted Nathanial from the beginning because he was Jacob's brother and Jacob had treated her sister, Rose, in a cruel manner and ended up leaving her to marry someone else. Daisy had thought it wasn't fair to judge Nathanial by his brother, but as it turned out, her mother had been right all along.

"You don't need to worry about anything with Bruno. He's very trustworthy."

"Hmm, that's what your *vadder* said."

"See? It must be true." Daisy quickly added, "Valerie asked me for a favor."

"Hmm?" Her mother stared at her, waiting to find out what it was.

"She asked me if I could show her *bruder* around because she doesn't feel up to it and her horse needs exercising."

"When does she want you to do that?"

"Tomorrow at ten in the morning."

"Okay. And he's coming to fetch you?"

"*Jah.* He is."

"*Gut!* Then I can meet him too."

Daisy's jaw dropped open. She hadn't figured on that. First her father had embarrassed her and tomorrow was going to be her mother's turn. "I'm only showing him around. I don't want him to think that he's being ogled and that you are seeing if he's worthy marriage material for me."

"There's no reason he'll think any of those things. He's a visitor to the community, so why wouldn't I want to meet him?"

Daisy bit her lip. "Okay. I guess that's true."

"Don't worry so. You seem uptight about something."

From the deep lines that formed in her mother's forehead, she looked like the one uptight about something.

"*Nee,* I'm not at all. I just want to be treated as an adult. You treat me like a child and so does *Dat.* Lily and I are grown up now. Girls our age have families and husbands."

"You like him a lot, don't you?" her mother asked.

"Who?"

"Bruno."

Daisy stared at her mother, wondering if it would be okay if she told her the truth. Sometimes she felt it was better if she kept things from her mother to save a lecture. "I do like him. How can you tell?"

She saw a slight smile forming around her mother's lips. "You told me you did."

"Oh, I don't remember."

"Vagueness is a symptom of the love disease."

Daisy grimaced. "Ooh. That's not very nice to call it a disease. I don't want to have a disease."

"It's the best kind of disease someone can have."

Now her mother was being weird.

"I better get some sleep. Oh, before I forget, Valerie said she was going to come and see you to talk about her helping out with fundraisers and doing volunteer work."

"*Wunderbaar.*"

"She's trying to take her mind off Dirk."

"Keeping busy is good."

Daisy stood up and kissed her mother on the cheek before she went upstairs to tell Lily all about her night.

Lily's door was closed and she hoped her sister was still awake. She opened the door and, as she did, light flooded in from the gaslight in the hallway. "Lily, are you awake?"

Lily sat up. "I'm awake. I was trying to stay awake to hear what happened and then I fell asleep."

Daisy sat down on the edge of her sister's bed. "I'm pretty sure I'm in love, and he likes me too. He asked me to show him around. No, wait, Valerie asked me to show him around, but he seemed pretty happy about it."

Lily rubbed her eyes. "When are you doing that?"

"Tomorrow morning."

"Does *Mamm* know?"

"*Jah,* she's okay with that."

"*Gut.* You're paving the way for me. If she lets you do things, she might let me do things."

"Yeah. I already told her she treats us like we're younger than we are."

Lily whispered, "She was angry with *Dat* when he told her that Bruno was driving you home. I heard them talking."

"What did she say?"

"I can't remember exactly, but I could tell she was angry. She was using that controlled tone, like she was stopping herself from shouting."

"The one where she gets really loud and then takes a few deep breaths and starts speaking quieter than she normally does?"

Lily giggled. "That's right, that's the one."

Daisy yawned. "I had a nice night. Valerie is so lovely, and that's probably why Bruno is so nice."

"Where are you going with him tomorrow?"

"I don't know. I don't even care." Daisy pulled off her prayer *kapp* and began to unbraid her hair.

"He might care."

"We'll just drive around. He just wants to see what's around and give Valerie's horse some exercise. It's no big deal." Everyone was annoying her. "I might go to bed. It's late and I've got an early start tomorrow morning."

"*Gut nacht,* Daisy."

"*Gut nacht.*" Daisy was pleased to get to the privacy of her own bedroom. This was the first thing that she could remember that she and Lily weren't sharing. She had a man she could fall in love with. It didn't seem right that her sister didn't have one too so they could share their joy and talk about things together. Lily had never been in love before, so how could Daisy feel comfortable talking to her about Bruno? It didn't feel right being happy without Lily feeling the same.

When she got back to her room, she threw her prayer *kapp* down on the dresser and picked up her hairbrush. After she brushed her long hair with a few extended strokes, she changed out of her dress and into her nightgown. Once she slipped in between the cool sheets, she put the guilt over her sister to one side and imagined what it would be like being married to Bruno. Of course, he would have to move from Ohio. She drifted off to sleep, smiling as visions of being married to Bruno, with many children, played out in her head.

CHAPTER 6

Daisy had woken at the crack of dawn after having dreams about Bruno. She was excited to be seeing him, for real, that morning. If she made a good effort to show how nice it was where she lived, there was a chance he might decide to stay on. Valerie had been trying to talk him into moving and she would help her. Valerie would benefit too if she had a family member close by.

"*Gut mayriye,* Daisy."

Daisy swung around and saw her father. "Morning."

He was closely followed by her mother, who always made breakfast for their father of a morning before he left for work.

"You're awake early, Daisy."

"That's because I had a good sleep."

As her father sat down at the table, he said, "Your *mudder* tells me you're showing Bruno around this morning?"

"I am. He wants to take Valerie's horse for a run, and Valerie thought he should see what there is to see. She's trying to talk him into moving here."

"We can always do with more young men here," her mother commented as she cracked two eggs into a bowl. "Can I get you anything, Daisy?"

Daisy normally made her own breakfast. *"Nee denke.* I'll get something later."

"You can't leave home with no food in your stomach," her mother said.

"I mean later, but before he comes. Don't worry. I won't go hungry." If she stayed in the kitchen, she would be inundated with questions about Bruno. "I'll fetch the eggs." She grabbed the basket and headed outside to be faced with a cold blast of wind. Even though it was cold, she knew it would be warm in the chicken house since it was protected on one side by the barn and the other by a wall of trees. It was nearly that time of year when they needed to move the chickens into the barn.

After she took her time collecting the eggs and talking to the chickens, she headed back into the house. Her father had finished breakfast and was just about to go to work and Lily was now awake and sitting at the kitchen table.

"I collected the eggs for you, Lily. I didn't top up the food or water though."

"Denke, I'll do that later."

Daisy was a bundle of nerves and knew she'd be that way until Bruno got there. The next couple of hours were a blur of talking to Lily, eating breakfast, washing up, and then cleaning the kitchen, after which, she paced up and down past the kitchen window while waiting for Bruno to arrive. From there, she had the best view of the driveway to see him as he approached. If she was fast enough, she could leave before her mother remembered she was going to talk with him.

"He's coming!" Daisy called out in excitement, totally forgetting her earlier plans of being discreet.

Lily jumped up from the kitchen table where she'd been mending one of her dresses and stared at the approaching buggy. Her mother entered the kitchen, smiled at Daisy, and then headed out the door. At this rate, her mother would be talking with Bruno before she did. Daisy smoothed down her dress, straightened her *kapp*, and hurried to catch her mother.

Her mother walked out the front door just as Daisy reached it. Bruno jumped down from the buggy and walked toward them.

"Guder mariye. You must be Bruno?" her mother said in a sweet voice, walking toward him.

"Jah, I am, and *guder mariye* to you. You're Mrs. Yoder?"

"I am."

They smiled at each other and each gave a polite nod.

"Oh, I've got your basket in the back." Bruno reached into the buggy and pulled out the basket, handing it to Nancy.

"Denke," Nancy said.

"Valerie said she'll drop the pie dish back soon, in a day or two."

"There's no rush. I have plenty," Nancy said.

Bruno's eyes traveled to Daisy, who was now standing beside her mother. "Are you ready, Daisy?"

"Jah. Bye, *Mamm."* Daisy walked toward the buggy, knowing her sister would be watching from the kitchen window. She'd find out later what Lily thought of him, but she hoped that Lily thought he was as fine as she thought him to be.

Bruno got into the seat beside her after saying a polite goodbye to her mother. "It's nice to see you again, Daisy."

"And you."

He turned the buggy to head back down the driveway. "Where to?"

"Go left. I'll show you the town center."

"I drove through it to get to Valerie's place when I arrived."

"Driving through is different from walking through. We'll start there and then I'll take you somewhere else. That's if you don't mind going for a walk."

"I don't mind at all."

As the buggy horse clip-clopped up the road, Daisy was pleased that she felt more relaxed than she had the night before.

"What was it like growing up with all girls?" Daisy asked.

He laughed. "I had a lot of *mudders*. And I had a lot of people telling me what to do."

"That doesn't sound good."

"I might have turned out a little too spoiled for my own good. Anyway, that's what my *mudder* keeps telling me. She says that's why …" He stopped abruptly.

Daisy guessed he was about to say 'that's why I'm not married.'

He continued, "That's why I'm the way I am."

"And what way is that?"

"I'm not going to tell you. You'll have to find out for yourself."

"How long will that take? I'm not a patient person."

He glanced at her. "We have something in common, then. I have no patience either. When I set my mind to something, it has to happen right away. Except, I can't be like that with

474

Valerie. I have to wait until she sees sense and realizes she should come back home with me. I don't want her to be sad."

"Maybe she'll never want to leave and go to Ohio. She likes it here."

"Anyway, changing the subject, didn't you say you have a twin?"

"*Jah,* she was busy in the kitchen this morning. She was baking bread and it was just at that stage where she couldn't leave it and that's why she couldn't come out and say hello."

"And what stage is that?"

"Er, what do you mean?"

"At what stage can't the bread be left?"

Daisy scratched her neck. "Just when it's being kneaded. She had flour up to her elbows." Daisy felt bad and decided never again to tell him even one little lie. She'd thought nothing of telling him something that wasn't exactly true, but then she had to tell a bigger lie to cover up the first one.

"I see. I'll meet her another time, then. Perhaps at the Sunday meeting."

"*Jah.*"

Soon they were driving by the river where there were local craft shops and fresh-produce markets.

"Do you like pretzels?" Daisy asked.

"I do."

"I bet you've never had pretzels like the ones they make here."

"I can't wait to try them. I hope they're as good as you say."

"Stop the buggy over there," Daisy directed as she pointed to another buggy that was parked nearby.

Once they were out on the sidewalk, Daisy looked up at him

and smiled. "Follow me." She showed him the town, taking him from one store to another.

"Now I've seen the stores, what else can you show me?"

She frowned at him. "We've still got a lot more of them to see."

He sighed. "Lead on."

Daisy hoped that they'd be together until nightfall. "Do you have to be back at any particular time?"

"*Nee,* I've got all day." He turned to her and smiled. "Valerie's hoping you'll convince me to stay on."

"I'll do my best. I'd like you to stay here too. What kind of things do you like?"

"Food."

"Everyone likes food."

"We haven't even had a pretzel yet."

Daisy laughed at him. "You're a typical man."

"Am I?"

"*Jah,* you are. As soon as we've finished looking through one more store, we can have something to eat."

"*Gut.* Something to look forward to."

Daisy giggled, hoping she wasn't laughing too much. She didn't want him to think she was a giggling silly girl. She wanted him to think of her as a woman worth marrying. She knew he was putting on an act, and that he really didn't mind shopping with her. "Let's have a look in the candy store."

"If I have to."

"*Jah,* you do." When they walked into the candy store, Daisy saw Nathanial Schumacher at the rear of the store. "I just remembered candy's bad for you. Let's go."

"*Nee,* if you don't mind waiting a moment, I'll take Valerie back some caramel fudge. It's her favorite."

"Okay." Daisy was stuck there so she turned aside, hoping Nathanial wouldn't see her. She turned and pretended to look at something on the shelves at the side of the store.

"Hello, Daisy, or is it Lily?"

It was too late. She hesitated and when she turned around, she noticed that Bruno was staring at her and then he looked over at Nathanial. Daisy had no choice but to respond to Nathanial, who had the worst timing in the world.

CHAPTER 7

"Oh, hello, Nathanial. I'm Daisy. What are you doing back here?"

Nathanial took his eyes from her and glanced at Bruno, who had moved to stand next to her. "I'm back doing some work, helping my *onkel.*"

"The *onkel* who makes the buggies?" she asked.

"That's right." He offered his hand to Bruno. "Hello, I'm Nathanial Schumacher."

Bruno leaned forward and shook his hand. "I'm Bruno Weber."

She had to act normal; she didn't want Bruno to know there had been anything between herself and Nathanial. "Bruno is visiting from Ohio."

"Really? I'm from Ohio too. From the edge of Ohio."

The two men chatted on about their geographical locations while Daisy just wanted to run away. Nathanial was the last person that she wanted to see.

"And you two are just out shopping, are you?" Nathanial asked.

Bruno answered, "Daisy is being kind enough to show me around."

"Bruno is Valerie Miller's *bruder*. Have you ever met her?"

"I can't say that I have. I don't know everyone, though."

"You come here quite a bit, do you?" Bruno asked Nathanial.

"I haven't been here for a couple of years now after a particularly nasty upheaval I had with someone in the community, but I won't go into that now." He smiled and looked directly at Daisy.

Daisy put her fingertips up to her face and cleared her throat. He was hinting, hoping Bruno would ask what he was talking about. It was the incident they'd had when Nathanial had taken her on a buggy ride. She was surprised he had the nerve to come back into the area and, even worse, to make reference to what happened.

"That's too bad," Bruno said. "I'm staying with my *schweschder* because her husband's just died."

"Ah, I'm sorry to hear that."

"I'm doing my best to make her see that she should come back home with me for good. She's all alone here now."

Daisy said, "She's not alone, Bruno. She's got so many friends in the community."

Bruno nodded. "You keep telling me that. Maybe I'll feel better when I see the evidence with my own eyes. I should stick around. Well, I will be until I know she's going to be okay."

"Daisy could be right. It takes a while to heal after someone has died. My *vadder* died not too long ago," Nathanial said.

"I didn't know that," Daisy said, suddenly seeing the softer side of him. "Your *vadder* would be Mark and Matthew's *onkel?*"

He nodded. "That's right. Mark and Rose were there at his funeral."

"I didn't even know they'd gone to Ohio." Since Rose had married, Daisy wasn't as close with her. In fact, she hardly ever saw her. "I guess I'm not as close to her as I once was."

"Daisy's older *schweschder,* Rose, is married to my cousin, Mark," Nathanial explained to Bruno.

"I guessed from the conversation that might have been the case," Bruno said. "If you two will excuse me, I'll look for some caramel fudge for Valerie. I think I can see some over there." He pointed to the other side of the store.

Daisy had no choice but to be alone with Nathanial. "What are you really doing here, Nathanial?"

"That's not a very nice way to speak to someone, especially for a deacon's *dochder.*"

Daisy shook her head, thinking that he should be pleased that she was speaking to him at all.

He stepped closer and whispered, "You've ruined my reputation and nearly ruined my life with the lies you told everyone about me."

"I didn't tell any lies; you attacked me."

"I didn't attack you." He turned to make sure no one could hear them. He stared back at her, and whispered, "I thought you wanted me to kiss you. I'd kissed girls before and that's how it always started out. You wanted me to kiss you and as soon as I tried, you jumped out of the buggy. Then you went around telling everyone I attacked you."

"Don't be ridiculous," she hissed in a low tone before she

glanced over at Bruno, hoping he'd heard none of the conversation.

Nathanial continued, "No one would believe me. There was no point trying to defend myself against your lies. One thing my *vadder* always said is that the truth always comes out eventually. I might act aggressively and say mean things, but I would never attack a woman—never. Neither would I attack anyone—male or female."

"Don't try to make me believe you're in the right."

"It seems we have a different interpretation of what happened. I believe I'm right and you believe you're right."

"If you see it like that, let's just leave it at that and not talk to each other again," she said.

He smiled wickedly. "That might make things a bit awkward since I'm here for the next six months."

Daisy tilted her chin high. "It won't be awkward at all. If I see you coming, I'm just going to walk the other way."

"And what do you think your boyfriend would think about what you have to say?"

Out of the corner of her eye, she could see Bruno heading back toward them. "Don't you dare say a thing," she whispered.

"I managed to find some," Bruno said when he joined them again with the fudge in his hands. "Would you like any candy, Daisy, before I take this to the register?"

Daisy shook her head. *"Nee, denke.* I'm fine."

"She's sweet enough, it seems," Nathanial said, which made Daisy sick to her stomach.

Bruno just stared at Nathanial as though he was trying to figure him out.

Suddenly, Nathanial said, "Have you two had lunch? If you

haven't, I'll take you both out for lunch—my treat. There's a place close by that I used to go to."

"I'm sorry, Nathanial. *Denke*, but Daisy and I have already made plans."

Daisy was relieved to hear Bruno's words and they made her fall more in love with him. He'd saved her from embarrassment. She wasn't going to be pushed around by Nathanial. Bruno was proving to be her perfect man. She looked at Nathanial to see how he took the refusal.

Nathanial looked annoyed. "Some other time, then. I'm sure I'll be seeing more of you, Bruno."

"I'd say so." He glanced over at Daisy. "And there might be other reasons for me to stay longer, other than my *schweschder's* well-being."

Daisy looked into Bruno's dark amber eyes and couldn't help but smile. She knew them looking at each other like that would enrage Nathanial further, but she couldn't help it—she hadn't planned to upset him.

"Another time?" Nathanial asked.

Bruno nodded. "Another time. Are you ready to go, Daisy?" Before they walked away, Bruno looked back at Nathanial, and said, "It was nice to meet you, Nathanial."

"I'll see you around, and you too, Daisy."

Daisy gave him a polite nod before she headed to the counter with Bruno to pay for the candy.

Once they were clear of the store, Daisy said, "I'm so glad you didn't take up his offer to eat with him."

"I've got you all to myself today and I'm not about to share you with another man. Besides that, I got the idea that something was wrong with him, like he didn't like seeing us together.

Do you two have some kind of history? He seemed jealous to see me with you."

Daisy shook her head. "He was here a while back and I think he liked my older sister, Tulip, but she married someone else. He could be still upset about that." Remembering she wanted to be more truthful, she added, "He took me on one buggy ride, but I didn't like how he treated me."

"Ah." He nodded. "It's obvious he still likes you. Are you sure he's not my competition to win your heart?"

Daisy giggled at him being so forthright. *"Nee,* not at all. He would be the last man I would be interested in. Anyway, let's not ruin the day by talking about him any further."

By now, Daisy knew without a doubt that Bruno liked her as much as she liked him. He'd as good as said so.

"That suits me just fine. Where are we going to eat?"

"I know a nice place." Daisy walked with him to the restaurant, glad that he dropped the subject of Nathanial so quickly, but something told her that Nathanial wasn't going to stop giving her a hard time. He seemed to have a chip on his shoulder as far as she was concerned.

CHAPTER 8

DAISY WASN'T hungry and her stomach churned. It had been awful running into Nathanial unexpectedly like that. She tried to ignore her irritation over the man. Instead, she'd turn her attention into making sure that Bruno saw that she'd make a wonderful wife for him.

"What shall we have?" He picked up the menu.

Even though she wasn't hungry, she'd have to force something down so Bruno wouldn't realize she was so distressed and upset over seeing Nathanial.

"I'll have the potato pie. I had it here once before and it was *wunderbaar,*" she said.

"Potato pie it is." He closed the menu and smiled at her. "You have the most incredible eyes, Daisy."

Daisy giggled. "They are just plain brown eyes."

"There's nothing plain about them; they're beautiful."

"Stop it! You're making me blush."

"I haven't said half of the things I'm thinking."

She touched the front of her prayer *kapp* to smooth down her hair. "Go on, tell me. What are you thinking?"

"Do you really want to know?"

"Jah, I do."

"You have the perfect shaped face; you're as beautiful as an angel. Are you an angel?"

Daisy giggled. "You're being silly. Anyway, all the angels in the Bible were men, weren't they?"

He laughed. "I guess that's true, but when I think of an angel, I think of a beautiful woman."

"There was Gabriel, and I can't think of any others. I don't think they all had names."

"I think you're right; that's the only name I can remember, too. Oh wait, I think there was also Michael."

They stared into each other's eyes.

"We have to order at the counter." Daisy stood up to put their orders in.

He reached out and grabbed her hand. "I'm paying for it, Daisy. This is my treat. No angel has ever paid for her own meal." Slowly, he released her hand.

Daisy sat down, now well and truly embarrassed. She felt her cheeks grow hot and she knew her face had turned bright red. This man was an answer to her prayers; he was everything she'd dreamed of except for the part about not being a twin. Had God gone to sleep when she'd added the part about how the man she loved would have to be a twin so her sister could marry his twin brother?

She fanned the menu against her face in an effort to cool it down while she watched Bruno leaning against the counter. He was tall and muscular, but he wasn't spectacularly attractive facially—his beautiful eyes and warm smile melted her heart just the same.

After he'd ordered the food, he sat back down and she placed the menu back on the table.

"How's your *schweschder* doing? It must be a comfort to her to have you visiting her. She must be devastated about losing Dirk. Dirk wasn't really that old and everyone's a little surprised that he died in the way that he did."

"Why? Has there been talk?"

"I hate to say it." Daisy pulled a face. "There has been a little bit of talk that he might have killed himself. Don't say anything to Valerie, though. She'd be upset enough without hearing that."

His gaze fell to the table. "I would never tell her anything like that. I wouldn't want to add to her grief."

"I guess it's something that will take a long time to get over."

"Maybe it's something that people never get over; they just learn to live with it."

She shook her head. "I think my mother wouldn't want to live if something happened to my father. You should see the way that they look at each other. I'm sure they're just as much in love as the day they married."

"That's nice. It would be nice if all marriages were like that."

"You don't think they are?" Daisy asked.

"Nee, they're not. I know for a fact that they're not."

"That's sad."

"That's life, I guess."

"Have you ever come close to being married?" Daisy asked.

"A couple of years back now."

Daisy was truly shocked. She'd expected a completely different answer. "Why didn't you go through with it?"

"I got very close. It was two weeks before the wedding and I called everything off."

Daisy was surprised. The same thing happened to Tulip. Wilhem, the man she had married, had also called off a wedding a couple of weeks before it had been due to take place. It had probably taken courage for him to call off a wedding, but at the same time, it made her feel uneasy. Perhaps he was a man who didn't know his own mind. "The girl must have been very upset."

"Yeah, she was. So upset she got married four months later to a friend of mine."

Suddenly finding herself laughing, Daisy felt much better. "I'm sorry, maybe I shouldn't laugh? I'm glad she found someone else, though. I wouldn't have wanted her to be upset. And are they both happy now?"

"They seem to be, but who really knows unless you're living in their home?"

"I suppose that's true. My two older brothers and my two older sisters are all married and they are really happy."

"Same with all my sisters. They're all married. So far, I've been happy not being married."

"Is your mother trying to marry you off?"

He laughed and seemed a little embarrassed. "How did you know that? Did Valerie say something?"

"*Nee,* she didn't. I just guessed from something you said before. Now I know that all your sisters are married, and I guessed your parents want you to marry soon. You'll have to carry on the family name because you're the only son."

"You're right. That's one of the reasons I was glad to get away and come here. There's a girl from home and she's got it into her mind that I should marry her. Mind you, she's had a little bit of help from my *mudder.* I've been sure to give her no encouragement at all."

"That's terrible. No wonder you're hiding at Valerie's place."

"That's just an added benefit of being here. The main reason is to make sure Valerie's okay."

"I understand. I was only joking."

The waiter brought their potato pies to the table along with a glass pitcher of orange juice.

"I forgot to ask what you wanted to drink. Is fresh orange juice okay?"

"Jah, that's good." Daisy was pleased that she was getting to know more about him. He was very open about himself, which Daisy liked.

When they were halfway through their pies, he said, "I might as well get this over now. I hope you and I can do something another day. Would you allow me to take you out again?"

Daisy swallowed the mouthful she was chewing. "I'd like that."

"Me too."

"Does that mean you want to go back to Valerie soon? Are we running out of time?"

He shook his head. *"Nee,* I've got all the time in the world. I think my *schweschder* will appreciate some time by herself."

"That's good. I've still got so many things to show you. I found it hard to know what to say to her yesterday. I didn't know whether to avoid talking about Dirk or not because I didn't want to make her cry. In the end, she did cry."

"Crying is unavoidable, I'm afraid, at times like these. She's got a lot of adjusting to do. This will be a new stage of her life. I'm doing all I can to make it easier for her."

"And that's why you want her to go back with you?"

"That's right." He popped another portion of pie into his mouth.

"That might be too many changes at the one time."

He swallowed. "I know, but at least I'll be there to keep an eye on her."

"I can keep an eye on her, along with the rest of my family."

"*Denke*, that's kind, and I know Valerie has got a lot of friends here, but is that the same as family?"

Daisy thought about her own family and how she'd feel if they weren't around. "I can't really say. I've grown up with always having Lily around. She's always gone everywhere with me except for the last few weeks."

"What's been different about the last few weeks?" He leaned forward, placing his chin on his knuckles after placing his elbow on the table.

Had she said too much? She moved what was left of her pie around her plate with her fork. "As you know, I live at home and help my *mudder* with her duties as well as the household duties."

"She does a lot of things for the community, doesn't she?"

"That's right. She's had so much work on that these days she sends Lily and I on separate errands." Looking up at him, she hoped that what she'd said didn't make her sound as though she was too young for him. Would he want to marry someone who still did errands for their mother? Or would he want a woman who worked and was industrious and had already saved money for her future family's life? At that moment, she realized she hadn't planned for her future. She'd been lazy and that couldn't be attractive to a man like Bruno. Her older sisters, Tulip and Rose, both had jobs long before they'd gotten married.

"That must keep you very busy, helping your *mudder.*"

"It really does. Too busy to get a job like my older sisters."

He leaned back in his chair. "And what kind of work would you like to do if you had to get a job?"

"I don't know. I'd do anything really. I'm a fast learner."

"I had many different jobs until I settled into what I'm doing now." He stretched out his hand, took hold of his glass, and drained the last of his orange juice.

"What kind of things did you do?" She took another sip of juice.

He placed his empty glass back onto the table. "I did all sorts of things. I was a cleaner, a laborer, I did anything and everything to get money together."

"And now you're happy and settled in what you're doing?"

"*Jah,* I am."

"That's not good."

He frowned and his mouth tilted to one side. "It's not?"

"*Nee.* I'm helping Valerie talk you into moving here. If you weren't happy in your job, it'd be easy to have you move here." She giggled.

He laughed. "Two against one?"

"I'm sure you'd like it here."

"Maybe I like it here already." He stared into her eyes so

much that she had to look away. "I'm sorry. I didn't mean to embarrass you."

"You didn't." She looked back at him. "Maybe you did a little."

He gave her a big smile. "Are you ready?"

"*Jah*, I'll take you somewhere special."

"Can't wait."

CHAPTER 9

DAISY STOPPED at the front of the house after Bruno had taken her home. She waited until he was out of sight and then ran into the house to find Lily. The first person she saw was her mother, who was sitting on the couch in the living room darning socks.

"There you are. You're just in time to help with the dinner. Join your *schweschder* in the kitchen."

"Okay."

"Wait!"

Daisy swung around to face her mother. *"Jah?"*

"Did you have a good time?"

"I did."

"Help Lily now and you can tell us all about it over dinner."

The last thing she wanted to do was tell her parents how things had gone with Bruno. Their outing had felt like a date and she didn't want to tell her parents what happened on her date. It was private.

493

Lily's face was beaming when Daisy saw her sitting at the kitchen table shelling peas. "I saw him just now and also earlier when he collected you."

"And? What do you think of him?"

"He looked handsome from a distance, but that's not really important. Not to me it isn't, anyway."

"Me either. Of course it isn't." She sat down next to Lily and helped with the peas. "We had a really good time and he wants to see me again."

"I'm happy for you. It's just that he doesn't live around here."

"He could move. Valerie moved for love."

"So, tell me all about your day. What's he like?"

"The only way I can describe him is that he's wonderful, because that's what he is. And before I tell you more, I must tell you that Nathanial is back."

"What do you mean he's back? Back in town?"

Daisy nodded. "I was showing Bruno all the stores by the river and Nathanial was in the candy store. I turned to leave, but Bruno said he wanted to get candy for Valerie. Nathanial walked up to us and …"

"What did you do?"

Daisy licked her lips. "It wasn't easy. I had to make like we had no qualms with each other. I introduced Bruno to Nathanial as though he was just someone normal because that was all I could do. I didn't want Bruno to think there was something strange going on. I couldn't tell him about what Nathanial did."

"That would've been hard to just act like nothing was wrong."

"It was. And after I introduced the two of them, Nathanial

asked Bruno and me to go to lunch with him. What do you think about that? He was trying to torture me."

"Oh no! How did you get out of it?"

"Bruno jumped in and said we had plans."

"That was good. He must've wanted to be alone with you." Lily shook her head. "That would be just like Nathanial to want to make you feel uncomfortable. I wonder what he's doing back here. Doesn't he know he's not wanted around these parts? I'm shocked that he showed his face. Do you think you should tell *Dat?*"

"*Nee.* Word will get out that he's here. If he's not sent away when he turns up at the Sunday meeting, there'll be nothing we can do about it. He blames me for everything and for having to leave last time. Soon after Nathanial was talking to both of us, Bruno decided to get his sister some candy and left the two of us alone."

Lily leaned forward. "Did you tell him to go away and leave you alone?"

"I didn't want to be that rude, but anyway, he blamed me for everything that happened between us. He said that I wanted to be kissed and many girls before me had been kissed and I had no reason to jump out of the buggy and run away."

Lily shook her head. "He's kissed lots of girls? That's just awful, Daisy. Do you think it's true? Maybe it's not. He could've just said that because he was mad."

"Does it matter?"

"Well, is that all he did? He only tried to kiss you? That doesn't sound that bad. You could've just said you didn't want to kiss him, rather than run away."

"You weren't there. Trust me, it wasn't good. It wasn't like he said, not at all. Anyway, I don't want to talk about him."

"Tell me more about Bruno."

"The rest of the day with Bruno was amazing." Daisy couldn't stop smiling. "He's just perfect; he's just the perfect man for me. He must've known I didn't want to have lunch with Nathanial and he told him we had other plans just like a real man would've said. Bruno stood up to him without being rude."

"Bruno looks a bit older than you."

"*Jah.* I don't know how old exactly, but I know he's quite a bit older. Do you think that matters?" Daisy didn't mind one little bit how old he was. Besides, he wasn't that old—not too old for her at all. This man was a great match for her and she knew it.

"There is that saying that if something looks too perfect, maybe it is."

Daisy frowned. "What do you mean?

"If he's so great, why hasn't he married before now?"

"He's never met anybody that he wanted to marry. Actually, he told me he came close a while ago and stopped before things went too far. Also, there's a woman who everyone wants him to marry and that's another reason he's here looking after Valerie."

Lily gasped and covered her mouth.

"What is it?" Daisy asked.

"What if he's doing what Jacob did to Rose? He could have been involved with that woman in the way that he shouldn't have been, and then he's run away and you're his next victim?"

Daisy narrowed her eyes at her sister. Why was she saying horrible things about Bruno? Didn't she want her to be happy?

"Do you think he's been involved intimately with this woman he's left behind?"

"I wouldn't say something like that, but if something seems too good to be true, maybe it is, and maybe he's not as perfect as he appears to be. Don't rush into anything. 'Marry in haste, repent at leisure.'"

Daisy arched an eyebrow. "Are you just saying this because he's not a twin?"

"*Nee.* Rose was fooled by Jacob, remember?"

"Of course I do. Something like that is hard to forget. Poor Rose was so upset."

"And do you want to be fooled in just the same way?"

"Of course I don't, but I don't think he's like that. He's a really good man."

"Why don't you get *Dat* to ask questions about him just to be sure? You think he's perfect, but Rose thought Jacob was before she married Mark, and then you also thought Nathanial was perfect once."

"*Nee,* I won't do that. I won't have *Dat* thinking something is wrong with Bruno because I would know—I would know in my heart."

"If you think so. I'm only trying to help."

"I know you are. I'm just sad that he doesn't have any brothers."

Lily giggled. "That was just a childish thing for us to think, Daisy. It was nice to think that we could live together forever, but we could live nearby each other and visit every day."

"*Jah,* we'll have to do that. We can't be separated too much, or I'd die."

Lily giggled. "Me too. I think you'll end up getting married to Bruno and I will meet someone at your wedding—maybe Bruno's cousin, if he has one."

Their mother walked into the kitchen and looked at the pile of peas in the container. "Is there any work going on in here or just a lot of talk?"

"We're working too, *Mamm,*" Daisy answered.

LATER THAT NIGHT, Daisy was in her room with Lily just before bedtime. Daisy pulled her long dark hair over one shoulder. She began to braid her hair, as was her nightly routine, into one long braid.

"Turn around. I'll do your hair."

Daisy turned around, flipping her hair over her back, pleased that she'd told Lily everything about Bruno. She would be careful, as Lily suggested. Being impulsive had never led her anywhere good in the past.

"I hope Nathanial doesn't try to ruin things with Bruno and you. Do you think he was jealous?" Lily asked.

"*Nee.* What happened was so long ago. He wouldn't have even given it two thoughts. Hopefully he's matured since then." His words at the candy store had shown otherwise, but Daisy pushed that out of her mind, preferring not to let anything ruin her good mood.

When Lily went into her own room, her words of earlier that day about Bruno not being perfect swirled in Daisy's head. She slipped between the covers of her bed and went over the day she'd had with Bruno. He seemed so perfect, but was she just setting herself up for a fall? She'd also liked Nathanial before she'd gone on that disastrous buggy ride with him a long time ago. What if Bruno was simply putting on a good act?

Daisy decided to be guarded just in case. She would not give her heart away too soon. He'd run from a woman in Ohio, so what if he was someone who ran when a relationship got serious? It was quite possible that it was so.

CHAPTER 10

WHEN NANCY and Hezekiah were getting ready for bed, Nancy asked, "What do you think of Valerie's *bruder,* Bruno?"

"He seems a man of good reputation from what I've heard so far. Do you want me to ask further about him?"

"Jah, I think that would be a good idea. You know what the twins are like—they don't have much sense about men or anything else."

"You don't trust them?"

"Nee. I don't trust them to make good decisions. I think they've proven that they don't always know how to make decisions."

"Valerie's *familye* is *gut.* I know that, but I'll keep asking. I don't think we've got anything to worry about there."

"Gut. See what you can find out, would you?"

"Of course I will. Daisy's already spent the day with him."

"Still, I'd like you to ask about him. I can tell she likes him. Why don't I ask him over for dinner with Valerie?"

"Okay. When?"

"I'll ask them at the Sunday meeting if they'll come for dinner on the following Monday."

"Fine by me," he said.

"Okay. I meant to have Valerie over soon anyway. She wants to talk with me about doing volunteer work."

"It works out good all around then."

"*Jah.*"

"Daisy seems quite serious about Bruno," he said.

"She can't be too serious about him; she's only just met him."

Hezekiah shrugged his shoulders. "Seems like it to me, though. She kept smiling throughout dinner and did you notice when we asked her about her day she deliberately didn't talk about him?"

"Now that you mention it, I can see that she didn't like to tell us much about him. Sounds like she wants to keep things to herself."

"Or not say his name in front of me," Hezekiah said. *"Vadders* are always the last to know anything."

Nancy giggled. "And *mudders* too. We'll have to see what Bruno's like when he's here for dinner."

"What you won't be pleased to hear is that Nathanial Schumacher is back here, staying for a few months while he's helping his *onkel.*"

"That's dreadful. When did he get here? Couldn't you have kept him away?"

"I can't do that."

"You could've told the bishop exactly what he did to Daisy."

"I said enough and besides, we don't know what he did to Daisy." He scratched his neck. "I don't like to say it, but …"

"You think she made the whole thing up?"

"*Nee*, I'm not saying that, but …"

"You think she might have exaggerated what happened?"

He grimaced. *"Jah*, I think it's possible. I didn't want to say anything to you about it before now. At the time, I was enraged with Nathanial, but when everything calmed down, I got to thinking what Daisy's like and … let's just say I have a question mark there."

Part of her wanted to be upset with her husband for thinking such a thing, but she'd had the same thoughts cross her mind too. Then again, he was Jacob's brother. "I think he's just like his older *bruder,* Jacob. They're bad seeds."

"You can't judge someone by their siblings. Every man has to stand on his own and be judged by his own works. *Gott* knows every man's heart and He's the judge."

"But meanwhile, we have to keep our *dochders* safe and away from men like Nathanial. We just can't take the risk."

"I agree, but at the same time, I can't point the finger at him and say he's done something when we don't have details and Daisy won't talk about it."

"She's embarrassed."

"I know, but she won't even tell you the full account of what happened that night, so it's hard for me to say anything to the bishop when I don't know the full story."

"She's said enough."

"Still, I don't have any reason to ask him to leave, and neither can I say anything to the bishop to cause him to ask Nathanial to leave. When it happened, I hinted to the bishop and he took note."

"He must be guilty. He left the community quickly when it all happened."

"I don't think he'll give Daisy any more trouble. Daisy seems fond of Bruno, so let's just leave things be. I'll keep an eye on Nathanial."

"Okay. I'll put Nathanial Schumacher out of my mind, and I'll invite Valerie and Bruno for dinner Monday night if they haven't made other plans."

Hezekiah smiled at his wife, leaned over, and kissed her on her cheek.

CHAPTER 11

DAISY WAS PLEASED to be going to the Sunday meeting because she knew she would see Bruno again. But ... she hoped Nathanial wasn't planning on causing trouble between herself and Bruno. It had been obvious that Bruno and she liked each other as more than just friends, and that had irritated Nathanial—she could see it on his face.

The meeting that Sunday was held at the Stoltzfus' house, old Mary's eldest son's place. Daisy sat down at the back of the living room next to Lily. They had both walked past Nathanial and he had smiled at them, but Daisy had looked the other way as soon as he'd done so. She hadn't meant to be rude; she was nervous and didn't want to give him any encouragement. Just before the meeting began, Valerie and Bruno walked in and took their seats. Before Bruno sat down, Daisy noticed he quickly looked around the room and saw where she was.

Lily leaned in close. "That's him, isn't it?"

"*Jah*, what do you think?"

"He seems all right, but he's not my type."

Daisy glared at her sister. They'd always had the same taste in everything so why wouldn't they have the same taste in men? "Why isn't he your type?"

"I don't know; he's kind of—too old or something."

"He's not that much older than us. Anyway, he mightn't be super handsome, but he doesn't need to be. He's perfect on the inside and that suits me just fine."

"That's all that matters," Lily said.

It had surprised Daisy that Lily hadn't been very encouraging.

"I hope Nathanial is not going to stay around too long," Lily whispered and then added, "Didn't you say he was working for his *onkel* for a few weeks?"

"Jah, but I was just hoping he would go sooner."

"Don't let it bother you, Daisy."

"I'll try not to."

Their mother, who was sitting directly in front of them, turned around and shot them a heated glare for whispering.

They kept quiet the rest of the meeting.

WHEN THE MEAL WAS SERVED, after the meeting was over, it was the twins' time to socialize.

All Daisy wanted to do was run over and talk to Bruno immediately, but she didn't want tongues to wag, so she restrained herself. Every now and again when she was talking to people, she would see Bruno looking in her direction.

Halfway through the meal, she saw her mother and father

talking to Bruno. She dug her sister in the ribs. "Look, Lily. I don't like the look of that."

"Why not? They're just being friendly with him since he's a visitor to the community."

"*Nee,* there's more to it than that. I should never have told *Mamm* about liking Bruno. Remember how pushy she was when she was trying to get Rose and Tulip married off?"

"*Mamm* would never be like that with us. She knows how sensible we both are."

"*Jah,* that's true," Daisy said with a giggle.

Lily said, "Do you want me to go over and see if I can hear what they're saying?"

"*Nee.* I'll go over and speak with him when they go. He'll tell me what they said."

"I'm sure there's nothing to worry about."

When her mother and father had finished speaking with Bruno, she casually walked over to him.

"How are you, Daisy? I was wondering when you were going to come and speak with me."

"Well, you could've come to me." Daisy laughed.

"I wasn't sure you'd want me to—only because people might talk."

"There's nothing we can do to prevent that happening. I'm not worried about that."

"That's good. If I'd known that, I would've been straight over to see you as soon as the meeting finished."

"I just noticed my parents were speaking with you."

"*Jah,* they invited me and Valerie to dinner."

Daisy was speechless. "Why did they ... I mean ..."

He laughed and touched her arm lightly. "I was a little surprised too, but pleased about it."

"When—when are you coming for dinner?"

"Tomorrow night."

Daisy was delighted that her mother was helping her with her new romance. That meant her mother and father approved of him. She already knew they liked Valerie a lot, and they must've liked Bruno just as much.

"I'll look forward to you coming. Did she say there would be anyone else there besides you and Valerie?" Daisy wondered whether her mother would be inviting the whole family—her brothers and their wives, and her two older sisters and their husbands.

He shook his head. "She didn't say. It'll be good to get to know your parents better. They seem nice, just like my parents."

CHAPTER 12

WHEN DAISY WOKE UP, she immediately remembered that Bruno was coming to dinner. This would be the first time that Lily would meet him, since they hadn't spoken at the Sunday meeting. She'd already worked out the dinner menu with her mother the night before. They were having roast chicken with bread stuffing, mashed potatoes, and coleslaw, and for dessert they were having fruit salad and tapioca pudding. She'd told her mother that she would do most of the cooking.

Her stomach churned at the thought of seeing Bruno again. She changed out of her nightdress, pulling on a clean dress. She wasted no time on her hair, figuring she'd fix it before Bruno arrived—for now she tucked her long braid under her prayer *kapp*. When she was done dressing, she headed downstairs.

"There you are," her mother said when she walked into the kitchen. "I let you sleep in and I was just about to wake you."

"Did I sleep in?" Daisy looked out the window to see a gray

overcast sky. She always slept in when the sky was gray like that. "I didn't mean to."

"Never mind. I had to send Lily to the store without you. There were a few things I needed."

"I could've gone with her."

"There's no use sending the two of you to do a job that only takes one. Now fix yourself some breakfast and then we'll start cleaning this *haus* from top to bottom. I don't want Valerie to think we live in a dirty place."

"The *haus* is already clean."

Her mother's face soured. "Not to my standards."

"What do you want me to do first?"

"Have something to eat and then we can start on the floors. After the floors are washed, it'll have to be the windows. We'll start the cooking at three."

"Okay."

When her mother went out of the room, Daisy fixed herself some eggs. She was a little disappointed to miss out on going to the store with Lily, but Bruno coming there tonight more than made up for it.

It was two o'clock in the afternoon and Lily still hadn't come home.

"I should go and look for her, *Mamm*."

"She should've been home hours ago."

Daisy nibbled on the end of her fingernail. "I hope she hasn't had an accident or something."

"She'll want to have had an accident if she comes home this late. Otherwise, she'll have no *gut* excuse for getting out of chores."

"I'm certain she'll have a reason. Let me go and look for her."

Her mother nodded. "Okay, but don't take too long."

When Daisy was halfway to the barn, she saw Lily coming up the driveway in the buggy pulled by their bay gelding.

She hurried toward her. "Where have you been, Lily?"

"Am I late or something?"

"Jah, and *Mamm's* furious."

"I lost track of the time. That's all."

"You better think of some reason why you were gone so long. You know how she likes to scrub the *haus* extra well before people come for dinner."

"How mad is she?"

"Very. You go and see her and I'll rub the horse down for you and unhitch the buggy."

"Denke, Daisy."

Lily jumped out of the buggy and, with the groceries in her arms, walked slowly to the house. Before she reached the door, it was flung open and their mother stood there scowling at Lily with her arms folded tightly across her chest.

When Daisy led the horse into the barn, she could hear her mother berating her sister. She did everything as quickly as she could so she could get back to the house.

Once she got back and entered the kitchen, Lily was nowhere to be seen. Her mother was mixing the bread stuffing for the chicken with her fingers.

"Where's Lily?"

"I sent her up to her room."

That meant Lily was in big trouble. "Can I go and see her?"

"Nee, you can't. You'll help me here."

Her mother was in one of those moods where she was not to be crossed.

Half an hour later, her mother disappeared from the kitchen and Daisy guessed she'd gone to see Lily. It wouldn't be nice if Bruno and his sister came to the house and sensed the tension. She hoped Lily and their mother would work things out right now.

Lily came down the stairs five minutes later with her mother walking close behind her. Lily was given the job of scrubbing the bathroom—the chore she and Daisy hated the most.

Later, when Lily and Daisy had a quiet moment, Daisy asked her why she'd been gone for so long in town.

"Like I said, I lost track of time. I looked around the stores and I stopped to have something to eat. I didn't know I was supposed to come right back as soon as I got the groceries. We normally look around the stores together."

"*Jah*, but tonight we've got people coming for dinner and that means scrubbing the *haus*."

"We clean it every day; it's fine."

"You and I know that, but *Mamm* doesn't."

The girls stopped talking when their mother came back into the kitchen.

"Less talk and more work, please. Our guests will be here soon and we don't want to have them waiting until late at night to be fed."

They all heard the front door open, and their mother rushed to greet their father.

"I hope she doesn't tell *Dat* that I was away so long."

"He won't mind. He'll tell *Mamm* she's fussing about things again."

Lily giggled. "She doesn't like it when he says that."

"You'll have to tell me honestly what you think of Bruno."

"*Jah,* of course I'll be honest. Why wouldn't I be?"

"I didn't mean that you wouldn't, but you might not tell me how you really feel about him because you know I like him so much."

"I'll be honest and tell you exactly what I think of him," Lily said as she picked up another pod of peas to shell.

CHAPTER 13

DAISY WAITED EXCITEDLY in the kitchen when she heard the buggy coming to the house. Her mother and father were in the living room and she and Lily were setting the table in the large dining room just off from the kitchen.

"What should I do?" Daisy asked Lily.

"Just wait here until they both come inside, and then go out into the living room."

Daisy nodded. "Okay. I'm so nervous I can't even think properly."

"Just relax; everything will be fine. Don't worry. You'll be all right—he obviously likes you."

"I guess so. He seems to like me."

Daisy did what her twin sister suggested; she stayed in the kitchen until she heard Bruno's voice in the living room and then she walked out to greet Bruno and his sister, Valerie.

Bruno looked handsome in his billowing white shirt paired with black pants held up by black suspenders. He'd made an effort to dress well—far different from the casual clothes he was wearing when she'd first met him at Valerie's *haus*.

"Daisy, it's nice to see you again," he said, smiling.

"Hello, Bruno. Hi, Valerie."

"Hello, Daisy. I was just telling Bruno how alike you and Lily are."

"*Jah*, they haven't met yet."

"I saw Lily yesterday at the meeting from across the yard, but I haven't spoken to her yet. It would be hard to tell the two of you apart." He turned to Mr. Yoder. "I guess you can tell which one is which?"

He laughed. "I can. I've had many years of practice. They are slightly different in the face, but even I can't tell who's who from a distance."

Right on cue, Lily walked into the room.

Daisy linked arms with Lily. "This is Lily."

"It's nice to meet you, Bruno. Hello again, Valerie."

"Hello, Lily," Valerie said.

Bruno smiled at her. "Hello, Lily. The resemblance is amazing."

Lily giggled. "I'm wearing the green dress and Daisy is wearing the purple dress."

"I'll remember that," he said.

"Dinner smells *wunderbaar*, Nancy," Valerie said.

"*Denke.* I hope it tastes as good."

Lily and Daisy sat on the couch next to Valerie, and Bruno sat on the couch opposite, next to the twins' parents.

"Why don't you go and make us some coffee, Daisy?" their mother suggested. "It'll be a little while before dinner."

"Of course." Daisy bounded to her feet.

"Shall I help?" Bruno said, standing up.

Daisy thought quickly. *"Jah,* I might need help carrying everything out."

The two of them hurried to the kitchen.

Bruno sat down at the kitchen table and watched Daisy make the coffee. "It was nice of your parents to invite us to dinner."

"They like Valerie, and it seems as though they might like you, too."

"How can you tell?'

"I can just tell."

"Do you want me to help you with anything there?"

"Nee, denke. You can help carry the tray in when everything's ready."

"I think I can manage that. When can we see each other again?"

She turned away from the stove where she'd just placed the pot to boil. She stared at him. "When would you like to do that?"

"Tomorrow?"

Daisy gave a quiet giggle. "I'll see if I can get away."

"There are a few repairs I want to make to Valerie's *haus.* I'll ask your *vadder* if you could come with me to show me the best places to buy the hardware."

"He might point out I don't know anything about hardware. Is that the best excuse you can come up with?"

"Can you think of a better one?" He smiled at her.

She shook her head. "Not quickly."

"That'll have to do, then."

She sat down at the table with him.

"Did you have any other plans for tomorrow?" he asked.

"*Nee.* Each day is pretty much the same for me. *Mamm* helps the community a lot, so she's always having us help her to either visit people or sew things that we can sell for charities."

"That's nice. It must feel good to be so useful to so many people. I know Valerie appreciates the help your *familye* has been."

"*Dat* says everyone needs a helping hand every once in a while and tomorrow it could be us."

"*Vadders* are so wise sometimes; mine says if one person in the community is hurting then we're all not well."

"Is he a part of the church oversight?"

"*Nee,* he's not. He was very strict when we were growing up. He's relaxed a little in his old age."

"What about your *mudder?*"

"She's a very kind and gentle woman—she's quietly spoken."

Lily walked into the kitchen. "Can I help with anything?"

"Are they getting thirsty?" Daisy asked, surprised to see her sister.

Lily said, "*Nee,* but they were talking about things and I thought I should make myself scarce."

"What were they talking about?" Bruno asked.

"They're talking about Valerie possibly selling the farm."

Bruno nodded. "That's something she's been wanting to talk over with someone like your *vadder.*"

Lily glanced at the bare table, and then the pot on the stove. Without saying anything, she gathered the tray, cups, teaspoons, and everything else they'd need for their coffee.

"*Denke,* Lily," Daisy said, glad that one of them was thinking straight. All she could think about was Bruno and wanting to be alone with him.

When the pot boiled, Daisy made the coffee and the girls followed Bruno back out to the living room.

THAT NIGHT, when Lily and Daisy were having their usual nightly chat in Daisy's bedroom, Lily leaned close to Daisy, and said, "I hope you didn't mind me coming into the kitchen. I didn't want to disturb you. I knew you'd want to be alone with him, but it wasn't right, me sitting there while Valerie talked about selling the farm and all that."

"Of course I didn't mind. I had a few minutes alone with him and he wants us to go somewhere tomorrow."

"I know. I heard him asking *Mamm* if he could come and collect you in the morning. That's *wunderbaar.* I could tell he really likes you. He couldn't stop smiling at you. I reckon you'll marry him."

Daisy's face lit up. "Do you think so?"

"I do. Then you'll have to help find someone for me. I'm not in a hurry. I'll take my time and find someone who suits me perfectly, just like Bruno suits you."

"He does suit me, doesn't he? And it was all so unexpected. One day I didn't even know him and the next day I'm in love with him."

"Are you in love?" Lily asked.

"*Jah,* I truly am. I can't stop thinking about him and when I'm with him, he makes me feel so happy. I can't imagine marrying anyone but him. The only thing is I don't want to move away and he doesn't live here."

"That's easy solved. Just tell him you won't marry him unless he moves here."

"Should I be that bossy? He might not like bossy women."

"Just be yourself, and you *are* bossy." Lily giggled.

"I guess I am, and if he loves me, he will move here. It'll help that Valerie wants to stay here too."

"I thought she was selling her farm. That's what she was talking about when I escaped into the kitchen."

"Bruno said she was thinking of selling the land and keeping the house."

"Can that be done?" Lily asked.

Daisy nodded. *"Jah,* people sell off parts of their land all the time."

"It'd be nice for Valerie to have her *bruder* living close by."

"Jah, it must be hard for her with her husband gone."

Lily agreed. "Especially with all that talk going around about him. I wonder if she knows what people are saying."

"I don't think she would," Daisy said.

"What do you think happened to Dirk?"

Daisy shook her head. "He's gone. That's all I know. The rest doesn't make any difference."

CHAPTER 14

WHEN HE COLLECTED Daisy the next morning, Bruno said he'd do his errands another day and today, Daisy could take him on a tour of the local countryside and show him all her favorite spots.

Daisy had proceeded to show Bruno all the places around the area that she could think of and, even though the day was cold, he thought it would be nice to have a walk down by the river on one of the many walking trails she'd mentioned. She hoped he might be romantic and hold her hand when no one was about.

She wanted nothing more than to marry him and be happy like her sisters were. Then she could really start her life and have her own home with her own children. It had been a childish fantasy that she would marry a twin so Lily and she could be together; she knew that now.

"Shall we park the buggy here?" he asked when they drew close to the river.

"*Jah*, this is perfect."

They got out of the buggy and then walked side-by-side down to the riverbank. It was a little muddy and Daisy was careful where she put her feet, so she didn't slip. Soon she heard the gurgling fast-running water of the river.

"Are you warm enough?" He glanced over at her.

She pulled her black shawl tighter around her shoulders to keep out the cool breeze coming up from the water. "I'm okay." As soon as she'd spoken those words, she regretted them. If she'd said she was cold then perhaps he would've placed his coat around her shoulders, or he might have put his arm around her to keep her warm. She'd think quicker next time.

When they were on the path parallel to the river, it was more level and solid underfoot.

"It's beautiful here," he said, staring out at the river.

"It's running fast today because we've had rain lately."

He sniffed the air. "I can smell wildflowers, or something."

"It could be. There are a few around, but not for long."

They walked on in silence for quite a while.

"Are you all right? You seem a little quieter today," Daisy said.

"I've got a lot on my mind."

"Like what?" Remembering her manners, she added, "Do you want to talk about it?"

"My *mudder* wants me to go home and I've still got a lot of things to organize for Valerie."

"Why? Like what?"

"Why does she want me home or what do I have to do for Valerie?"

"Both."

"Valerie has decided to go ahead with selling off most of her land. It's a bit of a nightmare and I don't think she's in any state to do all that alone. She'll keep the *haus* and a little land, enough to have a small garden and chickens."

"That's sad that she has to sell."

"It's the best outcome. It makes sense, since she can't work the land."

"And do you want to go home, Bruno, like your *mudder* wants?"

He stopped near the water and looked across it to the other side. *"Nee,* I don't want to go home. I wouldn't be able to see you if I went home." He looked back at her.

She smiled and looked away, glad that his quiet mood had nothing to do with her.

"Why does she want you to come home?"

"It's all to do with that girl I told you about. I don't know why they're pushing her onto me. They did it once before and it ended badly. I just want to choose my own *fraa.* What's wrong with that?"

"Nothing. That's how it should be. Parents can be too pushy sometimes. Anyway, how is Valerie today?"

"She's doing okay."

"I'm sure she's grateful and pleased that you've come to help out with everything."

"I guess she is. Let's sit here and look at the river so I can take my mind off all my troubles."

Daisy gave a little giggle as they sat down on a wooden seat.

"Why does your *mudder* like this girl so much?"

"I have no idea. Maybe it's because she's available and has all the attributes of a *gut fraa.* I mean, there's nothing wrong with her, she's perfectly nice, but totally unsuited to me. There's just no spark between us. Do you know what I mean?"

Daisy smiled and nodded, and then looked over the water and wondered if he felt a 'spark' with her. She felt it with him.

They talked some more and found out more about each other, until Daisy remembered she had to be home at a reasonable hour to help her mother.

"My *familye* has a dinner every week where we all gather. It used to be about once a month, but my *mudder* changed it to once a week. It's on tonight."

"That's a lovely idea."

"That's why I have to be home early to help with the dinner."

"We'll see each other again soon, won't we?"

"I hope so."

They stood and walked back to the buggy.

"How about Friday?" he asked.

Daisy nodded. "I'd like that very much."

"Good! It's nice that your *familye* keeps close together. My parents see everyone only at the meetings and community events because they're all so busy with their own families."

"Does it feel odd to be the only one out of your siblings not married?" Daisy asked, wondering how she'd feel if Lily married first, leaving her unmarried.

"It does sometimes. I'd like nothing more than a *fraa* and a *familye* to come home to after a hard day's work." He stopped still when they reached the buggy, and then looked down into her eyes.

She smiled at him, hoping he was about to ask her to marry him. Her parents might think that they hadn't known each other long enough, but she knew that it was right. He was the man for her. Many young people in the community got married after only knowing someone for a short time.

"Daisy, I'm so glad I came to stay with Valerie. I'm so pleased to have met you."

She waited for him to keep talking, but he didn't, so she said, "I'm grateful you came because I'm happy to have met you, too."

He looked into her face for a moment before he spoke again. "Let's go. I'll take you home before it gets too late. I need to keep in good standing with your parents."

As they both climbed into the buggy, Daisy couldn't help being a little disappointed that Bruno hadn't talked about marriage. Perhaps he would take time to think about what he wanted once he got Valerie settled.

CHAPTER 15

IT WAS nice to see her brothers and sisters happily married and their families growing. Daisy's niece, Shirley, had a baby sister, Lizzie. Her older brother, Trevor, and sister-in-law, Amy, had a baby boy, now six months old, whom they had named Stephen. Rose and Mark still didn't have any children because Rose had suffered two miscarriages in the past year, which she had become depressed about.

"Rose and I have an announcement to make," Mark said, as he stood up at the table at their family dinner.

Daisy hoped that he would say that Rose was finally expecting again.

Hezekiah said, "The last time you said that, you were announcing that you and Rose were going to get married. What is it this time?"

From a standing position, Mark reached out and grabbed Rose's hand. "Rose and I are having a *boppli.*"

Everyone let out delighted gasps and most people jumped out of their seats to congratulate and kiss the happy couple.

"And it's past the danger point. I'm halfway along." Rose sat with her shoulders back and a huge grin on her face.

Daisy couldn't speak because she was so pleased. She got up and kissed Rose quickly, and then kissed Mark, before she sat down. Everything had come easy for Rose except for having a baby. Hopefully, this baby would have no problems coming into the world. She'd lost the other two early in her pregnancies. Then there was Tulip who hadn't gotten pregnant at all, and she'd been married long enough to have a baby by now. She appeared to be hiding her personal disappointment. Maybe all the Yoder girls would have problems having babies.

Daisy had been right about Tulip being upset, because Tulip and Wilhem made their excuses and left right after dessert—not even waiting for coffee in the living room.

Daisy whispered to Lily, "I think Tulip's upset that she's not had a baby and she's been married long enough."

"I thought that too, and she left early. We had best not say anything to Rose because she would get upset about Tulip being sad. Rose should be feeling happy at this time."

"Agreed," Daisy whispered back. "Anyway, I've got something to tell you later."

"About Bruno?" Lily asked.

"Jah."

AFTER THEIR GUESTS had gone home that night, Hezekiah and Nancy went up to their bedroom, leaving the twins to do the washing up and the cleaning of the kitchen.

"Rose will have our fourth *grosskin.* Isn't it wonderful news? I thought she was getting big, but I didn't say anything because I didn't want to upset her in case she wasn't expecting."

"It's certainly is good news, but I couldn't help feeling a little sorry for Tulip. Did you notice how they left early?"

"*Jah,* I did, but there's nothing we can do about that. She'll have her *boppli* soon. It took Rose some time, so it'll probably take Tulip a while too."

Nancy took off her prayer *kapp* and unpinned her hair. She ran a brush through her long hair, which ended past her thighs. Her hair had only been cut once, when she was a teenager, because the weight of it had given her headaches. It took a good twenty minutes a night to brush her hair.

When Hezekiah was changed into his pajamas, he got into bed and propped himself up with the pillows. "There's something I have to tell you, Nancy, but I don't want you to get angry or upset."

The brush slipped out of Nancy's hand and bounced across the wooden floorboards. It was not a good way for her husband to start a conversation. Her eyes fixed onto Hezekiah, wondering what was wrong. Whatever he was about to say was not going to be good. "What is it?" She held her breath, bracing herself for what was to come.

"One of the twins has been seen alone with Nathanial."

She sighed with relief, leaned down, and picked up the brush. When she straightened up again, she said, "That was Daisy. She told me all about running into him at the candy store when she was out with Bruno."

"*Nee,* Nancy. It was Lily and they were in a café and they

were holding hands. I know for certain it was Lily because Daisy was elsewhere at the time the twin was spotted."

Nancy's mouth dropped open as she stared at her husband in disbelief. "And why are you only telling me about this now?"

"I didn't want to ruin dinner."

"Better ruining my dinner than ruining Lily's life. He caused you to have a heart attack and did goodness knows what to Daisy, and now he's paying everybody back by going after Lily."

"We don't know for certain …"

Nancy placed her brush back on the dresser and walked towards the door.

Hezekiah threw back the covers and got out of bed, getting to the door ahead of her and resting his hand on Nancy's. "Don't act in haste. No good will come of you being cross with Lily about this. This is something we have to think about more deeply." He led Nancy back to the bed and they both sat.

Nancy put her hand to her head. "I'm upset about it."

"I know, but we have to be smart about this, Nancy. Daisy told us she liked Bruno and now Lily obviously likes Nathanial, but has chosen not to tell us because she knows the fuss that happened between him and Daisy."

"I know that, Hezekiah. What are you trying to say? I want to go right in there now and ask Lily what's going on and ask her why she kept this a secret from us." Anger swirled in Nancy's head and she felt she was going to burst. She couldn't just sit there and do nothing.

"And what good would that do?"

She stared at her husband who sometimes seemed far too calm. "You want to let her sneak around behind our backs?"

"Many young people court in secret with no one looking over their shoulders."

"But he's not just any young man; he's no good."

"No one's all bad. He might have changed his ways. We don't know he hasn't transformed and repented of his ways."

"And if he hasn't? Are you willing to put our *dochder* at risk by allowing her to see more of this man who has a bad reputation?"

Hezekiah looked thoughtful and shook his head. "I don't know what to do right now. I only know that no good will come of lecturing Lily about it now. We have to be careful that we don't drive her further into his arms and away from us. I've seen things like that happen in other families."

Nancy gasped and covered her mouth with her hand. As the deacon, her husband was privy to many private matters between people in their community. "You're right; that's exactly what Lily would do. She'd run away with him. She's never really listened to what we have to say."

"Maybe the best thing we can do is to do nothing at all," Hezekiah suggested with amazing composure.

Nancy looked into her husband's eyes and was pleased that he was so wise and level-headed. He was right about saying nothing to Lily. She'd carefully monitor the situation and step in when necessary. If Lily thought she was in love with Nathanial, she was the kind of girl who would run away with him if told she wasn't allowed to see him again. Nancy would just have to trust that she had raised Lily properly and she wouldn't do anything silly.

"We'll pray about it and have faith that *Gott* will work things out for Lily. He'll guide Lily because we will ask Him to."

Nancy nodded and put her head on her husband's shoulder. He'd always been so sensible and had a special way of calming her down and making her think first, rather than reacting to a situation. It seemed as though every time she wanted to be happy and enjoy good news, the twins had a way of doing something dreadful to ruin everything. Why couldn't they be more normal?

THEY'D HAD their family dinner and everyone had gone home, but Daisy couldn't shake the fact that Bruno had been close to talking about marriage earlier that day at the riverbank and had stopped himself. It wasn't unusual in their Amish community to have quick courtships, and young people paired together fairly quickly. Why was he so hesitant?

Lily and Daisy were having their nightly conversation in Daisy's room.

"What did I do wrong, Lily? Should I have said something different? I was certain he was going to ask me to marry him. He even talked about the girl his *mudder* is trying to make him marry and he said there was no spark with her. Surely he wouldn't have told me that unless he felt he had a spark with me, don't you think?"

"I'm not sure."

"Do you think he only sees me as a friend?"

"I don't know."

Daisy groaned. "I wish I knew what was going on in his head. Sometimes I feel I'm sure he likes me and other times I don't know if he does or not."

"Maybe you were acting too keen. Remember, he said there was that woman chasing him—the one his *mudder* wants him to marry? Perhaps you shouldn't be so keen?"

"I'm just being myself and I don't think I've been like that. I don't want to play games. I might lose him if I do. Things should happen naturally."

"Lose him? Do you reckon you have him now? If you don't have him, you can't lose him."

Daisy scrunched up her face, trying to figure out Lily's logic. "What are you talking about?"

"If he knows you'll say yes to marrying him, he loses the thrill of the chase. Men are like hunters; they like the thrill of the chase and if he knows you're keen on him, there's no thrill there."

Daisy shook her head. *"Nee,* I think you're wrong."

"Has he asked you to marry him yet?"

"Nee, you know that he hasn't."

"Well, perhaps you should play a little harder to get? That'll make him more interested. Sometimes men want what they can't have and especially a man like Bruno who's been a bachelor for some time. He's used to passing women over and in doing so, he grows more and more picky with every woman he sees as not meeting his standards."

Lily's words cut into Daisy's heart like a knife. Perhaps there was some truth in what she said. She had shown Bruno she was keen on him and although she knew that he liked her too, was that enough for him to ask her to marry him? She had to be smarter about things if she wanted Bruno as her husband.

"Lily, I think some of what you say might be true."

"I know I'm right. Just because I've never had a boyfriend

doesn't mean that I don't know how these things work. If you act less keen, or if he thinks there might be someone else, he'll make sure to make you his wife. Men are territorial creatures. You don't have to say yes every time he asks you out."

"But he's only here for a short amount of time."

"He can stay longer if he wants. That's what you told me."

"Did I?"

"*Jah.*"

Although her sister's words seemed odd, she thought back to the first outing with Bruno. He had blocked Nathanial from his offer of lunch and perhaps that extra male attention from Nathanial had spurred Bruno on to keep seeing her. That showed her that maybe Lily was right about how men thought.

"So, if you're right, what do you think I should do now?" Daisy had no one else to ask and Lily seemed so confident in what she said.

"Don't act so keen on him. He won't want you as bad if he knows he can have you."

Daisy nodded. She wanted Bruno as her husband so badly she was willing to do what her sister suggested. If it didn't work, she could always go back to the way things were. "*Denke,* Lily. I'll think about it."

"Okay. *Gut nacht.*" Lily bounced out of her room without waiting for her to say good night back.

Daisy slipped further underneath her bedcovers, hoping her new plan was the right way to go.

CHAPTER 16

AFTER BREAKFAST, Hezekiah left for work at his brother's farm and Nancy sat at the table having a second cup of coffee. Lily was the first of the twins to come down for breakfast.

"Good morning, *Mamm*."

"Morning, Lily. It seems Daisy has taken to sleeping in."

Lily giggled. "Probably dreaming about Bruno."

Nancy smiled. "I think you could be right."

Lily poured herself a cup of coffee and sat down at the table with her mother.

After Lily had taken a sip, Nancy said to her, "And what about you? Have you found a boy that you like?"

"*Nee*, I haven't."

Nancy hesitated a moment. "*Nee?*"

Lily's brown eyes flickered as she stared at her mother. "*Nee.*"

Against Hezekiah's better judgment, she asked her straight out, "What about Nathanial Schumacher?" She wished she could be calm and patient like her husband had suggested but she couldn't.

"He'd be the last person I would want as my boyfriend, especially after what he did to Daisy."

"That's funny, because someone said they saw you in town with him the other day."

Lily smiled, and then said, "That was the other day when I was out by myself getting things from the store. I ran into him; he talked to me, and I had to say something to be polite."

"And was that all it was?

"*Jah*, that's all it was. Why do you ask?"

Nancy shook her head. She knew Lily was lying, but if she pushed her or told her what she knew, that they'd been seen holding hands, she could very well drive her daughter away and into Nathanial's arms just like Hezekiah had warned.

"It's nothing. You know how people like to talk." She reached out and patted her daughter gently on the hand. "Forget I said anything."

"Okay."

Lily drank her coffee and then fixed herself some breakfast. All the while, Nancy sat in the kitchen restraining herself from berating her daughter for having anything to do with Nathanial Schumacher. He was trouble, just like his brother, Jacob, had been trouble.

The awful thing was that the twins were very attractive, probably the most attractive girls in the community, and they were prey for men like Nathanial. She was pleased that Daisy had found a lovely man like Bruno. If only Bruno lived locally. As much as she wanted Daisy to stay close by, if it was in God's plan that she go to Ohio, she'd have to accept it.

Daisy walked into the kitchen rubbing her eyes. "That was exciting news last night, *Mamm.* You're about to have your fourth *grosskin.*"

"I couldn't be more happy."

Daisy sat down next to her mother. "You don't look very happy."

"I am. I'm just tired."

"Do you want me to make you some breakfast, Daisy?" Lily asked.

"Jah, please."

"One of you will have to go out and get the eggs."

Lily said, "I'll go out and get them after breakfast. We've got enough here to make Daisy something."

Nancy nodded.

"Can I have scrambled eggs, Lily?"

"Okay."

"And when do you see Bruno next?" Nancy asked.

"Friday. He's coming here to collect me at ten in the morning. Is that okay?"

Nancy nodded. "I like Bruno and he comes from a good family." She glanced over at Lily who was whisking the eggs and Lily didn't look at her. She felt like saying that she wasn't too happy about Nathanial and his family, but she bit the inside of her lip to stop herself from blurting out words that she might later regret.

"I'm so glad you and *Dat* like him. I think he's the man I'm going to marry. I'm certain of it."

"Well, don't rush into anything. You must be certain."

"I won't rush into anything, *Mamm,* don't worry."

"I'm not worried; I trust *Gott,* so I don't worry about you girls. I know both of you will make the right decisions in finding husbands. Because you know that the decisions you make now will affect the rest of your life. Your decision must be made with your head as well as your heart; you might love someone with your heart, but if you have doubts in your head, you should listen to them."

Lily set the eggs on the stove. "That's good advice, *Mamm*. I'll remember that when I find a man I like."

"*Jah*, that's good advice, and both my head and my heart think that Bruno is the right man for me."

"Wait a while, Daisy. Men can put on a good act for a while, but they can't keep up that act over time. Sooner or later their true personality will shine through," *Mamm* said.

"How did you know that *Dat* was the right one for you?" Daisy asked.

"I didn't have any doubt about it whatsoever, and we knew each other for a long time, which helped as well."

"When I was in my bedroom, I thought I heard Nathanial's name mentioned," Daisy said, looking between her sister and her mother.

"Your *schweschder* ran into him at the store the other day. Someone saw her with him and told me about it. The person thought that Lily and he might have something going on."

Daisy stared at Lily. "Is that true, Lily?"

"*Jah*, I didn't think to mention it. I said hello, he said hello, and that's about all."

"Why didn't you tell me? We tell each other everything."

"You've been so busy with Bruno, and that's all you ever want to talk about. I didn't want to make you upset by talking about Nathanial."

Daisy nodded. "I still want you to tell me everything that's happening with you."

"And I'll tell you anything important, but bumping into him wasn't important. Don't make a fuss."

"Okay. I didn't mean to make a fuss. Stop me if I talk about Bruno too much."

Lily giggled. "It's okay. I like hearing all about him. Since I don't have romance in my life, I like to hear about it from you."

Listening to her two daughters, Nancy wouldn't have thought that anything was wrong if she hadn't known better. She knew now that Lily was very good at lying and it disturbed Nancy to learn that. There was a chance that Hezekiah's source might have been mistaken, but Hezekiah wouldn't have told her about it unless he'd been quite certain. It had to be true, and many things about the scenario scared Nancy.

CHAPTER 17

GOING AGAINST LILY'S ADVICE, Daisy asked Bruno to the volley-ball game on Saturday afternoon.

When they were sitting together watching the three games that were playing, Daisy asked Bruno, "Are you going to have a game?"

"I think I'll just watch unless they need an extra person to play. I'd rather sit next to you."

When he smiled at her, her insides tingled with joy.

"In that case, I'll just watch too."

He leaned close to her and said, "If we weren't surrounded by so many people right now, I'd hold your hand."

She glanced at him and gave a little giggle. Then beyond Bruno, Daisy noticed that her sister, Lily, was sitting next to Nathanial, and another girl was sitting on the other side of him. They were laughing and joking as if Nathanial was a normal person, but he wasn't a normal person—he had treated her dreadfully.

"What's wrong?" Bruno asked.

"I'm just surprised to see Lily speaking with Nathanial."

"I know you said you went on a buggy ride with him, but is he an old boyfriend of yours or something? You seem to be disturbed by him in some way."

"I know some things about him, that's all—and those things aren't good. I told you a little bit about it the other day."

Bruno turned to look over at Lily. When he turned back, he said, "What shall I do? Do you want me to do anything? Shall we tell her we need to talk to her about something, or shall I tell her you want to see her?"

Daisy was pleased that he was only too willing to help even though he didn't know the full circumstances of the matter. He was once again showing that he was a man who would stand by her no matter what.

She shook her head. "I'm probably worried about nothing. I mean, they're not alone or anything. Marcy is talking to him as well, so it should be all right."

"Let's not let him ruin our night."

"Okay, I won't."

The rest of the night, Daisy did her best to enjoy Bruno's company, but she kept an eye on Lily. Wherever Lily was, Nathanial was not far away.

WHEN THE VOLLEYBALL was drawing to a close, Daisy asked Bruno, "Do you mind if we drive Lily home with us? I'm worried she'll have Nathanial drive her home, and that won't end well."

"Of course. I don't mind at all. We must keep her out of trouble."

"Denke. I'll just go tell her she can come home with us."

"Okay."

She walked over to Lily and managed to get her far enough away from Nathanial to speak to her in private. "You're coming home with us soon, Lily."

"Nee, I don't want to do that. You should go home with him —just the two of you."

"You'll be helping me, Lily."

"How will it be helping you?"

"Remember that you said if you like someone not to act too desperate toward him?"

"Jah?"

"Don't you see? I have just asked Bruno to take you home as well, and he'll wonder why I don't want to be alone with him. I'm trying to keep him on his toes."

"Good work, Daisy. I'm proud of you." She glanced over at Nathanial. "It doesn't hurt to have them think you're not interested in them."

"You'll come home with us then?"

"Of course I will. Just give me a few moments. Give me ten minutes."

"I'll meet you at Bruno's buggy."

Daisy hurried back to Bruno and glanced back at Lily to see her talking with Nathanial, and he didn't look at all happy. Daisy guessed that Nathanial had planned to take her home and Lily had just given him the news that he wasn't driving her home.

Daisy was pleased that she ruined things for Nathanial.

She'd have to make her sister see sense and do so without being obvious.

As soon as they got home, Lily jumped out of the buggy, thanked Bruno, and ran inside. This left Bruno and Daisy some time to say goodnight to one another.

"Daisy, would you be pleased if I stayed on for a few more months? I don't want to leave Valerie here alone and I've been offered six months' work at the horse auctions."

"Oh, Bruno. That would be *wunderbaar*," she said without realizing she'd touched him lightly on his hand.

He took hold of her hand, brought it up to his mouth, and pressed his lips gently onto her hand. She felt as though all her dreams had come true. Bruno was in love with her; she could see it in his eyes, now that he was staring at her.

"You should go inside right now, or I'll kiss you right on your beautiful lips."

She giggled. "I'm going."

He squeezed her hand a little before he released it.

"Bye," she said before she got out of his buggy.

"I'll see you soon, Daisy."

She walked inside and closed the door behind her. Her heart was thumping so hard that she could scarcely breathe. The man was in love with her. She was glad she hadn't followed Lily's advice about pretending not to be interested in him.

Looking around, she saw that her mother and father had already gone to bed. She hurried upstairs to tell Lily the good news that Bruno was staying for longer.

When she got to Lily's room, she saw that she wasn't there.

She went back into her own room to see if Lily was waiting to talk with her, but she wasn't there either. Daisy checked the dark kitchen and then the bathroom, but she wasn't anywhere in the house.

The only answer was that Lily had sneaked out of the house. *She must've gone to meet Nathanial. That's why she didn't protest too hard about coming home with me and Bruno. She must've pre-arranged to meet Nathanial somewhere.*

Fuming, Daisy paced up and down, wondering what to do. She could tell her parents, but her father had a weak heart. The only thing she could do was wait until Lily came home and then she'd confront her.

Daisy being so close to Bruno had driven a wedge between herself and Lily. They'd always shared everything and Lily had never kept anything from her before.

Her thrill about Bruno was now marred by her sister's disappearance. She went back into her sister's room and looked out the window. It was then that she noticed it was slightly open and once she looked out, she saw a tree close to the house that Lily must've climbed down. And that was probably the way she'd return.

Daisy slept in Lily's bed, knowing that once Lily came back through the window, she'd find out what was going on. She'd confront her.

Lily had to take the chance that Daisy would be so tired tonight she wouldn't notice they wouldn't be having their nightly talk. She felt bad for deceiving Daisy and her parents, but she knew they didn't like Nathanial, so she felt like she was trapped. In the end, she was an adult and old enough to make her own decisions. She'd had several long talks with Nathanial and she knew they had the wrong idea about him altogether.

She opened the window, grabbed the tree branch, and swung her body onto the trunk of the tree. Stepping down each branch, she got close enough to the bottom that she could let go of the branch. Losing her balance, she landed flat on her bottom. Immediately, she sprang to her feet and hoped her dress wasn't too dirty because her mother would see it and wonder how it got stained. With her hands, she dusted down her dress and straightened it.

Peeking around the corner of the house, she saw that Bruno was driving away and Daisy was walking back to the house. As soon as Lily saw that Daisy had gone inside, she scampered to the barn in the darkness. From the barn, she stuck to the fence line and hurried down the driveway. Nathanial said he'd wait for her at the crossroads not too far from her house. Thankfully, Valerie's house was in the opposite direction so Bruno would not see him waiting there.

By the time she reached Nathanial's buggy, she was breathless.

He laughed. "What took you so long?"

"I had to wait until Bruno left the house. Daisy and Bruno were sitting in the buggy talking for the longest time. Anyway, you're lucky I'm here at all since my family doesn't approve of you." She climbed up next to him.

"I guess you're right about that." He clicked the horse onward.

"Where are we going?"

"I thought we'd go somewhere for a bite to eat." He glanced over at her. "What do you think?"

She shook her head. "Not a good idea. Someone told my *vadder* that they saw us together and close together."

"Well, a bite to eat is out of the question, then, if we are to remain a secret."

"We could just drive around for awhile. Are you hungry?"

"No hungrier than I usually am. I'll live. Is this the first time you've had to sneak out of the house?"

"*Jah.* It's not something I plan to make a habit of."

"How will we see each other, then, if you don't keep sneaking out? It's going to take a long time for them to forget the lies your *schweschder* told about me."

"I haven't thought about it too much."

"Fair enough."

Lily giggled. It felt good to be out, away from her parents' control, and to be able to make some decisions for herself.

He glanced over at her again. "What's funny?"

"I feel free. Free to be me."

"Shouldn't you feel like that all the time?"

"I'd like to," Lily said. "But I don't see how that's going to happen as long as I'm living under my parents' roof."

"Get a job and move out."

"I couldn't get a job. I don't know how to do anything."

"Start by doing anything you can find, any job you can get, and then you work your way up."

Lily had always thought the only way out of home was to marry and get away that way. It had never occurred to her to get a job and have her own place. "If I got a job, would that give me enough money to rent a *haus?*"

"Well, if you have no skills you probably won't get much pay at first. Not in your first job. But you could share a place with someone. That's the best way to start."

"Like who?"

He chuckled. "Look on the Internet or on notice boards. People are looking for housemates all the time."

"That sounds like a good idea. Maybe I will get a job."

"It puzzles me why you haven't had one before now."

"*Mamm* keeps Daisy and me busy, that's why. Our days are full of things to do around the *haus* and then she's got us visiting people now."

"She's teaching you to be just like her. Is that what you want, Lily?" he asked.

"*Jah,* she's got a good life and I'd like to be just like her, just not as short-tempered and cranky."

At that moment, gentle rain began to fall.

"It's raining," Nathanial said. "I just hope it doesn't get any heavier."

"I love the rain. Let's stop the buggy and walk."

"No way in the world! Then I'd be responsible if you caught a cold, or pneumonia. I'd never forgive myself."

"You could visit me and bring me hot chicken soup."

He laughed as the rain started falling more heavily. "There's no way your parents would allow me to even see you, let alone bring you anything."

"I guess that's true. I can't believe that Daisy made the whole thing up. She obviously didn't think how it would affect you."

"She was trying to get back at me. That's what I reckon."

She stared into his face as he watched the road ahead of him. "Back at you for what?"

He turned to face her. "To tell you the truth, it was so long ago that I've forgotten."

Lily giggled.

"I'm going to pull off on the side of the road somewhere. I can't watch the road and see your pretty face at the same time."

"Just let the horse go where he wants."

"Yeah, and we'll end up in a ditch. And don't forget when it's raining branches have a habit of falling off trees."

"You can't have a very good horse then, if he'll pull the buggy into a ditch."

"There's nothing wrong with Jasper. I just bought him from one of my cousins."

Lily screwed up her nose. "He looks a bit old. Is he just about to be retired?"

"*Nee.* Wait until you see him in the day; he's a real beauty." He stopped the horse at the side of the road. Then he took her hand. "I'd like to kiss you, but I don't want you to run away screaming like your *schweschder* did."

Lily laughed. "I'm not my *schweschder.*"

"Are you sure?"

Lily nodded. "Quite sure."

"How do I know you're not Daisy out to get me into more trouble?"

"Because Daisy wouldn't sneak out at night, that's how you can know."

"Ah, so you're the bad twin—the evil twin." He chuckled.

"I wouldn't say that. I just want different things out of life and I'm just beginning to find that out. I want excitement. I want to do things other people don't normally do."

"Like run in the rain?"

"Jah, I'd like to run in the rain without a care in the world. And if I get sick, I will worry about that when and if it happens."

"I like the sound of that. You want to live for today and tomorrow can take care of itself."

Lily laughed, and then Nathanial joined in with her laughter.

"If I lived on my own I would run in the rain right now."

"What's stopping you?" he asked. "Apart from me not wanting you to get sick?"

"Oh, that's sweet."

"Not really. I just don't want you to get sick because then I would most likely catch your cold and then I'd be sick too. Seriously though, why can't you run in the rain because you're still living at home?"

Lily sighed. "My *mudder* is like a detective. She'd somehow find my wet clothes and she'd question me. I'm not a good liar and the whole thing wouldn't end well."

He squeezed her hands just slightly. "You should seriously consider making a life for yourself. You've never gone on a *rumspringa,* have you?"

"Nee."

"It figures," he said.

"Have you?"

"Yeah, not long back."

"Oh."

"We live a sheltered life. Not that I'm complaining, but I'm glad I know what else is out there."

"I don't want to know what else is out there. Why would I have to know if I'm only going to come back to the community anyway? It seems like a waste of time to me."

"I do hope you get a job, Lily. I think it would help you to get out and meet some different people. I think you'd love it."

She looked into his eyes and all that she saw was kindness. If she had believed Daisy, she wouldn't have gotten a chance to know him at all. "I'll definitely give it some serious thought. Next time I'm in town, I'll have a look at some noticeboards and see what jobs are on offer."

"*Gut.*" He looked into the dark night as the rain was falling more steadily. "Right now I'd feel better to get you home, Lily."

"Okay."

He turned the buggy around and headed back toward her house. "What's the deal with Bruno?"

"How do you mean?"

"He seems pretty interested in Daisy and haven't they only just met?"

"You think he likes her?" Lily asked.

"*Jah.* I told you I bumped into them, didn't I?"

"*Jah,* you did—at the candy store. She was showing him around."

"I reckon they'll marry."

"Maybe." Lily felt sick to the stomach at the thought of losing her twin and being left in the house alone with her parents. Their sole focus and attention would be on her. Besides that, she'd be lonely without her twin.

"This is about as close as I can go without everyone in your *haus* hearing the horse." He reached over the back and then handed her a thick coat. "Put this on."

"Won't you need it?"

"*Nee.* Put it over your head to keep dry."

She handed it back to him. "That's okay, it's not far."

He thrust it back into her hands. "Take it!"

"Okay." She gave a little laugh.

"I'll see you soon. Be safe."

"I will." She jumped down from the buggy, pulled the coat over her head, and hurried to the *haus.* The rain had eased and by the time she got to the bottom of the tree underneath her bedroom window, the rain had stopped.

Getting up that tree wasn't as easy as getting down. She left the coat at the bottom of the tree, intending to get it in the morning, tucked her dress into her knickers, and climbed up the tree.

Finally she reached the window. She clutched at it with both hands and then when she was deciding how to bring her legs in, a figure appeared before her. Her eyes met Daisy's.

CHAPTER 18

DAISY HAD WOKEN SUDDENLY when she heard a scratching sound. She'd sat up, remembering that she was in Lily's bed, waiting for her to come home and explain herself. She'd guessed the scratching noises were from Lily climbing up the tree to get back into her bedroom. Daisy squinted at the clock in the darkness to see that it was three o'clock in the morning.

She walked to the window and opened it fully. Lily clutched the window and their eyes met. Daisy pushed the window up higher and Lily made her way into the room.

"What the devil are you doing?" Daisy hissed.

With a flushed face, Lily asked, "Why are you in my room?"

"You went to meet Nathanial, didn't you?"

"Keep your voice down, or *Mamm* and *Dat* will hear you."

"What were you doing sneaking out to meet him?"

"He wanted to drive me home and he couldn't, so that's why I met with him. I was trying to help you out so you wouldn't appear too keen with Bruno."

"Well, isn't that making you seem too keen on Nathanial, since you were sneaking out to meet him in the middle of the night?"

"You've all made up your mind that you don't like him and you don't even know him."

"Why would I like him? I told you what he did to me."

"He told me all about it and I know you were exaggerating. You do that sometimes. He didn't stand up for himself back then, and now he regrets it. He said it's too late to do anything about it now. I think you were unfair to him."

"Lily, what sort of man would have you meet him late at night like this? Did you stop to think about that?"

"He loves me and that's why we wanted to meet with each other. What difference is it if it's the middle of the day, or if we meet at night?"

"In the middle of the day, there are people around, but at night, he can take you somewhere deserted."

"And what—murder me? Don't be so dramatic. You're just jealous because Nathanial didn't want you and that's why you made up that story about him."

Daisy said, "Are you accusing me of lying?"

"Shush! They'll hear you."

"I don't care if they do," Daisy hollered.

"I never thought you'd be so mean to me, Daisy. You think you're better than me now because you have a boyfriend—one that *Mamm* and *Dat* like."

"I never thought you'd be so stupid."

"Get out of my room," Lily yelled.

Their mother swung the door open. "What's going on? Why aren't you girls asleep?" She looked Lily up-and-down. "Get changed and get into bed, Lily, and Daisy, you go to your own room. We'll talk about this in the morning, and no more noise. Your *vadder* has to get up early in the morning."

Daisy rushed past her mother, went into her own room, and closed the door. She jumped into bed feeling sad and alone. She'd never had a fight with her sister; this had been their first one. Why couldn't her sister see that Nathanial was no good? And how could Lily accuse her of lying about what had happened with Nathanial? She'd only been trying to protect her twin.

NANCY WENT BACK to her own room and got back into bed.

"What was all that about?" Hezekiah asked her.

"Just a squabble. I'll get to the bottom of it in the morning." She leaned over and kissed her husband on his cheek. "Go back to sleep."

A minute later, Hezekiah was snoring. Nancy was worried to see her two girls fight. There was something seriously wrong. Seeing them annoyed with each other reminded her of the ongoing fight she was having with her own sister, Nerida. Maybe it was God's way of telling her she needed to pay Nerida a visit. It wasn't right that sisters didn't get along. She made up her mind to visit Nerida the very next day, and she'd try to make amends if Nerida was willing.

CHAPTER 19

NANCY LEFT the twins at home the next day. They still weren't speaking to one another, which was probably better than them yelling at one another. She'd given them jobs to do at the opposite ends of the house and hopefully that way it would break down any tension between the two of them. If they had a break from each other, they might calm down.

Nancy had no idea what their argument had been about, but guessed that Lily was a little upset that Daisy had Bruno and she had no one. Things couldn't have been easy for Lily because over the last few years they had grown used to the idea that they would marry twin brothers and they'd be together forever. Now that Daisy liked a man, it was tearing the girls apart. Nancy didn't like to see them at odds with one another, but neither could she offer a solution. It was bound to happen that one of the twins would find a man before the other. She'd had no idea that it would cause this big a problem between them.

Trying to relax, Nancy breathed in the fresh morning air. It had been raining the night before and the sweet scent of rain still filled the air. The colors of the landscape she passed looked so much brighter after a heavy downpour. The greens of the pastures were so much more vibrant, the roads darker, and her neighbors' red barns were now standing out in stark contrast to the trees behind them.

Her horse's hoofs swished through the puddles and Nancy skillfully navigated around some potholes made a little worse by the recent weather. As she got closer to Nerida's, she hoped the right words would come into her head when she was in front of her sister.

She stopped the buggy close to Nerida's house and when she'd tied the horse to the fencepost, she walked right up to the front door and knocked on it quickly before she could change her mind.

The door opened and Willow, her young niece, answered the door. "It's nice to see you, Aunt Nancy. Come in."

"Are you sure it's okay?"

"*Jah, Mamm* saw you coming from the kitchen window. She's waiting in the kitchen for you."

"Okay. Where's Violet?"

"She's upstairs writing a letter. I'll go and tell her you're here, but I think *Mamm* wants to talk to you by herself first." Willow wrapped her arms around Nancy. "I'm glad you're here."

"Me too, Willow. It's been too long."

Nancy closed the front door behind her and headed into the kitchen.

Nerida was sitting at the table with her hands firmly clasped in front of her. "Hello, Nancy. What brings you here today?"

Nancy walked forward. "I've come to say I'm sorry. It's silly that we have such a rift that's been developing between us because of ... I barely remember how it started." Nancy knew very well how it started, but didn't want to dredge it all up again.

"You can sit down." Nerida motioned with her hand toward the chair opposite.

Nancy pulled out the chair and sat down.

Her younger sister continued, "I was very hurt by what happened."

Nancy nodded. "I was irritated by you and I won't say that I wasn't, but I shouldn't have let that come between the two of us. It doesn't really matter that you gave your girls similar names to my girls'."

Nerida shook her head. "Are we going to start this whole thing over again? My *dochders'* names are nothing like your girls' names."

"But don't you see that they are? My girls have flower names and then you called your daughters Violet and Willow."

Nerida rolled her eyes and sighed. "I don't have to explain myself, but I will. I'd always liked the name 'Violet,' and while I realize it is a flower, it's also a color. I have always liked the name 'Willow,' which is a tree and not a flower. When I named them, I didn't name them purposely to copy your flower idea."

"I told you how I felt when you were considering calling your *boppli* Violet. And yet, you went ahead with the name. You were always copying me when we were children and I thought you'd stop when we became adults."

"I didn't think you would be that upset about it. Anyway, I copied you when we were younger because I looked up to you.

You're my only *schweschder*. I wasn't going to copy my brothers, was I?" Nerida raised her eyebrows and her mouth lifted upward into a kind smile.

Nancy gave a little laugh. "I suppose not."

"Was I that annoying?"

Tears came to Nancy's eyes as she remembered the good times they'd had growing up together. "You weren't annoying at all; we had fun. It was only when you got older that you became annoying."

"I didn't copy you or imitate you deliberately. I guess I thought the things that you did were good ideas. I can't even remember how I copied you back then, but I must've because I can remember you complaining about it when we were teenagers."

"It doesn't matter any more." Nancy wiped a tear from her eye. "I was silly to get annoyed with you and let this huge rift develop."

Nerida smiled. "*Jah,* you were. We should've been close and our *kinner* would now be closer than they are."

In her heart, Nancy still believed that her sister had copied her idea and nothing Nerida could say or do would persuade her into believing otherwise. All the same, as much as she was irritated by what her sister had done, they were sisters and she was prepared to put the past aside to have Nerida and Nerida's husband, John, and their two girls, Violet and Willow, back in her life and the life of her family.

CHAPTER 20

WHILE THEIR MOTHER was out trying to make things right with
Nerida, Daisy didn't want a similar rift to develop between
herself and Lily.

She walked over to Lily, who'd been given the job of
washing the windows outside the house.

"What do you want?" Lily asked when she saw Daisy
approaching.

"You don't have to speak like that."

"Well, I think I do. You've shown that you don't care about
me now that you're seeing a lot of Bruno."

"Is that what this is about?"

Lily threw the wet sponge on the ground. "You tell me."

"You know what Nathanial is like."

"I don't, and I can do anything I want. No one cares about
me anyway."

"You're only saying that to be dramatic, or do you think
Mamm and *Dat* don't care about you now?"

"You'll get married soon and then everyone will be married except me. It didn't turn out like we always said it would. We were supposed to be married at the same time."

"And if I could've kept my word, I would've, but Bruno doesn't have a twin."

"Did you ever stop and think that he might not be the right person for you? We haven't traveled to all the different communities yet like we said we would. If we do that, we could find twins."

"*Nee!*" Daisy shook her head. "I can't, now that I have met Bruno."

"Bruno, Bruno, Bruno—that's all I ever hear about anymore. That's all you ever speak about all the time. I'm sick of it!" She picked up the metal bucket full of water and threw it down on the ground.

Once the water drained, Lily picked up the bucket and hurled it at the window in anger. The window shattered and glass went everywhere.

Daisy looked on in horror as the scene unfolded.

"I'll go away and then you'll be happy." Lily pulled a sour face at Daisy before stomping down the driveway with her hands curled into fists.

Daisy carefully picked up the larger pieces of glass and laid them down together so she could cover them in newspaper later. Instead of running after Lily, she figured she would give her time to cool down. It was clear that nothing she could say at this point would make any difference. Once she was back in the house, Daisy found some brown paper that they used for making dress patterns and then she found some tape. She taped up the glass in the paper and then threw it in the trash.

Once she'd cleaned up as best she could, she looked around the yard and down along the driveway, but she couldn't see Lily anywhere.

Lily was down the driveway and just about to turn onto the road when she remembered Nathanial's coat at the bottom of her bedroom window. How would she explain that if anyone found it? That was a disaster waiting to happen. She turned around and headed back to the house hoping Daisy wouldn't see her. It was unfortunate that the window broke because she hadn't thrown the bucket very hard. It must've been a weak or faulty window. Maybe the bucket hit the window in the wrong place.

When she got back to the house, she couldn't see Daisy anywhere. Directly under her bedroom window at the back of the house, she found Nathanial's coat, from the night before, just where she'd left it underneath the tree. After she had looked around about her to make sure no one was watching, she grabbed it and curled it into a tight ball. She headed into the barn where she'd hide the coat until she went somewhere to meet Nathanial again.

She tucked the coat behind the drum of chicken feed, and then sat down on a bail of hay and cried. It felt like Daisy had left her already and the only person who understood her was Nathanial and her parents didn't approve of him. How was her life ever going to get any better? It seemed as though Daisy would definitely marry Bruno, and what would become of her? Nathanial was right. She'd have to get a job and make a life on her own. It was a hard thing to do since she'd always had her twin with her every day of her life. Lily stretched her hands above her head and yawned. It had been a tough couple of days.

She arranged some hay bales together, lay down on them, and slowly closed her eyes.

Then, she sat up quickly. All she wanted to do was see Nathanial, the only person who understood her. He'd understand why she broke that window. She grabbed his coat, spread it out, and then she wrapped it around her to keep herself warm. Being in his warm coat comforted her.

NANCY'S BUGGY horse clipped-clopped steadily up the driveway. Nancy immediately noticed the brown paper covering the window at the front of the house. Before she unhitched the buggy, she rushed into the house to see what was going on.

"What on earth happened to the window?" she asked Daisy when she found her in the kitchen.

Daisy swung around looking incredibly guilty.

"Lily and I had an argument and then there was an accident with the window and it's broken."

"I can see that it's broken, but how could that possibly have come about?"

Daisy shrugged her shoulders and her perfectly shaped mouth kept tightly closed. Nancy had never been able to figure out which twin did what. They'd always covered for one another and clearly that wasn't about to change even though they were at odds with one another.

"Where's Lily now?" Nancy demanded.

"She was upset and went for a walk. I'm sure she'll be back soon."

Nancy sighed. "We'll have to get someone out to fix the

window. Your *vadder* won't be too happy about it when he gets home."

"Sorry, *Mamm.*"

Nancy gritted her teeth. "Sorry won't fix the window!"

"*Jah,* you're right." Then Daisy smiled brightly. "How did things go with Aunt Nerida?"

"Make me a cup of tea while I unhitch the buggy, then I'll tell you all about it."

"Is it good news, then?"

"*Jah.* Well, it's not bad news."

HOURS LATER, it was growing dark and Lily still hadn't come home. Daisy got more worried. What if she'd driven Lily into Nathanial's arms?

Daisy was helping her mother with dinner. "Where could Lily be? It's past time for her to get home. It's nearly time for *Dat* to get home."

"You know her better than anybody. Where do you think she'd be?" her mother asked.

Daisy bit her lip. "I'll take the buggy out and look for her."

"Okay, but don't go by yourself. Stop by Valerie's house and see if Bruno will go with you."

"Great; okay."

CHAPTER 21

Nancy took Daisy by the arm. "Come on. I'll help you hitch the buggy. Try to find her before your *vadder* gets home because I don't want him to get worried."

"I will."

Together they got the buggy ready before it got dark. They used the fastest horse, not the one her mother had just taken out that day to visit Nerida. A fresher horse could travel better.

Daisy was upset. She should've let things cool off more before she spoke to Lily. Valerie's house was on the way to the Schumachers' house.

When Daisy arrived at Valerie's, she jumped down from the buggy, hurried over, and knocked on the door. She had hoped that Bruno would answer the door, but it was Valerie.

Seeing the look on Daisy's face, Valerie asked, "What's wrong?"

"I was wondering if I might be able to borrow Bruno for a short time?"

"Is something wrong?" Valerie asked again.

By this time, Bruno was at the door standing next to his sister.

"Daisy, what's going on?"

"It's Lily. She's disappeared and hasn't come home. We had a dreadful argument. I'm trying to find her before my *vadder* gets home. He tends to worry and he's got a problem with his heart."

"Okay. I'll come with you. Don't worry; we'll find her." He looked back at his sister. "You go ahead and eat dinner; don't worry about me. I'll grab something later."

Valerie walked out the door and stood on the porch as they were both getting into the buggy. "Is there anything I can do, Daisy?"

"Please pray that she'll be safe."

"I will."

Bruno had immediately taken control and sat in the driver's seat.

As they headed down to the main road, he asked, "Where are we going?"

"The Schumachers' *haus.* Nathanial is staying at Matthew Schumacher's—they're cousins."

"Is this the same Nathanial I met the other day?"

"*Jah.* She's developed a friendship with him but I think she's only doing it to upset me."

Bruno glanced at her and she shook her head.

"Don't ask. It's a long story."

"I didn't ask anything. Can you think of anywhere else she might be?"

"If she's not there, we could just check with all our friends. I don't know where else she would be."

"Don't worry, we'll find her."

"Denke for coming with me."

"I'm glad you asked me."

WHEN THEY PULLED up at the Schumachers' house, Daisy said, "You stay here. I'll run in and see if she's inside, or if she's been here."

"Okay."

Daisy knocked on the door, trying not to look worried.

Matthew opened the door and, knowing which twin stood before him, said, "Hello, Daisy."

"Hi, Matthew. Lily wouldn't happen to be here, would she?"

"Nee. Why?"

"She's missing."

Matthew yelled over his shoulder, "Nathanial, have you seen Lily Yoder?"

"Not today I haven't."

Relief washed over Daisy. If Nathanial was here, it meant that Lily wasn't with him. Then again, if Lily wasn't with him, where could she possibly be?

"She's missing!" Matthew yelled again to Nathanial, who came to the door as quick as a flash.

"Is that right, Daisy? Is Lily missing?"

"I'm sure it's nothing to worry about. She's probably just at someone's *haus* visiting and she forgot to tell us."

"Then why do you look so worried?" Nathanial asked.

"Because she is my *schweschder,*" Daisy said a little too harshly.

Matthew suggested, "Why don't we join you, and that way we can cover more ground?"

Daisy agreed, glad that Matthew knew all of Daisy and Lily's friends. They decided that Daisy and Bruno would call at all the houses south of the Schumacher property, and Mark and Nathanial would do the ones to the north. Then they'd meet back at the Yoders' house when they were finished. By now, Daisy's father would be home and would know about Lily's disappearance.

When Daisy got back into the buggy, she explained the plan to Bruno.

As the buggy traveled back down the road, Bruno asked, "Is that a good thing that she wasn't with Nathanial?"

"I am relieved in a way, but I'm worried because I still don't know where she is."

"I'm sure there's nothing to worry about; she's probably just visiting a friend or something."

Daisy shook her head. "We had a dreadful fight and a window even got broken. We never ever had an argument before—it was terrible."

TWO HOURS LATER, they got back to the house without Lily. Nancy rushed out to the buggy.

"We've just found her. She came back here just five minutes ago."

"That's a relief," Bruno said.

"Where was she?" Daisy asked, now finding herself annoyed at Lily for wasting all their time.

"I don't know. She hasn't said yet. She's inside talking to your *vadder.*"

"I'll take Bruno home and come back."

Bruno said, "Why don't I bring the buggy back in the morning? I can put the horse in Valerie's stable overnight. You stay here now; you're tired."

Her mother stepped forward. *"Denke,* Bruno. I think it would be a good idea."

"You don't have to thank me." He gave Daisy's mother a big smile, and then said to Daisy, "I'll see you in the morning, early."

Bruno left, and before Nancy and Daisy got back inside the house, Nathanial and Matthew drove up in Matthew's buggy. Daisy had temporarily forgotten that they were out looking for Lily.

"Mamm, that's Nathanial and Matthew Schumacher. They were helping us look for Lily."

Nancy raised her eyebrows. "Ask them if they want to come in for a hot chocolate."

Nancy went back into the house and Daisy rushed over and thanked the two young men for looking for Lily.

"She's in the house; she's okay. I've just got home myself this minute, so I don't know where she's been or anything."

"She's all right, though?" Matthew asked.

Daisy nodded.

"I'm glad she's okay," Nathanial said.

"Would you like to come in for a hot drink?"

"We won't stay, Daisy. We've both got to get up early for work in the morning," Matthew said.

"Denke very much for looking. You saved Bruno and me hours looking for her."

CHAPTER 22

DAISY WALKED into the kitchen and saw Lily sitting down next to their father.

"Are they coming inside, Daisy?" her mother asked.

Lily looked up at Daisy anxiously. *"Nee,* I can't face anyone."

Daisy shook her head. "They said they had to get up early for work tomorrow."

"I should go to bed," Lily said.

Daisy ignored Lily's words, turned around, and walked out of the room and hurried upstairs before Lily.

Daisy got ready for bed behind her closed door. She took off her prayer *kapp,* and changed into her nightgown. She was too exhausted to brush out her hair as she normally did.

When she'd just dozed off, she felt someone rocking her shoulder. She opened her eyes to see Lily.

"I'm sorry, Daisy."

Daisy sat up in bed. "What made you so angry?"

"I just thought no one cared about me and it looks like you'll soon be married to Bruno and then what will happen to me? Of course, I want you to be happy, but I want me to be happy as well. I want us both to be happy together like always. Everything is changing."

Daisy imagined how she would feel if Lily had found a man to marry before she had met Bruno. "I understand, Lily. It's hard because we've always been so close, and things are changing. I think Bruno likes me as much as I like him and we'll probably marry, but I can't say when."

"You'll marry him and probably soon."

Daisy giggled.

"Can we be friends again?" Lily asked.

"Always. Even when we were arguing, we were closer than two people could ever be."

In the warm glow from the light flooding out of Lily's room across the hall, Daisy saw Lily's sad face break into a smile.

"You know what I found out from tonight?" Daisy asked.

"What?

"I'm pretty sure Matthew is very keen on you."

"I kind of thought that he was, but so is Nathanial."

"Matthew is much nicer," Daisy assured her.

"I know."

"I guess you have to make up your own mind about that."

"Can we talk more tomorrow?"

Daisy nodded. *"Jah,* and then you can tell me where you disappeared to tonight."

Lily gave a little giggle before she leaned over and gave her sister a tight hug. "Are things back to normal between us?" Lily asked.

"Of course they are."

When Lily walked out of her room, Daisy slipped back under the covers wondering how she would feel if Lily got married first. Although she liked Bruno, she still didn't know if Bruno liked her enough to marry her. He'd come close to marrying once before and hadn't followed through with it. Perhaps a private talk with Valerie would give her some insight.

WHEN NANCY GOT into bed with her husband, she whispered, "With all the fuss over Lily, I forgot to tell you I visited Nerida today."

"How did that go?"

"I think it went well. We're probably not back to being the best of friends, but I think we made a good start."

"Did you apologize to her?"

"For what? Do you think I was in the wrong?"

"It was so long ago that I don't remember what happened or if there was a 'right and wrong' situation. Sometimes both people can be in the wrong and in the right depending on which person is viewing the situation. Being right isn't important when it's about family, and in saying that, I'm not thinking that you were in the wrong."

Nancy listened hard to her husband as he struggled to dig himself out of the hole that he had just dug for himself. Even though she knew she'd had cause to be angry with Nerida, in hindsight, she probably should have kept her opinions to herself.

"I would certainly do things differently now. I would keep my mouth shut for one thing."

"It's often best that we hold our tongues and think before we say things."

"Do you think I should've kept quiet?" Nancy asked.

"I'm speaking about people in general. Our words can hurt deeply."

"Jah. I've learned that lesson the hard way."

"Tell me what you said to Nerida?"

"I just said I'm sorry that we haven't been speaking and I'd like things to go back to the way they were."

"And she accepted that?"

"It'll take time to get back to where we were, but we had a good talk. I think we'll be okay."

"I'm pleased. What made you take the step of visiting her?"

"Lily and Daisy were fighting, and then I saw how silly they were being. It upset me that two of the people I love most in the world were fighting."

"That's how our Heavenly Father must feel when his children fight among themselves."

"That's true. I didn't think about it like that. We've missed out on many years together and our *kinner* could've been closer."

"Looks like things are working out for everybody, then," Hezekiah said.

"I hope so. I hope this is the end of Daisy and Lily quarreling. Daisy was very concerned when Lily disappeared."

"We all were."

CHAPTER 23

Daisy was awake early the next morning so she'd be able to take Bruno back to Valerie's when he brought the buggy back from the night before. Daisy's father had just left for work, and Lily still wasn't awake.

She sat across from her mother as they both ate breakfast.

"Are you and Lily getting along better? I heard you whispering and giggling last night. Did you patch up your differences?"

"I think so. I think she feels left out that I've got Bruno and she's got no one."

"I was worried that she might like Nathanial."

Daisy shook her head. "I don't think she likes Nathanial. I think she was just pleased that he was showing her some attention. I think that's all over with now."

"She's come to her senses about him?"

"I think so. In fact, I'm sure she has."

"That must be hard for her that you've got someone and she

doesn't. You've always been so close and done everything together. I was afraid this would happen one day. I didn't think there would be a big falling out between you, but I knew one of you would be sad without the other. You both built up in your minds that you would live in the same place and marry brothers."

"And marry *twin* brothers," Daisy corrected her mother.

"It wasn't likely to ever be like that."

"I suppose not," Daisy had to agree.

"Do you know where Lily went last night?"

"I think she just went for a walk. She hasn't really said."

"Sometimes it's good to be alone to think things through. Do you know what time Bruno is getting here?" her mother asked.

"It would have to be early, before he goes to work. I suppose there was no hurry to get the buggy back."

"Well, everyone was too upset to think straight last night."

The sound of hoofbeats distracted them. Daisy ran to the window and was pleased to see that it was Bruno.

"I'll be back soon, *Mamm.* I just have to drop him back at Valerie's."

"I'll see you when I see you."

Daisy threw on her black shawl and hurried out to Bruno.

"How are you feeling this morning?" he asked when she climbed into the buggy next to him.

"I'm feeling fine. Lily and I are okay now; we sorted everything out."

"What was the problem?"

Daisy shook her head. "It's a little complicated."

He gave a quick laugh. "Things between families usually

are." He turned the buggy around and headed down to the road. "Take my *mudder* for instance; she wrote me a letter saying she wanted me to come home."

"Ach nee! Are you going home soon—sooner than you said?"

He smiled at her. "I've got a letter back in Valerie's buggy that I will send to her today, and that letter tells my *mudder* that I have met someone very special and that is why I need to stay here longer."

Daisy's face lit up. "You said that to your *mudder?"*

"I put that in a letter and I just wondered if it's okay with you if I send that letter? I mentioned you by name, if you don't mind."

Daisy's heart flooded with gladness. This man was telling his mother about her by name. "I don't mind at all."

"Valerie's got a phone in the barn and my *mudder* could've called, but she prefers to write. I'm going to the post office when I get a chance today and I'll post that letter."

"How's Valerie?"

"If you don't need to go home right away, how about you stop by and talk to her?"

"I was thinking of doing that. Is she awake?"

"Jah. She is. I'm running a little late for work, but I've already got my buggy hitched and ready to take me to work." He gave a little laugh. "When I say 'my' buggy, I mean Valerie's buggy. She's been good enough to allow me to use it while I'm here."

"I'll stay on and speak with her before I go home."

"Daisy, I won't be able to see you much because of how much I'll be working, but would you come and have a picnic with me on Sunday afternoon after the meeting?"

"*Jah,* I'd like that."

"I'll arrange everything. I don't want you to lift a finger."

"Okay."

When Bruno drove away, Daisy knocked on Valerie's front door.

"Coming." Valerie opened the door. "Daisy!"

"I hope you don't mind me coming to say hello. Bruno said you were awake."

"Please come in. I'm getting sick of my own company. Come and sit with me. Have you had breakfast?"

"I have."

"How about a cup of tea?"

"I can always do with a cup of hot tea."

"Good. I have just boiled the water."

Daisy sat down at the kitchen table, watching Valerie make the tea. "How have you been?"

"I guess I'm doing okay; I'm adjusting. I don't know what I'll do when Bruno goes back; he's been such a good help to me."

"It's good that he might be staying here for a few more months."

"It's a blessing." Valerie placed a cup of tea in front of her. "Do you have milk or sugar?"

"*Nee,* just black is fine for me, *denke.*"

"How is Lily doing? She disappeared or something for a while last night?"

"She's okay now. We had a bit of an argument and a window got broken accidentally. It was a bit of a fuss, but we're okay now. Everyone was panicked looking for her, but she hadn't gone far at all."

"That's good." Valerie sat down alongside her.

Daisy wondered what to say to her; she was used to talking to much younger women and Valerie was closer to her mother's age. "Bruno tells me that his mother had a woman lined up for him to marry."

Valerie laughed. *"Jah.* That seems to be what mothers do."

"Did your *mudder* match you with Dirk?" Daisy nearly spilled her tea. It wasn't the wisest thing to bring up the subject of Valerie's late husband just weeks after he had been found dead, although, Valerie had spoken of him before and hadn't minded. "I'm sorry. I shouldn't have mentioned your husband. I'm so stupid sometimes. *Mamm* always says I speak before I think."

"Don't be sorry about that. I want to talk about him. I feel that he's close to me when I speak of him."

Relieved, Daisy listened while Valerie told her all about Dirk and how they had met. Valerie shed a few tears, which brought sympathy tears to Daisy's eyes.

"It wasn't all smooth sailing in our marriage. Most marriages are like that. It's not easy getting used to living with another person."

Daisy nodded and sipped on her hot tea.

"But the problem at the start of our relationship didn't help at all."

"Do you want to talk about it?" Daisy asked.

Valerie didn't wait to be asked twice and lunged into her story. "Dirk had always loved me. I didn't love him because there was someone else in my life and Dirk knew it."

"What happened and how did you come to marry Dirk? Did you realize it was he who you really loved all along?"

"Nee. The man I loved went to another county and married

someone else quite quickly. I was devastated and it took me a long time to get over it. Dirk was there for me. I wasn't in love with him when we married, but I grew to love him. It was a different kind of love to the love I had for that first man. I can't even describe how that love was. It was something all-encompassing and I'm sure not many people experience that kind of love." Valerie's whole body trembled. "Unfortunately, it must have all been one-sided. It was all going on in my head and wasn't real. If it had been real, there's no way he could've married anyone else."

Daisy found Valerie's story quite sad. "I find it all confusing. So many people tell me different things about love. I know some married couples aren't happy, and others are. Some start off happy and then don't remain that way."

"It's a complicated thing," Valerie said, now smiling.

"I suppose it was good that that first man moved away. It would've been hard to see him all the time with another woman."

"*Jah,* you're right. It would've been dreadful, but he eventually left my mind and my heart after he betrayed me. I felt hurt at first, but nothing lasts forever—not pain, anyway."

"I'm glad." Valerie was such a kind and gentle person that Daisy didn't want to see her upset.

"Have you ever experienced love at your young age, Daisy?"

Daisy carefully set her teacup back on the saucer. "Between you and me, I like your *bruder.*"

Valerie laughed and Daisy was relieved that she was taking the news well. "I could tell that from the moment you walked in the door—that there was something between the two of you."

That was something Daisy needed to know. She didn't want

to be like Valerie and think that the man she loved felt the same and then find out that he'd married somebody else. She couldn't think of anything worse.

"*Jah,* well, I don't know if we could call it love, but I like him, strongly."

"You seem a very good match."

"Do you think so? You don't think I'm too young for him?"

"Age has little to do with it. He's attracted to your personality and the way you light up the room when you walk into it with your cheerfulness."

Daisy giggled. "I didn't know I did that."

Valerie swiped her hand through the air. "So many people are stuffy and boring, and so serious. That gets tiresome after a while."

"It does, doesn't it?"

"If I had been blessed enough to have a daughter, I would have wanted her to be just like you."

"You would make a *wunderbaar mudder,* Valerie, and your *dochder* would've been blessed to have you in her life."

Valerie laughed. "Denke. I've grown used to the fact that that is something that I will never have."

Daisy cleared her throat. "If you don't mind me asking, did you have something medically wrong with you that made you not able to have *kinner?*"

"No, nothing. If I did have anything wrong with me, I didn't know about it."

"Maybe Dirk had the problem."

"Maybe. We'll never know because he refused to get tested, and then we ran out of time. It just wasn't meant to be."

"Tulip's going through that right now. She desperately wants to have a baby and nothing is happening. It seems to be making her upset. I haven't talked to her about it, but I know she desperately wants to have a *boppli.*"

"She's got plenty of time before she needs to start worrying about it. It can take years sometimes. I wouldn't want to see anyone childless."

"I guess it's something that most people just take for granted," Daisy said.

"You're right, Daisy. I know I did. It was the natural progression of getting married. There was so much pressure on young people to get married back then. The next thing was to have *bopplis.*"

Daisy took another sip of her tea, wondering what her future would bring. She didn't mind too much if she didn't have any children, because she already had nieces and one nephew, and she knew she would get a whole lot more too. "Were you under pressure to marry Dirk?"

"I suppose I was under pressure to marry somebody. Everyone married so young back then, at seventeen and eighteen. I was nearly twenty and didn't want to remain unmarried. Since I was the oldest girl in the *familye,* I felt a certain amount of pressure to make a good example and there was also the financial burden I was to my parents." Valerie shook her head. "Nothing was said, but I knew that once I married and left the family home there would be one less mouth to feed."

"But also one less person to do all the chores," Daisy pointed out.

Valerie chuckled, "Very true, but there were plenty of girls in the family to do the chores."

"If you don't mind me saying, Valerie, I think it's a bit awful that you felt you had to move out of your home for financial reasons. Couldn't you have gotten a job?"

"Very few women worked back then. It's not like it is today where most women work out of the home. They were different times."

"I'm glad I didn't live back then. If I did, *Mamm* and *Dat* would've already given up on me and probably kicked me out."

"Or they would have found you someone to marry two years ago."

"*Jah, Mamm* likes to match-make, I know that for sure and for certain."

"Yet, she hasn't found anyone for you?" Valerie laughed. "She mightn't want you and Lily to leave since you're the last two—the youngest."

Daisy giggled. "I think she would love us to go. Half the time I think Lily and I drive her crazy."

"I can't see how that would be true," Valerie said.

"It is." Daisy took another sip of tea.

"I've got cookies somewhere. Would you like some?"

"*Nee denke*, I'm fine."

"More tea?"

"*Nee*, I've not finished this one yet." Daisy took the last mouthful and set the teacup down. "I should go now."

"Can't you stay longer, Daisy?"

Daisy was a little surprised that she'd want her to stay. "Okay, if you want me to. There's nowhere that I have to be in particular."

"I'd like if you could stay a little longer."

"Then I might have that second cup of tea."

Valerie stood and took hold of the teacup in front of her. "I'll find those cookies too."

When Daisy left an hour later, she was pleased she'd stopped by to visit Valerie. Once she'd gotten past the initial awkwardness, it had been just like talking with a friend her own age, and Valerie had seemed better afterward.

As she drove the buggy home, down the narrow, winding tree-lined roads, her thoughts went to Tulip and how she must feel watching Rose so happy about being pregnant. Now that Daisy wasn't getting along with Lily all that well, she realized she wasn't as close to Rose and Tulip as she would like to be. Now was a perfect time to change that.

CHAPTER 24

Daisy arrived back home with a plan. She called Tulip and told her they'd all collect her and then continue on to visit Rose. Tulip loved the idea.

Daisy ran into the house and found her mother and Lily in the kitchen. *"Mamm,* guess what?"

Her mother stopped sweeping and leaned on the broom. "What is it that's got you so excited?"

"You, me, and Lily are going to visit Rose. We'll collect Tulip on the way. We haven't visited her since she told us she's pregnant. I've called Tulip and she's getting ready."

"I think it's a great idea," Nancy said. "Have you called Rose?"

"Nee, not yet."

"Why don't you call Rose to see if she's got anything on today? She might be busy."

"Can't it be a surprise? Mark and she only have one buggy between them, and she's not going to walk anywhere in her condition, especially since she's had two miscarriages. She said she was going to rest until the *boppli's* born. She'll be home for certain."

"All the same, she might have visitors. Call her and see if we can stop by."

"Okay." Daisy hurried out to the barn to make the call. It was a waste of time to call Rose to see if she was going to be home and Daisy knew it, but her mother always had to do things a certain way—her way.

When Daisy came back into the house to deliver the news that Rose was home and looking forward to their visit, her mother had come up with another idea.

"You and Lily will stay home today and clean the *haus.* I will collect Tulip and go on to visit Rose on my own. What's more, as punishment, you're both not allowed to leave the *haus* for a week and you'll come straight home after the meeting on Sunday."

"But *Mamm,* Bruno has a special thing planned for us on Sunday after the meeting. He's making us a picnic. And besides that, it was my idea for us all to visit Rose."

"You can call Bruno and tell him it'll have to be postponed."

"But *Mamm,* I think he's going to propose."

"You should've thought about that before you broke the window."

Lily jumped in and said, "I broke the window. It had nothing to do with Daisy. I picked up the bucket and hurled it in a temper—a filthy rotten temper."

"It doesn't matter to me who threw it," *Mamm* said.

"Daisy shouldn't be punished the something that I did. It's not fair."

"Both of you are being punished for acting like children when you're old enough to act like young ladies." She shook her head at them. "What time did you tell Tulip we were coming?"

"At eleven," Daisy answered.

"I should hurry."

They watched at the doorway while their mother went on the visit to Rose that Daisy had planned.

"It's so unfair," Lily said.

"I know, I can't believe she'd do it. It's my idea. I just wanted us to spend more time with Rose and Tulip. Also, I don't mind staying home today, but Sunday was going to be special—I'm certain of it. Now that's all been ruined thanks to *Mamm.*"

Lily smiled. "Don't worry. Perhaps she'll change her mind before then. She wants us married, so she'll see sense before Sunday. Why don't we cook a really nice dinner and clean the *haus* well?"

Daisy sighed and then shook her head. *"Nee,* it won't make a difference. She'll expect nothing less. I think we're done for. It's no use. She's never gone back on her word when she's punished us before. We're being treated like children."

NANCY DROVE off laughing at her two daughters, who stared at her out the window with deliberate sad faces. They had no idea they were about to get a visitor. Earlier that morning, Hezekiah had arranged to have the glass replaced in the broken window by placing a phone call to the Bontragers, the local Amish glaziers.

Ed Bontrager had said he'd send his oldest son, Elijah, out that morning. Elijah would be perfect for one of her daughters, and since Daisy only had eyes for Bruno, Nancy had a hunch that Elijah could be the man to take Lily's mind off Nathanial. The Bontragers were quiet and kept to themselves. There were five boys all close in age. Nancy figured Elijah was around the same age as Tulip—just a little older than the twins. Ed's wife had died years ago and Ed had never remarried.

Nancy pulled up the buggy at Tulip's house and waited for her to come out. It had been a while since she'd had some quiet time with just Tulip and Rose without the constant mindless chatter of the twins. Rose would want to talk about her coming baby and Nancy wanted to share that joy with her, while reassuring Tulip that her turn would come soon.

Two hours later, the girls were up to their armpits in housework when they heard loud hoofbeats working their way to the house. They both hurried to the door, thinking it was their mother back early, and they were surprised to see the oldest Bontrager boy, Elijah, in a wagon.

He jumped down and waved and the girls walked toward him.

"Hello there. You've got a broken window?"

"Jah, we do," Daisy said while Lily stood still, gawking at him.

"I've come to measure it."

"You're going to fix it?" Lily asked as she stepped forward.

He smiled. "I am. I'll measure it first and then go back to the factory and cut the glass. You'll have a new windowpane by the end of the day."

"Wunderbaar!" Daisy glanced at her sister who was looking very interested in Elijah.

He was tall and fair-haired, and his build was slight rather than the solid build she knew her sister preferred, but surely his relaxed, friendly manner and good character made up for his physique.

"Lily, why don't you show Elijah the broken window? I've got that pot on the stove I've got to watch."

"Jah, right this way, Elijah."

Daisy smiled as she watched her twin sister walk to the front of the house with Elijah. She had nothing on the stove and Lily had played along without missing a beat, thanks to the like minds the twins shared.

"How did the window break?" he asked, standing there staring at it.

"It was just my clumsy sister. She was washing the floor and the end of the broom smashed into the window."

He took hold of the jagged pieces of glass left in the window and carefully placed them on the ground. Then he looked in the window. "It was broken from the outside."

Lily did her best act of looking surprised. "Was it?"

"Jah, it was."

She followed his gaze to the metal bucket just to the side in the garden.

"I'm not really sure what happened," she said, fluttering her lashes.

He gave her a smile before he took his tape out of the pocket of his work pants. She stood back a little and watched him take the measurements. He then crouched down and set the tape on the ground and jotted the measurements on a small notepad.

"That's the smallest notepad I've ever seen."

He looked up at her. "That's all I need. Just a few measurements and the width of the glass." He held it up in the air and then stood. "And it fits in my pocket."

"Do all your brothers work in the glass business?"

"Most of us, but not all of us. Here." He held the small pad and pen out to Lily. "Hold this for me, would you?"

She took it from him while he took a couple more measurements. Then he spun around and took the notepad from her.

He didn't seem interested in her at all, and was only polite. Most of the young men gave her more attention and it bothered her that he didn't.

"Denke. That's all I need for now."

"That's it?"

"Jah." He gave her a polite nod and then strode off toward his wagon.

She hurried after him. "What's the process now then—with the glass?"

"Like I said, I take the measurements back and cut the glass. I'll be back later."

"Can I come and watch?"

He stopped suddenly and turned around to face her. "It's dangerous in the factory if you don't know what you're doing."

"I could watch from a safe distance."

"My *vadder* wouldn't like it."

A cheeky grin spread across Lily's face. "Do you always do what your *vadder* wants?"

"Jah, I do." He climbed into the wagon and said over his shoulder, "It's his factory."

Lily stood there and watched him leave. Her cute flirty act had always worked in the past, particularly with Nathanial.

WHEN ELIJAH RETURNED with the glass, Lily headed out to talk with him. He had parked his wagon as close to the window as he could.

"Don't you need two men to lift that?"

"*Nee*, I can do it by myself, Daisy."

"It's Lily. And I just asked because it must be heavy."

"I do it all the time by myself. It's not a big window."

"Oh, you must be very strong. Can I see your muscles?" She stepped forward with an outstretched hand to touch his bicep and he moved away.

"Nope."

While he untied the ropes that secured the glass in the back of the wagon, Lily wondered how she could engage him in conversation. There were only so many questions she could ask about glass. "You don't go to many of the young people's outings."

"That's because I'm not young."

Lily laughed. "You're young enough."

"I've got other things to do."

Lily stepped closer with her hands behind her back. "Like what?"

"Working keeps me busy."

"You can't work all the time," she said.

He answered without looking up at her. "I don't, but when I'm not working I just want to sit and do nothing."

"Well, that just sounds boring. You need to enjoy yourself

more." She was pleased when he finally took his eyes off what he was doing and looked at her.

"You might want to move back a few steps because I'll need to swing the glass that way."

She frowned and stepped back. "Is this far enough?"

He looked across at her. "Yep, that'll do it." After he slipped on some large gloves, he took hold of the glass and carried it to the window.

Lily was so offended at the way he was treating her, she went into the house and closed the door behind her. She stomped into the kitchen where she found Daisy.

"Why are you looking so angry?"

"He's a bit rude."

"Why?"

Lily repeated their conversation.

"Try something different. Just go out there and act naturally. I bet you did that coy flirty thing."

Lily pouted. "I didn't."

"I reckon you did. You flirted with him and that works on people like ... well, like some people we know, but the nice men probably respond to something different."

Lily was furious again with Daisy. "So go out there and change my personality, you mean?"

"If you like him just talk to him." Daisy turned away from her.

"What's got you so cranky?" Lily asked.

"You have! And I'm not the one who broke the window."

"Shh, he'll hear you."

Daisy spun around "So? Did you tell him I did it?"

Lily grunted, turned around, and marched out of the

kitchen, hoping to see Elijah look at her the way other boys looked at her. It seemed that he didn't even 'see' her at all.

"Finished yet?" Lily asked as she flounced around the corner of the house.

"All done."

When she saw him smiling at her, she said, "It's nice to see your smile."

"I'm smiling because my job is finished and it's a job done well."

Lily nodded. "My parents will be pleased that you've done a good job."

"I aim to make people happy."

"Do you?" Lily stepped forward, trying to make him think of her as a pretty girl and a potential girlfriend.

He laughed at her. "What are you playing at, young Lily?"

Lily's mouth turned down. He thought of her as nothing more than a silly young girl. She opened her mouth and couldn't think of anything to say.

"I'm sorry. Is it Daisy? You're both so much alike."

She shook her head and looked at the ground. "It's Lily."

"I'll get a bag and get rid of the glass."

"Leave it. I can get rid of it," Lily said, just wanting him to go. He wasn't attracted to her, so what was the point of him hanging around?

"It's fine; I can do it," he said, heading back to the wagon.

"I'm sure you've got better things to do," she called after him.

He turned around. "Well, we did have another job come in and they're waiting for me at the workshop."

"I can do it."

"Okay. I'll see you around D—I mean Lily."

She lifted a hand in the air in a half-hearted attempt at a wave. Why didn't Elijah find her appealing? It was odd and annoying.

NANCY CAME HOME LATER that day, after the glass had already been replaced and Lily had removed the shattered pieces.

"How is Rose?" Daisy asked as she made her mother a cup of tea.

Lily sat down at the kitchen table next to their mother. "I still can't believe you visited them without us. It was Daisy's idea, too."

"I thought it might teach you two a lesson."

Lily grimaced. "A lesson in what?"

"If you haven't figured that out yet, maybe you need some more lessons like that."

Daisy pulled a face at her sister, communicating to her to be quiet. "Go on, *Mamm*, how were Rose and Tulip?"

Lily pouted and crossed her arms over her chest.

"Rose and Mark are buying their own *haus*. They'll be in it before their firstborn comes. You should've seen Rose's face. She's so excited."

"We would've seen her face if you had allowed us to go with you," Lily said.

Nancy stared sternly at Lily. "You should've thought of that before you broke the window."

When her mother turned back to Daisy, Lily rolled her eyes as she mouthed what her mother had just said—making sure her mother didn't see, of course. "When we are no longer under 'house arrest' we shall go and see her by ourselves," Lily told Daisy.

"Okay. I'll look forward to that."

When Daisy was seated and they all had tea, Nancy said, "Elijah came to fix the window, I see."

"Why didn't you tell us he was coming?" Daisy asked.

"Did he fix the window? It looks like it's done."

Lily answered, *"Jah, Mamm,* it's all fixed and it's as good as new."

"I didn't tell you because I wanted you to be yourselves when Elijah came here."

Lily and Daisy exchanged looks, not knowing what their mother meant and not wanting to ask.

"Who else would we be, *Mamm?"* Lily asked.

"He's nice, don't you think?" Nancy looked at Daisy first and then her gaze rested on Lily.

"Jah, he's nice," Lily answered.

"Gut! I've invited the Bontragers for dinner next week."

"All of them?" Daisy asked.

"Jah. And I've also invited Valerie and Bruno."

Daisy smiled upon hearing that Bruno would be joining them. Her mother always had a plan for everything she did. Did she think that Valerie and Ed Bontrager might be a match, or Elijah and Lily—perhaps both? The smug way her mother was acting, Daisy knew she was up to something. It would do no good to ask; her mother would deny that she plotted and planned such things. She'd insist that it was too early for Valerie to consider another man. The more Daisy thought about it, the more she saw that Valerie and Ed might be a good match, but only some years along when Valerie adjusted to life without her late husband.

"Why are you staring into space, Daisy?" her mother asked.

"I'm thinking about Valerie and if she might ever marry again."

"*Nee*, not soon at any rate. It'd be far too early for Valerie to even look at another man. *Nee*, I'm sure that part of her heart died when her husband died. Although, I never saw Valerie and Dirk as belonging together—they were an odd match."

"Who did you see Valerie with, then?" Daisy asked.

"Maybe someone like Ed Bontrager?" Lily said, causing Daisy to burst out laughing.

It was obvious that Lily had the same thoughts about what their mother was plotting.

Their mother ignored them and picked up her teacup, taking a couple of sips of hot tea while looking straight ahead.

CHAPTER 25

WHEN DAISY and Lily were sitting in the back row at the next Sunday meeting, Daisy noticed that Lily was doing a lot of glancing in Nathanial's direction. Nathanial was sitting on the opposite side of the room, so it made it obvious when Lily turned her head to the far right to look at him. Matthew Schumacher and Elijah Bontrager were both sitting toward the front.

Either Matthew or Elijah would be a much better match. Daisy hoped her sister would listen to reason and to what people were telling her. Her sister's life would be ruined if she got involved with Nathanial. Nathanial's brother had been involved with a girl and they'd had to get married. Daisy's heart would be broken if her sister was ever placed in the position where she had to marry a man. She wanted Lily to be sensible about her choice of a husband.

There was no divorce among the Amish—there was no turning back when they made their decisions to marry. It had to be a forever choice. They both had to choose men they could grow old with because that was exactly what they would do—either that, or live in separate houses and never marry again. Daisy was more than certain that Bruno was the right man for her, and if he ever asked her to marry him, she would jump at the chance before he changed his mind. Daisy looked over at Bruno when she should've been concentrating on the bishop's words.

AFTER THE MEETING WAS OVER, Bruno asked Daisy, "How long have we got before you have to go home?"

Daisy glanced over her shoulder at her parents. "Whenever they say they're ready to go home."

"Daisy, I wanted to do this somewhere romantic, someplace where we'd both remember it forever, but my heart can't wait. Marry me? Would you consider marrying me, Daisy?"

She stared into his dark amber eyes. "I will marry you, Bruno."

They ducked behind the buggy and Bruno pulled her close to him. "I've wanted to hold you in my arms since the first time we met."

Daisy giggled, but she couldn't speak. Her tummy was full of butterflies flapping their wings hard.

"We'll talk more about this soon. Perhaps if we get a chance to be alone on Tuesday night when we're over for dinner."

"*Nee, Mamm's* invited the Bontragers—Ed and his boys. There are so many of them that I don't think we'll have a chance for a private word. I think I'll be allowed out on Thursday, though."

He took her hand and held it. "Thursday night, we'll talk more. I'll come and collect you as soon as I finish work for the day. Can you clear that with your parents?"

Daisy nodded. "Where will we live?" She didn't want to spoil the moment, but neither did she want to move away from her family.

"That's something we'll need to discuss before we speak to the bishop, or tell your parents."

"I don't know if I can keep something from Lily."

"Will Lily keep quiet about it?"

Daisy shook her head. *"Nee,* not at all."

Bruno laughed. "Try to keep it from her if you can."

"I will."

Bruno peered around the side of the buggy. "I think your parents are looking for you." He squeezed her hand. "I'll see you on Tuesday night."

Daisy nodded and went to her parents quickly before she got into trouble for going missing.

DURING THE TUESDAY night dinner at the Yoder house, Daisy could tell by the way that Ed and Valerie looked at one another that there was some kind of history between them. Perhaps they had once dated. She made a mental note to ask her mother about it later. Could Ed have been the mystery man who Valerie had loved so long ago?

When everyone had taken their seats at the long wooden table, Hezekiah Yoder cleared his throat. "If everyone can stop talking, we might say a prayer of thanks for the food."

Everyone did as he suggested and closed their eyes.

When they had all opened their eyes, Nancy said, "Everyone can help themselves, unless someone would like me to serve them? How about you, Valerie, would you like some help?"

As soon as Valerie answered that she would help herself, the room was awash with many different conversations. Bowls of mashed potatoes, coleslaw, and meat were passed across and around the table as everyone helped themselves.

The Bontrager boys were all good talkers and they were entertaining; each seemed to have a funny story to tell. Elijah seemed to be the quietest of all, or maybe it was just because he was preoccupied the whole night by Lily, who had made sure she sat next to him.

CHAPTER 26

ON THURSDAY AFTERNOON, Daisy waited anxiously for Bruno. She'd managed to keep their secret—the first she'd ever kept from Lily. Lily had been distracted by talking constantly about Elijah, even more so after the Bontragers had come for dinner on Tuesday night. It seemed that their mother's plan of averting Lily's attention from Nathanial had worked, and Daisy hoped that Lily's attraction to Elijah was greater than her attraction to Nathanial.

When Daisy saw Bruno's buggy approach the house, she said goodbye to Lily and her parents and headed out to meet him.

"Hello, Daisy."

Seeing his smiling face made her heart glad. She stepped into the buggy and sat beside him. "Hello."

"I'm going to take us somewhere so we can talk about our plans. Are you hungry?"

"Always."

"I'll take us to a diner so we can have something to eat while we talk."

Later, when they had ordered burgers and were sitting across the table from one another, he began, "I've given things a lot of thought and I think it would be best if we live here. I'll have to get a permanent job somewhere ..."

"Really? You'll stay here?"

"Would you have been willing to come back to Ohio with me?"

"I would've, but it would be awful to leave my *familye*, and leave Lily. We've never been apart, not even for a day."

"Problem solved. I might have a permanent job offer where I'm working now, but it's too early to tell. The boss said he'd know in a couple of weeks if he could put me on staff. I've got a small business built up back home, but I could sell that to my friend who's looking after it now."

"I thought you said your job here had already become permanent."

"I'm talking longer term. Right now it's kind of permanent for the short term."

Daisy smiled and took a deep breath. "Everything's working out so well."

"I'd have to get a *haus* here. I've nearly got a deposit saved and if I get a good price for my business, we might have enough to buy a small *haus*. It won't be anything grand, but we can do work on a place and fix it."

"We might be able to stay with *Mamm* and *Dat;* we've got loads of space."

"We could do that, or we could stay with Valerie, but neither

604

of those options suits me. I think we need to start off life in our own place. Does it matter to you if it's only a small *haus*?"

"Anything. Anything would be perfect as long as we'll be together."

He reached across the table and took hold of her hand. "I was hoping you'd say that."

"When would we marry?"

"I figured in December. That'd give me a chance to get things organized."

Daisy added up the months. It was only four months away, but that was enough time to sew all the clothes for the wedding and give her mother plenty of time to plan everything. *"Mamm* is going to be so excited. She really likes you."

He raised his eyebrows. "That's good."

"So does everyone else."

"And you?"

Daisy giggled. "Of course I feel that way."

He smiled at her and his warm amber eyes crinkled at the corners.

ON THEIR WAY home after they had talked about their wedding and the life they'd have together, Bruno made a suggestion. "It might be a good idea if we tell your parents tonight."

"Really? So soon?"

"Don't you want to?"

"Jah, I'm glad. I don't think I could've kept the secret much longer."

Daisy walked into the house with Bruno. She never thought

she'd find the perfect man for her so soon, and the best thing was that her parents approved of him already.

NANCY KNEW from the look on Daisy's face when she walked through the front door with Bruno what they had come to say.

"Hello, *Mamm, Dat ...*"

Daisy had stars in her eyes as she glanced up at Bruno as the young couple stood before them. Hezekiah and Nancy were seated.

"Sit down," Hezekiah said to the young couple whose faces glowed with youthful anticipation.

Once they were seated, Bruno said to Daisy, "Do you want me to talk?"

Daisy nodded.

"I asked Daisy to marry me and she said she would."

"Oh, I'm so pleased." Nancy jumped to her feet and spread her arms out. Daisy stood up and they hugged, and then Bruno stood as Nancy hugged him. Hezekiah shook Bruno's hand and then hugged his daughter.

"That makes your *vadder* and I happy, Daisy."

Bruno chuckled. "I'm happy I meet with your approval."

Nancy took a step back. "Are you taking her back to Ohio?"

"*Nee,* I'll try not to as long as I can find work around here."

"He's going to sell his business in Ohio. He's already got a buyer."

"That *is* good news," Hezekiah said as he sat back down again.

Nancy knew Hezekiah couldn't have been more delighted, but Nancy also knew Lily would be sad. Not only would she be the only child left at home, but she'd also never been apart from her twin sister for any length of time. She'd have to watch Lily carefully to make sure she didn't jump in to a marriage and make a silly mistake just to keep up with her older sisters.

"Does Lily know?" Nancy asked.

"*Nee,* and it has been very hard to keep something quiet from her."

"What's this?" Lily asked as she walked into the room.

"I just told *Mamm* and *Dat* that Bruno and I are getting married."

Lily stopped still with her mouth gaping open. "You are?"

"*Jah.*"

"When?"

"We figure in December or thereabouts," Bruno said.

Finally, Lily smiled. "That's *wunderbaar.*" She hurried to her sister and threw her arms around her and also gave Bruno a hug. Then she sat down on the couch opposite the happy couple, in between her parents. "Does that mean you're moving, Daisy?"

"*Nee,* Bruno can find work here and he thinks the job he has now might be a permanent one."

"Phew! That is good news. Where will you live?" Lily asked.

"We'll buy something somewhere. It'll only be small to start with," Bruno said. "Depending on how much I get for my business back in Ohio when I sell it."

"It sounds like you've got everything worked out."

Bruno nodded and gazed at Daisy. "We have."

"Probably not everything," Daisy said. "But we know what direction we're going in."

"You've set your sails in the right direction?" Lily asked with a giggle, causing Nancy to laugh as well.

"Bruno, I have to explain why we're laughing. Hezekiah always talks about sailing and rivers when he's giving the girls advice."

Hezekiah's mouth turned down at the corners as he turned his head toward his wife. "I give *gut* advice and talking about sailing is something that the girls can relate to."

"We've never gone sailing, *Dat*," Daisy said.

"Neither have I, but there is a certain life current that you can go along with or you can fight against."

"I know what you mean, Mr. Yoder. Many things can be related to water. It's a life force, and it's important which way you set your sails in life," Bruno said.

Lily shook her head. "Men!"

Everyone laughed.

LATER THAT NIGHT, after Bruno had gone home and Hezekiah was up in his bedroom, Nancy sat down in the kitchen with the twins.

"*Mamm,* we'll have to start making clothes for the wedding, but I don't want the wedding to stop us making clothes for Rose's *boppli.*"

"We can do it all," Nancy replied to Daisy. "Are you feeling left out, Lily?"

Lily screwed up her face. "*Nee.* I'm happy for Daisy. Bruno is lovely. I only wish I'd met him first," she said, nudging Daisy in a joking manner.

"It wouldn't have mattered one bit because he's in love with everything about me, not just the way I look."

The girls giggled.

"I just don't want you running into the arms of a man who's totally unsuitable when Daisy gets married and you find you're lonely."

Lily's eyes sparkled. "Hopefully I won't be lonely for long."

Nancy shook her head. "That's exactly what I'm worried about."

Lily sighed at her mother's words. "I'll make a good decision."

"I hope so. There are so many *gut* men around and I hope you can sort the suitable from the unsuitable."

"Is this about Nathanial, *Mamm?* You've never liked him, have you?" Lily asked.

Nancy frowned. "It's not about liking him. He's not got a good reputation. Just ask Tulip, and then there's what happened with Daisy too."

Daisy looked down at her hands in her lap. She knew Lily didn't believe that Nathanial had tried to attack her.

"Who do you think is suitable for me?" Lily asked her mother.

"Matthew Schumacher or Elijah Bontrager. Either of them would be my idea of a good choice."

"Well, just as well it's my choice when I choose a husband."

Nancy lowered her head while keeping her eyes fixed on Lily. "What do you mean?"

"I'm saying that it's my choice who I marry, isn't it?"

"I'm only trying to protect you from making a mistake."

"You didn't make a big fuss like this with Daisy."

"I think I did."

"*Jah,* she did," Daisy said, remembering the dreadful night when she'd jumped out of Nathanial's buggy and walked all the way home.

"*Gut nacht, mudder.*" Lily stood up. "Don't be concerned about me. I've got the perfect man in mind."

"Who?" her mother and Daisy chorused.

"You'll both have to wait and see. You didn't tell me you were getting married to Bruno, Daisy. I was the last to find out, so you'll be the last to find out when I get married." Lily flounced out of the room.

"Well, what do you think of that?" Nancy asked Daisy.

Daisy shook her head. "I didn't mean to upset her."

"It couldn't be avoided. Who was she talking about just now?"

Daisy bit her lip and thought of all the men who paid her attention. "From the way she was talking, it's not Nathanial."

"I agree."

"I hope she makes the best choice."

"I'm sure she will, *Mamm.*" Daisy stood up, leaned over, and kissed her mother on the cheek.

NANCY SAT ALONE at the kitchen table. She'd have Tulip talk to Lily about Nathanial—that, coupled with Daisy's knowledge of him, should be enough to change her mind about him if she still liked him.

Looking at the kitchen table, Nancy was upset that neither of the twins had thought to take their cups and saucers to the sink to wash them out. What kind of wives would they make when they had to run their own households? She'd raised them better than that. Perhaps it was all the excitement of Daisy's news that made them act in a selfish manner.

After she had washed the dishes from the tea, she walked up the stairs to her bedroom with a little smile tugging at her lips. Tomorrow she'd have Daisy's wedding to plan, and after that, she would carefully direct her remaining headstrong daughter to a suitable man—or, at least, she'd try.

Several weeks later.

BEFORE HE'D LEFT for work, Hezekiah had brought the treadle sewing machine from one of the spare rooms to the living room. The twins and their mother were settled down for a day of sewing in the living room. Fabric was spread out from one end of the room to the other. Daisy had planned to have all her sisters as her special wedding attendants, but Rose declined as the date of the wedding coincided with her due date. Because of that, Tulip had suggested to Daisy just to have Lily. They were in the middle of sewing Daisy's blue wedding dress and a dress for Lily along with Bruno's suit, when they heard the phone from the barn.

"I'll get it," Lily called out as she jumped to her feet.

"I wonder who that could be," Daisy said.

"I hope it's not someone with a problem," Nancy said. "I'm too busy to help them today."

"Lily and I can do the sewing if it is."

Lily rushed back inside. "It was *Onkel* John."

"What's happened?" Nancy asked.

"It's Aunt Nerida. She fell off the roof and is in the hospital."

Nancy leaped to her feet. "Is she going to be okay?"

"*Jah.* She's got a broken leg. John called from the hospital and they're fixing it now."

"Call me a taxi, Lily. I must go to the hospital and see her."

Lily ran out of the room and Nancy raced upstairs to change into clothes more suitable for being seen in public. Once she had a nice dress on, and her hair properly fixed under her *kapp,* she headed downstairs.

"Do you want us to come with you, *Mamm?*"

"*Nee,* you two keep sewing or we'll never get it all done."

"But we want to come with you," Lily said.

"It only takes one of us and she's my *schweschder,* so you two continue on here and I'll tell you how she is when I return. If I'm late, don't forget to start cooking the evening meal."

"We will, *Mamm,*" Daisy said.

On the way to the hospital in the taxi, Nancy was worried. If Lily had been correct in saying that Nerida had fallen off the roof, she could've died falling from such a height. And what if she had died before they had made amends? Nancy was thankful that they had talked recently, and each had made an effort in getting back to the relationship that they once had.

Nancy made inquiries at the front desk and was told that Nerida was still in the emergency area. Without waiting for permission, she hurried to the area marked 'emergency.' Making her way through the curtained-off beds, she heard

John's voice behind a curtain. She pulled the curtain aside and saw Nerida lying on the bed.

"You came," Nerida said, looking up at her.

Nancy stepped through the curtain and closed it behind her. "Of course I came." She turned to John. *"Denke* for calling and letting me know."

"It's a bad break," John said.

"It's broken in a couple of places. I landed on a cement feeding trough that John was about to move."

"What were you doing on the roof?"

"Cleaning out the gutters. The trees are so close to the house and with all the rain we had recently damp patches started appearing on the edges of the ceiling."

"Oh, that's not good."

"I told her she should've waited for me to do it," John said.

"You have too much to do already," Nerida told him. "I won't be doing it again, that is for sure and for certain," Nerida said.

"Are you in pain?" Nancy asked her.

"Only when I move. It'll probably be set in plaster. They're deciding what to do with me now."

"It'll either be that or a steel rod or two," John said.

Nancy shook her head. "I find it hard to believe you got up on the roof."

"I didn't get on the roof. I just put a ladder up to the gutters and then emptied them. I do it all the time."

"Nancy, we both have something to ask of you, if you wouldn't mind."

"Anything, anything at all."

"Would you look after the girls until I'm back on my feet?" Nerida asked.

Nancy thought it an odd thing to ask because their two girls were more than old enough to look after themselves. She had to agree because of the rift that she was trying to mend. "We'd love to have them come stay. Is that what you meant? You want them to stay with us?"

"*Jah,* if you wouldn't mind. We know you're busy with Daisy's wedding and Rose's *boppli* due soon. It's asking a lot."

"*Nee,* it's not. I would be more than happy to have them stay. Daisy and Lily would love it as well. And we've got more than enough spare rooms. They can have a room each."

John chuckled. "Don't look after them too well or they might not want to come back."

Nancy giggled. "Don't worry, there'll be more than enough chores to go around with Daisy's wedding coming up. How long will you be in the hospital?"

"It depends what they need to do to get me better. If they put those rods in, I could be in for a lengthy stay. I'd like to know the girls are looked after, and I need John by my side. I'm not *gut* with hospitals, or pain."

"Where are Violet and Willow now?"

"They're at home," John said.

"Shall I collect them on the way? From here the taxi would go right by your place."

"I can bring them over tonight when I leave here," John said.

Nancy figured John might want to say goodbye to them and tell them exactly what was going on with their mother, so she didn't insist on collecting them.

"I should go. I don't want to get in the way when the doctor comes back."

"Okay. *Denke* for coming to see me, Nancy. It means a lot."

Nancy turned to John, "Bye, John."

"I'll see you tonight some time, Nancy. I'm not sure when."

"Okay." Nancy leaned over and gave her sister a quick kiss on her forehead before she left.

WHEN NANCY WALKED through the front door at home, the two girls looked up at her.

"You weren't very long, *Mamm,*" Daisy said.

"How is she?" Lily asked.

Nancy collapsed into a chair. "She's got a bad break and they might have to put rods in her bones to hold them together."

Lily screwed up her face. "Oooh, that sounds awful,"

"*Jah,* it wouldn't be very pleasant at all. The good news is that Violet and Willow will be coming to stay with us until Nerida gets better."

"That's *wunderbaar.*" Lily clapped her hands while Daisy agreed.

"We'll have to make up two beds for them with fresh linen."

"I can do that," Lily said.

"Aren't they old enough to stay at home on their own? *Onkel* John would be there too. I mean, I'm pleased they're coming to stay, but it's odd," Daisy said.

"Nerida asked me and she needs peace of mind. She knows if they're with me, they'll be fine. She wants John to stay by her side at the hospital."

"I can understand that," Daisy said.

"I'll go and put fresh linen on the beds now," Lily said as she jumped to her feet.

"Can I get you something to eat, *Mamm?*" Daisy asked

"Jah. I'd like that and a hot cup of tea."

"You sit down and don't do anything until you recover. You look pale."

Nancy sat down while one daughter made the beds and the other one got her something to eat. Sometimes the twins surprised her and on a day like today, she needed all the help she could get with the shock of her sister falling off the roof.

IT WAS JUST after they finished eating dinner that night that John and the girls arrived.

"Denke for having us," Violet said to Nancy when she walked through the door with a small bag under her arm.

"Jah, Aunt Nancy. *Denke* for having us stay," Willow added.

"It's our pleasure. Any time." She looked up at John. "Have you had anything to eat yet?"

"Jah, I've already eaten."

"We had dinner ready for *Dat* when he came home from the hospital."

Willow said, "He was gone so long that we were worried about him and didn't know what had happened. Half the time we waited in the barn so we could answer the phone quickly."

John explained, "I was calling them, but someone hadn't hung up the receiver properly and that's why my calls weren't getting through."

Nancy looked over her shoulder when she heard the twins greeting their cousins. "Girls, show Willow and Violet to their rooms, would you?"

"Jah, Mamm," Daisy said.

Hezekiah walked out of the kitchen and shook John's hand.

"Can you sit down with us, or are you tired from your day at the hospital?"

"I can stay a few minutes. I am tired."

"How about a hot cup of tea?"

"That would be appreciated, *denke*, Nancy."

John and Hezekiah sat in the living room while Nancy made the tea. When she heard laughter coming from upstairs she wondered what she had gotten herself in for, going back to having four girls under the one roof. The blessing of the situation was that if the cousins were still there after Daisy's wedding it meant that Lily wouldn't be the only girl left at home. The cousins would be good company for Lily.

The Wedding Day

DAISY OPENED her eyes to see three sets of eyes peering back at her. "What are you all doing?" They were her two cousins and her twin sister, Lily.

Lily bounced up and down on her bed. "It's your wedding day."

"*Jah*, and the sun's shining. It's gonna be a *gut* day," Willow said.

Daisy glanced out the window between the gap in the curtains. There was rarely sun at that time of year. "There's no sun."

Willow giggled. "The sun is shining in your heart because

you're so in love with Bruno." She drew her hands to her heart and fluttered her lashes, causing Violet and Lily to laugh.

"How about some privacy?" Daisy asked.

"You won't have any privacy when you're married living in that tiny *haus* that you and Bruno bought," Lily said.

Daisy groaned and pulled the sheet over her head. Lily promptly pulled it away. "Get up."

"*Jah,* rise and shine," Willow said.

"We'll make you breakfast," Violet said.

"We don't want you fainting on your wedding day from lack of food," Lily said, pulling the covers off Daisy all together.

Daisy knew she couldn't win against the three of them. "Okay, okay, I'm coming. I'm getting out of bed right now."

"Don't get changed into your wedding dress yet or you might spill something on it," Lily suggested.

"*Jah,* I was just going to put my dressing gown on for the moment and eat breakfast in that."

"Let's go," Lily said as Violet grabbed Daisy's dressing gown and handed it to her.

"What about a shower? You don't want to be all stinky," Willow said.

"I had one last night," Daisy replied.

Willow frowned.

"Do I smell, or something?" Daisy sniffed the air.

"*Nee,* but have another one anyway."

Daisy sighed. "I'll eat, then shower, and then one of you will surely tell me what I should do after that."

The three girls giggled while Daisy pulled on her dressing gown.

"Aren't you excited, Daisy?" Willow asked, as the three of them followed Daisy down the stairs.

"I am. I never thought the day would come. I've been looking forward to it for months."

"You'll be a married lady in a few hours," Violet said.

"*Jah*, you'll be Mrs. ... What's his last name?" Willow asked.

"Weber," Lily said.

"You'll be Mrs. Weber. Mrs. Daisy Weber. Or, Mrs. Bruno Weber. How does that make you feel, Daisy?"

"Um, old, I guess."

Nancy walked into the kitchen as the girls were eating. "Hurry up, girls. In just under an hour the benches and tables are arriving. How are you feeling, Daisy?"

Daisy knew her mother was stressed with so much work needing to be done to get the house ready for the hundreds of guests who'd be attending the wedding that morning. "I'm getting a little nervous now."

"You should be. Marriage is a big step."

"*Denke, Mamm,*" Daisy said.

"Not to be taken lightly," her mother added.

"*Jah*, Daisy knows all that, *Mamm.* You're only making her more nervous," Lily said.

"Lily, have you seen your *vadder* this morning?"

"*Nee*, I only just woke up. Is he missing?"

She shook her head. "I think he's outside somewhere."

"Have you and *Dat* eaten, *Mamm?*" Daisy asked.

"*Jah*, we ate earlier." Nancy hurried out of the kitchen.

"Your *Mamm* seems more nervous than you," Willow said to Daisy.

"She was like this at Rose's and Tulip's weddings too. She

likes everything to be just so and she won't let anyone else do anything."

Lily added, *"Jah,* and she has to be in charge of everything. The big boss lady."

Daisy finished the last mouthful of food. "I'll talk to *Mamm.*" She hurried out of the kitchen while she heard Lily grumbling about having to do the washing up.

Daisy found her mother heading up the stairs. *"Mamm."*

Her mother looked behind her. *"Jah?"*

"Can we talk?"

"Okay." She turned around and came down the stairs. "I thought you'd want to talk sooner or later."

They sat on the couch together. "This will be the last time I talk with you as a single woman."

Nancy nodded and took a deep breath. "Well, I've had this talk with Rose and then with Tulip."

"What talk?"

Nancy frowned. "About what to expect on your wedding night."

Daisy was horrified. *"Mamm!* Stop it."

"Stop what?"

"I know about all that stuff." Daisy put her hand to her head.

Her mother looked relieved. "You do?"

"Jah, I've heard all about it and I know what to expect, so stop worrying." Daisy put her hand over her mouth and giggled.

"Well, you might laugh, but no one bothered to have that talk with me and it was a shock to me on …"

"Enough!" Daisy blocked her ears. "I don't want to hear it, *Mamm.*"

Nancy laughed.

When Daisy took her hands away from her ears, she said, "I didn't want to talk about that. I just wanted to say *denke* for being such a *gut mudder*. I hope that I will be just as good with my *kinner*."

Nancy stared at her and Daisy could see her mother's eyes become misty.

"*Denke*, Daisy. I did my best. I did my best with all of you. Sometimes I was sure you girls must think I'm just a cranky old cow."

Daisy giggled. "Well, sometimes. I'm only joking. You were never a cow, and never too cranky. Just normal cranky when we did horrible things." Daisy hugged her mother and Nancy hugged her back.

Hezekiah walked in the front door. "The men are here with the benches. Daisy, you're not dressed!"

"It doesn't take me long to get ready."

"You better go now," Nancy said to Daisy.

The other three girls, all giggling and seemingly talking at once, came out from the kitchen into the living room.

"Take Daisy up and help her get ready, girls," Nancy ordered.

The four girls ran up the stairs while Hezekiah and Nancy smiled at one another. A wedding day was a good day.

DAISY RAN her hands over the soft fabric of her blue wedding dress. One cousin braided her hair while the other tied her pinafore apron at her back.

Lily stepped back and looked at her sister. "You look beautiful."

"You would say that, Lily, because you look exactly the same," Violet said.

Lily giggled. "I know that, silly."

"Anyway, you do look beautiful, Daisy."

"*Denke,* Violet." Daisy put her hand on her stomach to quell the nerves that had just kicked in. She hoped she'd feel better when she saw Bruno. He was her dream come true.

Nancy poked her head through the door. "Five minutes."

"I'm nearly finished with her hair," Violet said.

"Oh, Daisy, that looks lovely. The dress turned out really well."

Daisy breathed out heavily and was just about to say something to her mother when she shut the door.

"*Mamm's* more nervous than you are, Daisy."

"Only five more minutes," Daisy muttered to herself.

"Five more minutes to change your mind," Willow said.

"Willow, that's a dreadful thing to say. Why would she change her mind? She wants to marry Bruno, don't you Daisy?" Violet asked.

The cousins' squabbling made Daisy laugh. "I do want to marry Bruno. And I won't be changing my mind."

Violet shook her head at her younger sister.

Once Violet finished braiding Daisy's hair, Lily placed the white organza prayer *kapp* on top of Daisy's head.

"There you go, even more beautiful," Lily said. "Now let's go."

Daisy went down the stairs first and Bruno was waiting at the bottom. The room was buzzing with low conversations and crowded with many people. As Daisy's gaze swept over the benches, she saw that every space was filled. There were even people on the porch and lining the sides of the room.

They walked to the front and stopped in front of the bishop. After a quick glance behind her, Daisy was comforted when she saw her mother and father. They'd sat next to Bruno's parents. Tulip and Rose were there with their husbands, and her two older brothers were there with their wives. Rose was looking particularly glum and very, very pregnant.

It seemed as though Rose was still a little cross that Daisy hadn't waited to have the wedding until after her baby was born. Daisy figured she'd waited long enough to marry Bruno and she couldn't wait a few more weeks to start her new life.

Malcolm Tyler, who had a rich baritone voice, was chosen to sing a hymn in High German. Daisy closed her eyes as she listened to his beautiful lilting tones. When he was finished, the bishop delivered a short sermon on life and marriage. Then he read verses from Genesis and told the story of how man was created in God's image. Then the time came for Daisy and Bruno to exchange their agreements with one another. They were finally pronounced married.

Daisy looked into Bruno's amber eyes and thought back to the first day she saw him. In her heart, she'd known even back then that there was something special about him. Another thing that made her pleased was that her mother hadn't pushed them together, and neither had her mother met him first. Daisy had found him all on her own, and somehow, that had made everything that little bit more special.

. . .

LATER WHEN THE wedding feast was underway, Nancy was distressed to see Nathanial continually looking in Lily's direction. "There is no way on *Gott's* green earth that I will ever allow Lily to marry that man."

Hezekiah replied, "What are you talking about, Nancy? Matthew would be perfect for Lily. If another woman doesn't ..."

Matthew Schumacher was Mark's younger *bruder* and Mark had married their oldest daughter, Rose.

Nancy frowned and looked over at Lily again to see Matthew sitting next to her. Seeing Matthew and Lily talking happily distracted her from her dislike of Nathanial. "I've always liked Matthew."

"I've always liked him too," Hezekiah said.

Nathanial now had competition in winning Lily's heart. And both Matthew and Nathanial had to watch out for Elijah Bontrager.

"Just as well Violet and Willow have come to stay. Lily will need the distraction of more girls in the *haus*."

Hezekiah shook his head. "More girls in the *haus*? Is that what we really need?"

"That's what we've got until Nerida gets stronger and her leg mends. And I think it's a blessing for Lily to have the girls there."

Laughing, Hezekiah reached out and took hold of Nancy's hand. "One day we'll be on our own again, but it might be in our old, old age. If we last that long."

"I think you might be right, but I'm grateful for every day we've got together."

"Me too. You've made every day of my life much brighter since I met you. You've made me a happy man."

Nancy was too choked up to speak. If she lost Hezekiah, she didn't know what she'd do. All she could do was smile at him. He knew how she felt since she told him all the time. "We've been blessed," she managed to say, and he looked into her eyes and smiled.

Moments later, Nancy looked over at her newly married daughter, Daisy, who was staring at her new husband. She closed her eyes and prayed that Bruno would stay in their local community and not take Daisy back to Ohio with him. They had bought a house, but most of his family was in Ohio and that was enough for Nancy to find reason to worry. She closed her eyes again, this time more tightly, and gave her concerns to God. He would watch over them all.

"All will be well," Hezekiah said quietly.

Nancy opened her eyes and looked at him.

"Daisy and Bruno will be okay."

"I know. Daisy has made a good choice in Bruno," Nancy said.

"He's her perfect match, just like you're mine."

Nancy giggled like a young girl. Hezekiah always made her feel better. She took her mind off scenarios that might never occur, and concentrated on enjoying the remainder of the wedding celebration. However, the cogs in the deep recesses of her mind were still turning over regarding Lily—her next matchmaking project. Daisy had found her own husband, but Lily sorely needed her help. That was a project for another day.

$\sim$

The remaining 3 books - Amish Lily, Amish Violet and Amish Willow are also available in a box set paperback edition. (3 books-in-1)

Amish Love Blooms Books 4- 6

A NOTE FROM SAMANTHA

I hope you have enjoyed the first three books in the Amish Love Blooms series.

It's often said that the order of the children in a family have an influence on their personalities. To a degree I believe that is true. I've tried to reflect that with the twins who have escaped the responsibilities the older ones had.

Originally I had planned for this to be a four book series, but I loved writing the books so much and wasn't ready to say goodbye to the family. It worked out perfectly to have Nerida ask for her sister's help in finding husbands for her daughters. Then of course, I couldn't leave Valerie, a widow, without finding her own second chance love story. Her story is in the very last book, Amish Willow.

Samantha P

www.SamanthaPriceAuthor.com

Printed in Great Britain
by Amazon

75401461R00376